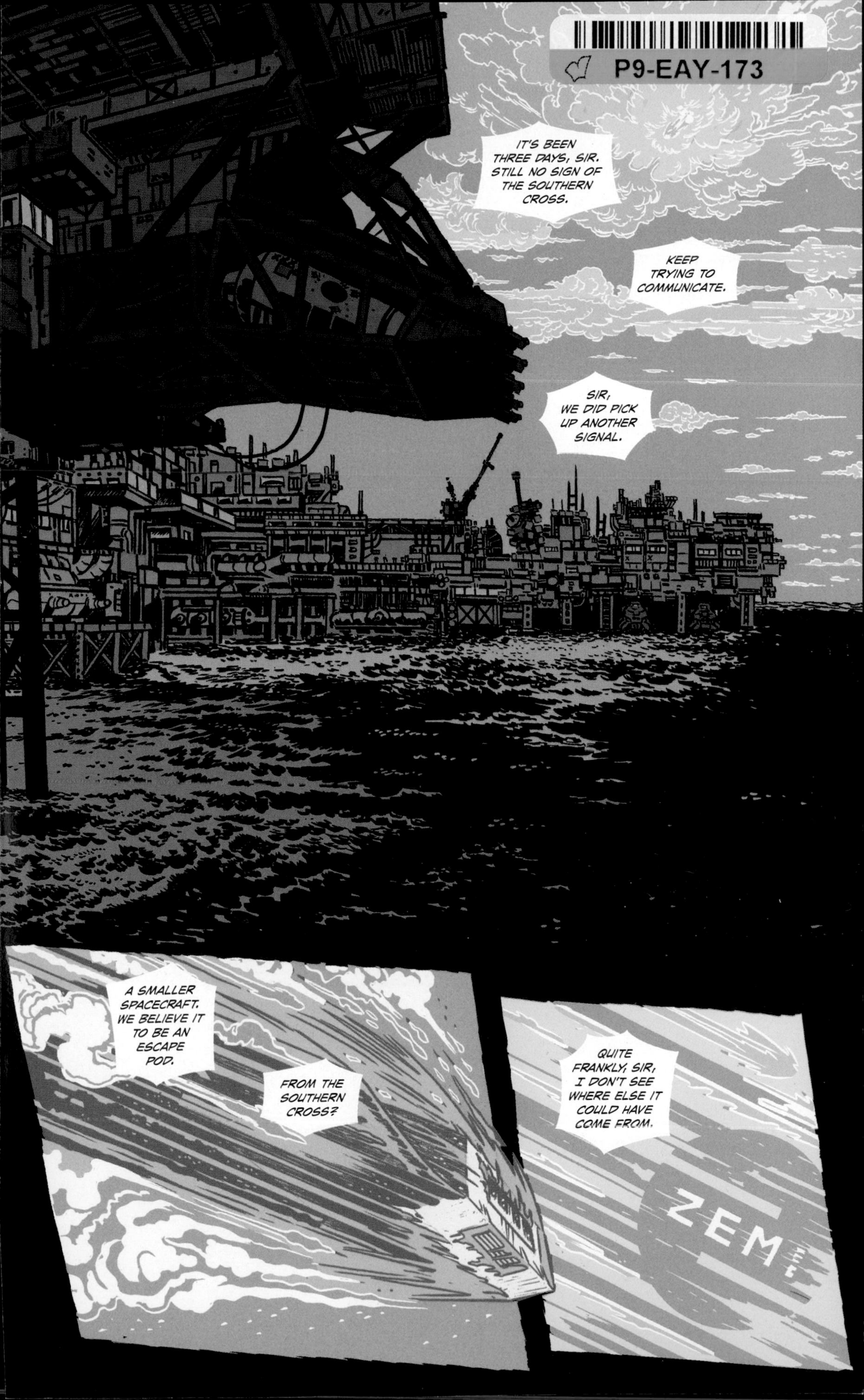
IT'S BEEN THREE DAYS, SIR. STILL NO SIGN OF THE SOUTHERN CROSS.
KEEP TRYING TO COMMUNICATE.
SIR, WE DID PICK UP ANOTHER SIGNAL.
A SMALLER SPACECRAFT. WE BELIEVE IT TO BE AN ESCAPE POD.
FROM THE SOUTHERN CROSS?
QUITE FRANKLY, SIR, I DON'T SEE WHERE ELSE IT COULD HAVE COME FROM.
ZEM!

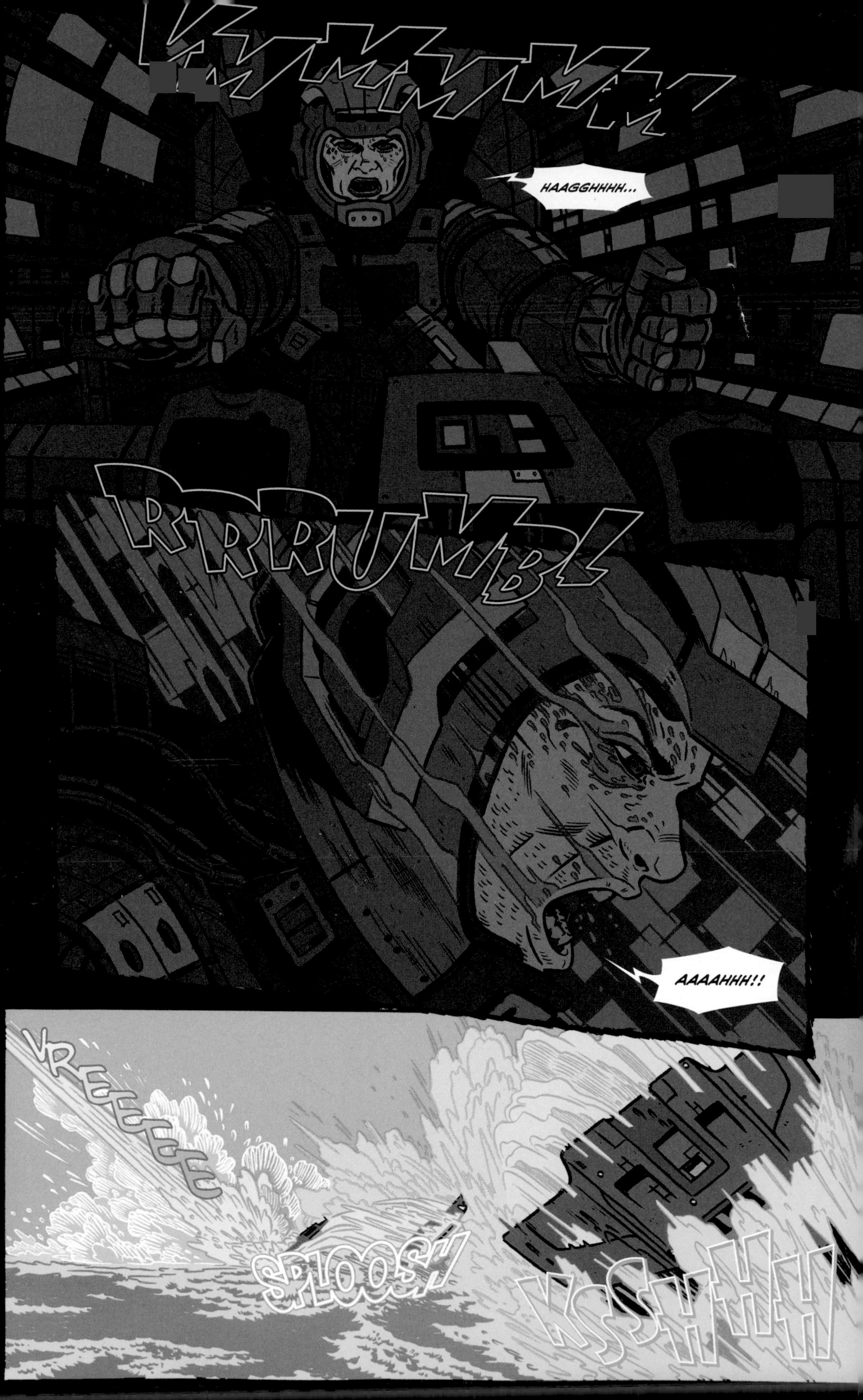
HAAGGHHHH...
RRRUMBL
AAAAHHH!!
SPLOOSH

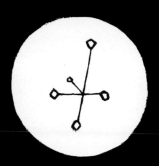

DEDICATED TO THE MEMORY OF OUR PAL,

# DARWYN COOKE

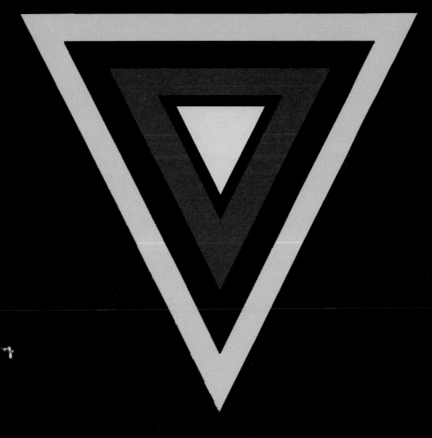

# SOUTHERN
# CROSS

**BECKY CLOONAN**
STORY/COVER

**ANDY BELANGER**
ART

**LEE LOUGHRIDGE**
COLOURS

**SERGE LaPOINTE**
LETTERS

**IMAGE COMICS, INC.**
Robert Kirkman—Chief Operating Officer
Erik Larsen—Chief Financial Officer
Todd McFarlane—President
Marc Silvestri—Chief Executive Officer
Jim Valentino—Vice-President

Eric Stephenson—Publisher
Corey Murphy—Director of Sales
Jeff Boison—Director of Publishing Planning & Book Trade Sales
Chris Ross—Director of Digital Sales
Jeff Stang—Director of Specialty Sales
Kat Salazar—Director of PR & Marketing
Branwyn Bigglestone—Controller
Sue Korpela—Accounts Manager
Drew Gill—Art Director
Brett Warnock—Production Manager
Leigh Thomas — Print Manager
Tricia Ramos—Traffic Manager
Briah Skelly—Publicist
Aly Hoffman—Events & Conventions Coordinator
Sasha Head—Sales & Marketing Production Designer
David Brothers—Branding Manager
Melissa Gifford—Content Manager
Drew Fitzgerald—Publicity Assistant
Vincent Kukua—Production Artist
Erika Schnatz—Production Artist
Ryan Brewer—Production Artist
Shanna Matuszak—Production Artist
Carey Hall—Production Artist
Esther Kim—Direct Market Sales Representative
Emilio Bautista—Digital Sales Representative
Leanna Caunter—Accounting Assistant
Chloe Ramos-Peterson—Library Market Sales Representative
Maria Eizik—Administrative Assistant
IMAGECOMICS.COM

SOUTHERN CROSS™, VOLUME 2
First Printing, July 2017. Copyright © 2017 Becky Cloonan & Andy Bélanger. All rights reserved.
Published by Image Comics, Inc. Office of publication: 2701 NW Vaughn St., Suite 780, Portland, OR 97210.
Contains material originally published in single magazine form as Southern Cross #7-12.
SOUTHERN CROSS™ (including all prominent characters featured herein), its logo and all characters likenesses are
trademarks of Becky Cloonan & Andy Bélanger, unless otherwise noted. Image Comics® and its logos are registered
trademarks and copyrights of Image Comics, Inc. All rights reserved. No part of this publication may be reproduced or
transmitted, in any form or by any means (except for short excerpts for review purposes) without the express written
permission of Becky Cloonan, Andy Bélanger or Image Comics, Inc. All names, characters, events and locales in this
publication are entirely fictional. Any resemblance to actual persons (living or dead), events or places, without satiric
intent, is coincidental.
Printed in the United States.

For information regarding the CPSIA on this printed material call: 203-595-3636 and provide reference # RICH - 747529

For international rights inquiries, contact: foreignlicensing@imagecomics.com

ISBN: 978-1-5343-0043-9

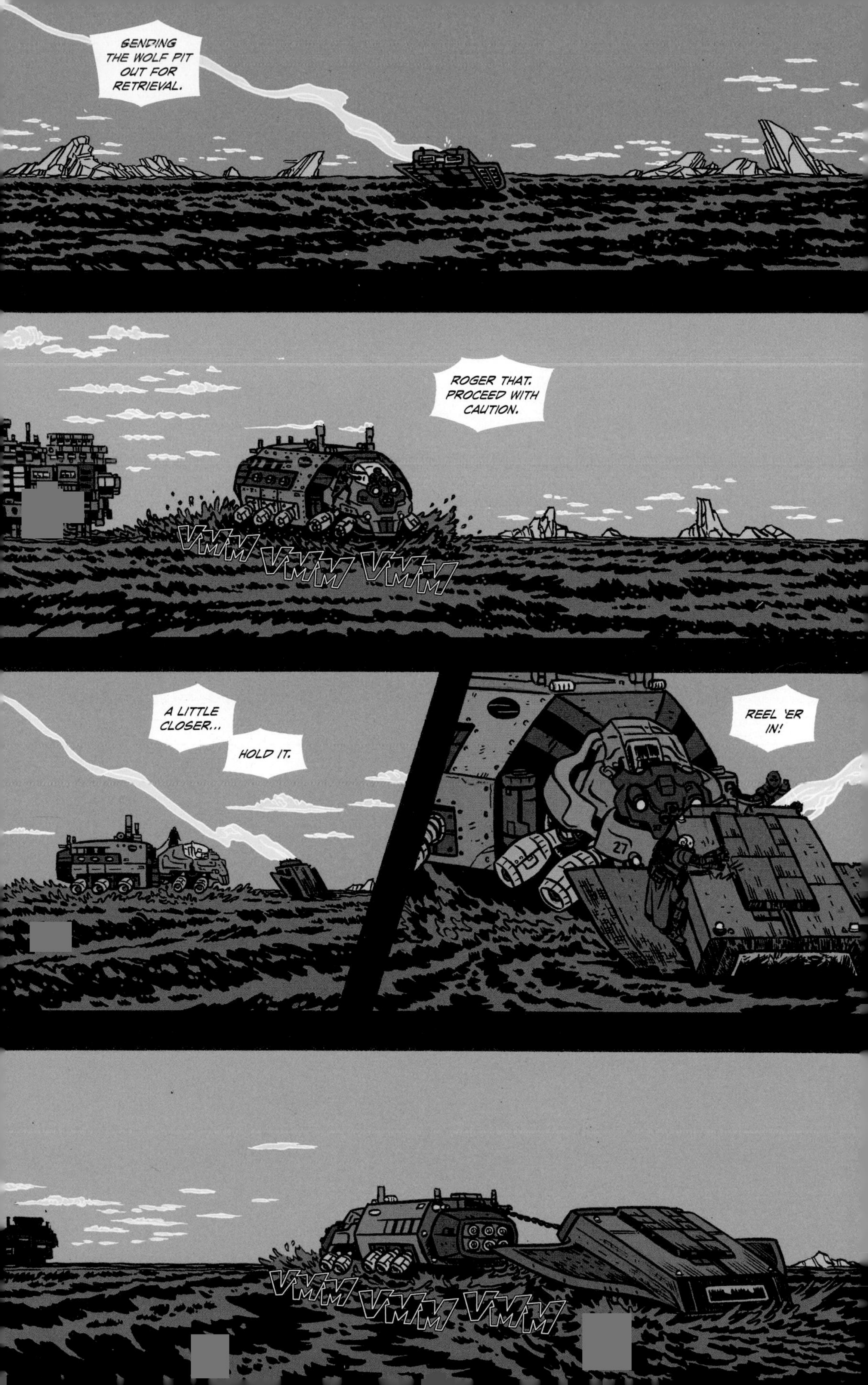
SENDING THE WOLF PIT OUT FOR RETRIEVAL.
ROGER THAT. PROCEED WITH CAUTION.
VMMV VMMV VMMV
A LITTLE CLOSER...
HOLD IT.
REEL 'ER IN!
27
VMMV VMMV VMMV

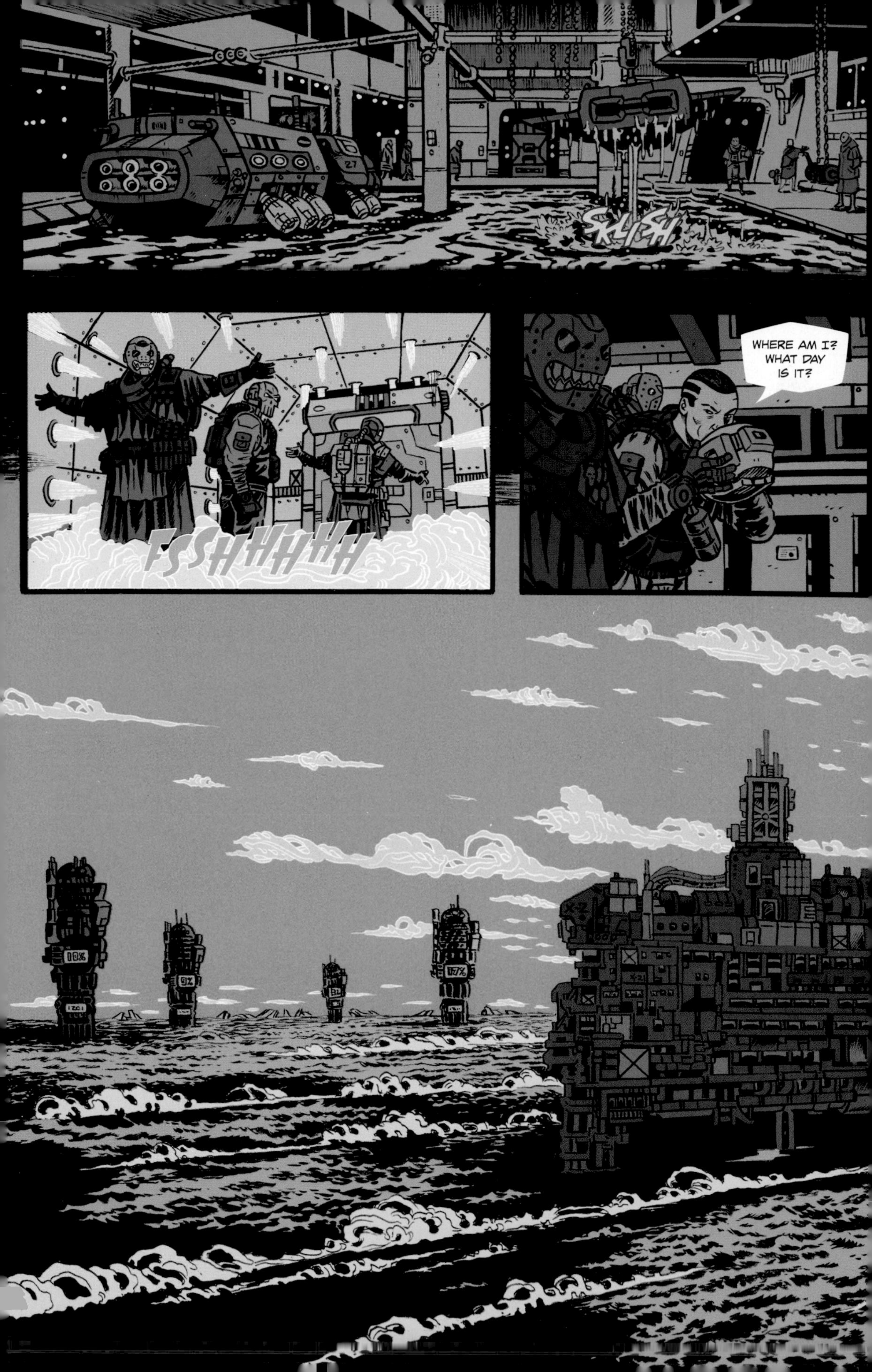
SKLISH
FSHHHHHH
WHERE AM I? WHAT DAY IS IT?

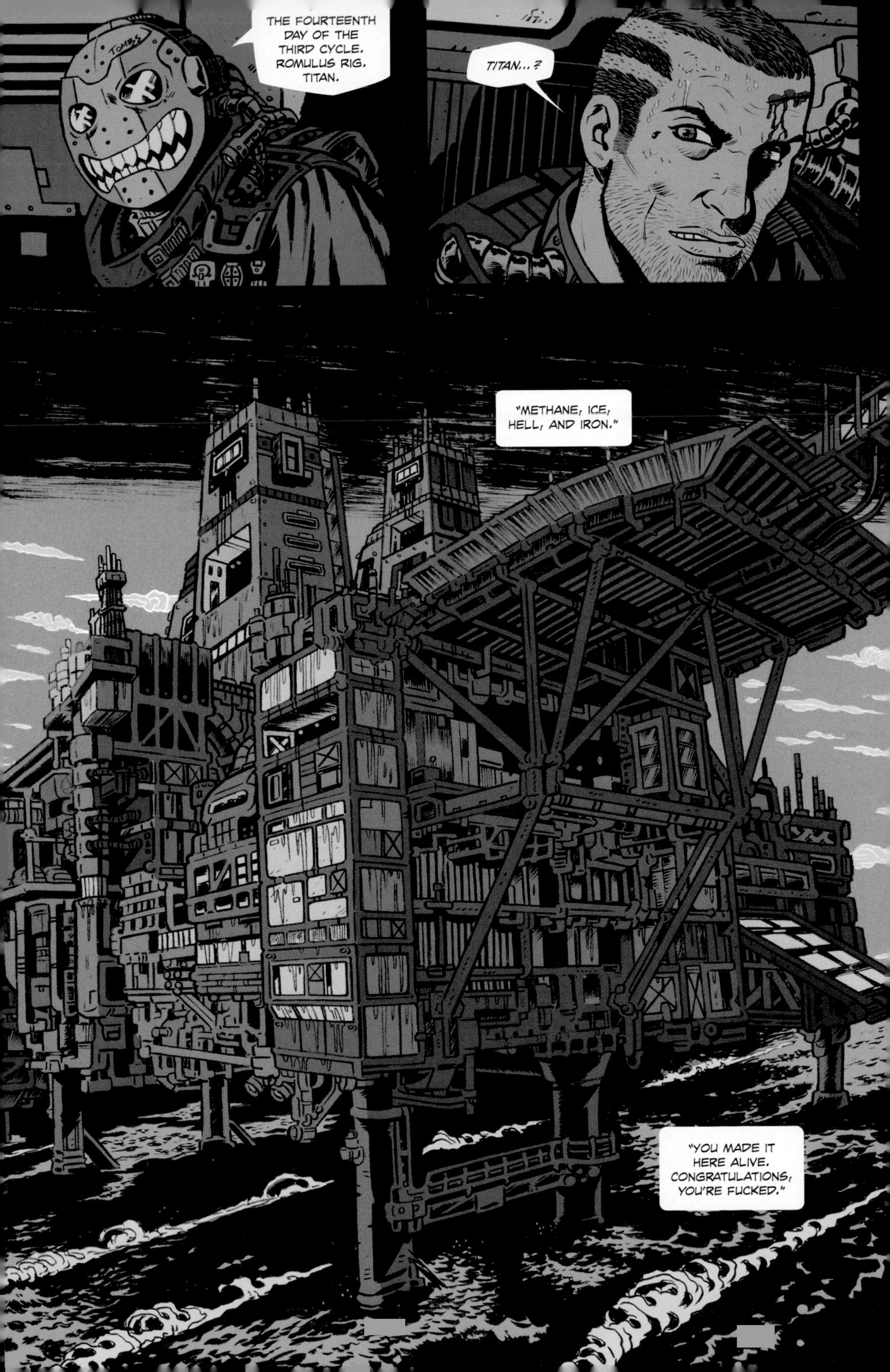
TOMBS
THE FOURTEENTH DAY OF THE THIRD CYCLE. ROMULUS RIG. TITAN.
TITAN...?
"METHANE, ICE, HELL, AND IRON."
"YOU MADE IT HERE ALIVE. CONGRATULATIONS, YOU'RE FUCKED."

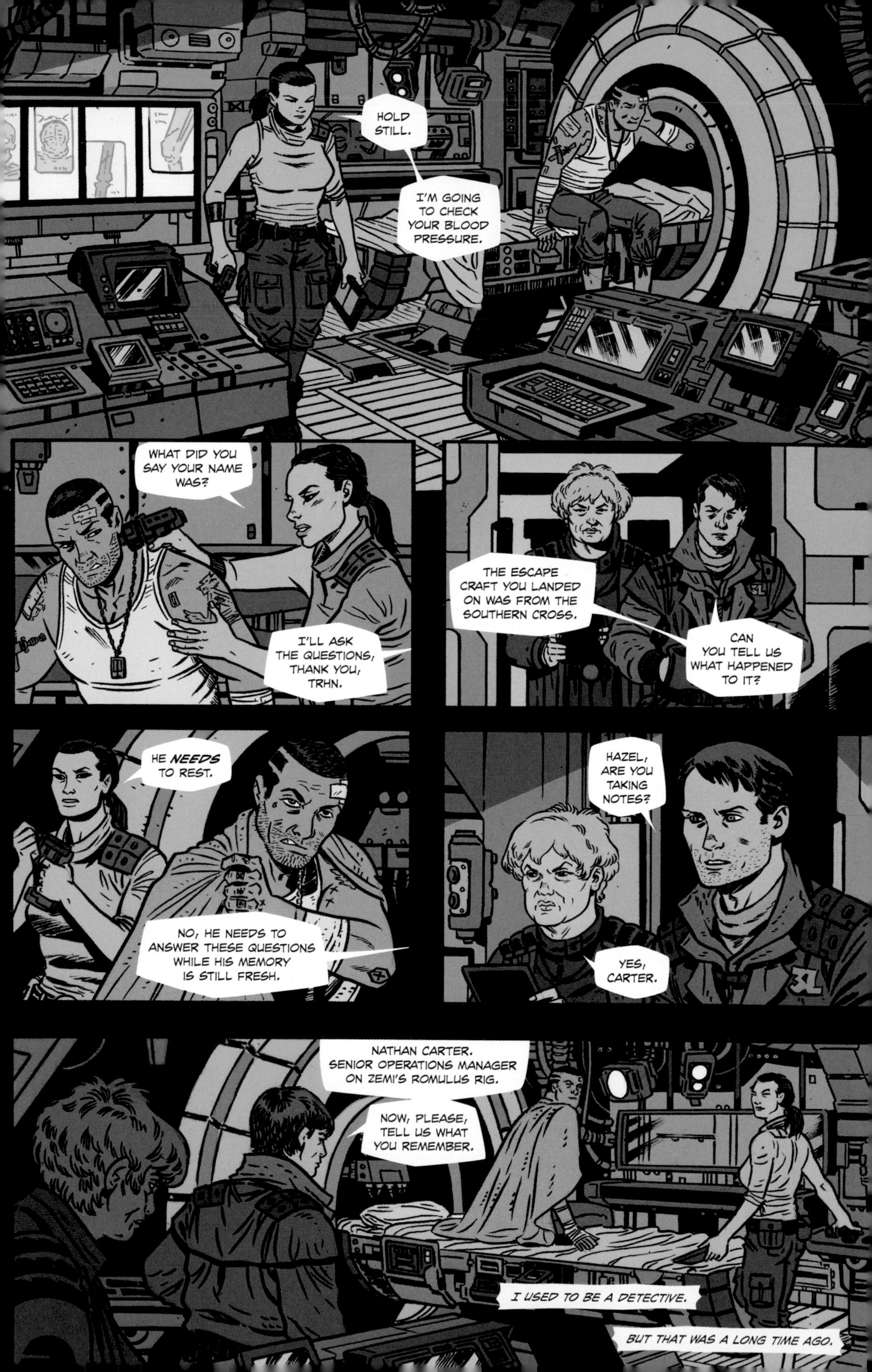

HOLD STILL.
I'M GOING TO CHECK YOUR BLOOD PRESSURE.
WHAT DID YOU SAY YOUR NAME WAS?
I'LL ASK THE QUESTIONS, THANK YOU, TRHN.
THE ESCAPE CRAFT YOU LANDED ON WAS FROM THE SOUTHERN CROSS.
CAN YOU TELL US WHAT HAPPENED TO IT?
HE NEEDS TO REST.
NO, HE NEEDS TO ANSWER THESE QUESTIONS WHILE HIS MEMORY IS STILL FRESH.
HAZEL, ARE YOU TAKING NOTES?
YES, CARTER.
NATHAN CARTER. SENIOR OPERATIONS MANAGER ON ZEMI'S ROMULUS RIG.
NOW, PLEASE, TELL US WHAT YOU REMEMBER.
I USED TO BE A DETECTIVE.
BUT THAT WAS A LONG TIME AGO.

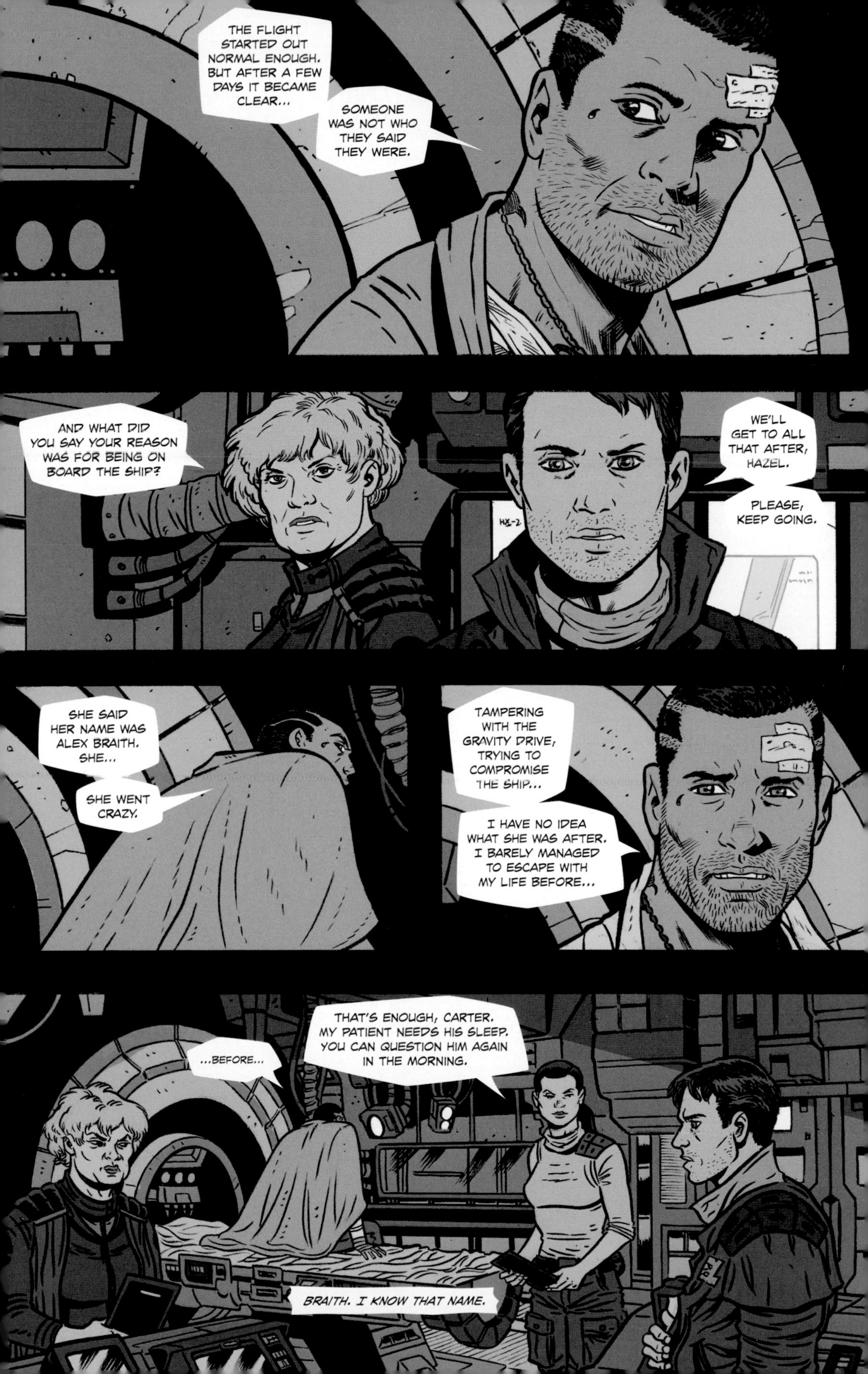
THE FLIGHT STARTED OUT NORMAL ENOUGH. BUT AFTER A FEW DAYS IT BECAME CLEAR...
SOMEONE WAS NOT WHO THEY SAID THEY WERE.
AND WHAT DID YOU SAY YOUR REASON WAS FOR BEING ON BOARD THE SHIP?
WE'LL GET TO ALL THAT AFTER, HAZEL.
PLEASE, KEEP GOING.
SHE SAID HER NAME WAS ALEX BRAITH. SHE...
SHE WENT CRAZY.
TAMPERING WITH THE GRAVITY DRIVE, TRYING TO COMPROMISE THE SHIP...
I HAVE NO IDEA WHAT SHE WAS AFTER. I BARELY MANAGED TO ESCAPE WITH MY LIFE BEFORE...
...BEFORE...
THAT'S ENOUGH, CARTER. MY PATIENT NEEDS HIS SLEEP. YOU CAN QUESTION HIM AGAIN IN THE MORNING.
BRAITH. I KNOW THAT NAME.

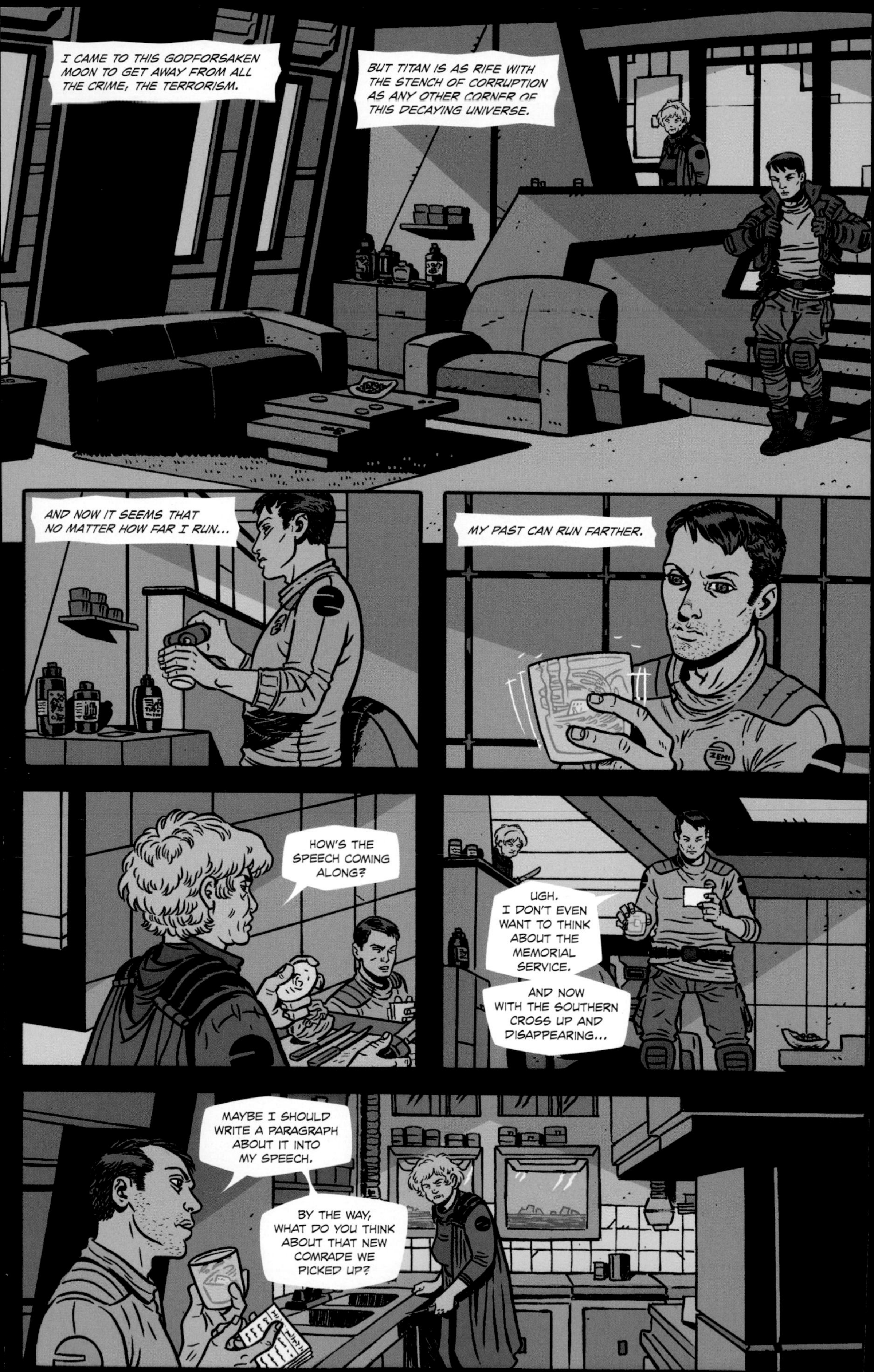
I CAME TO THIS GODFORSAKEN MOON TO GET AWAY FROM ALL THE CRIME; THE TERRORISM.
BUT TITAN IS AS RIFE WITH THE STENCH OF CORRUPTION AS ANY OTHER CORNER OF THIS DECAYING UNIVERSE.
AND NOW IT SEEMS THAT NO MATTER HOW FAR I RUN...
MY PAST CAN RUN FARTHER.
HOW'S THE SPEECH COMING ALONG?
UGH. I DON'T EVEN WANT TO THINK ABOUT THE MEMORIAL SERVICE.
AND NOW WITH THE SOUTHERN CROSS UP AND DISAPPEARING...
MAYBE I SHOULD WRITE A PARAGRAPH ABOUT IT INTO MY SPEECH.
BY THE WAY, WHAT DO YOU THINK ABOUT THAT NEW COMRADE WE PICKED UP?

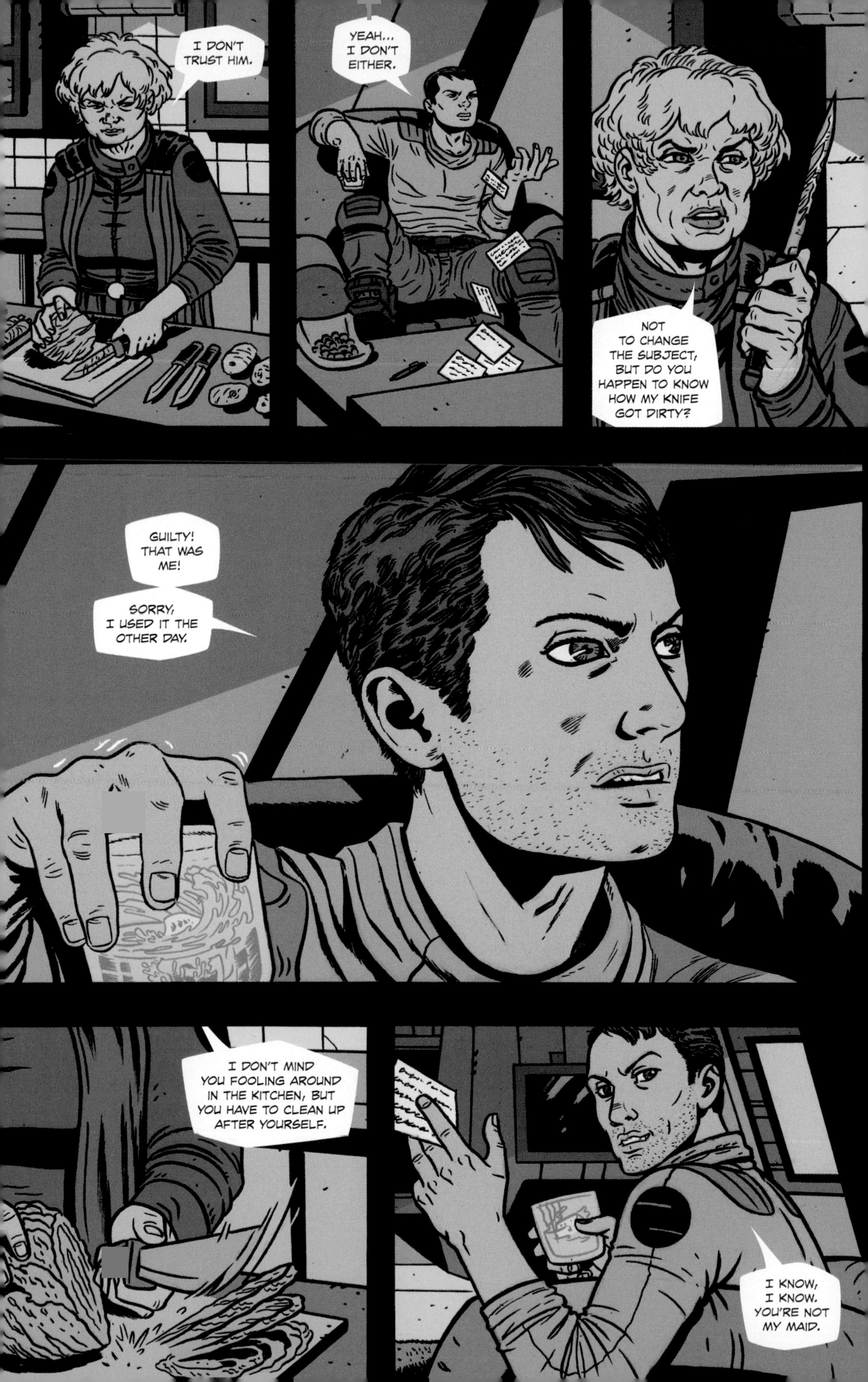
I DON'T TRUST HIM.
YEAH... I DON'T EITHER.
NOT TO CHANGE THE SUBJECT, BUT DO YOU HAPPEN TO KNOW HOW MY KNIFE GOT DIRTY?
GUILTY! THAT WAS ME!
SORRY, I USED IT THE OTHER DAY.
I DON'T MIND YOU FOOLING AROUND IN THE KITCHEN, BUT YOU HAVE TO CLEAN UP AFTER YOURSELF.
I KNOW, I KNOW. YOU'RE NOT MY MAID.

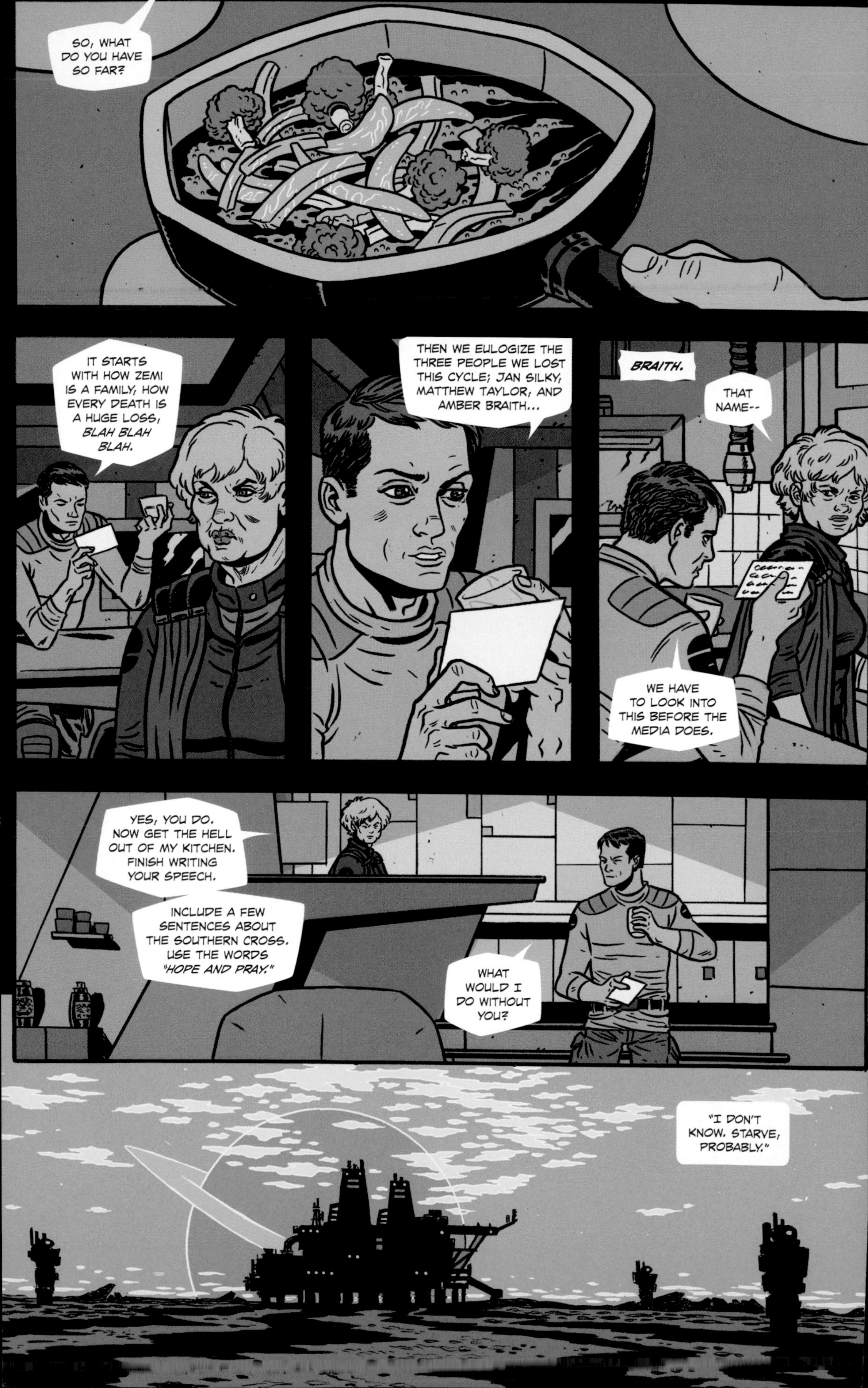
SO, WHAT DO YOU HAVE SO FAR?
IT STARTS WITH HOW ZEMI IS A FAMILY, HOW EVERY DEATH IS A HUGE LOSS, *BLAH BLAH BLAH.*
THEN WE EULOGIZE THE THREE PEOPLE WE LOST THIS CYCLE; JAN SILKY, MATTHEW TAYLOR, AND AMBER BRAITH...
*BRAITH.*
THAT NAME--
WE HAVE TO LOOK INTO THIS BEFORE THE MEDIA DOES.
YES, YOU DO. NOW GET THE HELL OUT OF MY KITCHEN. FINISH WRITING YOUR SPEECH.
INCLUDE A FEW SENTENCES ABOUT THE SOUTHERN CROSS. USE THE WORDS *"HOPE AND PRAY."*
WHAT WOULD I DO WITHOUT YOU?
"I DON'T KNOW. STARVE, PROBABLY."

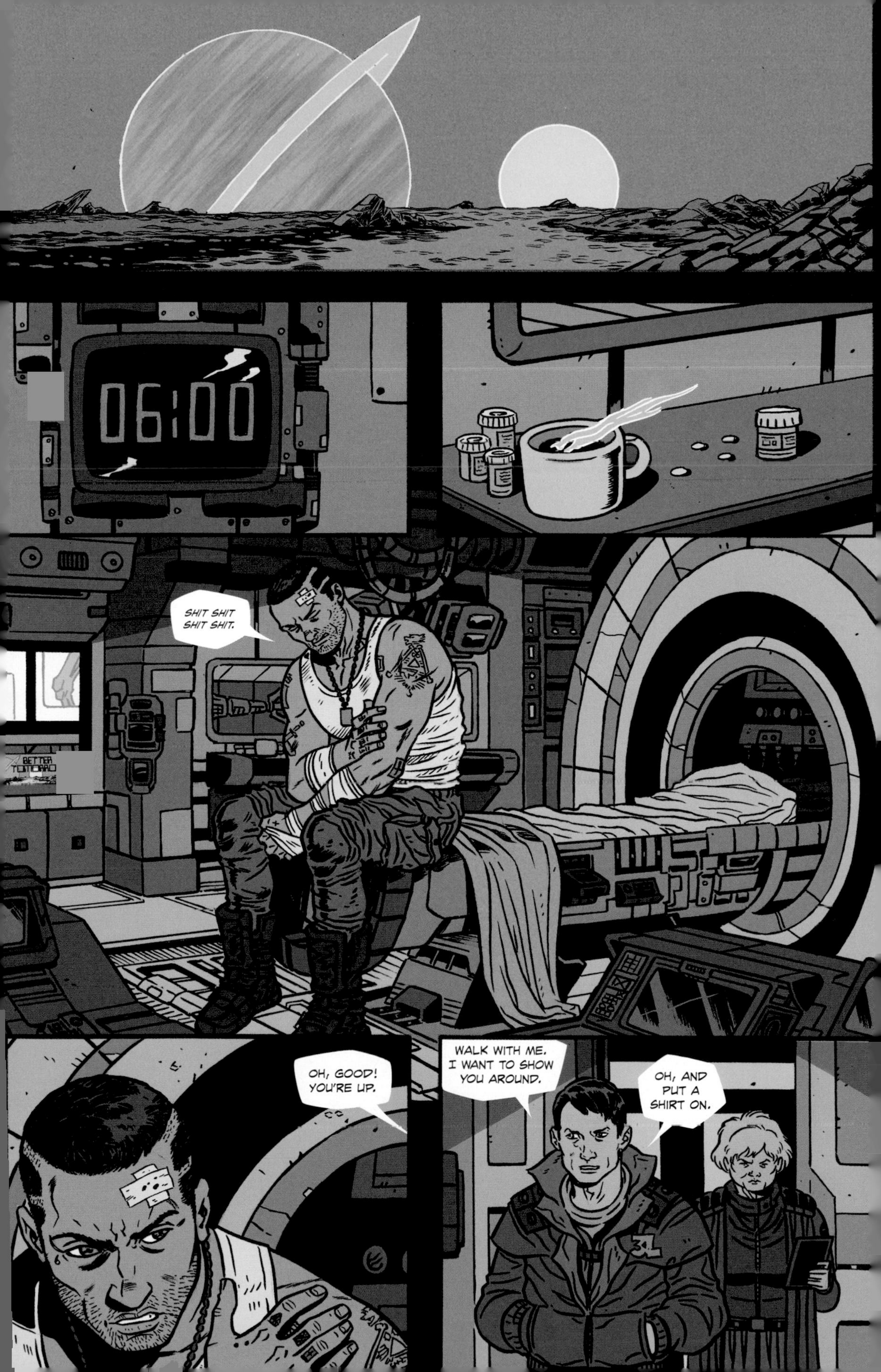
06:00
SHIT SHIT SHIT SHIT.
BETTER TOMORROW
OH, GOOD! YOU'RE UP.
WALK WITH ME. I WANT TO SHOW YOU AROUND.
OH, AND PUT A SHIRT ON.

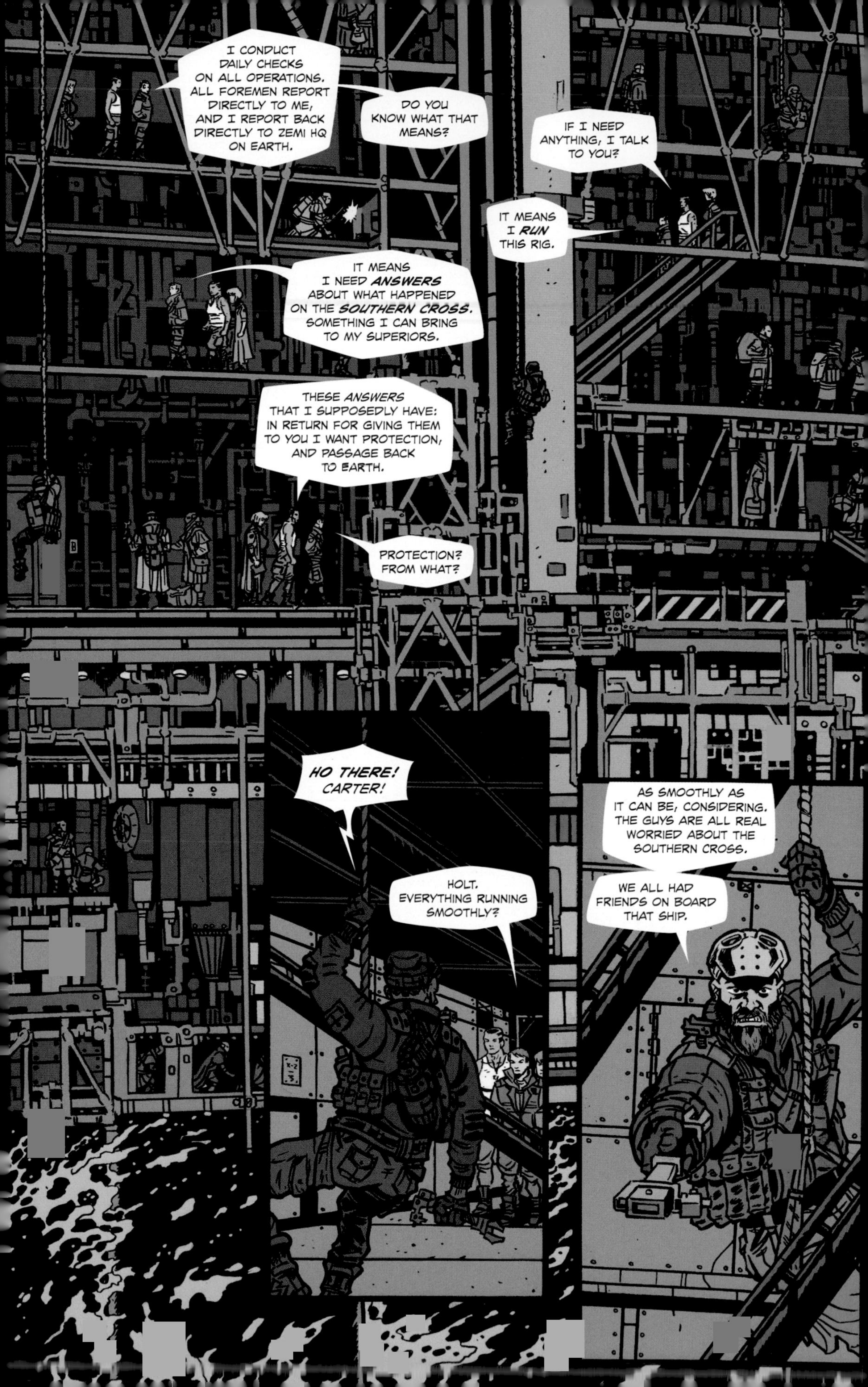
I CONDUCT DAILY CHECKS ON ALL OPERATIONS. ALL FOREMEN REPORT DIRECTLY TO ME, AND I REPORT BACK DIRECTLY TO ZEMI HQ ON EARTH.
DO YOU KNOW WHAT THAT MEANS?
IF I NEED ANYTHING, I TALK TO YOU?
IT MEANS I RUN THIS RIG.
IT MEANS I NEED ANSWERS ABOUT WHAT HAPPENED ON THE SOUTHERN CROSS. SOMETHING I CAN BRING TO MY SUPERIORS.
THESE ANSWERS THAT I SUPPOSEDLY HAVE: IN RETURN FOR GIVING THEM TO YOU I WANT PROTECTION, AND PASSAGE BACK TO EARTH.
PROTECTION? FROM WHAT?
HO THERE! CARTER!
HOLT. EVERYTHING RUNNING SMOOTHLY?
AS SMOOTHLY AS IT CAN BE, CONSIDERING. THE GUYS ARE ALL REAL WORRIED ABOUT THE SOUTHERN CROSS.
WE ALL HAD FRIENDS ON BOARD THAT SHIP.

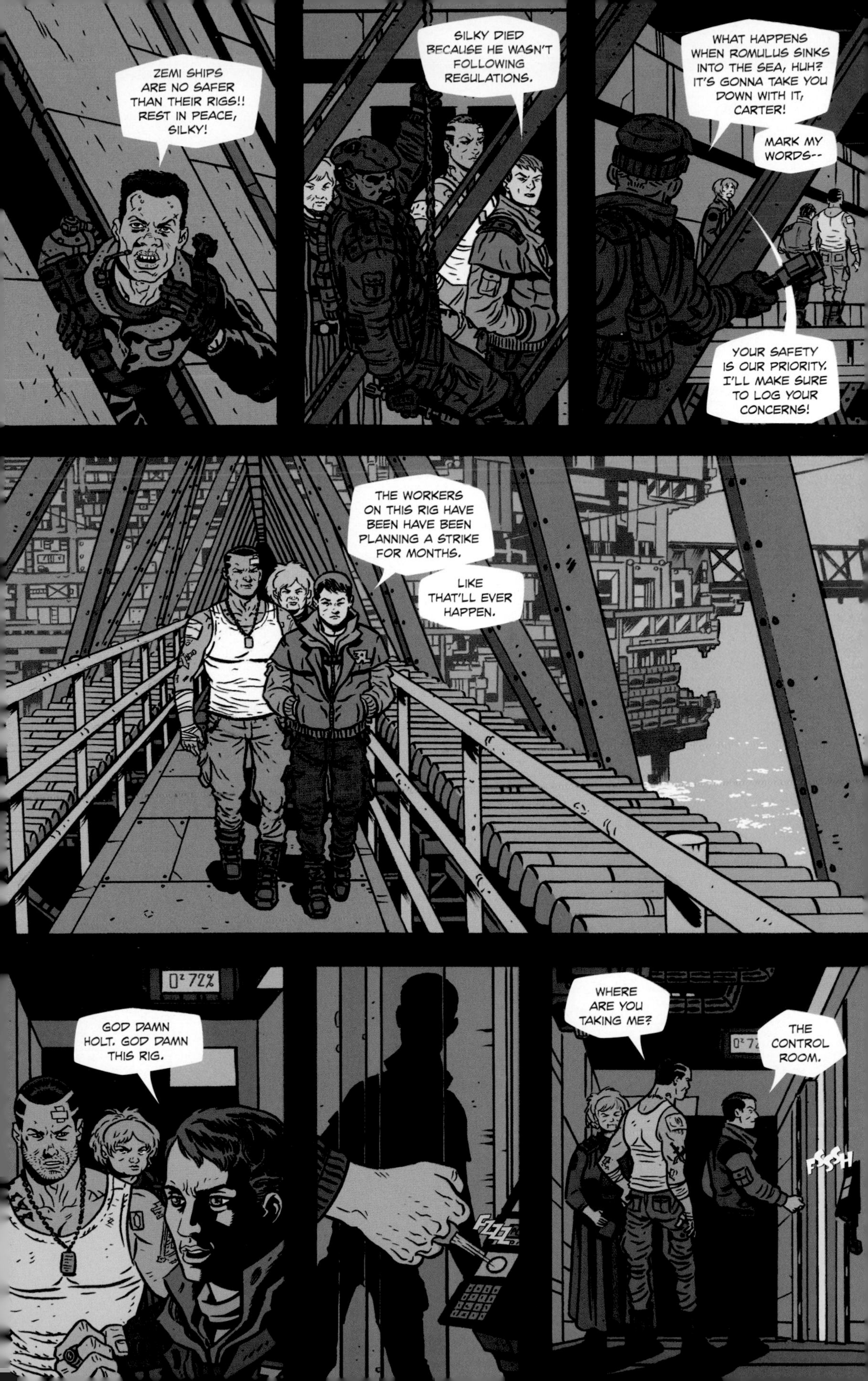
ZEMI SHIPS ARE NO SAFER THAN THEIR RIGS!! REST IN PEACE, SILKY!
SILKY DIED BECAUSE HE WASN'T FOLLOWING REGULATIONS.
WHAT HAPPENS WHEN ROMULUS SINKS INTO THE SEA, HUH? IT'S GONNA TAKE YOU DOWN WITH IT, CARTER!
MARK MY WORDS--
YOUR SAFETY IS OUR PRIORITY. I'LL MAKE SURE TO LOG YOUR CONCERNS!
THE WORKERS ON THIS RIG HAVE BEEN HAVE BEEN PLANNING A STRIKE FOR MONTHS.
LIKE THAT'LL EVER HAPPEN.
O² 72%
GOD DAMN HOLT. GOD DAMN THIS RIG.
WHERE ARE YOU TAKING ME?
THE CONTROL ROOM.
FSSSH

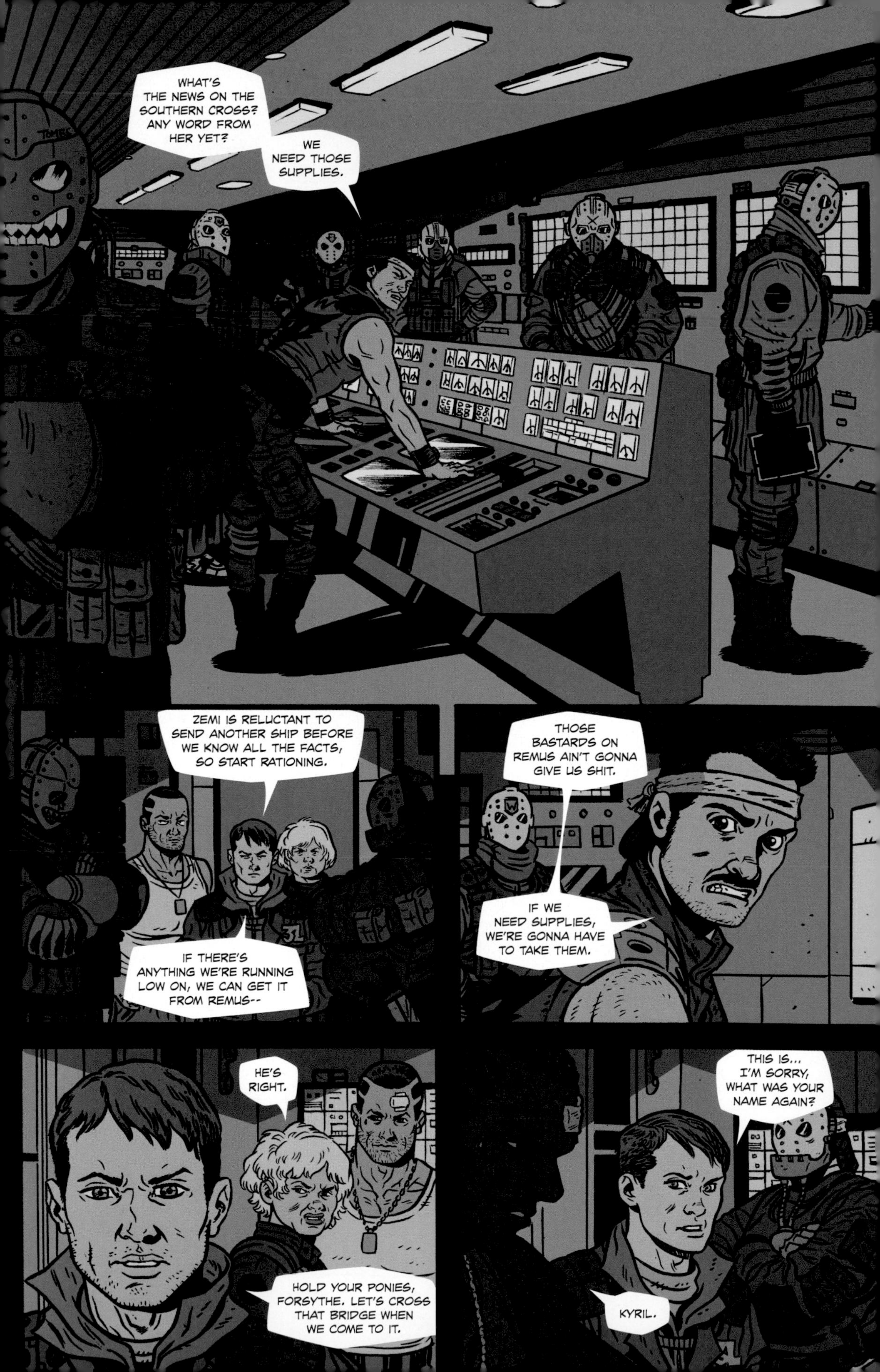
WHAT'S THE NEWS ON THE SOUTHERN CROSS? ANY WORD FROM HER YET?
WE NEED THOSE SUPPLIES.
ZEMI IS RELUCTANT TO SEND ANOTHER SHIP BEFORE WE KNOW ALL THE FACTS, SO START RATIONING.
IF THERE'S ANYTHING WE'RE RUNNING LOW ON, WE CAN GET IT FROM REMUS--
THOSE BASTARDS ON REMUS AIN'T GONNA GIVE US SHIT.
IF WE NEED SUPPLIES, WE'RE GONNA HAVE TO TAKE THEM.
HE'S RIGHT.
HOLD YOUR PONIES, FORSYTHE. LET'S CROSS THAT BRIDGE WHEN WE COME TO IT.
THIS IS... I'M SORRY, WHAT WAS YOUR NAME AGAIN?
KYRIL.

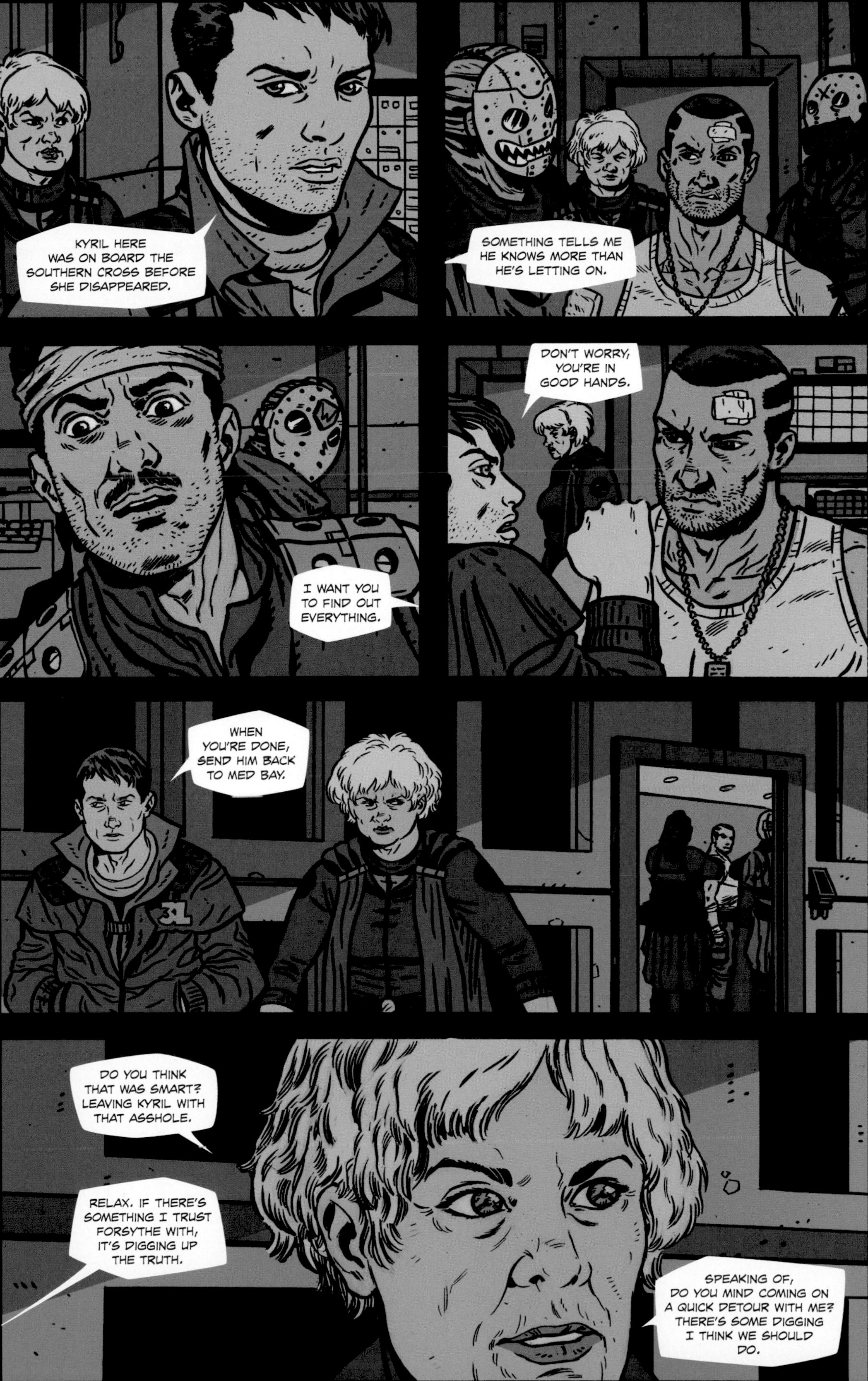
KYRIL HERE WAS ON BOARD THE SOUTHERN CROSS BEFORE SHE DISAPPEARED.
SOMETHING TELLS ME HE KNOWS MORE THAN HE'S LETTING ON.
I WANT YOU TO FIND OUT EVERYTHING.
DON'T WORRY, YOU'RE IN GOOD HANDS.
WHEN YOU'RE DONE, SEND HIM BACK TO MED BAY.
DO YOU THINK THAT WAS SMART? LEAVING KYRIL WITH THAT ASSHOLE.
RELAX. IF THERE'S SOMETHING I TRUST FORSYTHE WITH, IT'S DIGGING UP THE TRUTH.
SPEAKING OF, DO YOU MIND COMING ON A QUICK DETOUR WITH ME? THERE'S SOME DIGGING I THINK WE SHOULD DO.

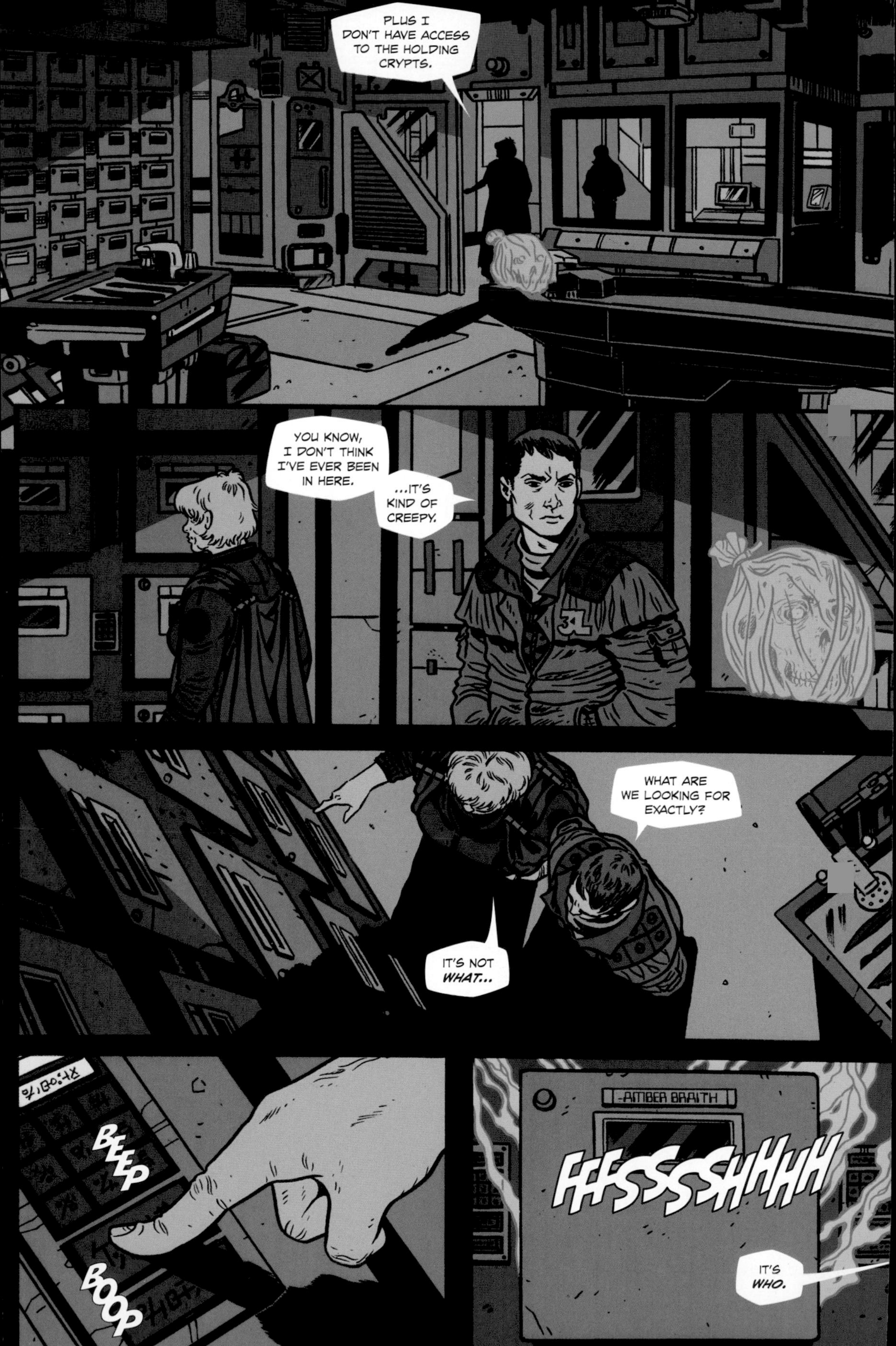
PLUS I DON'T HAVE ACCESS TO THE HOLDING CRYPTS.
YOU KNOW, I DON'T THINK I'VE EVER BEEN IN HERE.
...IT'S KIND OF CREEPY.
WHAT ARE WE LOOKING FOR EXACTLY?
IT'S NOT *WHAT*...
BEEP
BOOP
AMBER BRAITH
FFFSSSSHHHH
IT'S *WHO*.

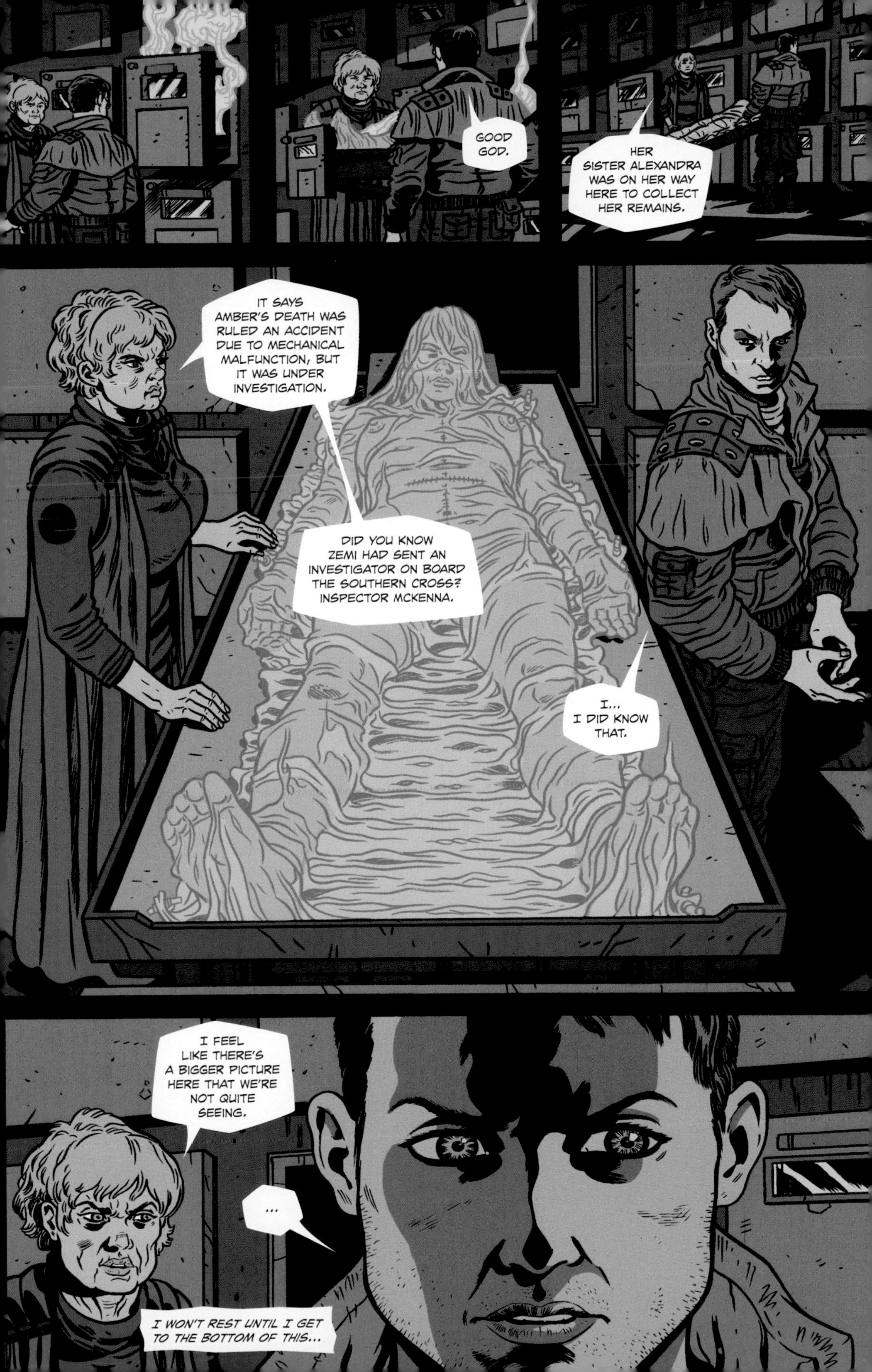
GOOD GOD.
HER SISTER ALEXANDRA WAS ON HER WAY HERE TO COLLECT HER REMAINS.
IT SAYS AMBER'S DEATH WAS RULED AN ACCIDENT DUE TO MECHANICAL MALFUNCTION, BUT IT WAS UNDER INVESTIGATION.
DID YOU KNOW ZEMI HAD SENT AN INVESTIGATOR ON BOARD THE SOUTHERN CROSS? INSPECTOR MCKENNA.
I... I DID KNOW THAT.
I FEEL LIKE THERE'S A BIGGER PICTURE HERE THAT WE'RE NOT QUITE SEEING.
...
I WON'T REST UNTIL I GET TO THE BOTTOM OF THIS...

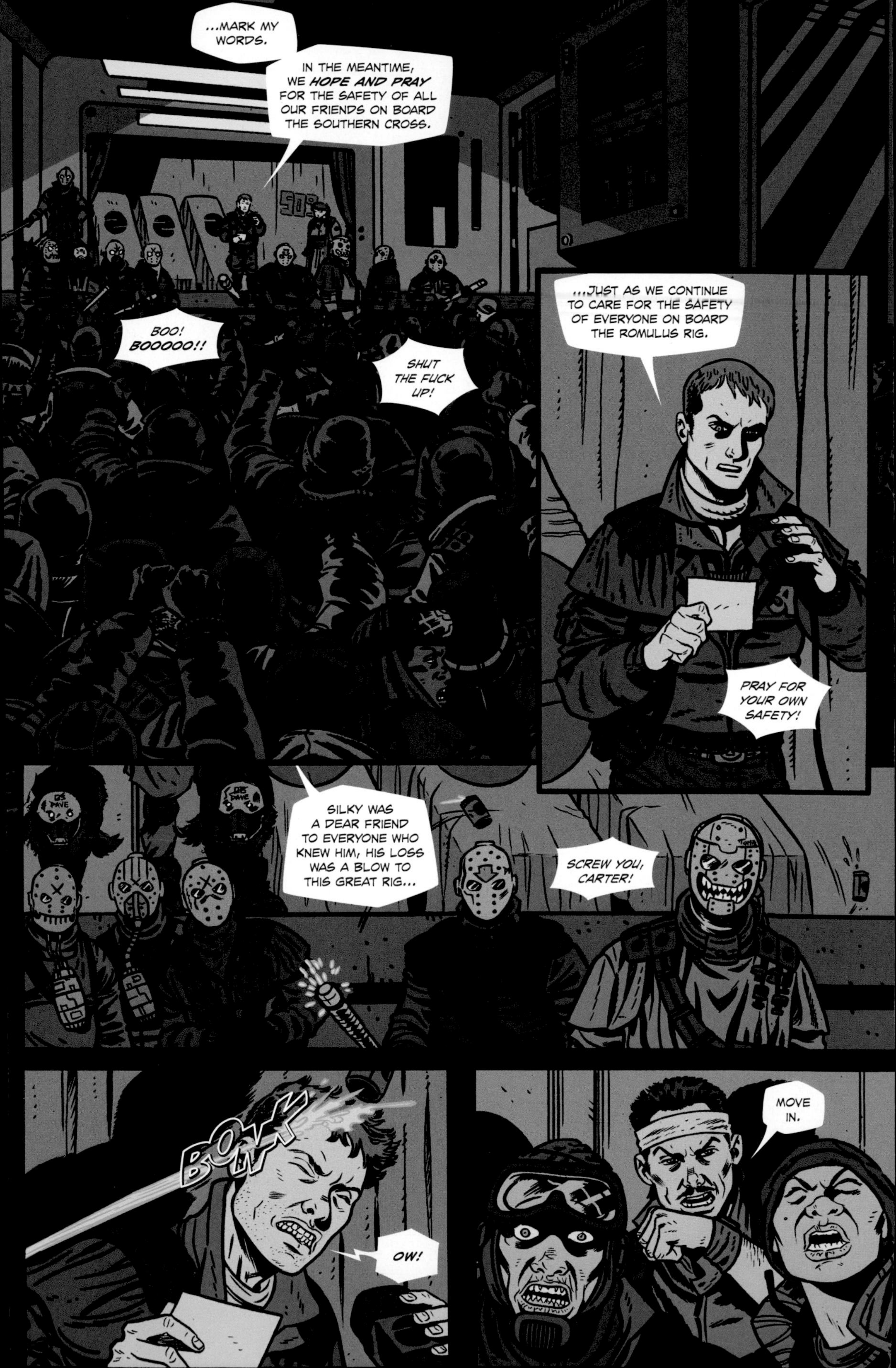

...MARK MY WORDS.
IN THE MEANTIME, WE HOPE AND PRAY FOR THE SAFETY OF ALL OUR FRIENDS ON BOARD THE SOUTHERN CROSS.
BOO! BOOOOO!!
SHUT THE FUCK UP!
...JUST AS WE CONTINUE TO CARE FOR THE SAFETY OF EVERYONE ON BOARD THE ROMULUS RIG.
PRAY FOR YOUR OWN SAFETY!
SILKY WAS A DEAR FRIEND TO EVERYONE WHO KNEW HIM, HIS LOSS WAS A BLOW TO THIS GREAT RIG...
SCREW YOU, CARTER!
BOKK
OW!
MOVE IN.

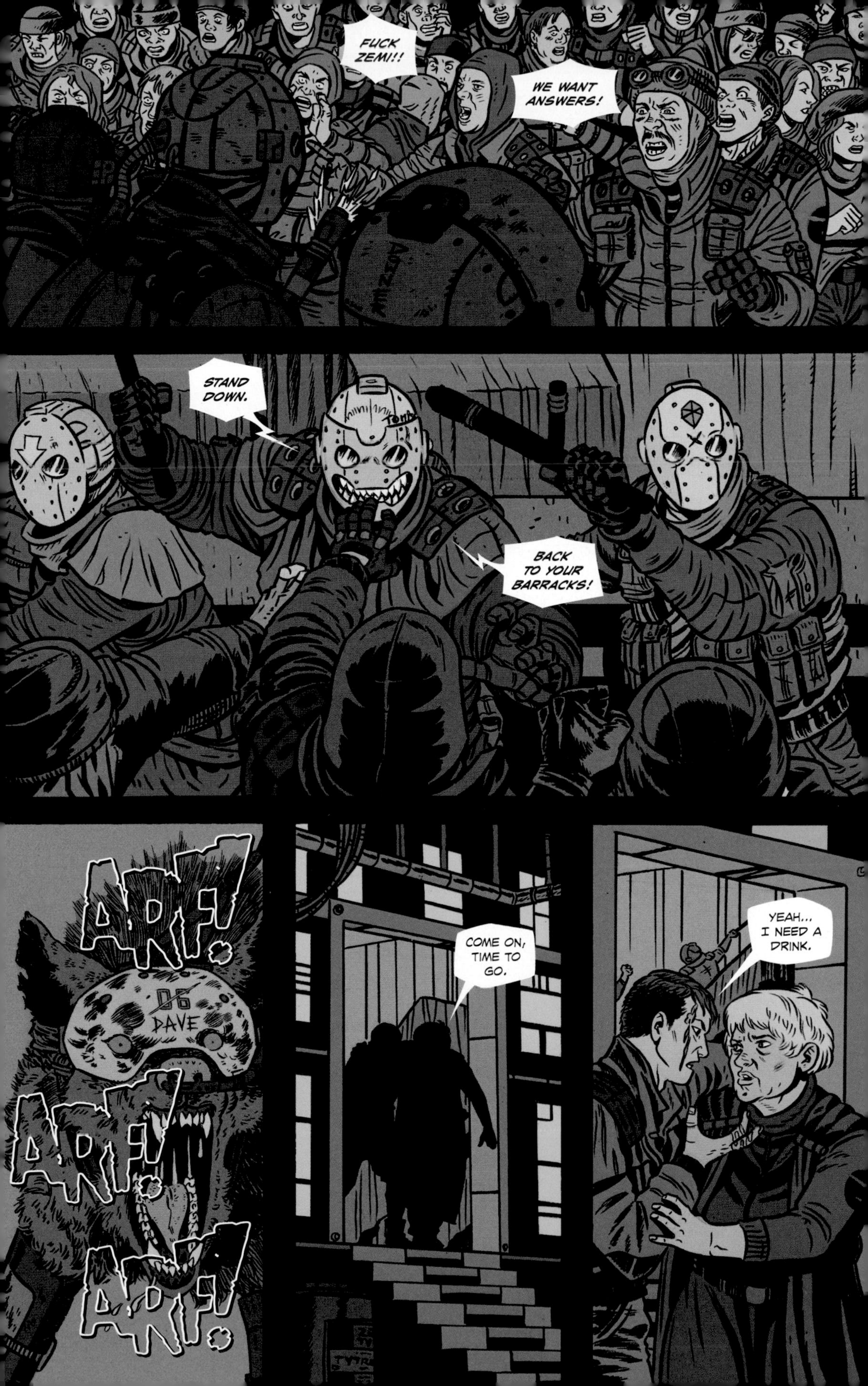
FUCK ZEMI!!
WE WANT ANSWERS!
STAND DOWN.
BACK TO YOUR BARRACKS!
ARF!
ARF!
ARF!
COME ON, TIME TO GO.
YEAH... I NEED A DRINK.

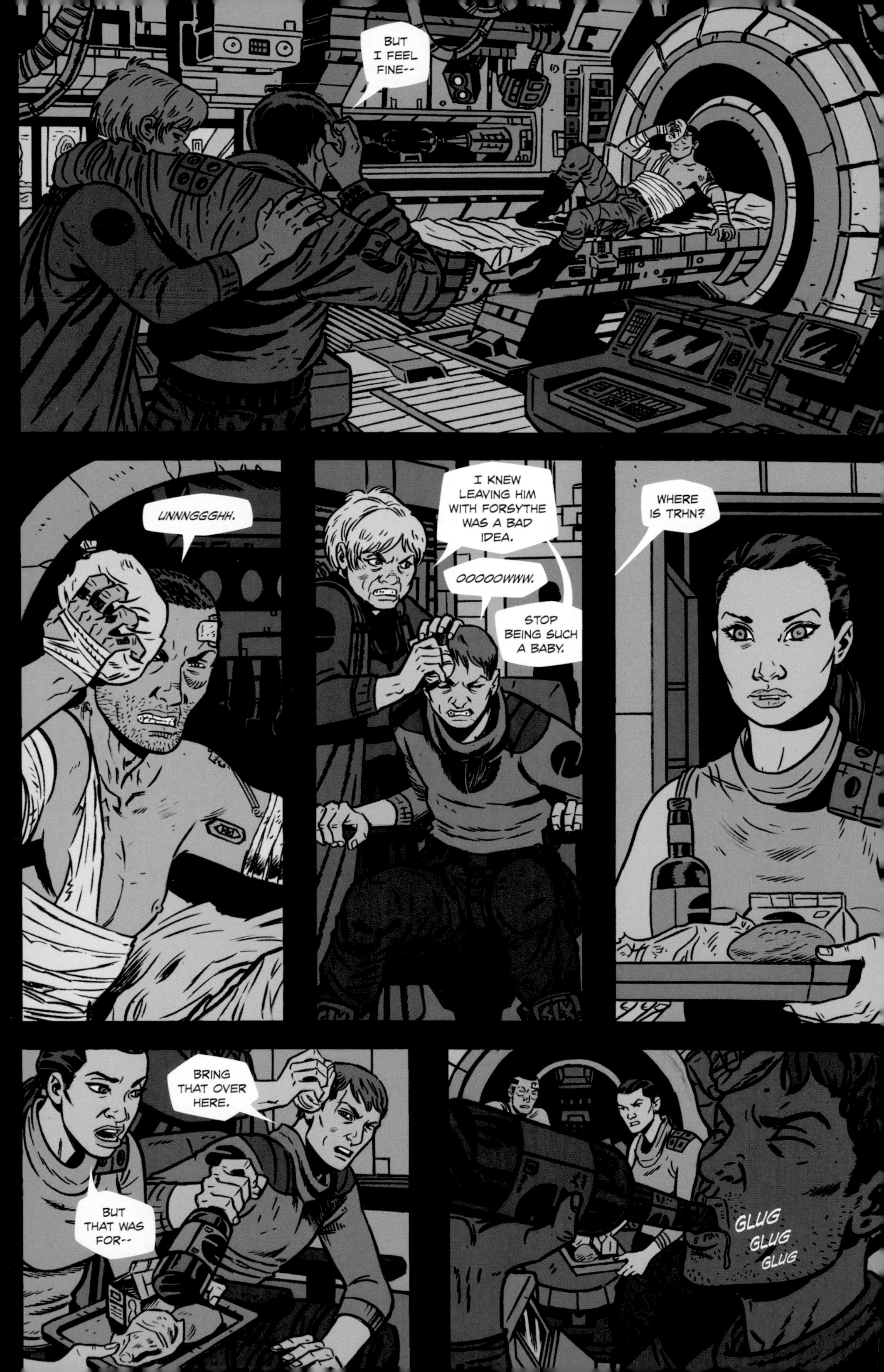
BUT I FEEL FINE--
UNNNGGGHH.
I KNEW LEAVING HIM WITH FORSYTHE WAS A BAD IDEA.
OOOOOWWW.
STOP BEING SUCH A BABY.
WHERE IS TRHN?
BRING THAT OVER HERE.
BUT THAT WAS FOR--
GLUG
GLUG
GLUG

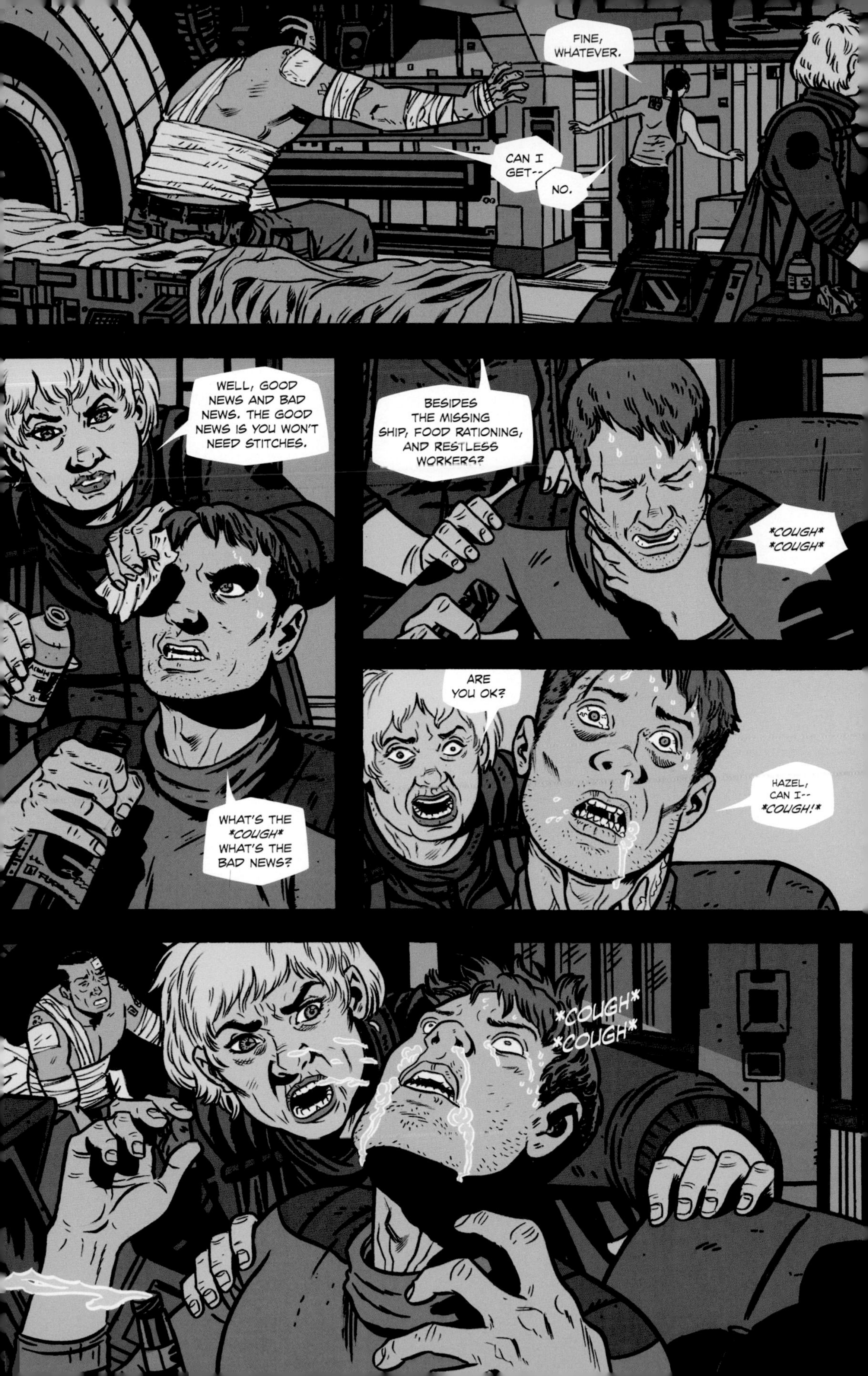
FINE, WHATEVER.
CAN I GET--
NO.
WELL, GOOD NEWS AND BAD NEWS. THE GOOD NEWS IS YOU WON'T NEED STITCHES.
WHAT'S THE *COUGH* WHAT'S THE BAD NEWS?
BESIDES THE MISSING SHIP, FOOD RATIONING, AND RESTLESS WORKERS?
*COUGH* *COUGH*
ARE YOU OK?
HAZEL, CAN I-- *COUGH!*
*COUGH* *COUGH*

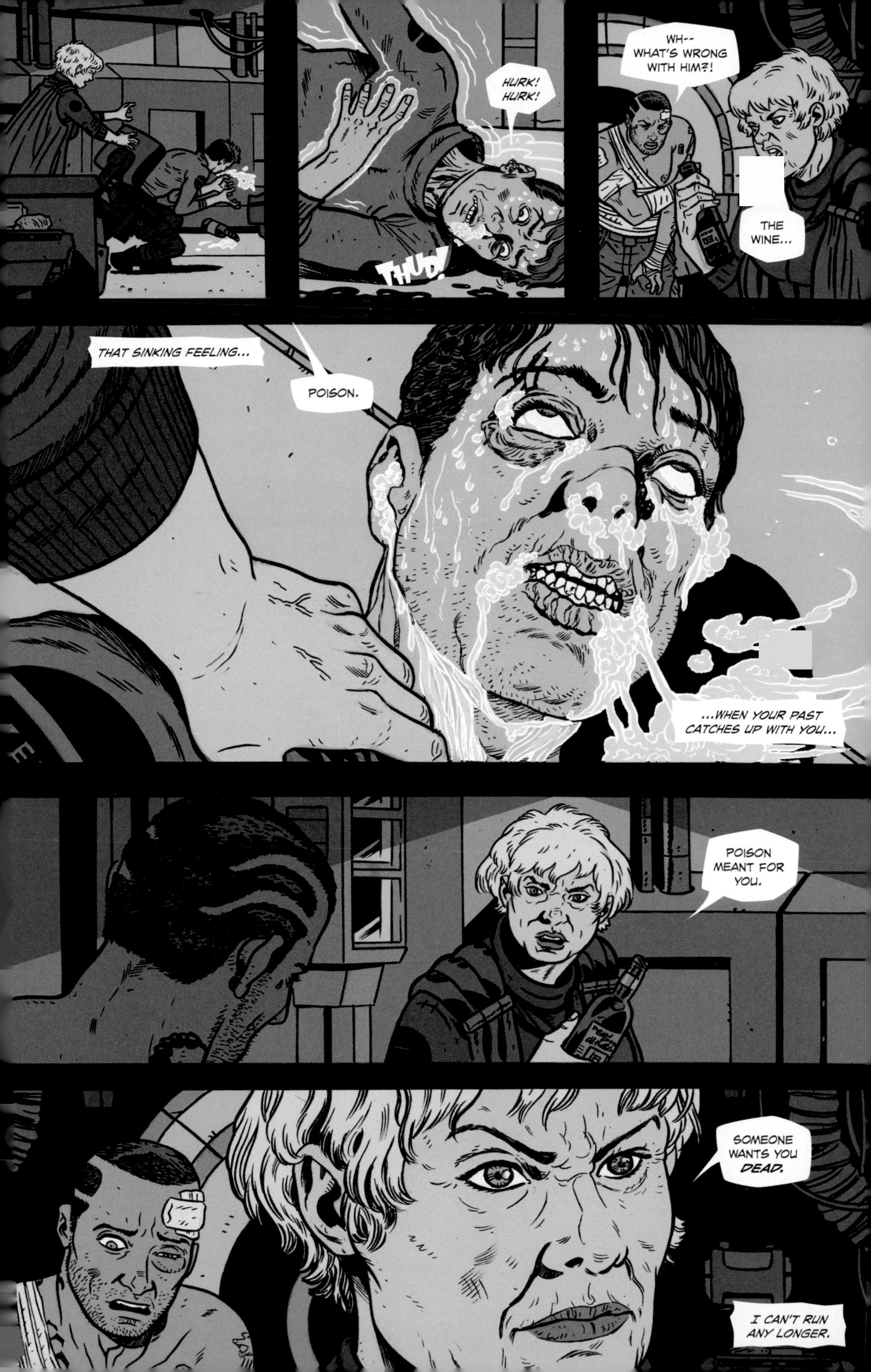
HURK!
HURK!
THUD!
WH--
WHAT'S WRONG
WITH HIM?!
THE
WINE...
THAT SINKING FEELING...
POISON.
...WHEN YOUR PAST
CATCHES UP WITH YOU...
POISON
MEANT FOR
YOU.
SOMEONE
WANTS YOU
DEAD.
I CAN'T RUN
ANY LONGER.

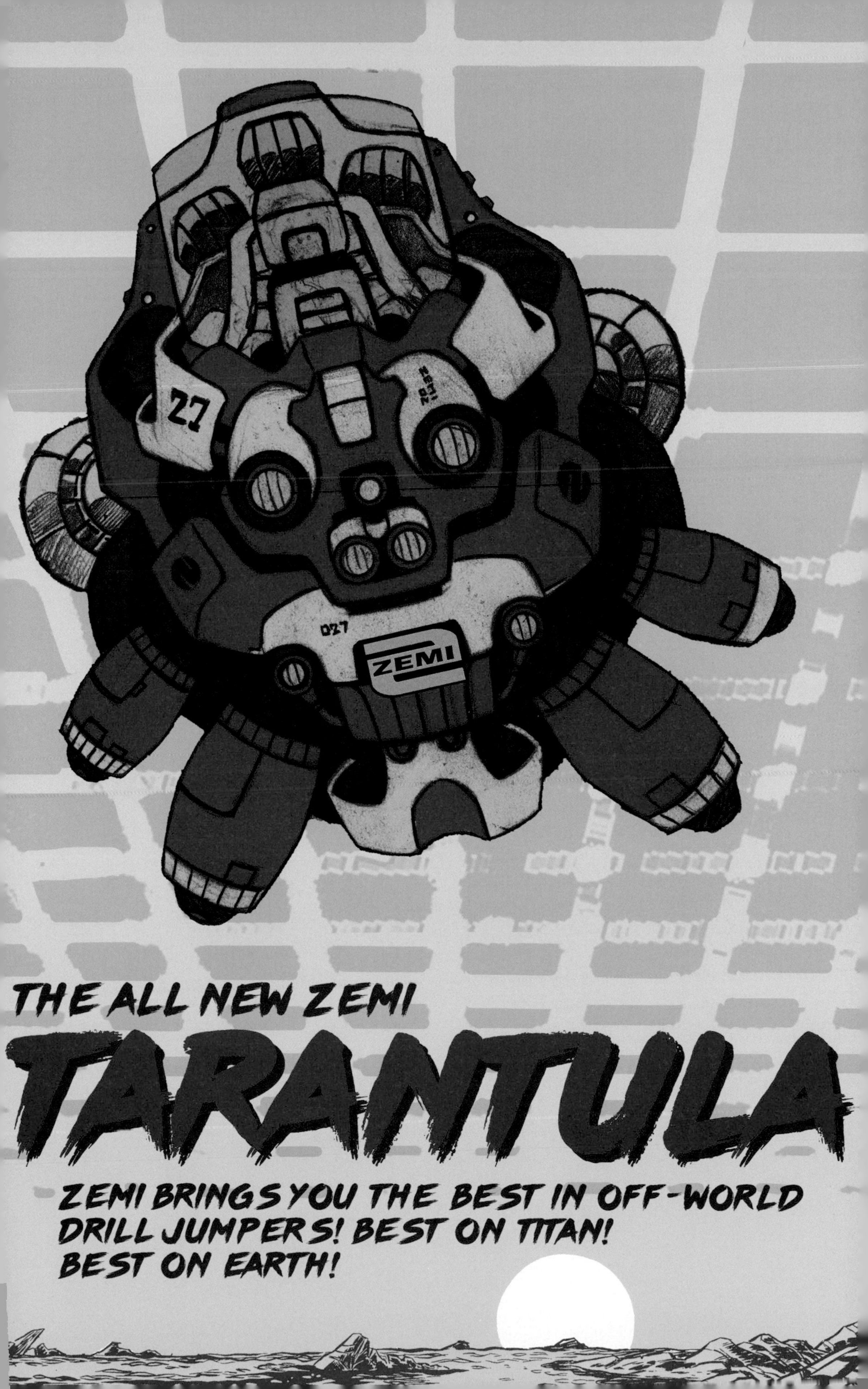
27
027
ZEMI
THE ALL NEW ZEMI
TARANTULA
ZEMI BRINGS YOU THE BEST IN OFF-WORLD DRILL JUMPERS! BEST ON TITAN! BEST ON EARTH!

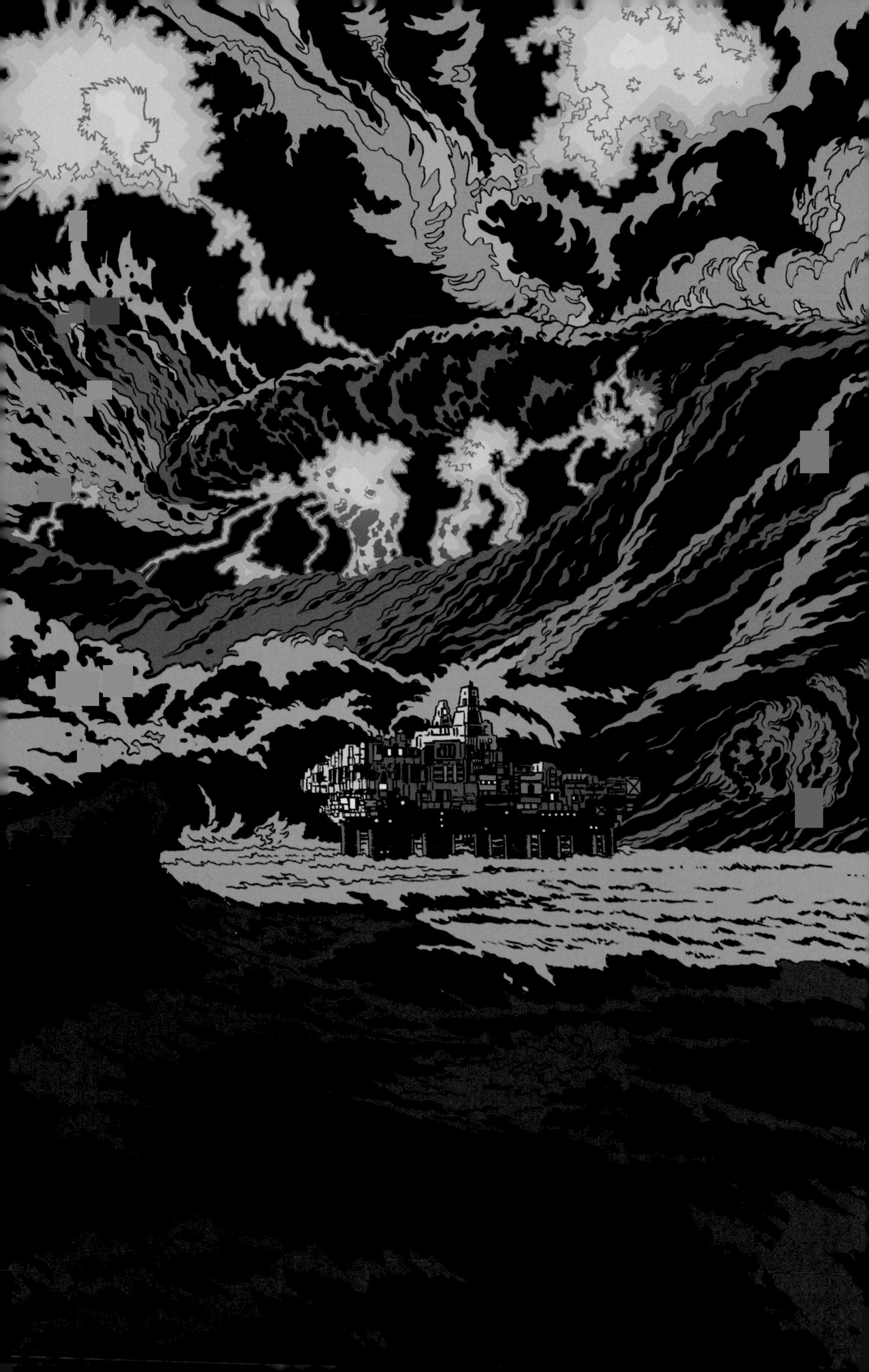

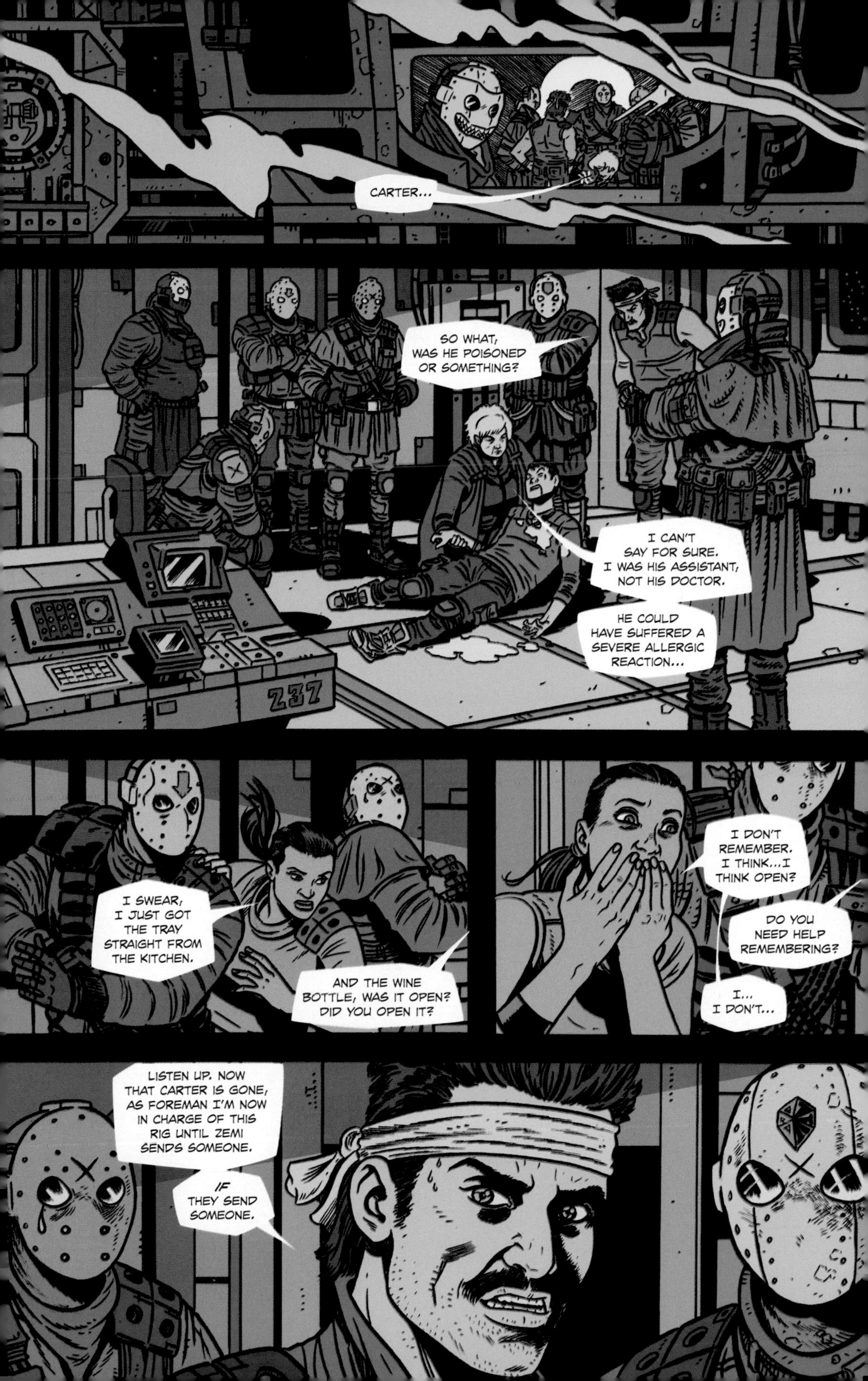
CARTER...
SO WHAT, WAS HE POISONED OR SOMETHING?
I CAN'T SAY FOR SURE. I WAS HIS ASSISTANT, NOT HIS DOCTOR.
HE COULD HAVE SUFFERED A SEVERE ALLERGIC REACTION...
237
I SWEAR, I JUST GOT THE TRAY STRAIGHT FROM THE KITCHEN.
AND THE WINE BOTTLE, WAS IT OPEN? DID YOU OPEN IT?
I DON'T REMEMBER. I THINK...I THINK OPEN?
DO YOU NEED HELP REMEMBERING?
I... I DON'T...
LISTEN UP. NOW THAT CARTER IS GONE, AS FOREMAN I'M NOW IN CHARGE OF THIS RIG UNTIL ZEMI SENDS SOMEONE.
*IF* THEY SEND SOMEONE.

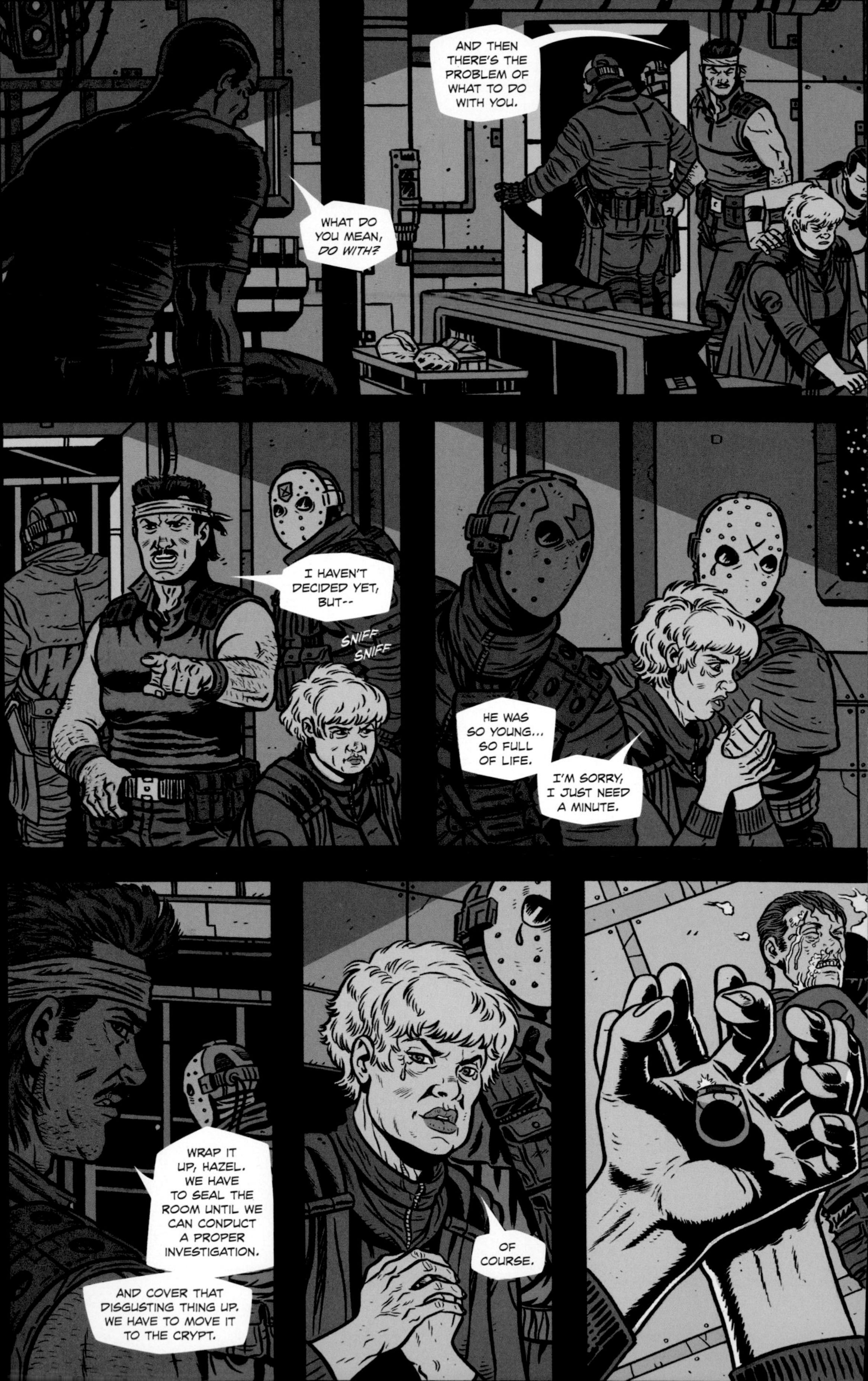
AND THEN THERE'S THE PROBLEM OF WHAT TO DO WITH YOU.
WHAT DO YOU MEAN, DO WITH?
I HAVEN'T DECIDED YET, BUT--
SNIFF SNIFF
HE WAS SO YOUNG... SO FULL OF LIFE.
I'M SORRY, I JUST NEED A MINUTE.
WRAP IT UP, HAZEL. WE HAVE TO SEAL THE ROOM UNTIL WE CAN CONDUCT A PROPER INVESTIGATION.
AND COVER THAT DISGUSTING THING UP. WE HAVE TO MOVE IT TO THE CRYPT.
OF COURSE.

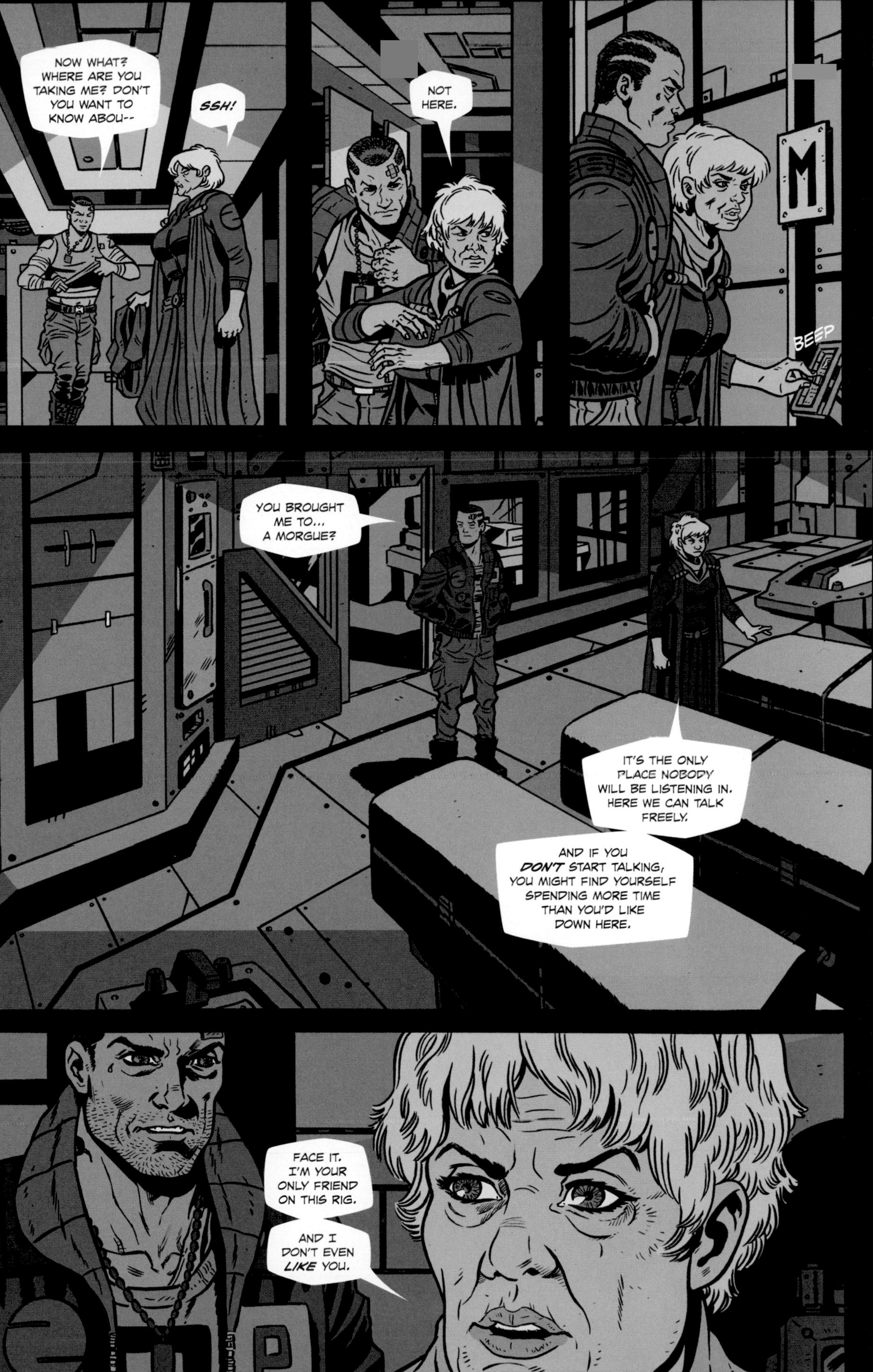
NOW WHAT? WHERE ARE YOU TAKING ME? DON'T YOU WANT TO KNOW ABOU--
SSH!
NOT HERE.
M
BEEP
YOU BROUGHT ME TO... A MORGUE?
IT'S THE ONLY PLACE NOBODY WILL BE LISTENING IN. HERE WE CAN TALK FREELY.
AND IF YOU DON'T START TALKING, YOU MIGHT FIND YOURSELF SPENDING MORE TIME THAN YOU'D LIKE DOWN HERE.
FACE IT. I'M YOUR ONLY FRIEND ON THIS RIG.
AND I DON'T EVEN LIKE YOU.

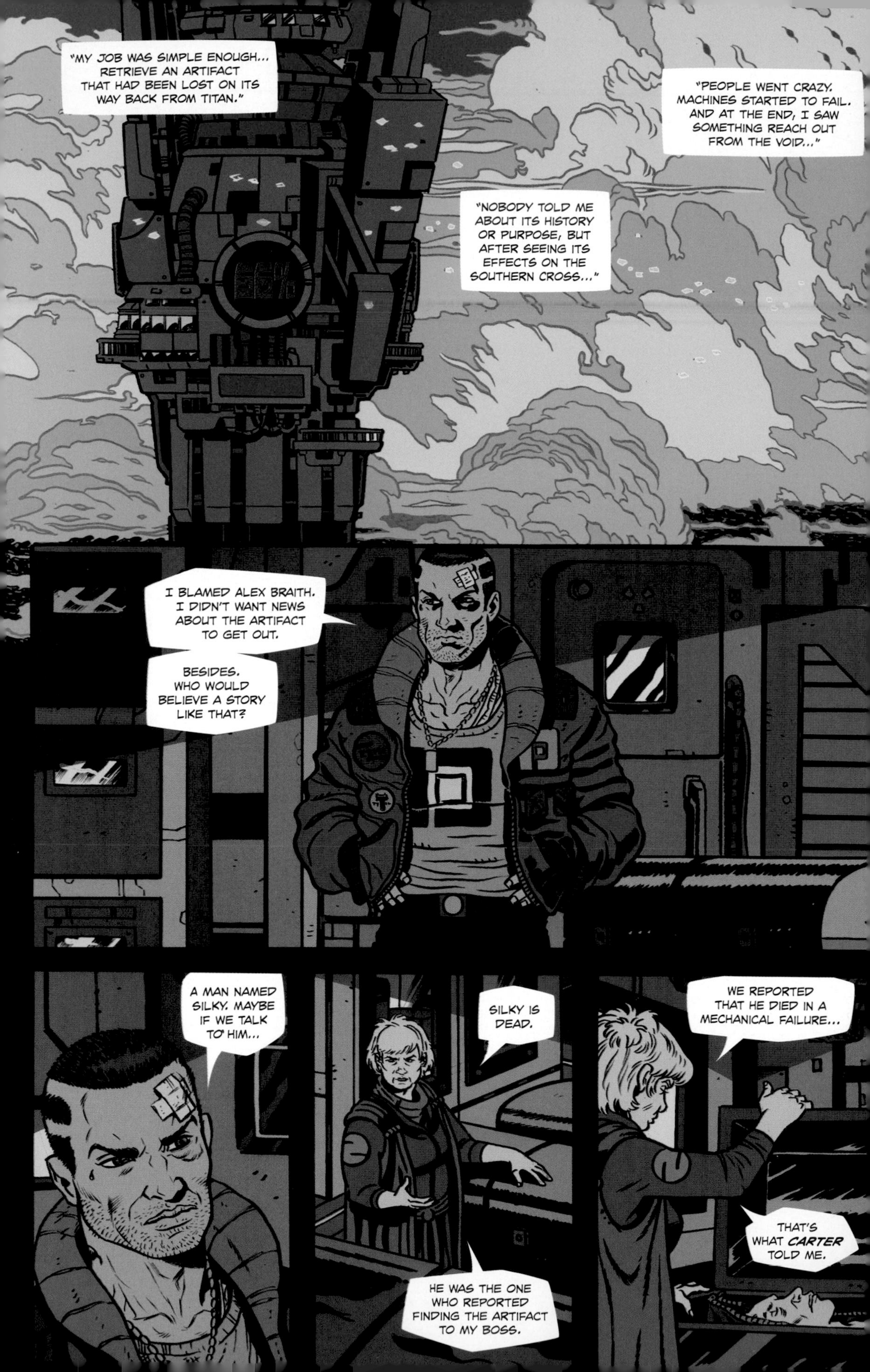
"MY JOB WAS SIMPLE ENOUGH... RETRIEVE AN ARTIFACT THAT HAD BEEN LOST ON ITS WAY BACK FROM TITAN."
"NOBODY TOLD ME ABOUT ITS HISTORY OR PURPOSE, BUT AFTER SEEING ITS EFFECTS ON THE SOUTHERN CROSS..."
"PEOPLE WENT CRAZY. MACHINES STARTED TO FAIL. AND AT THE END, I SAW SOMETHING REACH OUT FROM THE VOID..."
I BLAMED ALEX BRAITH. I DIDN'T WANT NEWS ABOUT THE ARTIFACT TO GET OUT.
BESIDES. WHO WOULD BELIEVE A STORY LIKE THAT?
A MAN NAMED SILKY. MAYBE IF WE TALK TO HIM...
SILKY IS DEAD.
HE WAS THE ONE WHO REPORTED FINDING THE ARTIFACT TO MY BOSS.
WE REPORTED THAT HE DIED IN A MECHANICAL FAILURE...
THAT'S WHAT *CARTER* TOLD ME.

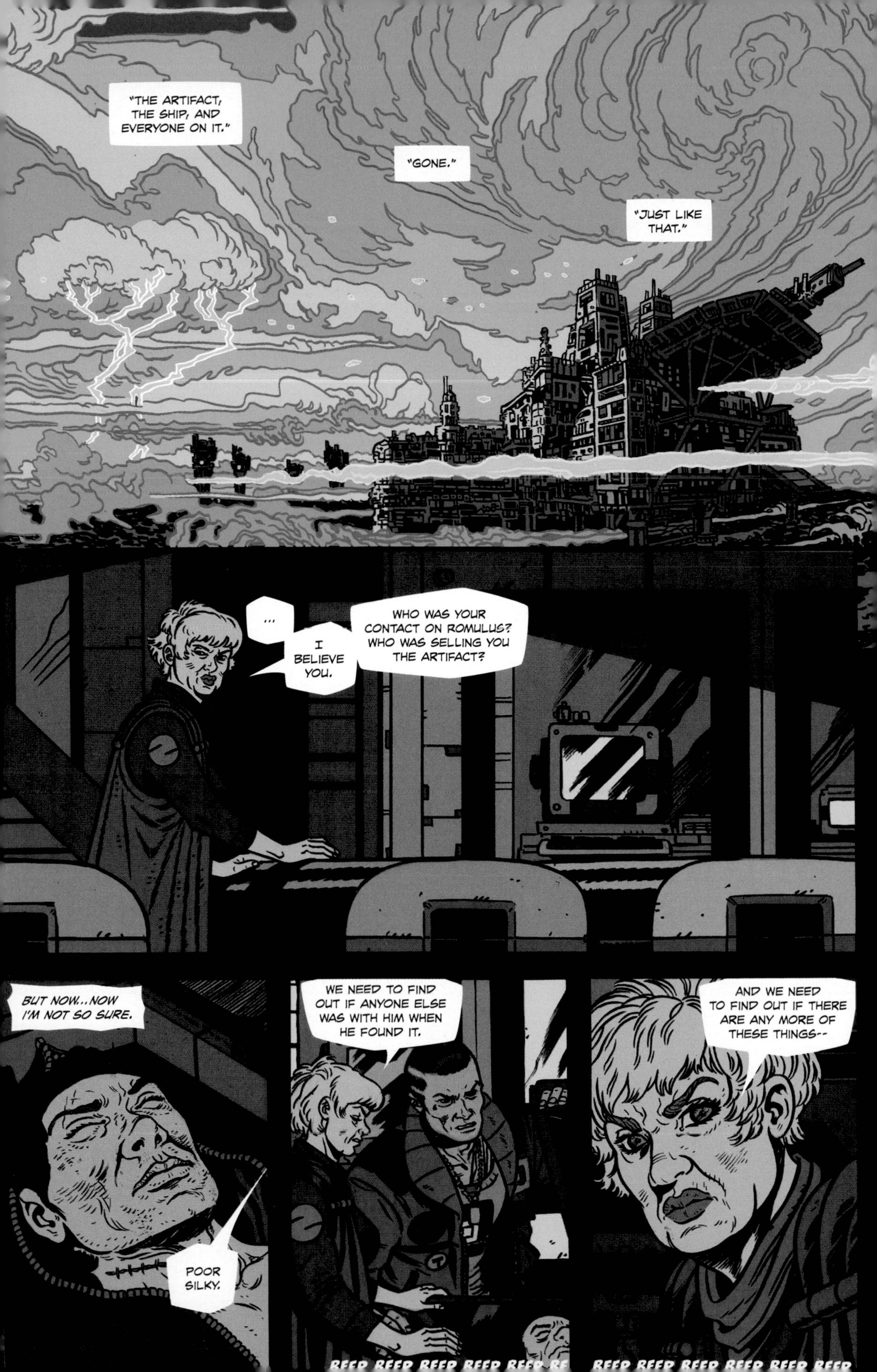

"THE ARTIFACT, THE SHIP, AND EVERYONE ON IT."
"GONE."
"JUST LIKE THAT."
...
I BELIEVE YOU.
WHO WAS YOUR CONTACT ON ROMULUS? WHO WAS SELLING YOU THE ARTIFACT?
BUT NOW...NOW I'M NOT SO SURE.
POOR SILKY.
WE NEED TO FIND OUT IF ANYONE ELSE WAS WITH HIM WHEN HE FOUND IT.
BEEP BEEP BEEP BEEP BEEP BE
AND WE NEED TO FIND OUT IF THERE ARE ANY MORE OF THESE THINGS--
BEEP BEEP BEEP BEEP BEEP BEEP

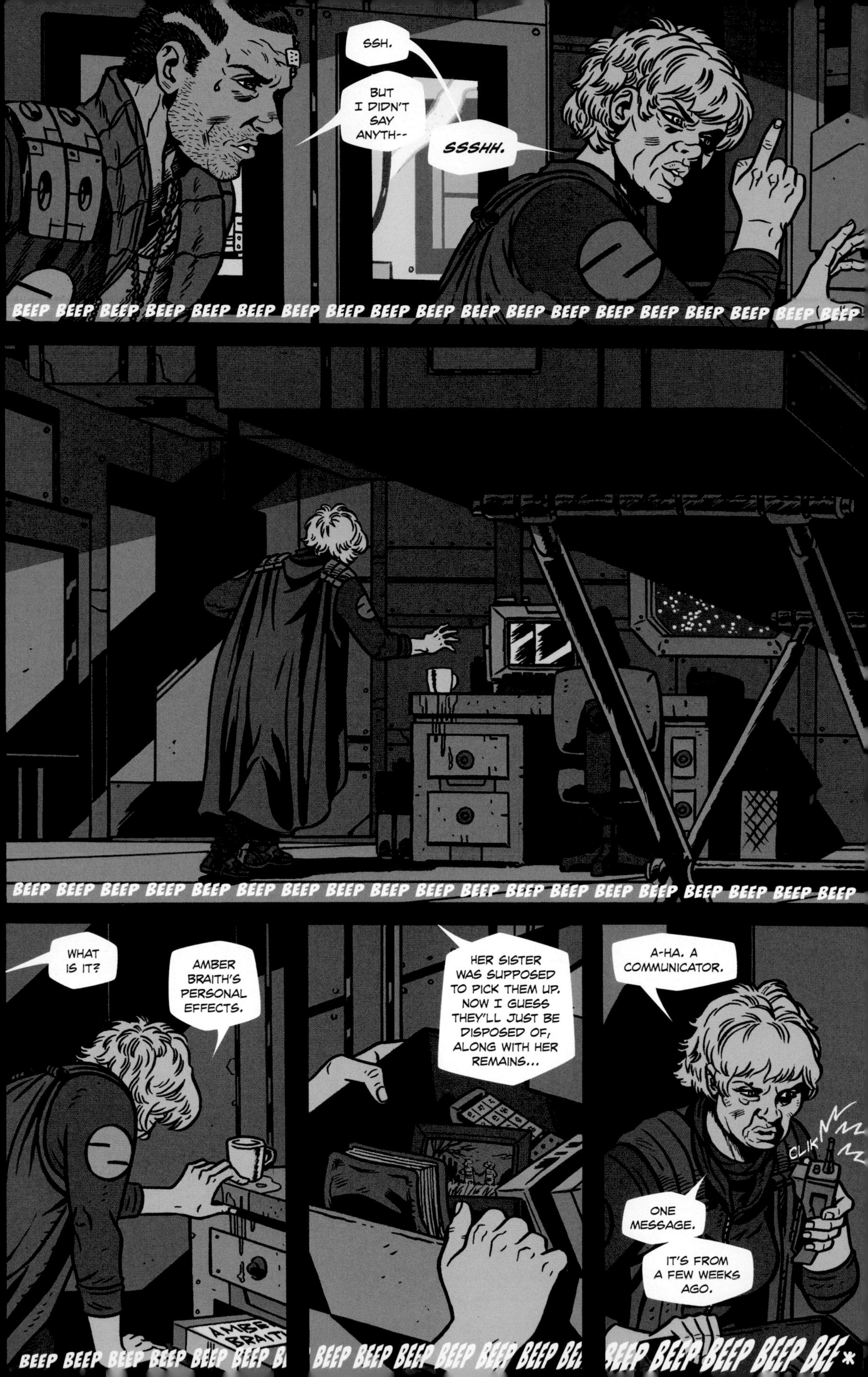
SSH.
BUT I DIDN'T SAY ANYTH--
SSSHH.
BEEP BEEP BEEP BEEP BEEP BEEP BEEP BEEP BEEP BEEP BEEP BEEP BEEP BEEP BEEP BEEP BEEP BEEP BEEP
BEEP BEEP BEEP BEEP BEEP BEEP BEEP BEEP BEEP BEEP BEEP BEEP BEEP BEEP BEEP BEEP BEEP BEEP BEEP
WHAT IS IT?
AMBER BRAITH'S PERSONAL EFFECTS.
HER SISTER WAS SUPPOSED TO PICK THEM UP. NOW I GUESS THEY'LL JUST BE DISPOSED OF, ALONG WITH HER REMAINS...
A-HA. A COMMUNICATOR.
CLIK
ONE MESSAGE.
IT'S FROM A FEW WEEKS AGO.
BEEP BEEP BEEP BEEP BEEP BEEP
BEEP BEEP BEEP BEEP BEEP BEEP
BEEP BEEP BEEP BEEP BEE*

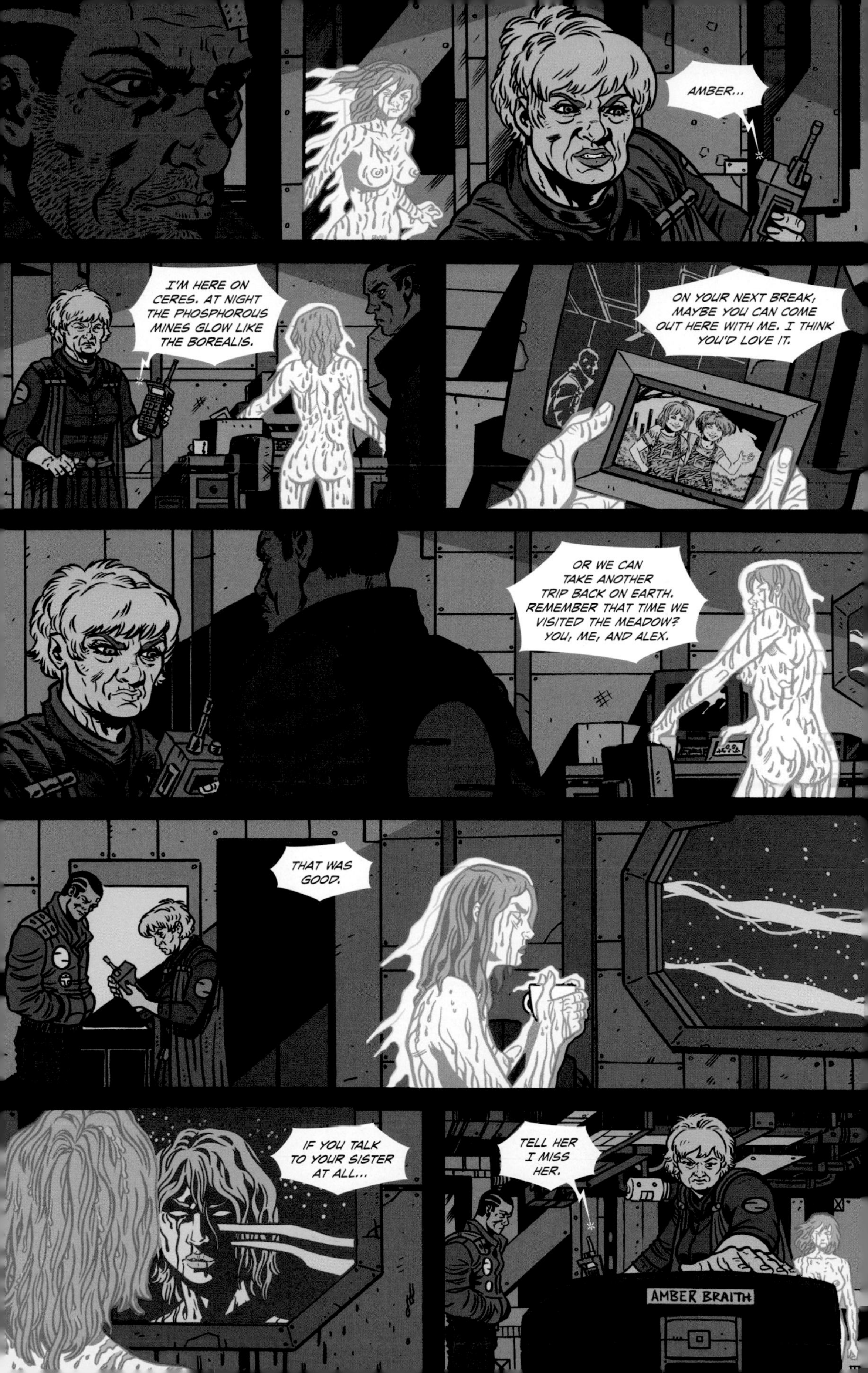
AMBER...
I'M HERE ON CERES. AT NIGHT THE PHOSPHOROUS MINES GLOW LIKE THE BOREALIS.
ON YOUR NEXT BREAK, MAYBE YOU CAN COME OUT HERE WITH ME. I THINK YOU'D LOVE IT.
OR WE CAN TAKE ANOTHER TRIP BACK ON EARTH. REMEMBER THAT TIME WE VISITED THE MEADOW? YOU, ME, AND ALEX.
THAT WAS GOOD.
IF YOU TALK TO YOUR SISTER AT ALL...
TELL HER I MISS HER.
AMBER BRAITH

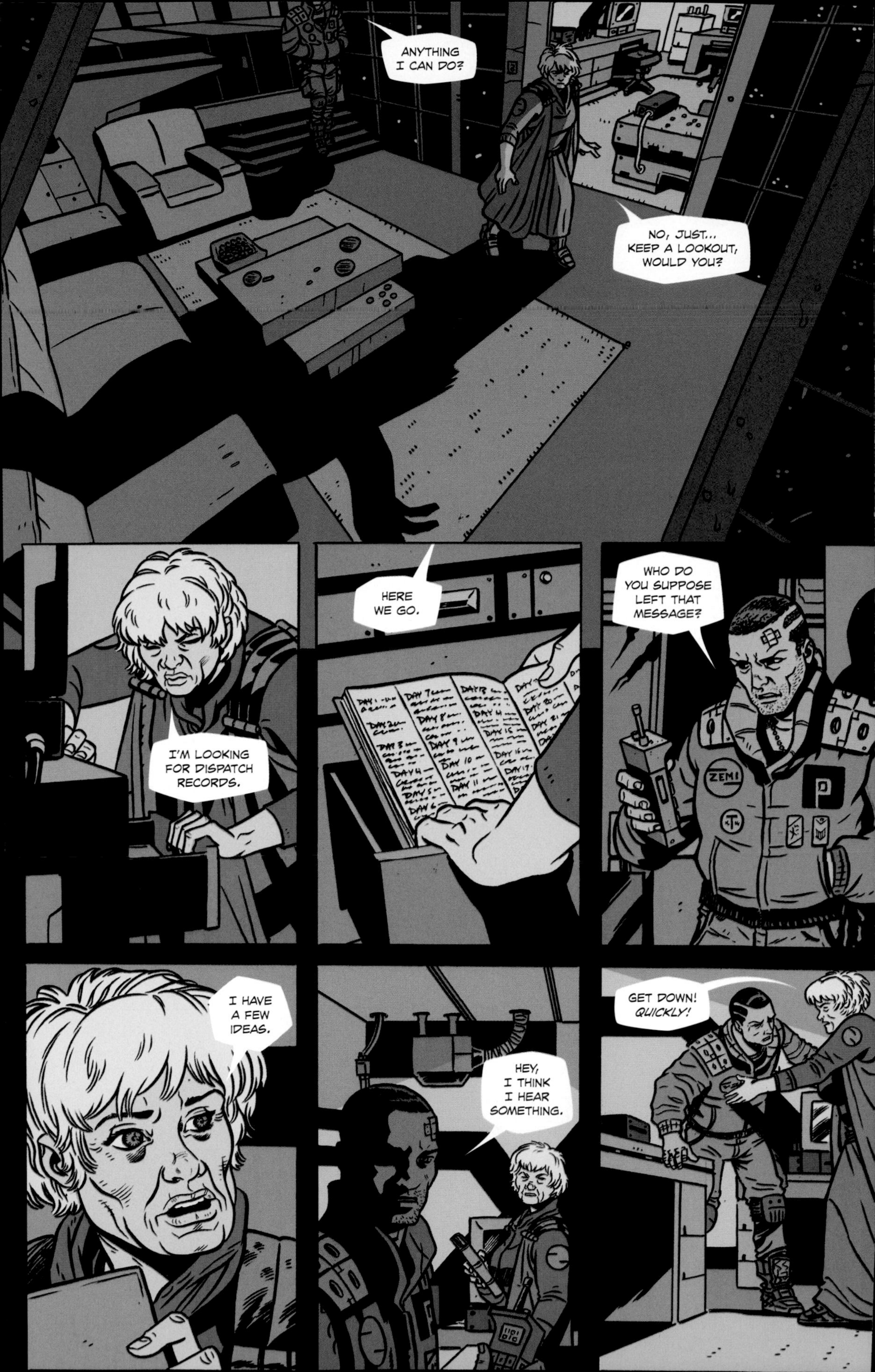
ANYTHING I CAN DO?
NO, JUST... KEEP A LOOKOUT, WOULD YOU?
I'M LOOKING FOR DISPATCH RECORDS.
HERE WE GO.
WHO DO YOU SUPPOSE LEFT THAT MESSAGE?
ZEMI
I HAVE A FEW IDEAS.
HEY, I THINK I HEAR SOMETHING.
GET DOWN! *QUICKLY!*

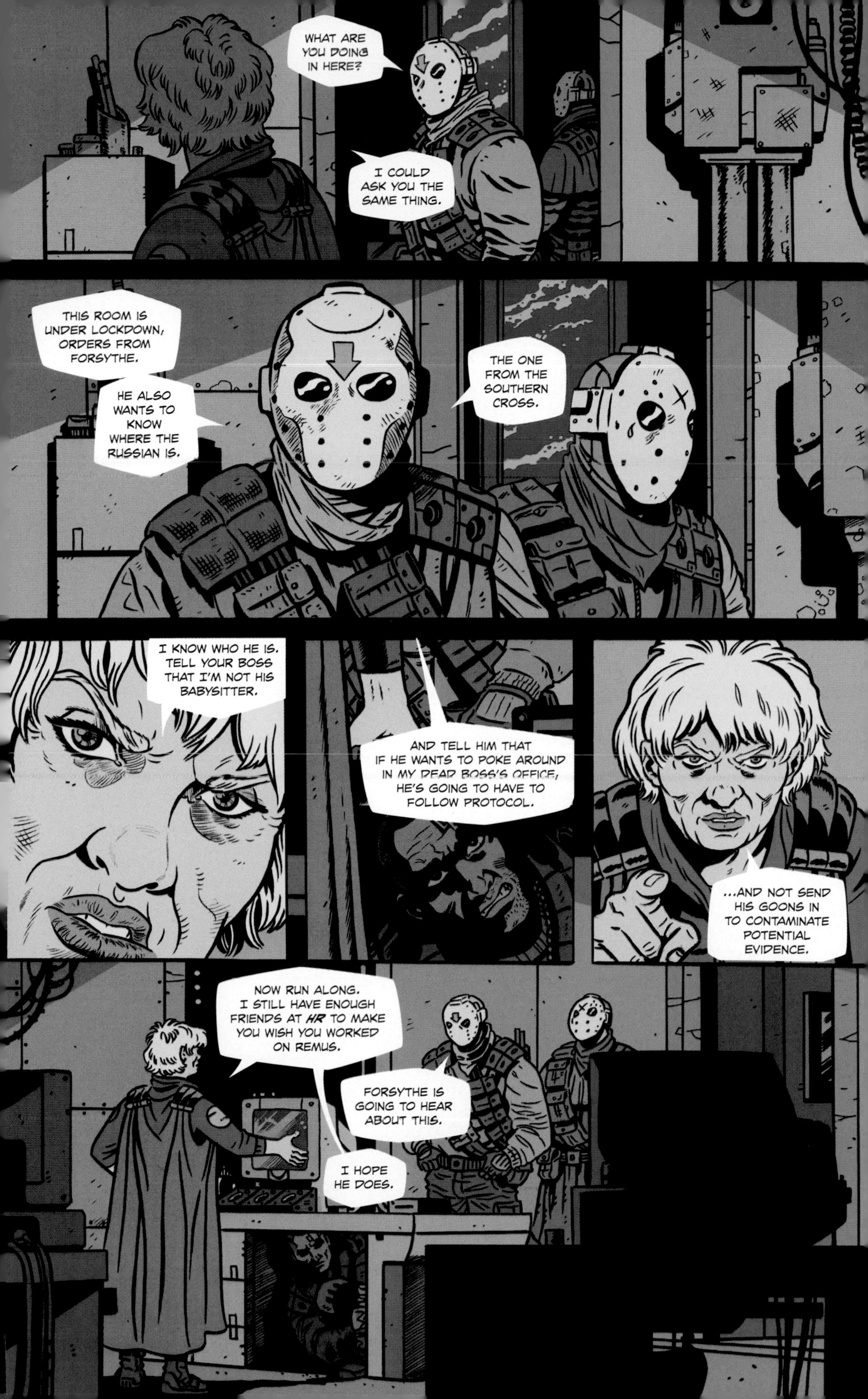

WHAT ARE YOU DOING IN HERE?
I COULD ASK YOU THE SAME THING.
THIS ROOM IS UNDER LOCKDOWN, ORDERS FROM FORSYTHE.
HE ALSO WANTS TO KNOW WHERE THE RUSSIAN IS.
THE ONE FROM THE SOUTHERN CROSS.
I KNOW WHO HE IS. TELL YOUR BOSS THAT I'M NOT HIS BABYSITTER.
AND TELL HIM THAT IF HE WANTS TO POKE AROUND IN MY DEAD BOSS'S OFFICE, HE'S GOING TO HAVE TO FOLLOW PROTOCOL.
...AND NOT SEND HIS GOONS IN TO CONTAMINATE POTENTIAL EVIDENCE.
NOW RUN ALONG. I STILL HAVE ENOUGH FRIENDS AT *HR* TO MAKE YOU WISH YOU WORKED ON REMUS.
FORSYTHE IS GOING TO HEAR ABOUT THIS.
I HOPE HE DOES.

CAN I COME OUT NOW?

SSSSSK

OH, YEAH. THEY'RE GONE.

TOOK YOUR SWEET TIME ON THAT ONE.

WHAT'S THE PLAN, ANYWAY?

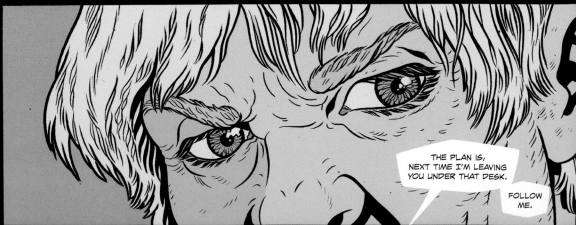

THE PLAN IS, NEXT TIME I'M LEAVING YOU UNDER THAT DESK.

FOLLOW ME.

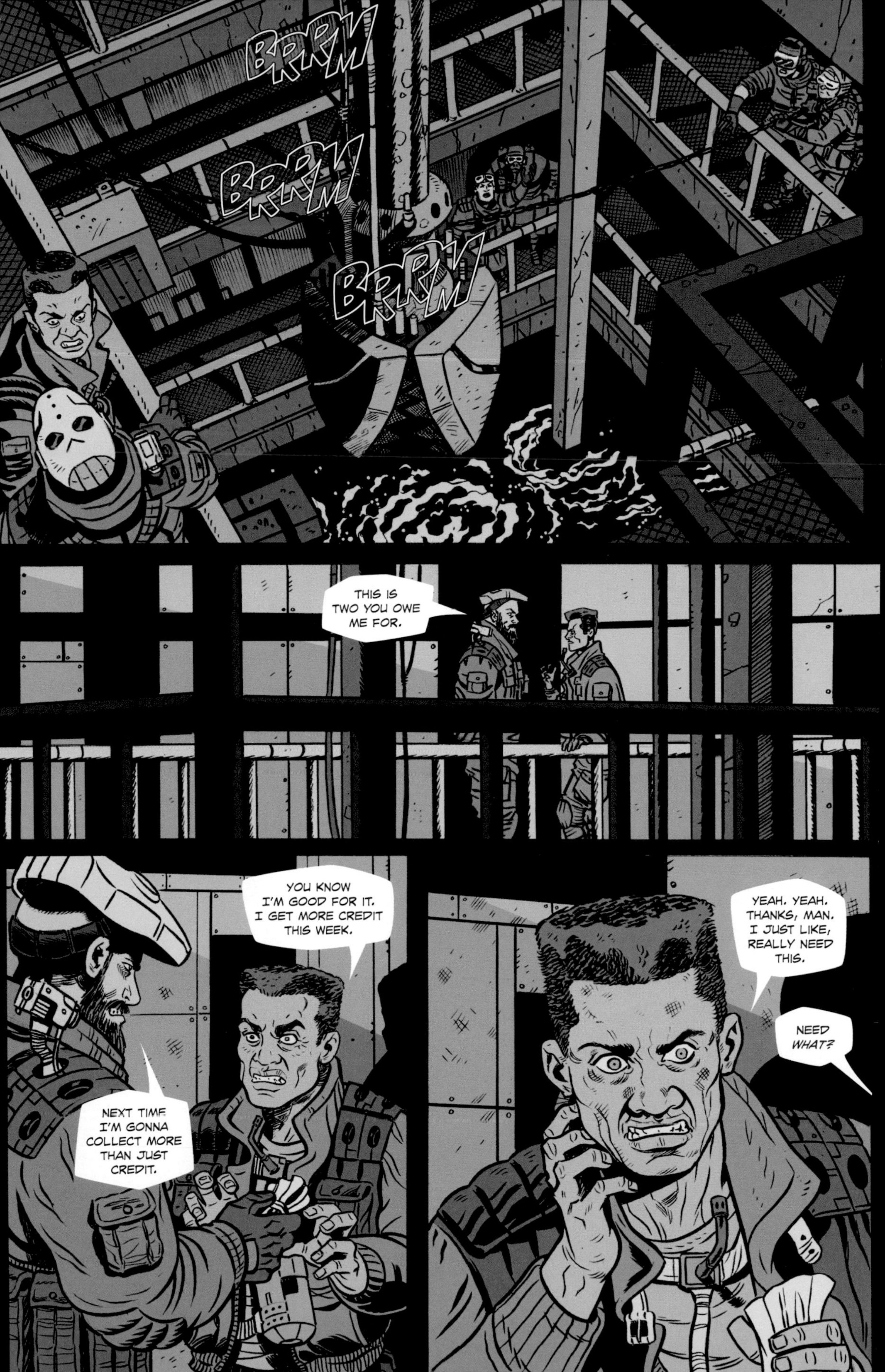
BRRM
BRRM
BRRM
THIS IS TWO YOU OWE ME FOR.
YOU KNOW I'M GOOD FOR IT. I GET MORE CREDIT THIS WEEK.
NEXT TIME I'M GONNA COLLECT MORE THAN JUST CREDIT.
YEAH. YEAH. THANKS, MAN. I JUST LIKE, REALLY NEED THIS.
NEED *WHAT?*

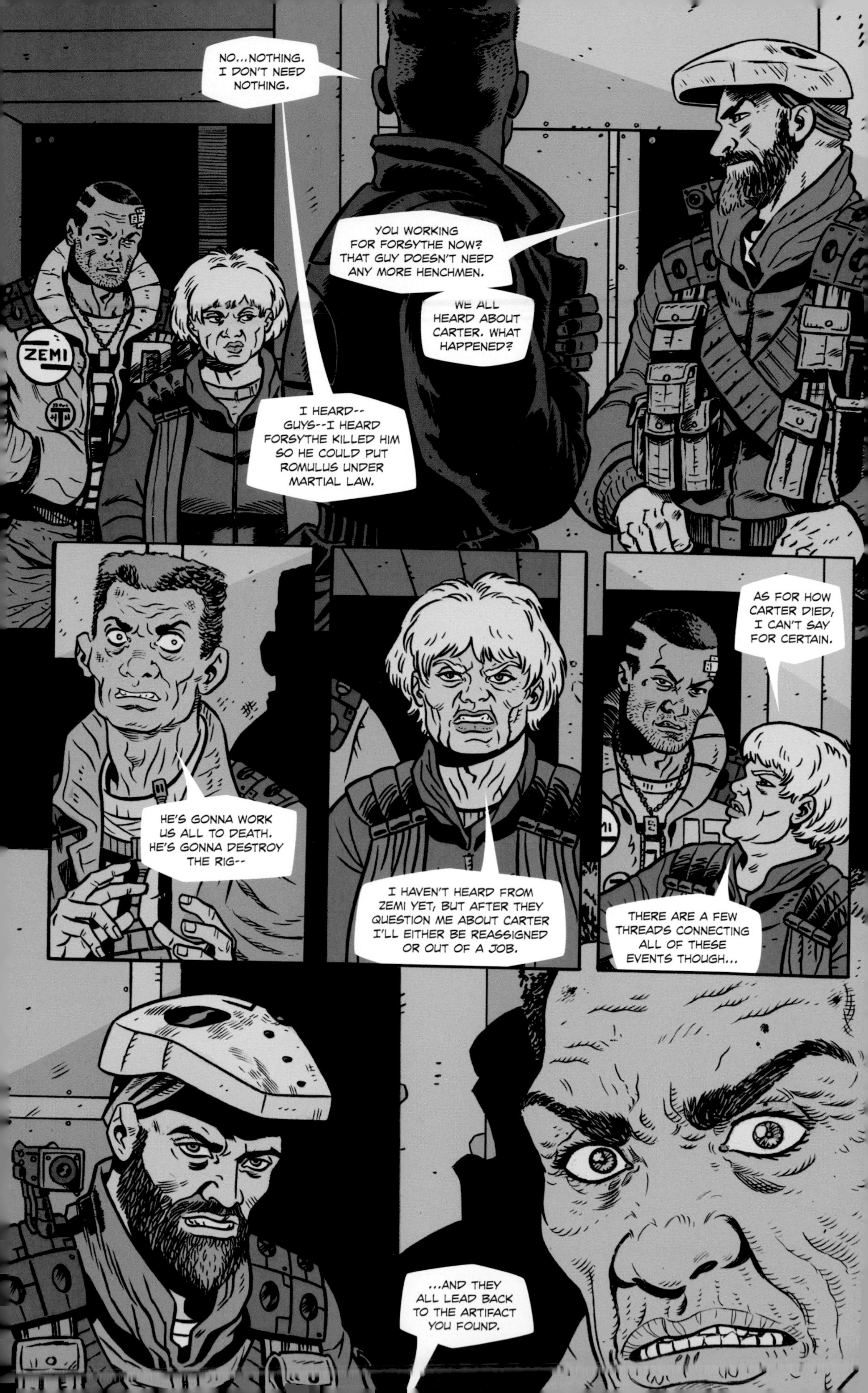
NO...NOTHING. I DON'T NEED NOTHING.
YOU WORKING FOR FORSYTHE NOW? THAT GUY DOESN'T NEED ANY MORE HENCHMEN.
WE ALL HEARD ABOUT CARTER. WHAT HAPPENED?
I HEARD-- GUYS--I HEARD FORSYTHE KILLED HIM SO HE COULD PUT ROMULUS UNDER MARTIAL LAW.
HE'S GONNA WORK US ALL TO DEATH. HE'S GONNA DESTROY THE RIG--
I HAVEN'T HEARD FROM ZEMI YET, BUT AFTER THEY QUESTION ME ABOUT CARTER I'LL EITHER BE REASSIGNED OR OUT OF A JOB.
AS FOR HOW CARTER DIED, I CAN'T SAY FOR CERTAIN.
THERE ARE A FEW THREADS CONNECTING ALL OF THESE EVENTS THOUGH...
...AND THEY ALL LEAD BACK TO THE ARTIFACT YOU FOUND.

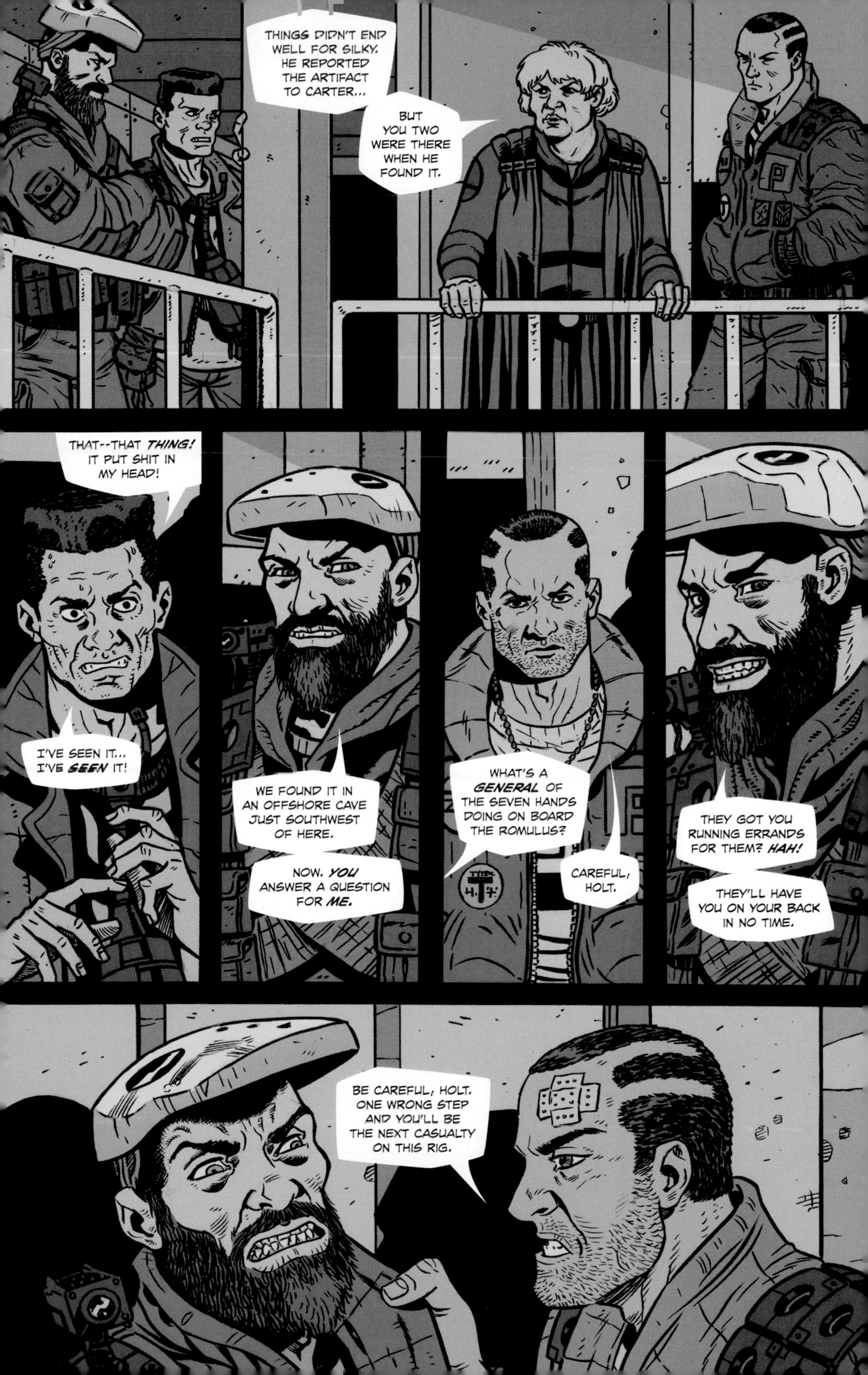
THINGS DIDN'T END WELL FOR SILKY. HE REPORTED THE ARTIFACT TO CARTER...
BUT YOU TWO WERE THERE WHEN HE FOUND IT.
THAT--THAT *THING!* IT PUT SHIT IN MY HEAD!
I'VE SEEN IT... I'VE ***SEEN*** IT!
WE FOUND IT IN AN OFFSHORE CAVE JUST SOUTHWEST OF HERE.
NOW. ***YOU*** ANSWER A QUESTION FOR ***ME.***
WHAT'S A ***GENERAL*** OF THE SEVEN HANDS DOING ON BOARD THE ROMULUS?
CAREFUL, HOLT.
THEY GOT YOU RUNNING ERRANDS FOR THEM? ***HAH!***
THEY'LL HAVE YOU ON YOUR BACK IN NO TIME.
BE CAREFUL, HOLT. ONE WRONG STEP AND YOU'LL BE THE NEXT CASUALTY ON THIS RIG.

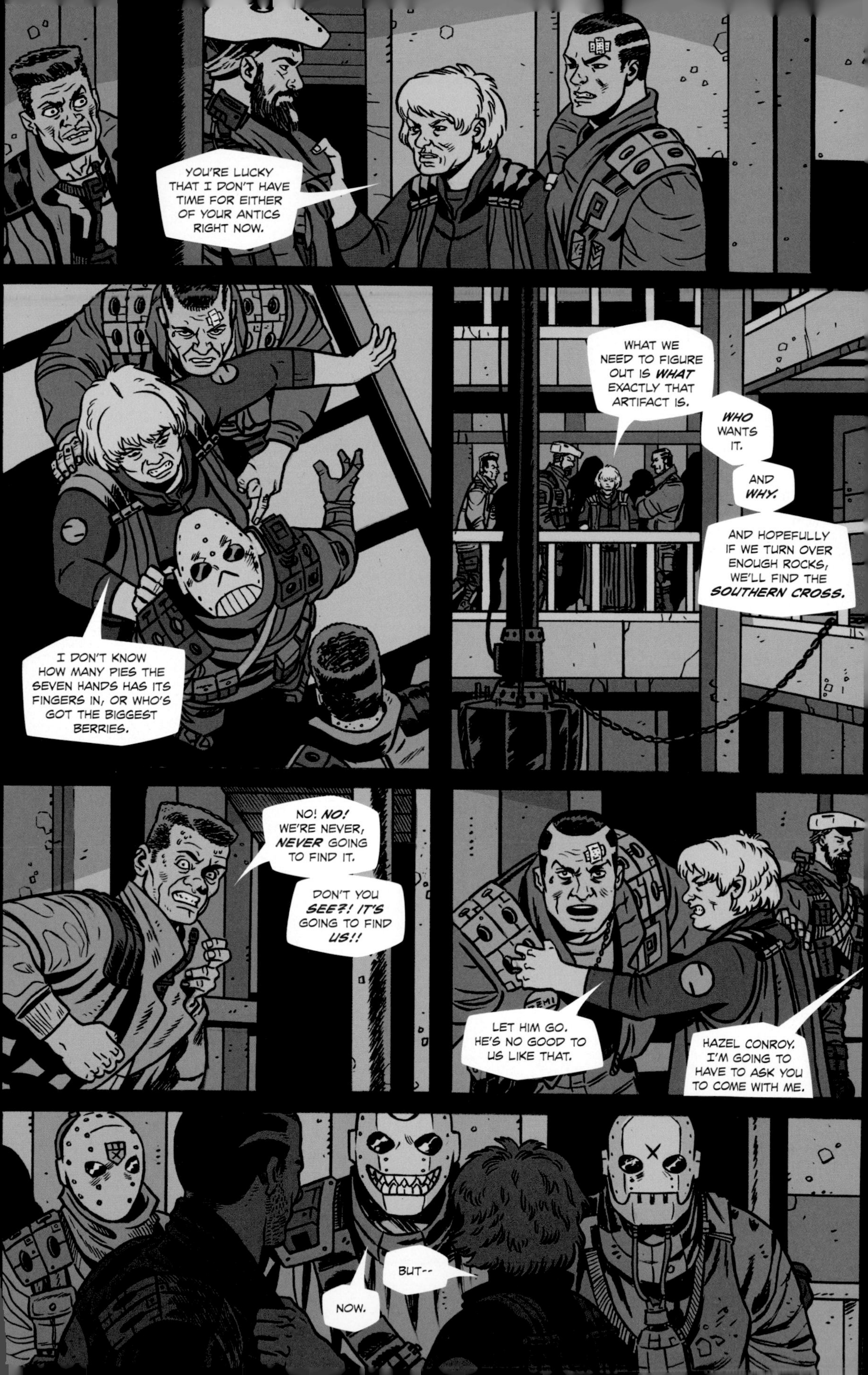

YOU'RE LUCKY THAT I DON'T HAVE TIME FOR EITHER OF YOUR ANTICS RIGHT NOW.
I DON'T KNOW HOW MANY PIES THE SEVEN HANDS HAS ITS FINGERS IN, OR WHO'S GOT THE BIGGEST BERRIES.
WHAT WE NEED TO FIGURE OUT IS WHAT EXACTLY THAT ARTIFACT IS.
WHO WANTS IT.
AND WHY.
AND HOPEFULLY IF WE TURN OVER ENOUGH ROCKS, WE'LL FIND THE SOUTHERN CROSS.
NO! NO! WE'RE NEVER, NEVER GOING TO FIND IT.
DON'T YOU SEE?! IT'S GOING TO FIND US!!
LET HIM GO. HE'S NO GOOD TO US LIKE THAT.
HAZEL CONROY. I'M GOING TO HAVE TO ASK YOU TO COME WITH ME.
BUT--
NOW.

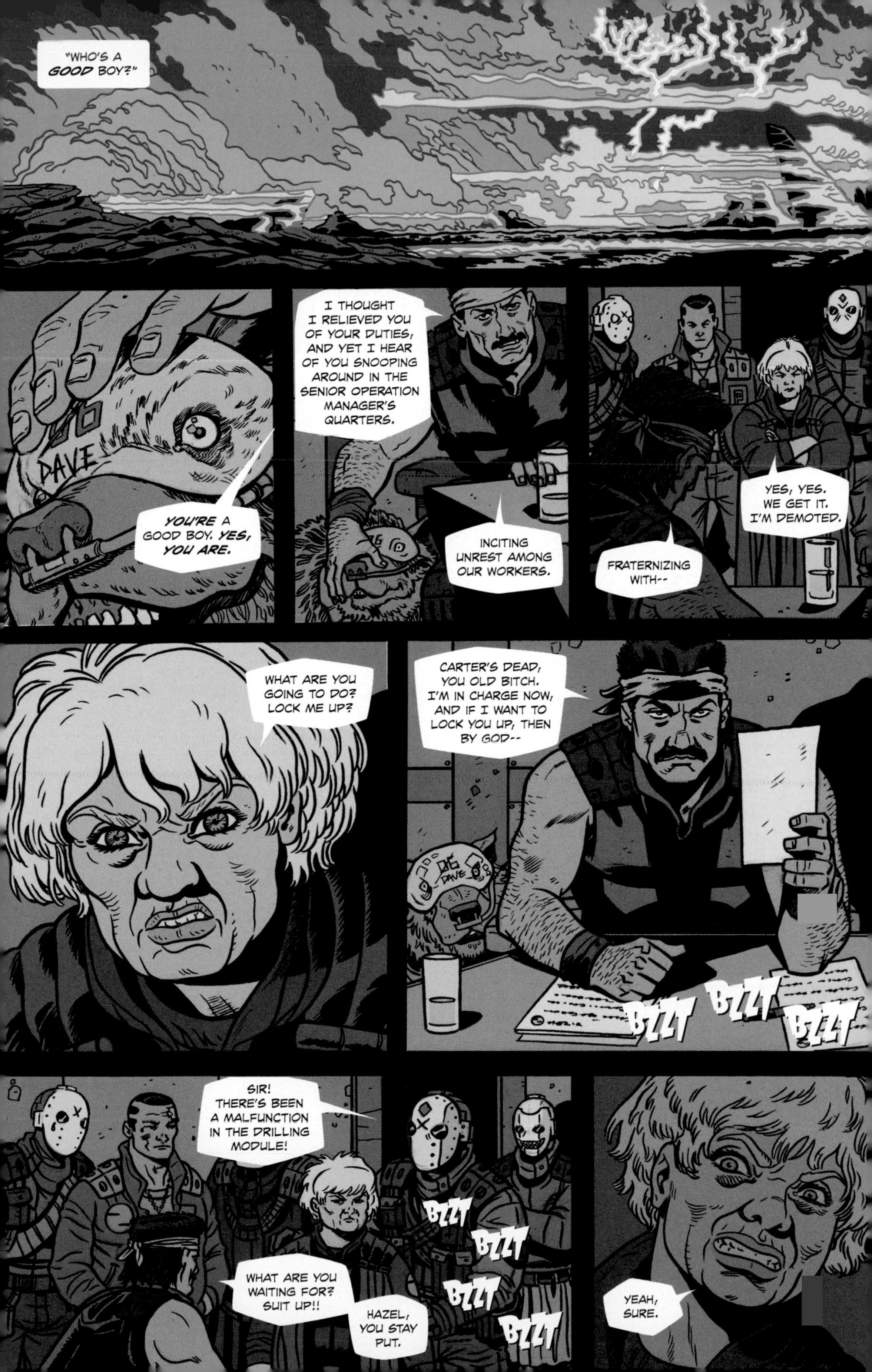
"WHO'S A *GOOD* BOY?"
*YOU'RE* A GOOD BOY. *YES, YOU ARE.*
DAVE
I THOUGHT I RELIEVED YOU OF YOUR DUTIES, AND YET I HEAR OF YOU SNOOPING AROUND IN THE SENIOR OPERATION MANAGER'S QUARTERS.
INCITING UNREST AMONG OUR WORKERS.
FRATERNIZING WITH--
YES, YES. WE GET IT. I'M DEMOTED.
WHAT ARE YOU GOING TO DO? LOCK ME UP?
CARTER'S DEAD, YOU OLD BITCH. I'M IN CHARGE NOW, AND IF I WANT TO LOCK YOU UP, THEN BY GOD--
BZZT BZZT BZZT
SIR! THERE'S BEEN A MALFUNCTION IN THE DRILLING MODULE!
BZZT BZZT BZZT BZZT
WHAT ARE YOU WAITING FOR? SUIT UP!!
HAZEL, YOU STAY PUT.
YEAH, SURE.

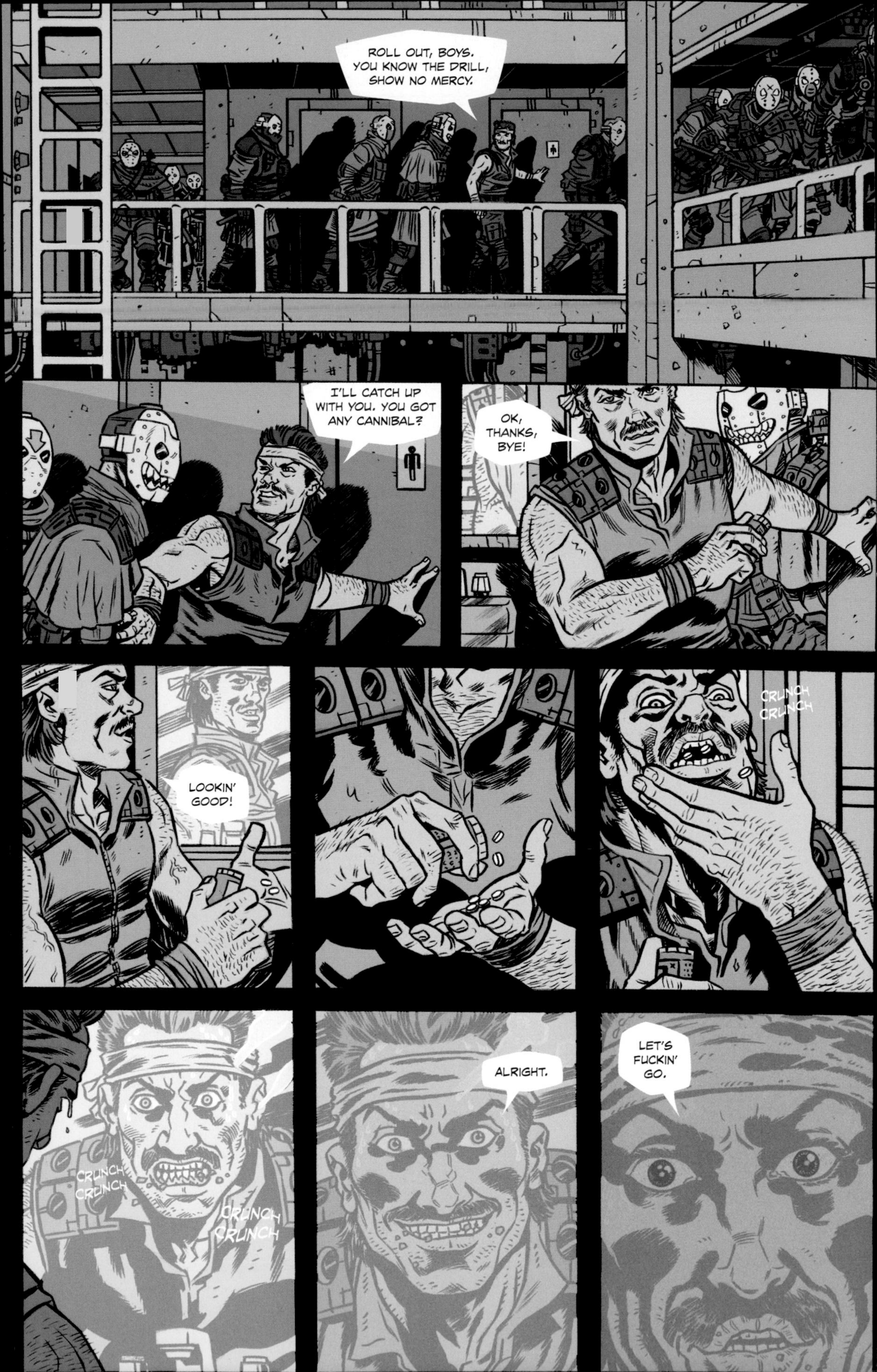
ROLL OUT, BOYS. YOU KNOW THE DRILL, SHOW NO MERCY.
I'LL CATCH UP WITH YOU. YOU GOT ANY CANNIBAL?
OK, THANKS, BYE!
LOOKIN' GOOD!
CRUNCH CRUNCH
CRUNCH CRUNCH
CRUNCH CRUNCH
ALRIGHT.
LET'S FUCKIN' GO.

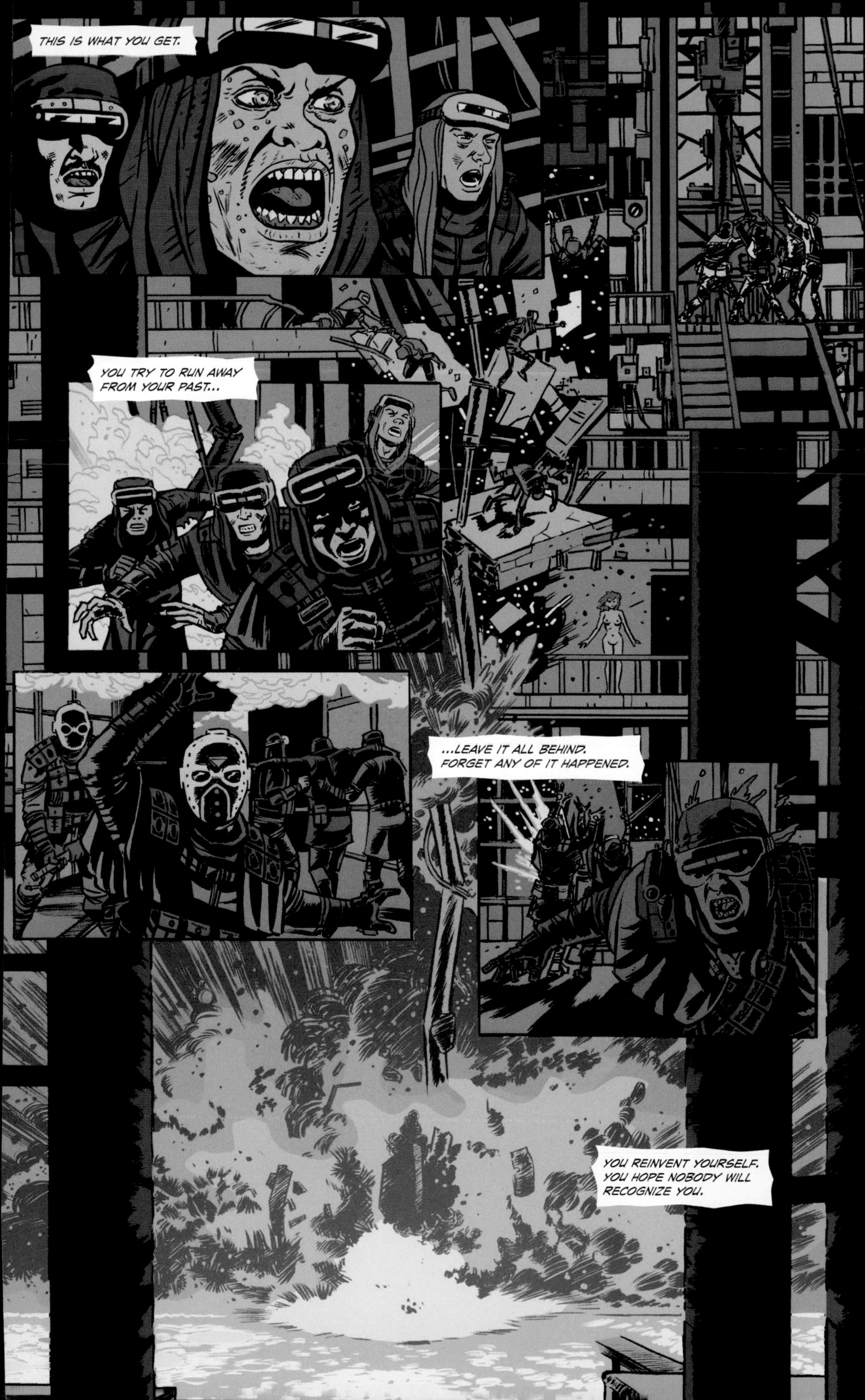
THIS IS WHAT YOU GET.
YOU TRY TO RUN AWAY FROM YOUR PAST...
...LEAVE IT ALL BEHIND. FORGET ANY OF IT HAPPENED.
YOU REINVENT YOURSELF. YOU HOPE NOBODY WILL RECOGNIZE YOU.

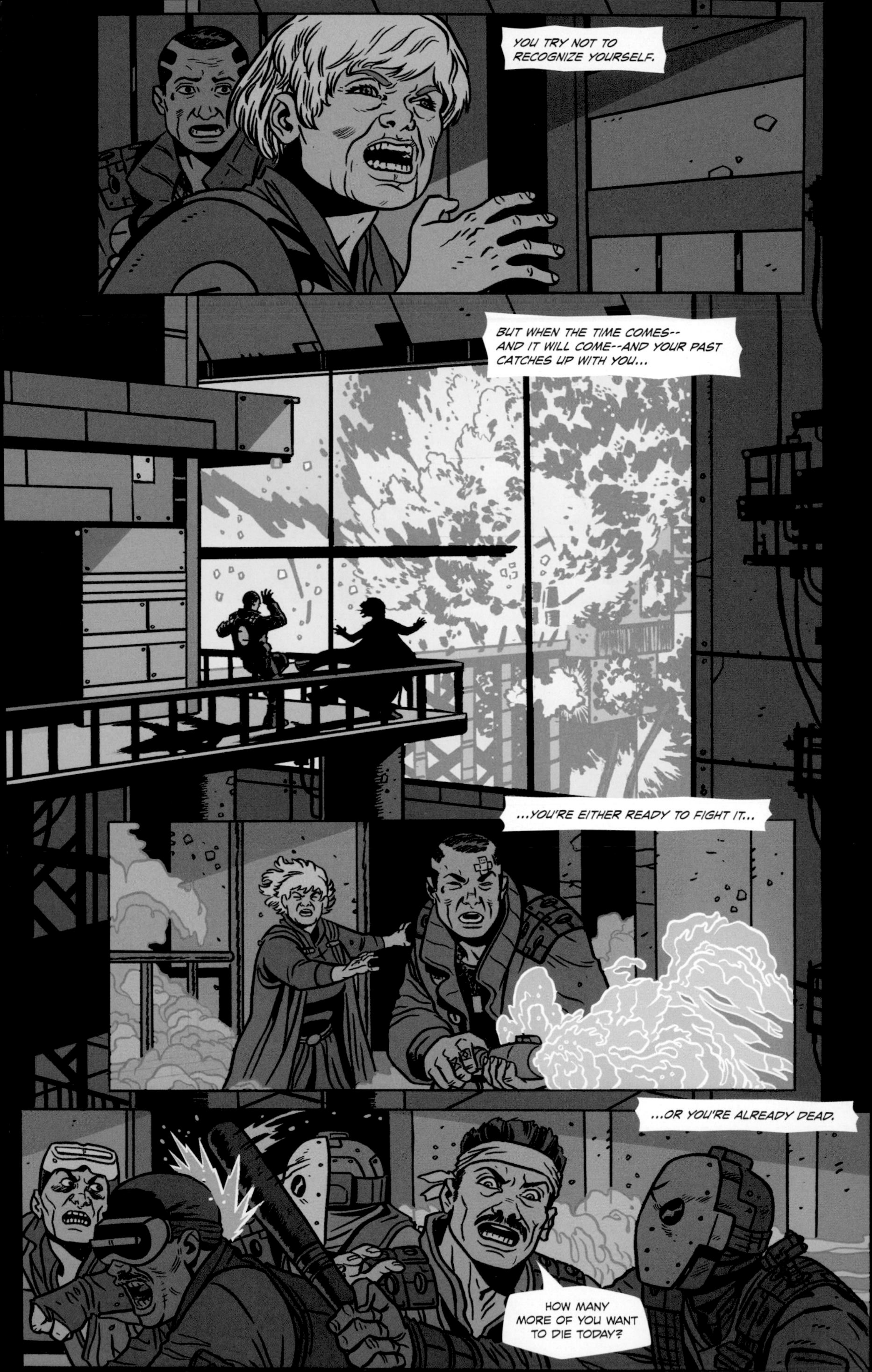
YOU TRY NOT TO RECOGNIZE YOURSELF.
BUT WHEN THE TIME COMES-- AND IT WILL COME--AND YOUR PAST CATCHES UP WITH YOU...
...YOU'RE EITHER READY TO FIGHT IT...
...OR YOU'RE ALREADY DEAD.
HOW MANY MORE OF YOU WANT TO DIE TODAY?

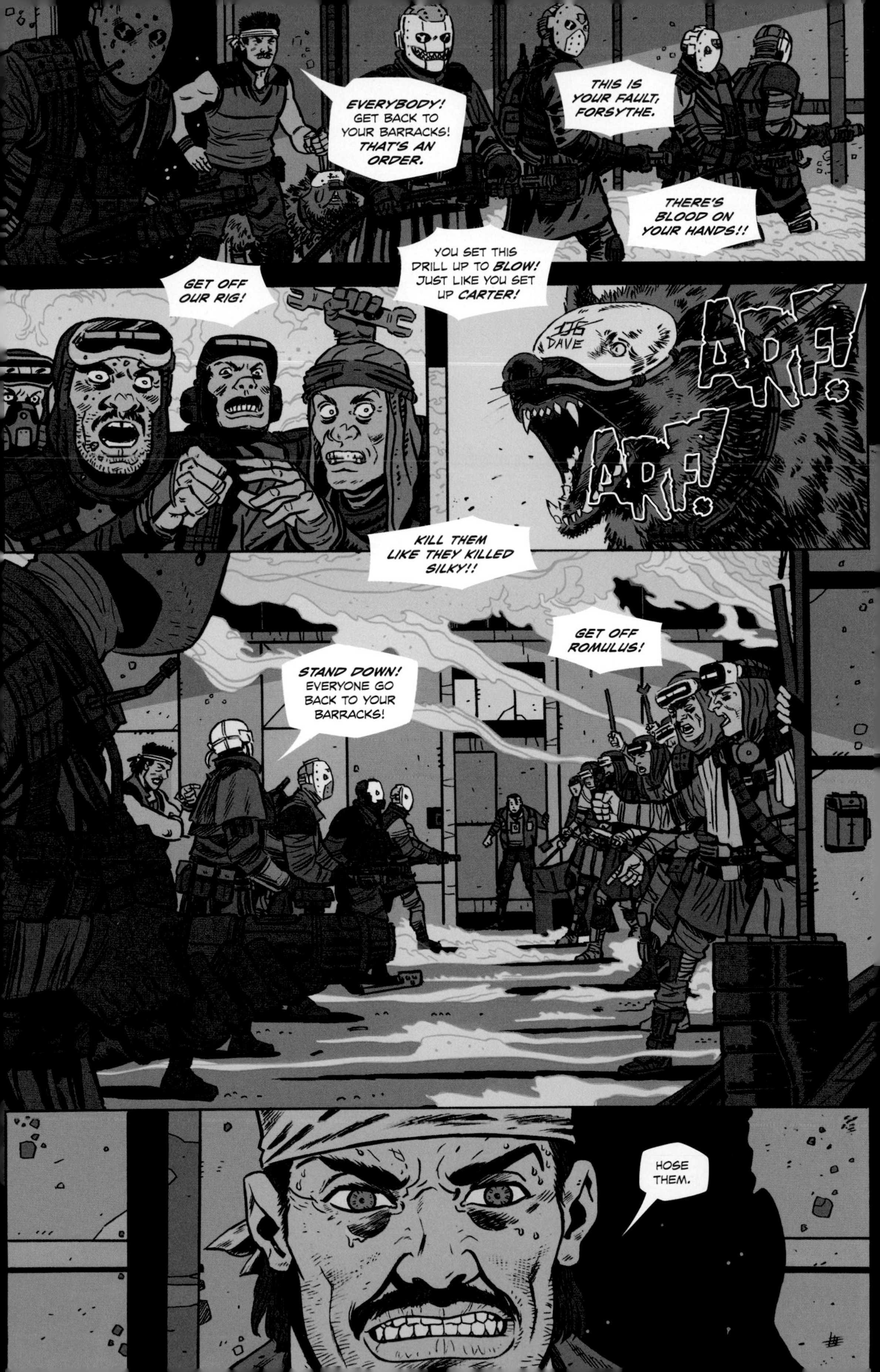
EVERYBODY! GET BACK TO YOUR BARRACKS! THAT'S AN ORDER.
THIS IS YOUR FAULT, FORSYTHE.
THERE'S BLOOD ON YOUR HANDS!!
YOU SET THIS DRILL UP TO BLOW! JUST LIKE YOU SET UP CARTER!
GET OFF OUR RIG!
DAVE
ARF! ARF!
KILL THEM LIKE THEY KILLED SILKY!!
GET OFF ROMULUS!
STAND DOWN! EVERYONE GO BACK TO YOUR BARRACKS!
HOSE THEM.

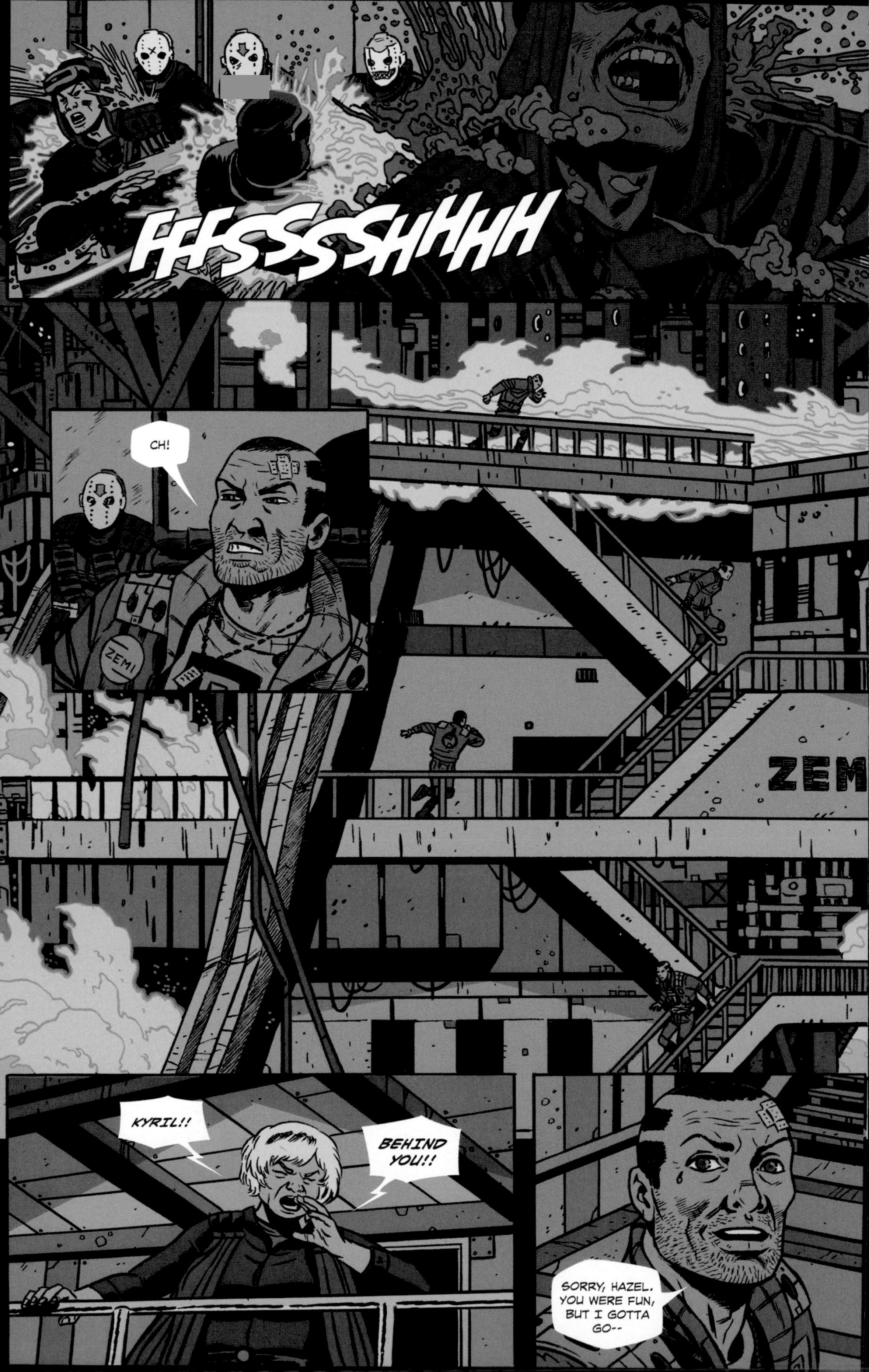
FFFSSSSHHHHH
CH!
ZEMI
ZEM
KYRIL!!
BEHIND YOU!!
SORRY, HAZEL. YOU WERE FUN, BUT I GOTTA GO--

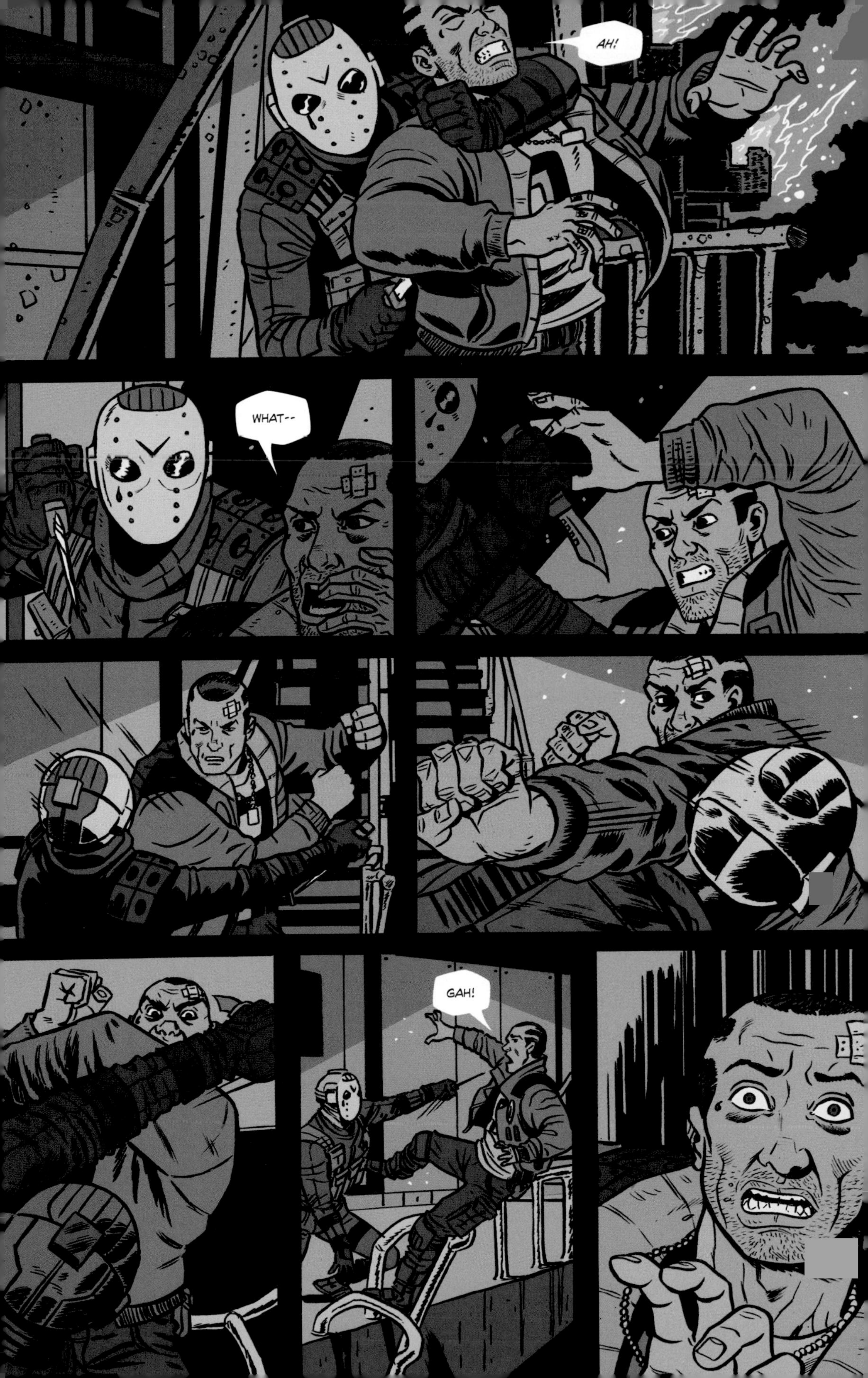
AH!
WHAT--
GAH!

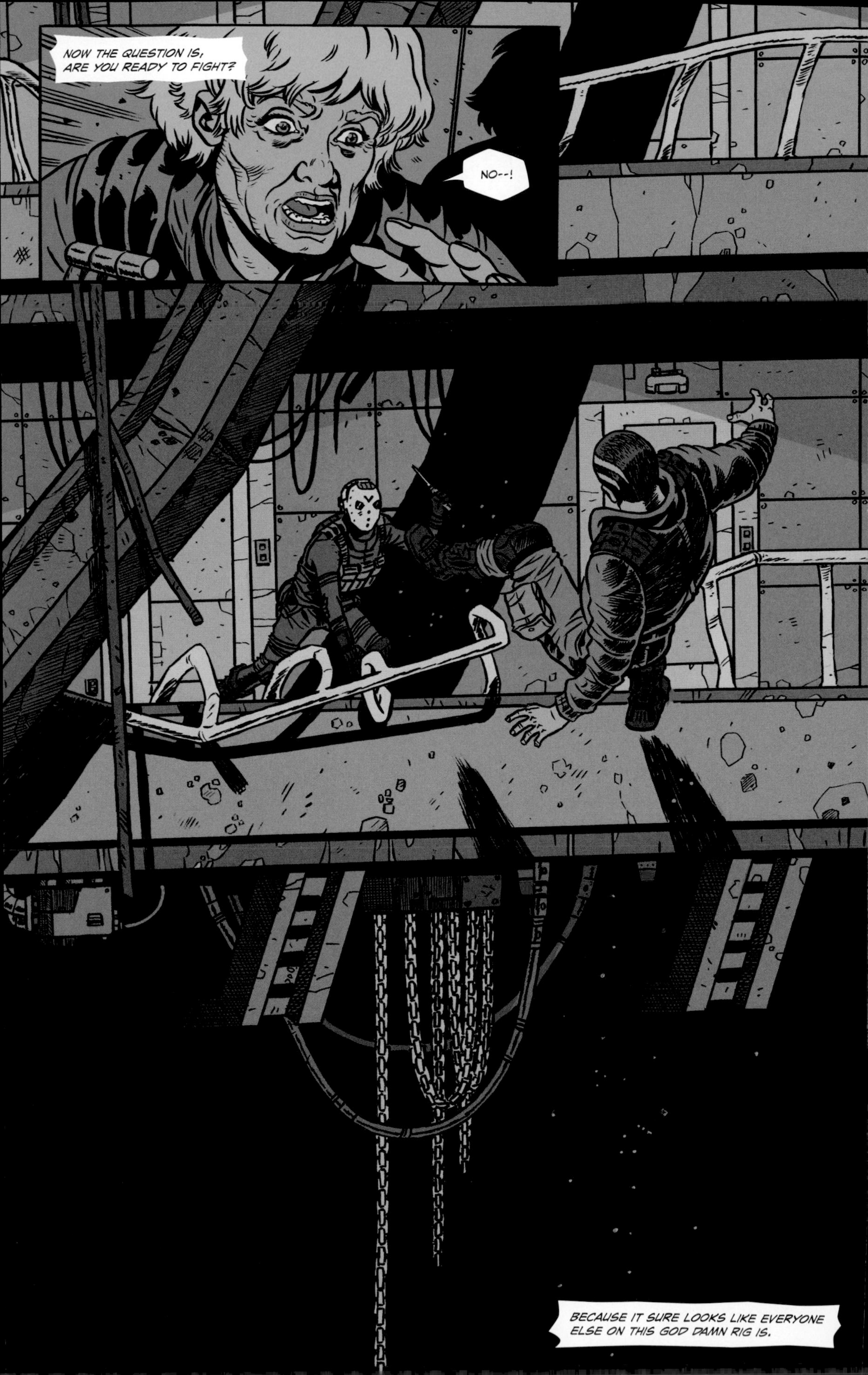
NOW THE QUESTION IS,
ARE YOU READY TO FIGHT?
NO--!
BECAUSE IT SURE LOOKS LIKE EVERYONE ELSE ON THIS GOD DAMN RIG IS.

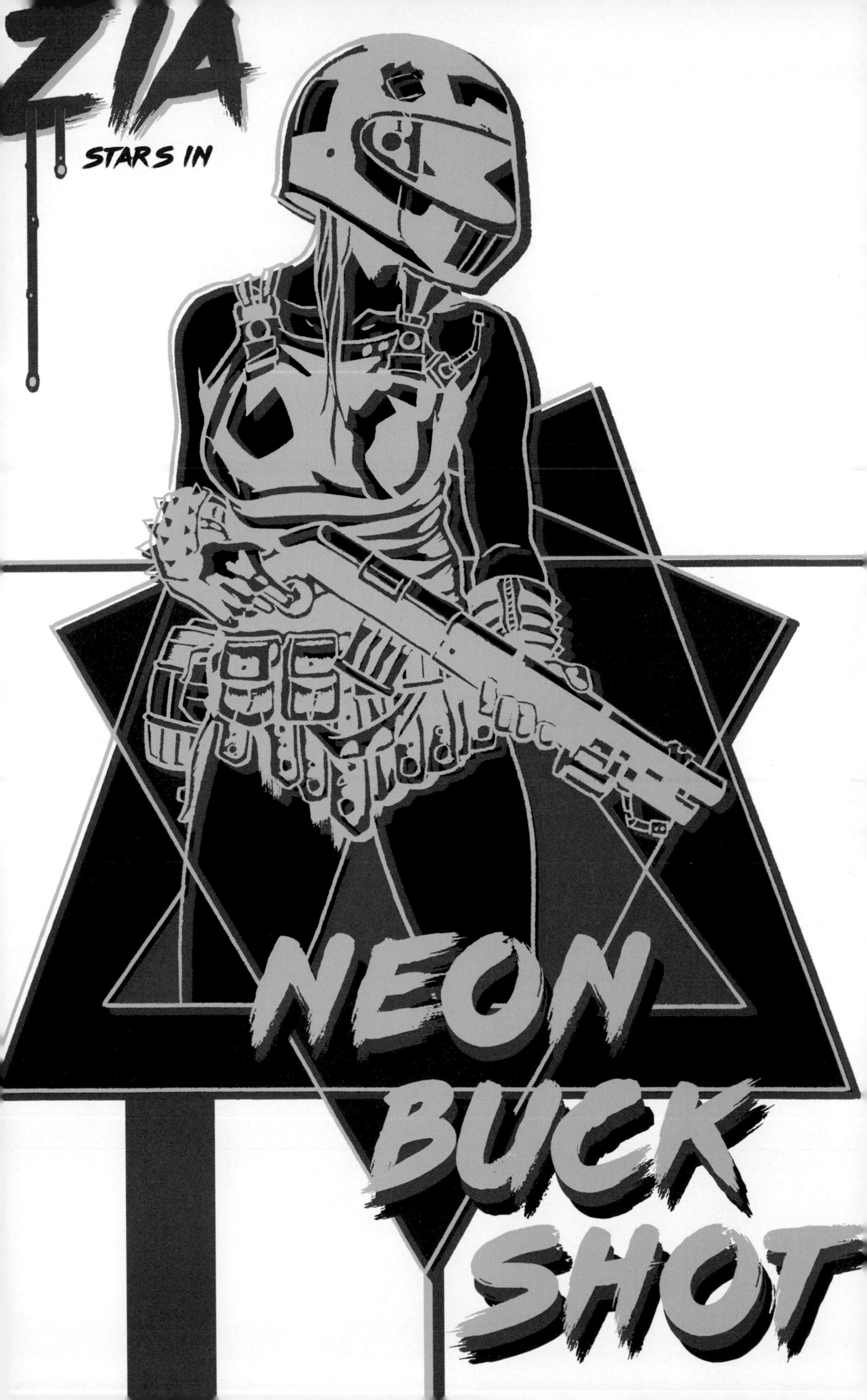
ZIA
STARS IN
NEON
BUCK
SHOT

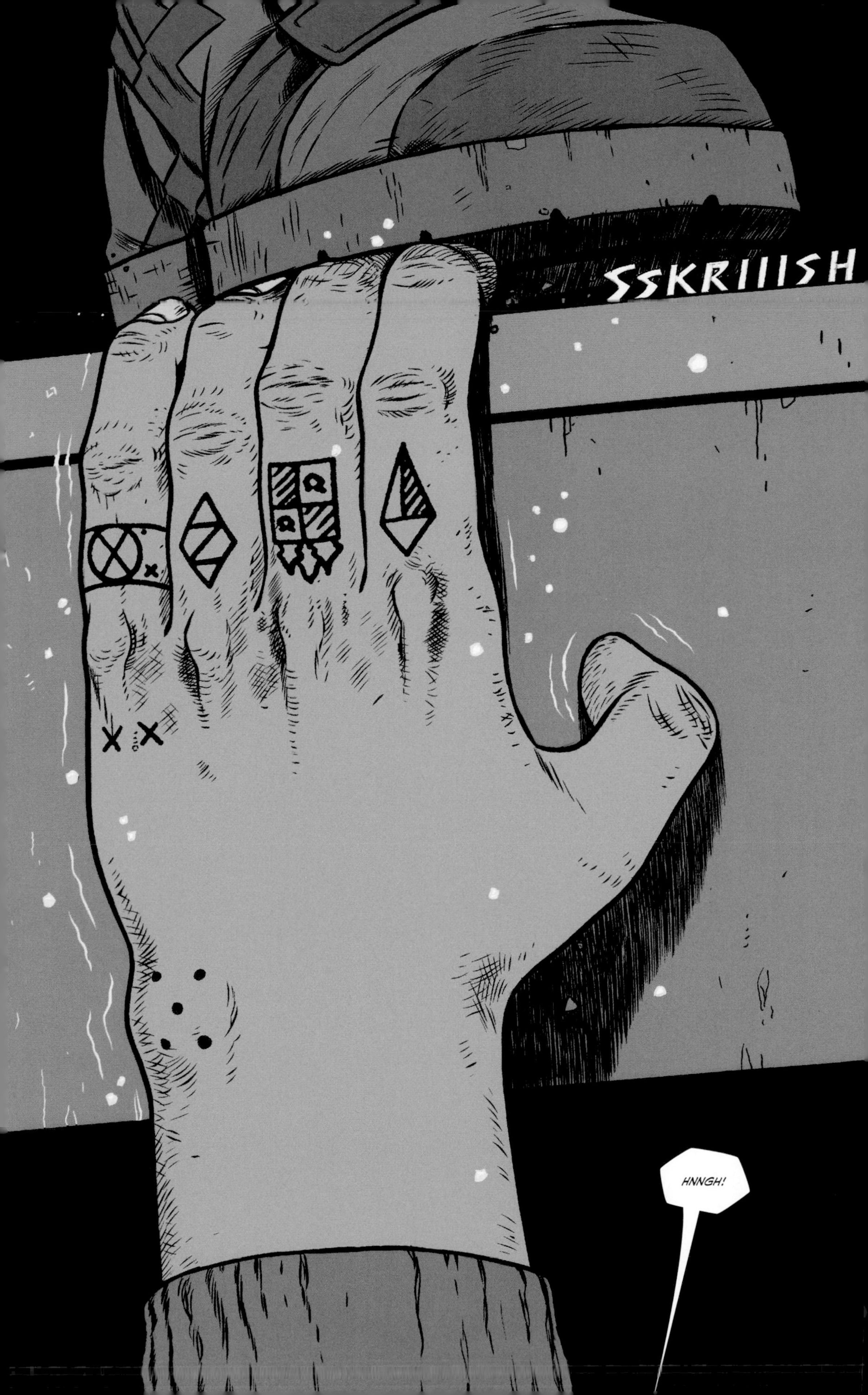
SSKRIIISH
HNNGH!

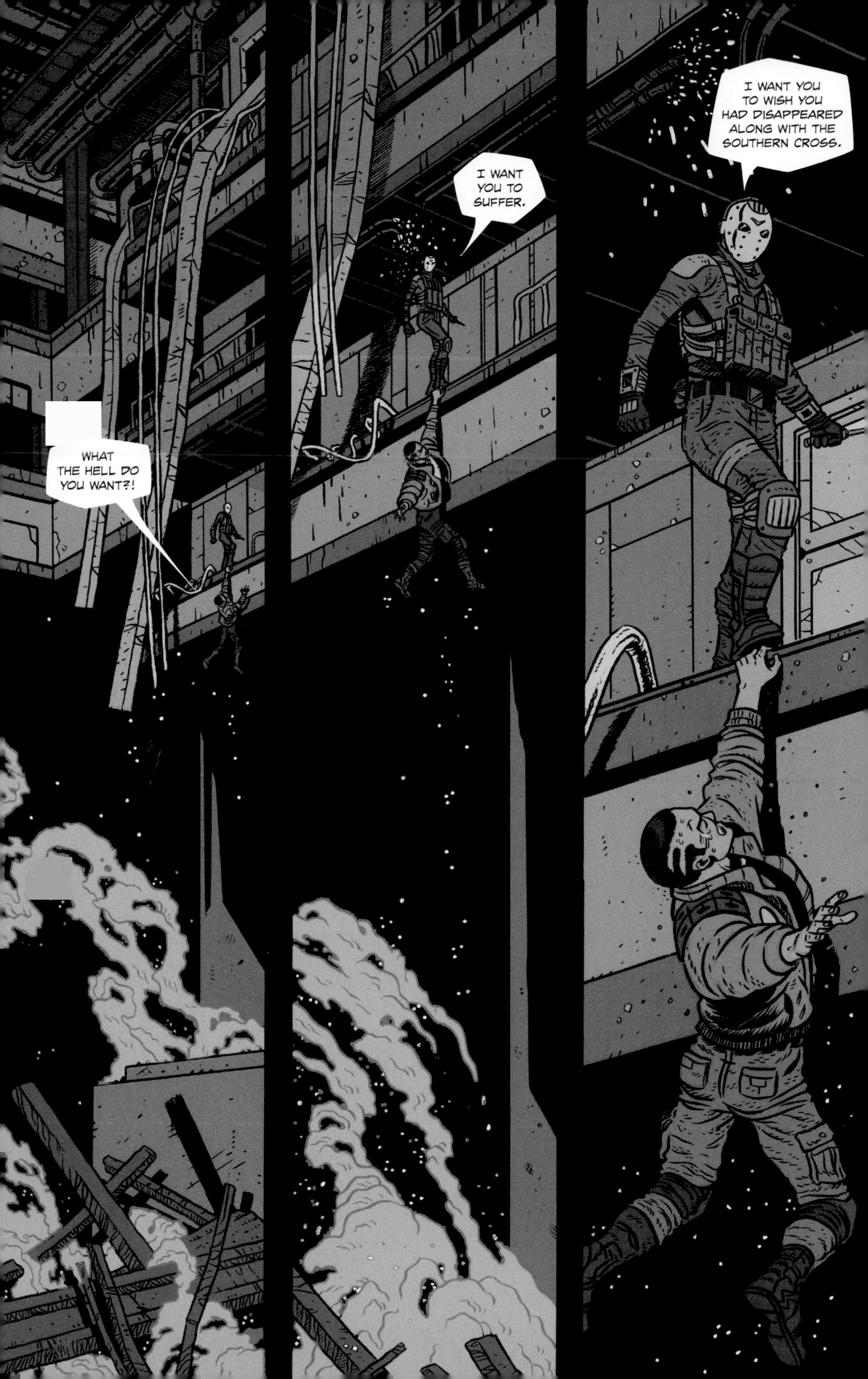
WHAT THE HELL DO YOU WANT?!
I WANT YOU TO SUFFER.
I WANT YOU TO WISH YOU HAD DISAPPEARED ALONG WITH THE SOUTHERN CROSS.

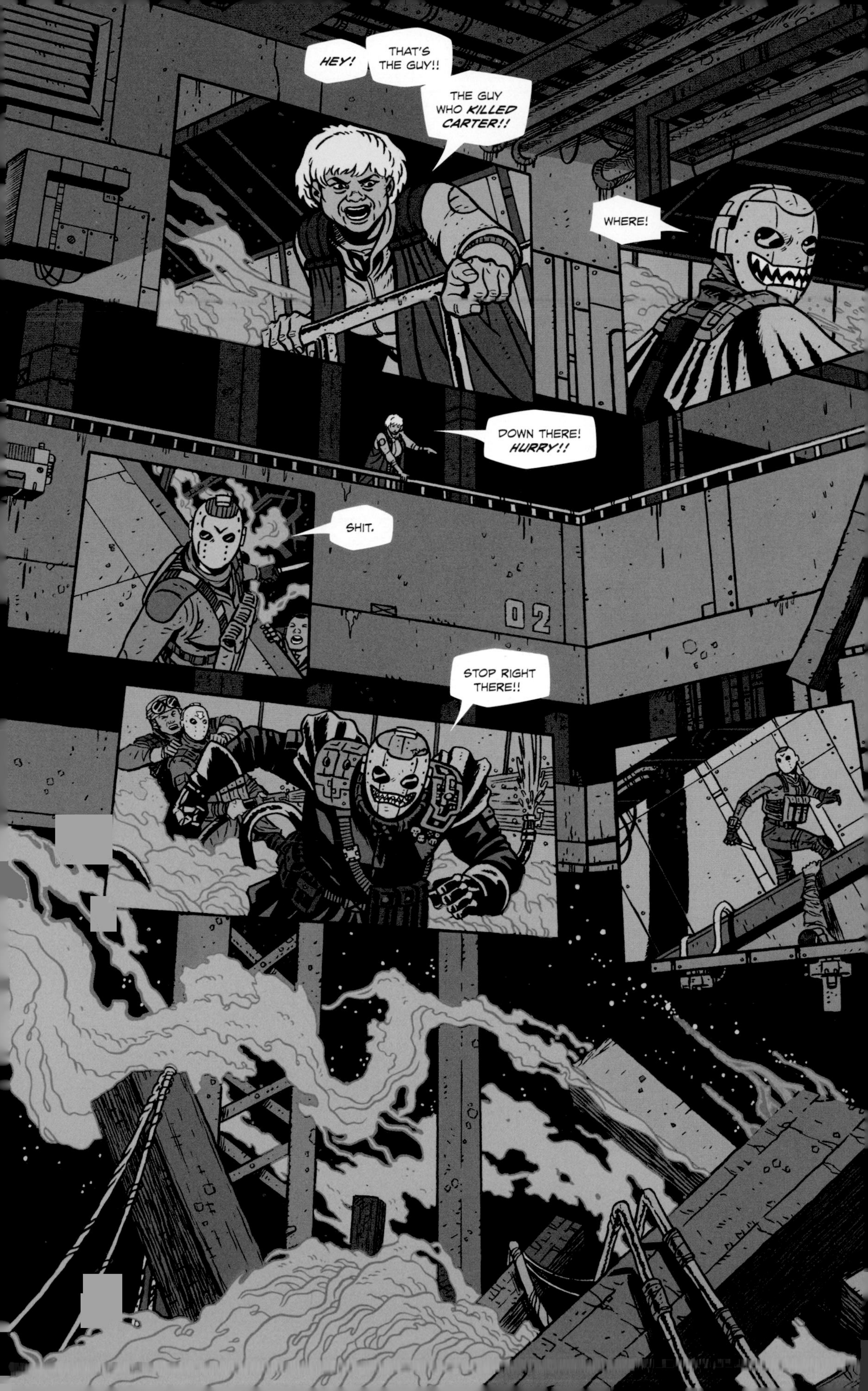
HEY!
THAT'S THE GUY!!
THE GUY WHO KILLED CARTER!!
WHERE!
DOWN THERE! HURRY!!
SHIT.
STOP RIGHT THERE!!

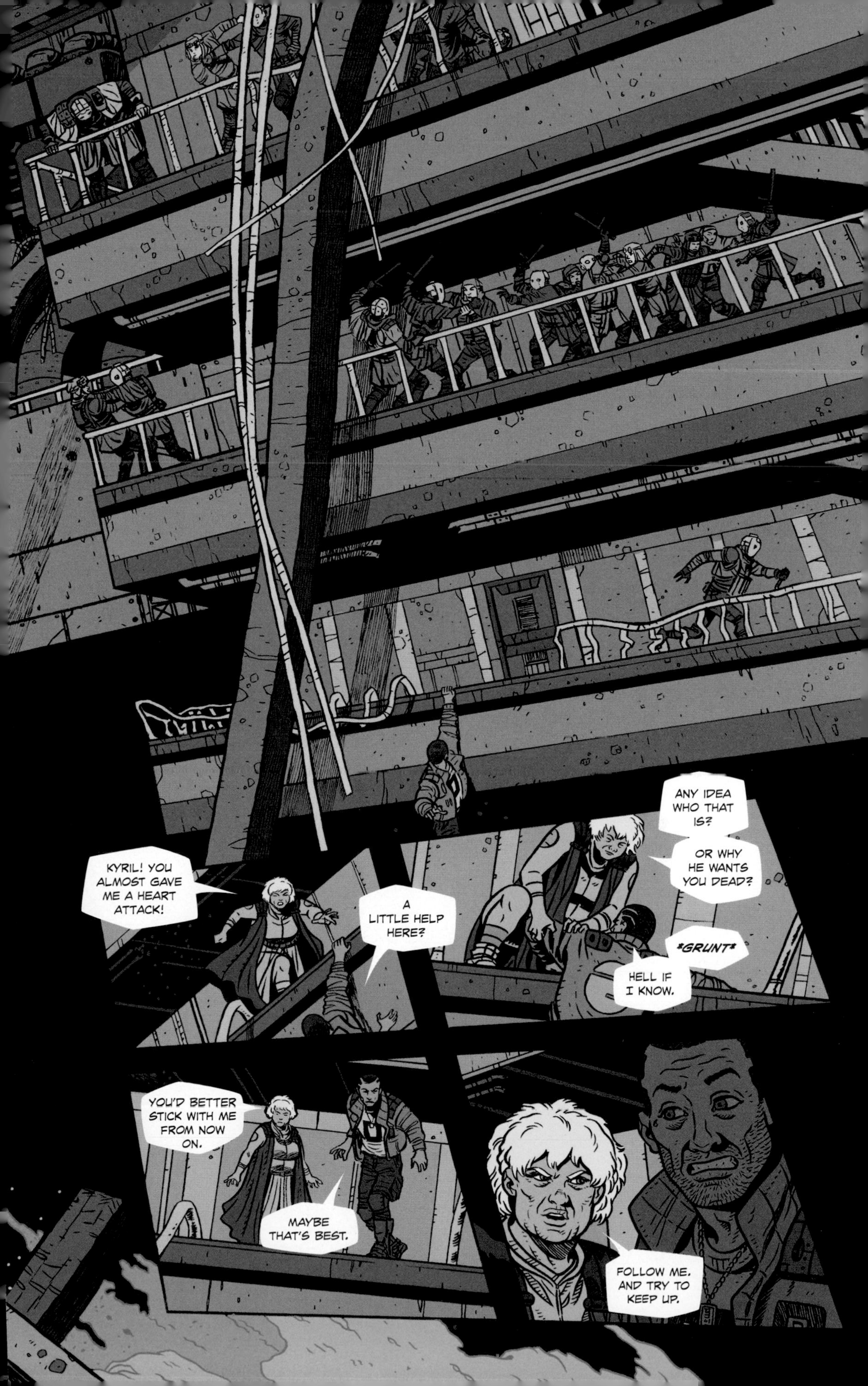

KYRIL! YOU ALMOST GAVE ME A HEART ATTACK!
A LITTLE HELP HERE?
ANY IDEA WHO THAT IS?
OR WHY HE WANTS YOU DEAD?
*GRUNT*
HELL IF I KNOW.
YOU'D BETTER STICK WITH ME FROM NOW ON.
MAYBE THAT'S BEST.
FOLLOW ME. AND TRY TO KEEP UP.

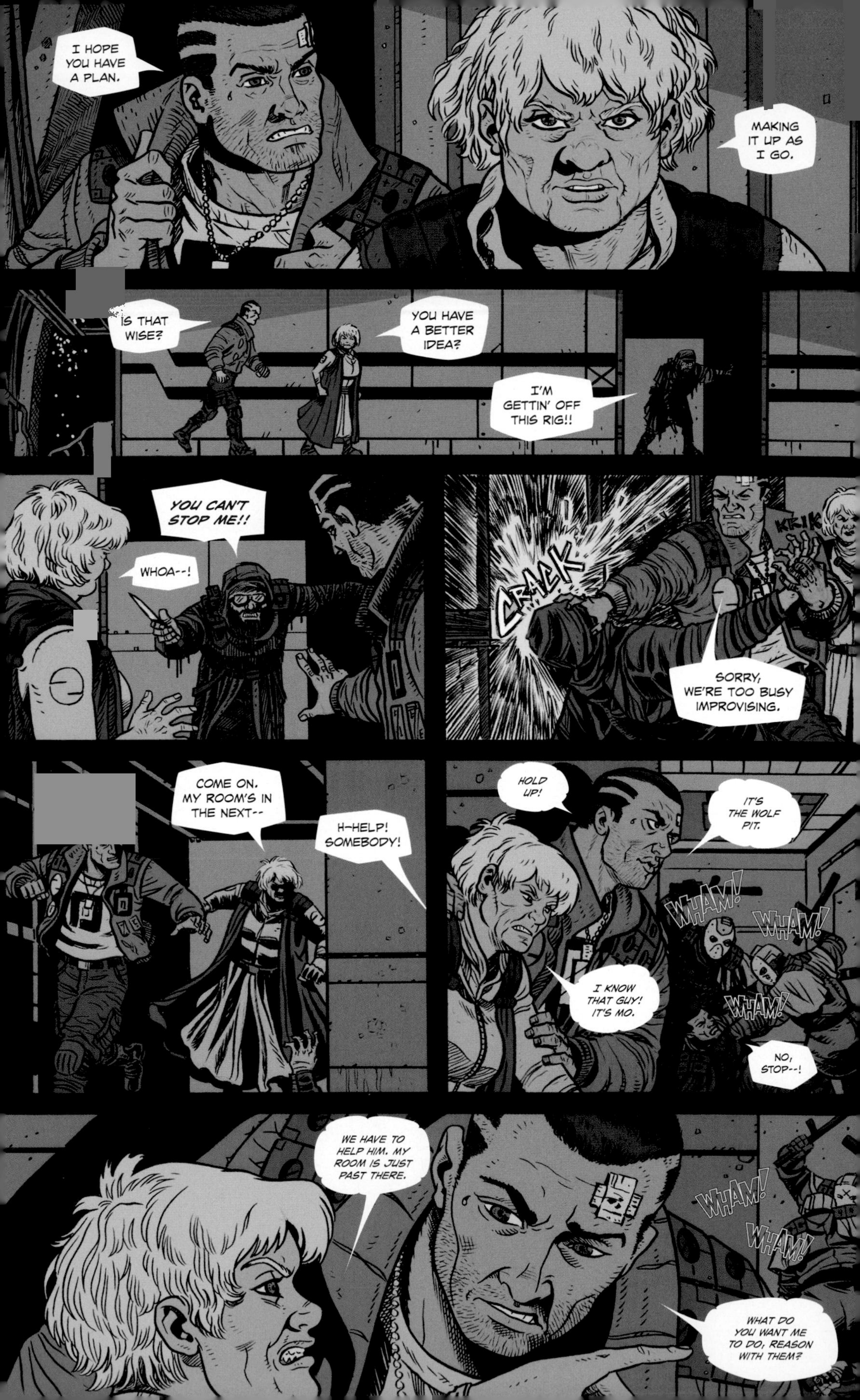
I HOPE YOU HAVE A PLAN.
MAKING IT UP AS I GO.
IS THAT WISE?
YOU HAVE A BETTER IDEA?
I'M GETTIN' OFF THIS RIG!!
YOU CAN'T STOP ME!!
WHOA--!
CRACK
KRIK
SORRY, WE'RE TOO BUSY IMPROVISING.
COME ON. MY ROOM'S IN THE NEXT--
H-HELP! SOMEBODY!
HOLD UP!
IT'S THE WOLF PIT.
WHAM!
WHAM!
I KNOW THAT GUY! IT'S MO.
WHAM!
NO, STOP--!
WE HAVE TO HELP HIM. MY ROOM IS JUST PAST THERE.
WHAM!
WHAM!
WHAT DO YOU WANT ME TO DO, REASON WITH THEM?

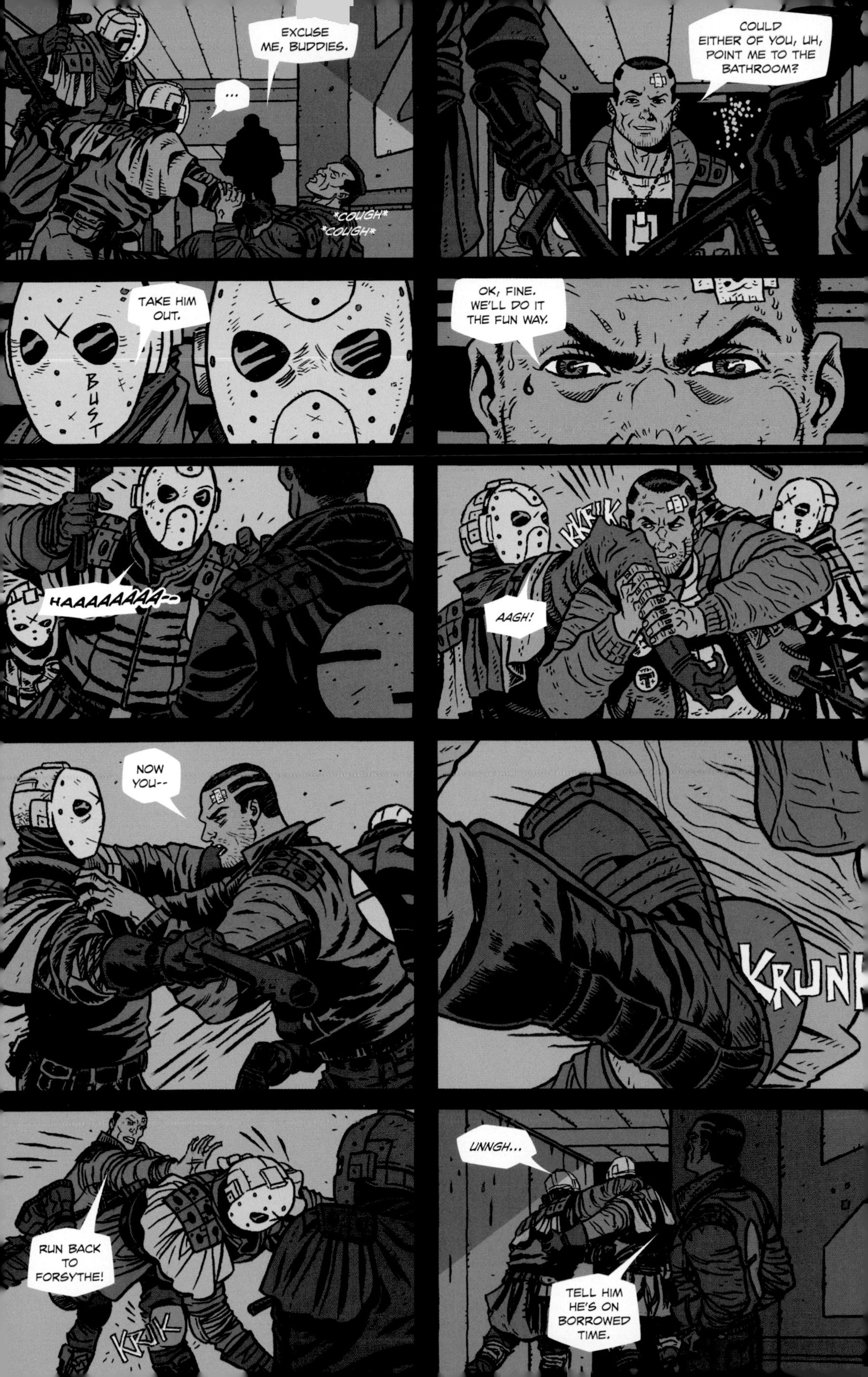
EXCUSE ME, BUDDIES.
...
*COUGH*
*COUGH*
COULD EITHER OF YOU, UH, POINT ME TO THE BATHROOM?
TAKE HIM OUT.
BUST
OK, FINE. WE'LL DO IT THE FUN WAY.
HAAAAAAAA--
KKRIK
AAGH!
NOW YOU--
KRUNK
RUN BACK TO FORSYTHE!
KRUK
UNNGH...
TELL HIM HE'S ON BORROWED TIME.

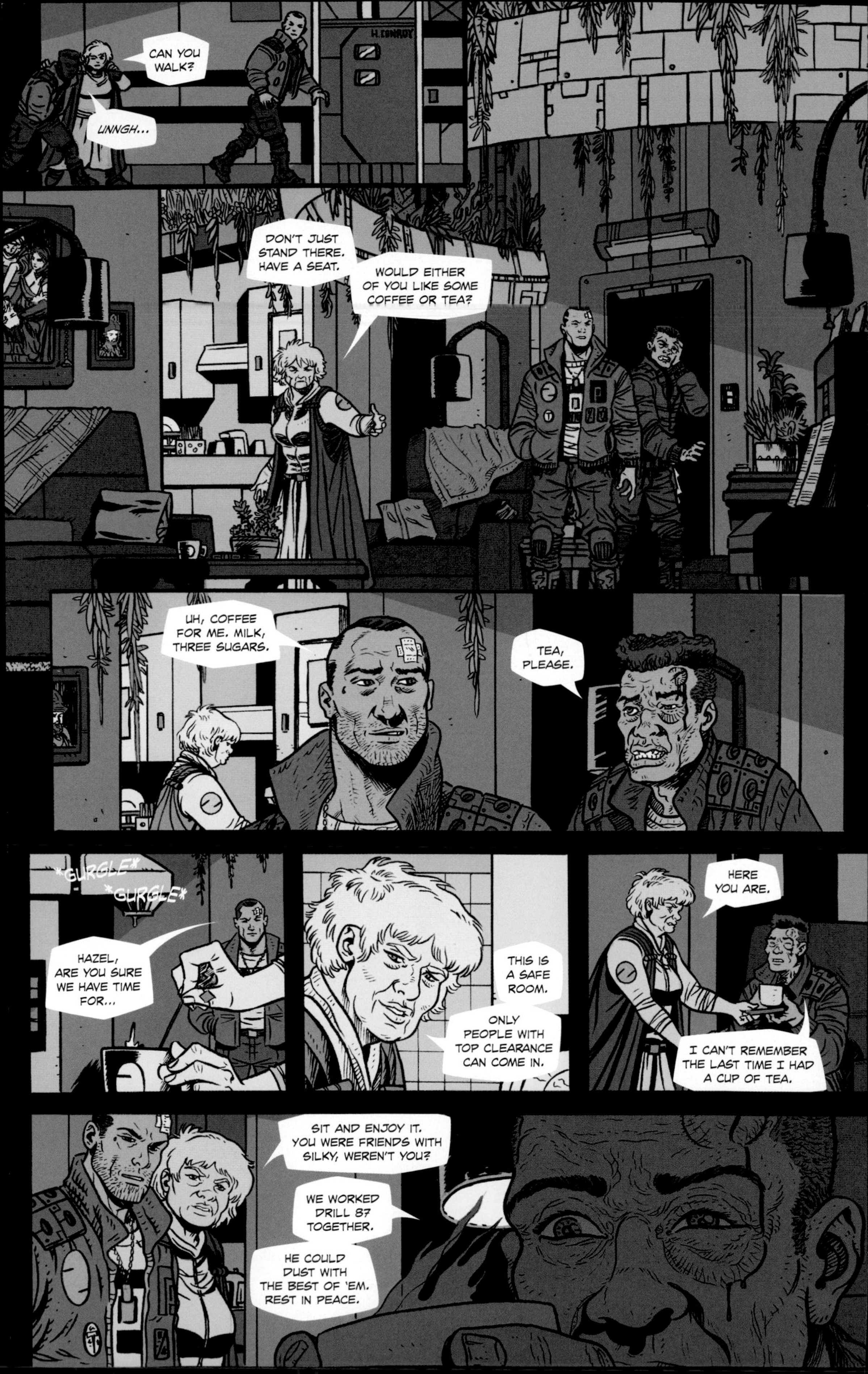
CAN YOU WALK?
UNNGH...
H. CONROY
DON'T JUST STAND THERE. HAVE A SEAT.
WOULD EITHER OF YOU LIKE SOME COFFEE OR TEA?
UH, COFFEE FOR ME. MILK, THREE SUGARS.
TEA, PLEASE.
*GURGLE*
*GURGLE*
HAZEL, ARE YOU SURE WE HAVE TIME FOR...
THIS IS A SAFE ROOM.
ONLY PEOPLE WITH TOP CLEARANCE CAN COME IN.
HERE YOU ARE.
I CAN'T REMEMBER THE LAST TIME I HAD A CUP OF TEA.
SIT AND ENJOY IT. YOU WERE FRIENDS WITH SILKY, WEREN'T YOU?
WE WORKED DRILL 87 TOGETHER.
HE COULD DUST WITH THE BEST OF 'EM. REST IN PEACE.

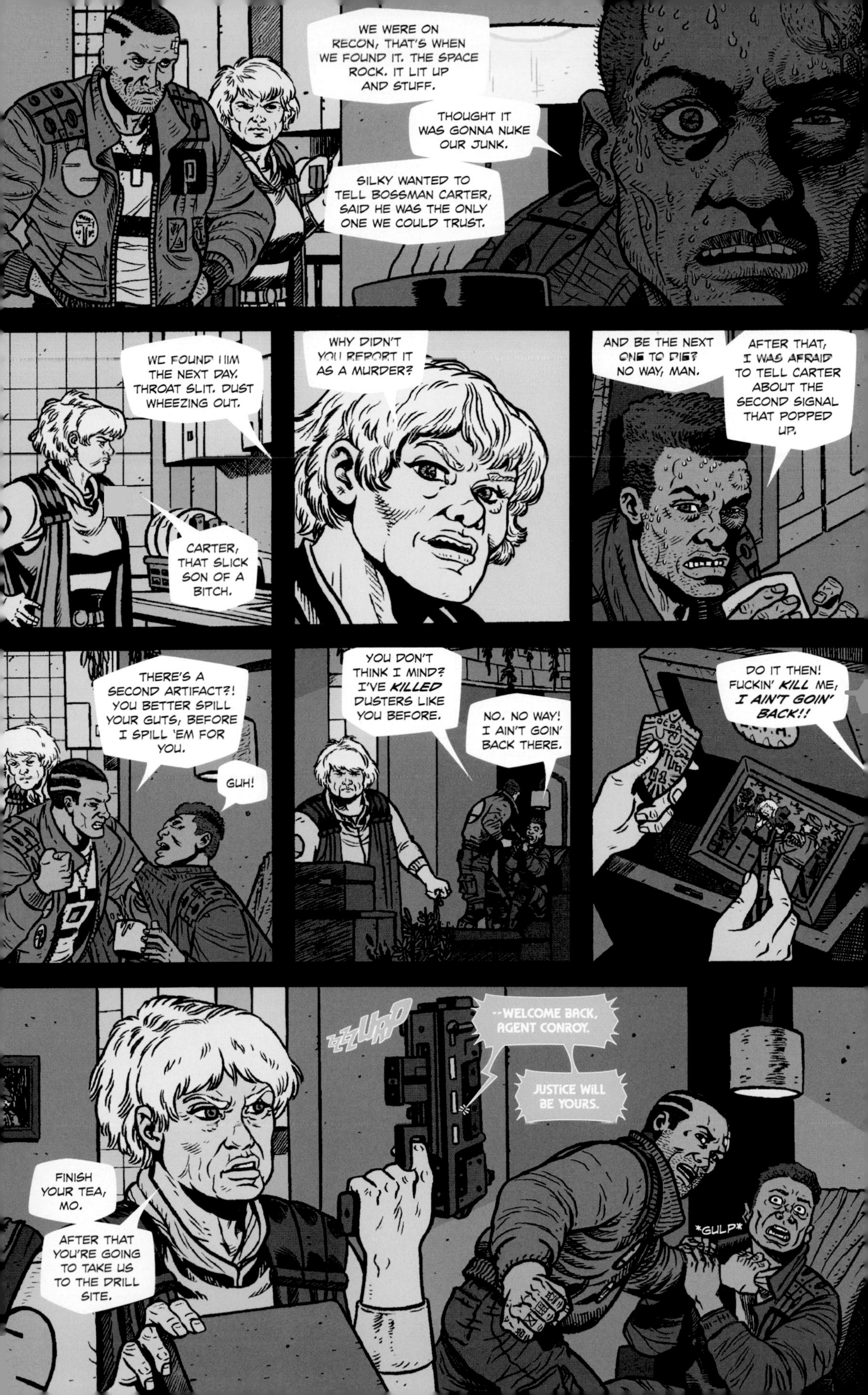
WE WERE ON RECON, THAT'S WHEN WE FOUND IT. THE SPACE ROCK. IT LIT UP AND STUFF.
THOUGHT IT WAS GONNA NUKE OUR JUNK.
SILKY WANTED TO TELL BOSSMAN CARTER, SAID HE WAS THE ONLY ONE WE COULD TRUST.
WE FOUND HIM THE NEXT DAY. THROAT SLIT. DUST WHEEZING OUT.
CARTER, THAT SLICK SON OF A BITCH.
WHY DIDN'T YOU REPORT IT AS A MURDER?
AND BE THE NEXT ONE TO DIE? NO WAY, MAN.
AFTER THAT, I WAS AFRAID TO TELL CARTER ABOUT THE SECOND SIGNAL THAT POPPED UP.
THERE'S A SECOND ARTIFACT?! YOU BETTER SPILL YOUR GUTS, BEFORE I SPILL 'EM FOR YOU.
GUH!
YOU DON'T THINK I MIND? I'VE *KILLED* DUSTERS LIKE YOU BEFORE.
NO. NO WAY! I AIN'T GOIN' BACK THERE.
DO IT THEN! FUCKIN' *KILL* ME, ***I AIN'T GOIN' BACK!!***
ZZZZURRP
--WELCOME BACK, AGENT CONROY.
JUSTICE WILL BE YOURS.
FINISH YOUR TEA, MO.
AFTER THAT YOU'RE GOING TO TAKE US TO THE DRILL SITE.
*GULP*

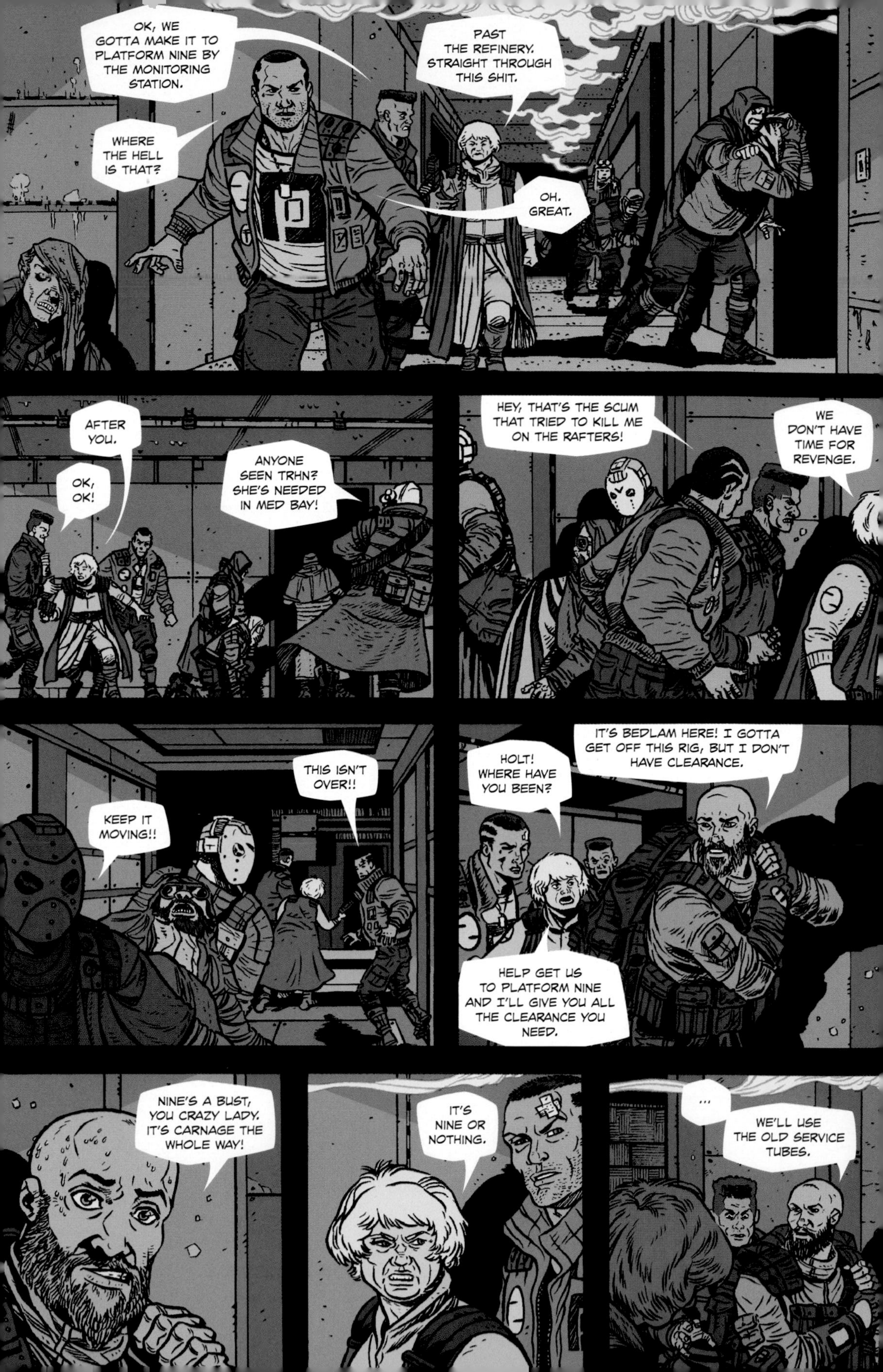
OK, WE GOTTA MAKE IT TO PLATFORM NINE BY THE MONITORING STATION.
WHERE THE HELL IS THAT?
PAST THE REFINERY. STRAIGHT THROUGH THIS SHIT.
OH. GREAT.
AFTER YOU.
OK, OK!
ANYONE SEEN TRHN? SHE'S NEEDED IN MED BAY!
HEY, THAT'S THE SCUM THAT TRIED TO KILL ME ON THE RAFTERS!
WE DON'T HAVE TIME FOR REVENGE.
KEEP IT MOVING!!
THIS ISN'T OVER!!
HOLT! WHERE HAVE YOU BEEN?
IT'S BEDLAM HERE! I GOTTA GET OFF THIS RIG, BUT I DON'T HAVE CLEARANCE.
HELP GET US TO PLATFORM NINE AND I'LL GIVE YOU ALL THE CLEARANCE YOU NEED.
NINE'S A BUST, YOU CRAZY LADY. IT'S CARNAGE THE WHOLE WAY!
IT'S NINE OR NOTHING.
...
WE'LL USE THE OLD SERVICE TUBES.

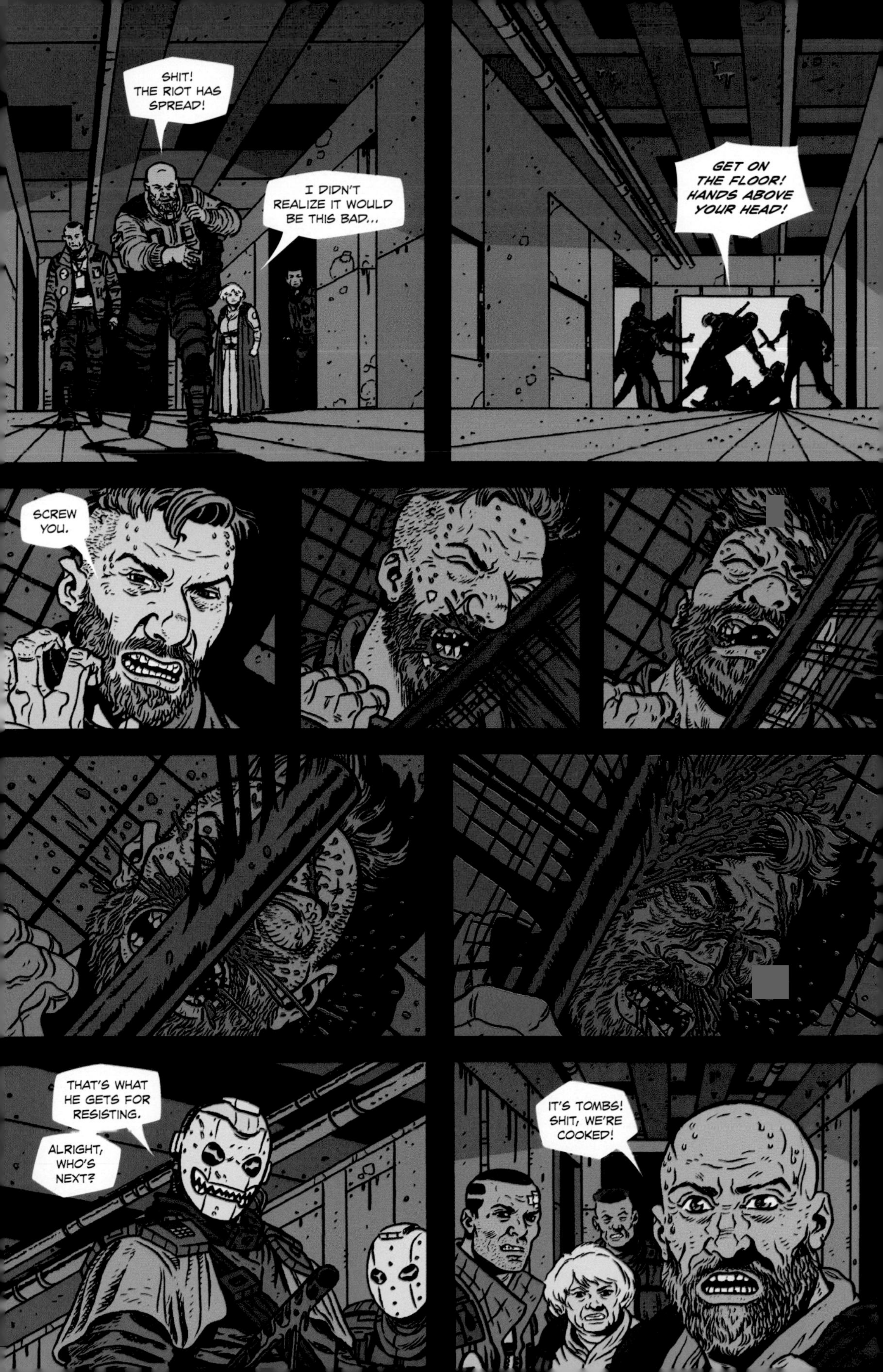
SHIT! THE RIOT HAS SPREAD!
I DIDN'T REALIZE IT WOULD BE THIS BAD...
GET ON THE FLOOR! HANDS ABOVE YOUR HEAD!
SCREW YOU.
THAT'S WHAT HE GETS FOR RESISTING.
ALRIGHT, WHO'S NEXT?
IT'S TOMBS! SHIT, WE'RE COOKED!

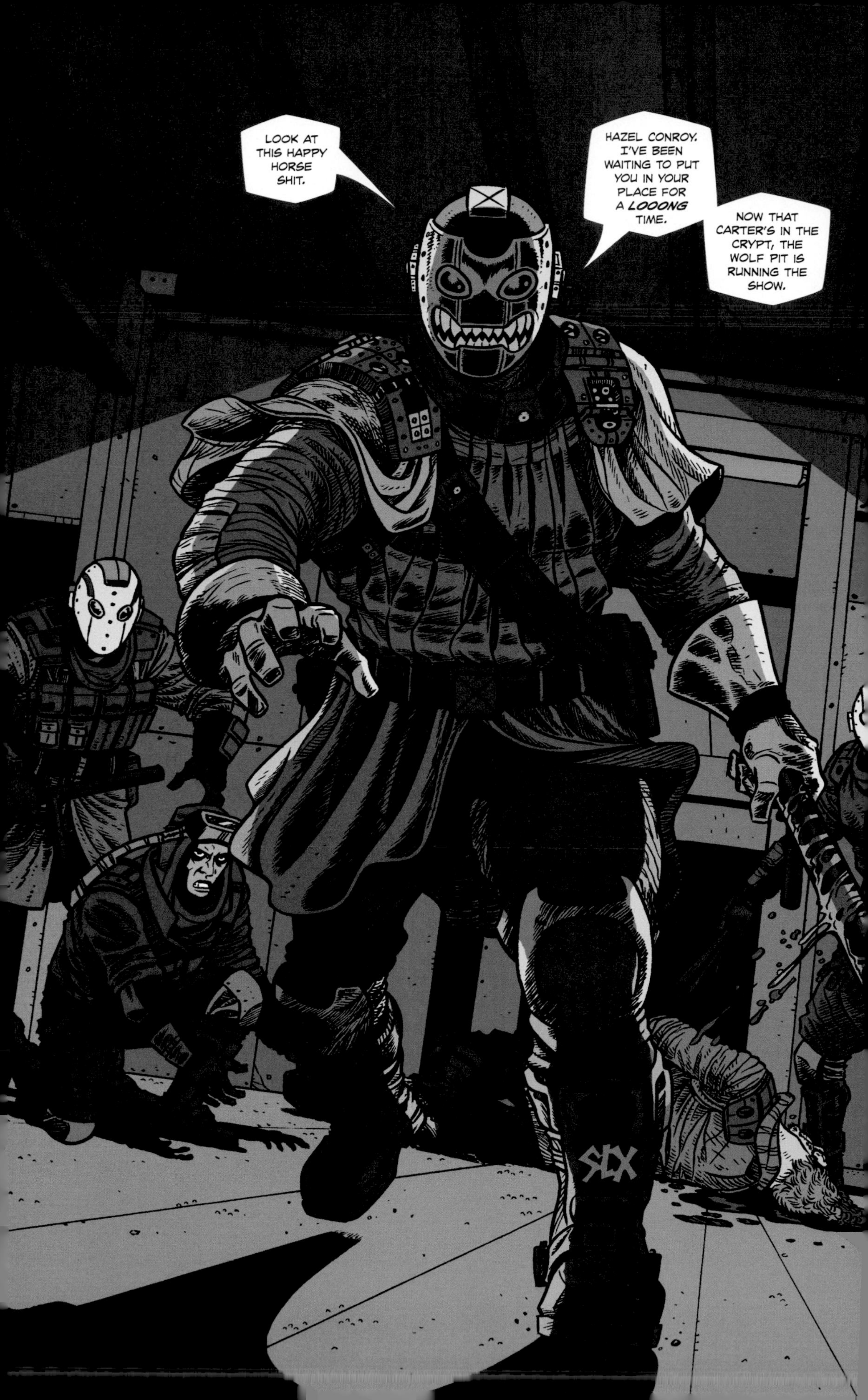
LOOK AT THIS HAPPY HORSE SHIT.
HAZEL CONROY. I'VE BEEN WAITING TO PUT YOU IN YOUR PLACE FOR A *LOOONG* TIME.
NOW THAT CARTER'S IN THE CRYPT, THE WOLF PIT IS RUNNING THE SHOW.
SLX

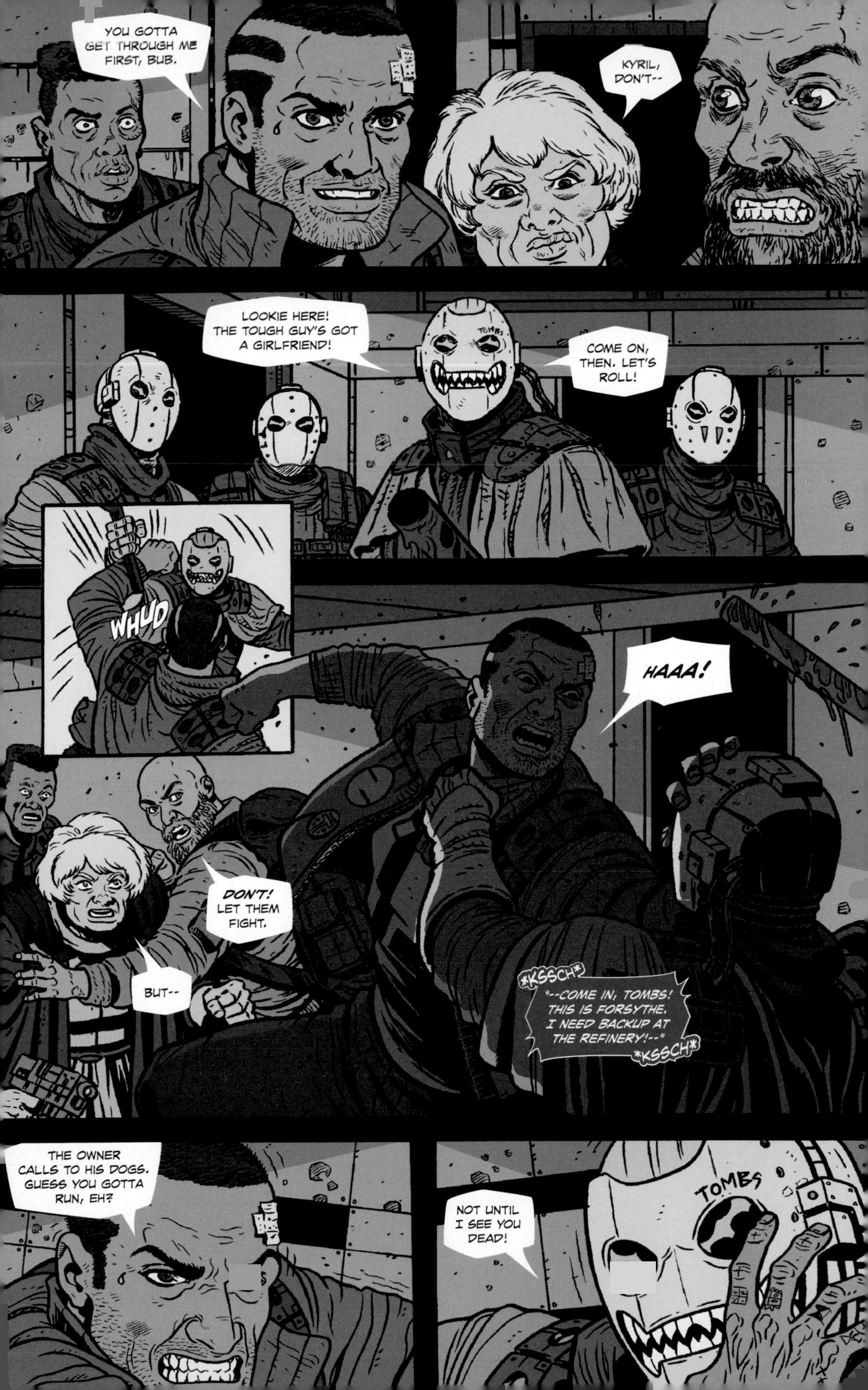

YOU GOTTA GET THROUGH ME FIRST, BUB.
KYRIL, DON'T--
LOOKIE HERE! THE TOUGH GUY'S GOT A GIRLFRIEND!
TOMBS
COME ON, THEN. LET'S ROLL!
WHUD
HAAA!
DON'T! LET THEM FIGHT.
BUT--
*KSSCH*
"--COME IN, TOMBS! THIS IS FORSYTHE. I NEED BACKUP AT THE REFINERY!--"
*KSSCH*
THE OWNER CALLS TO HIS DOGS. GUESS YOU GOTTA RUN, EH?
NOT UNTIL I SEE YOU DEAD!
TOMBS

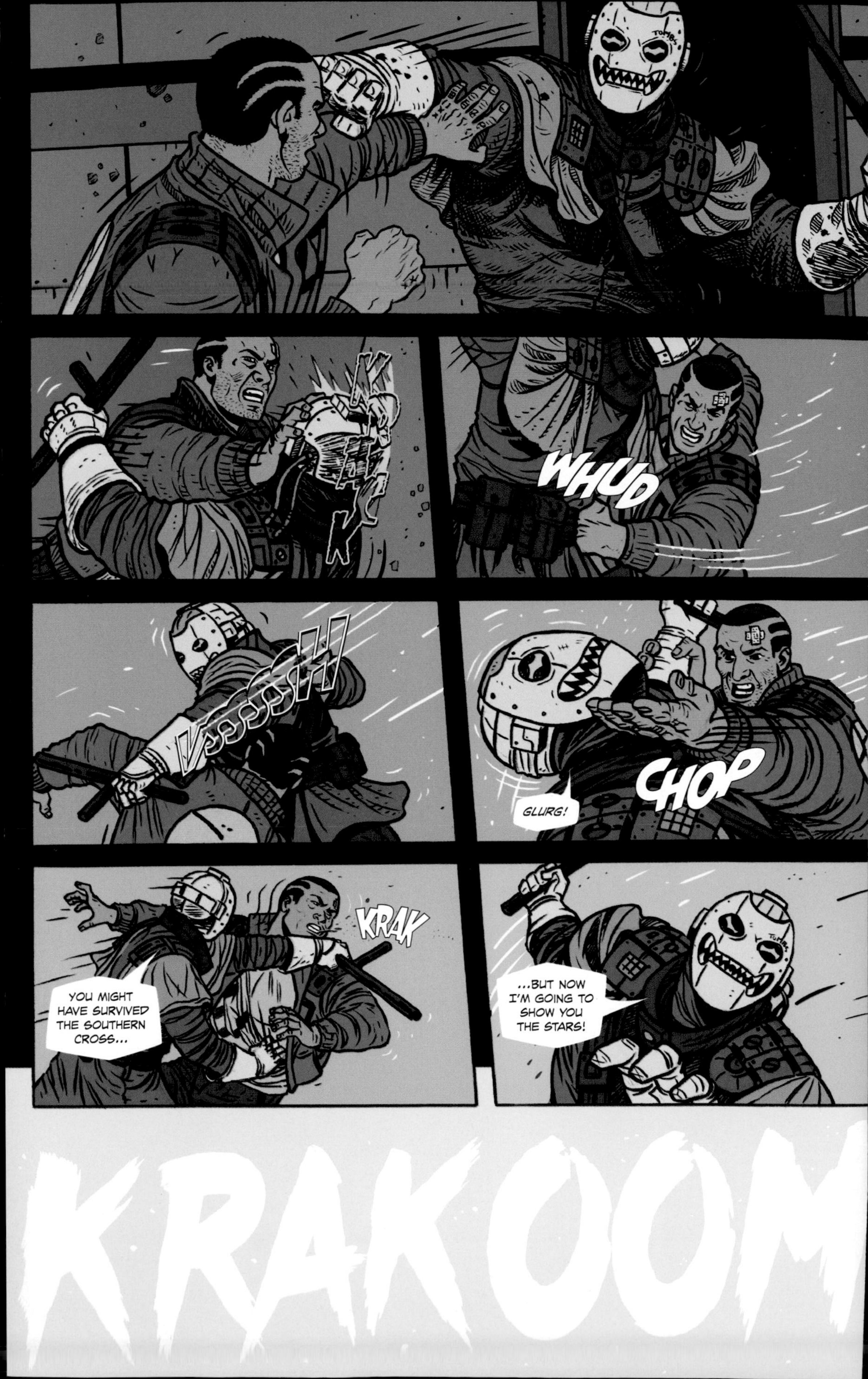
WHUD
CHOP
GLURG!
KRAK
YOU MIGHT HAVE SURVIVED THE SOUTHERN CROSS...
...BUT NOW I'M GOING TO SHOW YOU THE STARS!
KRAKOOM

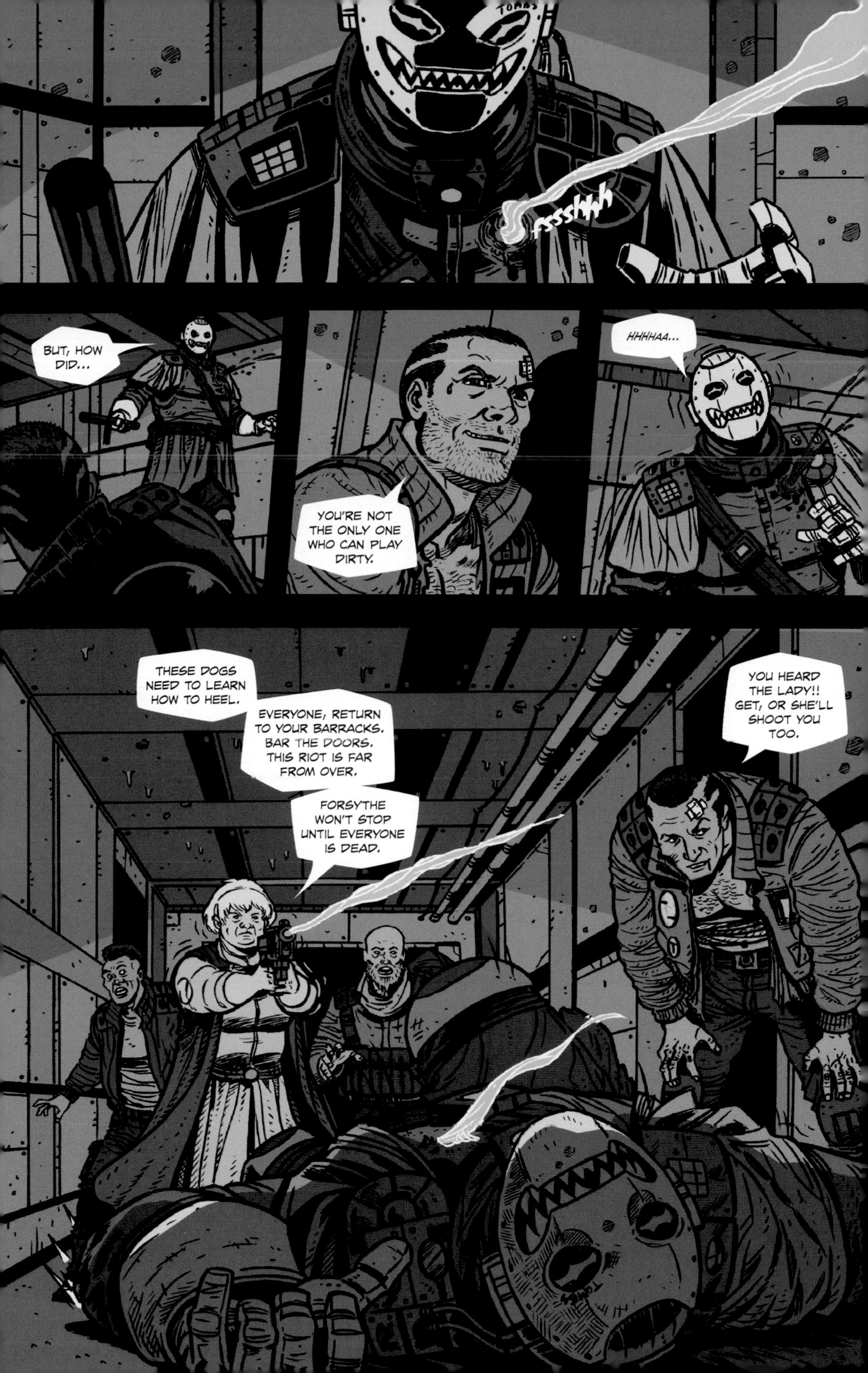
fssshhh
BUT, HOW DID...
YOU'RE NOT THE ONLY ONE WHO CAN PLAY DIRTY.
HHHHAA...
THESE DOGS NEED TO LEARN HOW TO HEEL.
EVERYONE, RETURN TO YOUR BARRACKS. BAR THE DOORS. THIS RIOT IS FAR FROM OVER.
FORSYTHE WON'T STOP UNTIL EVERYONE IS DEAD.
YOU HEARD THE LADY!! GET, OR SHE'LL SHOOT YOU TOO.

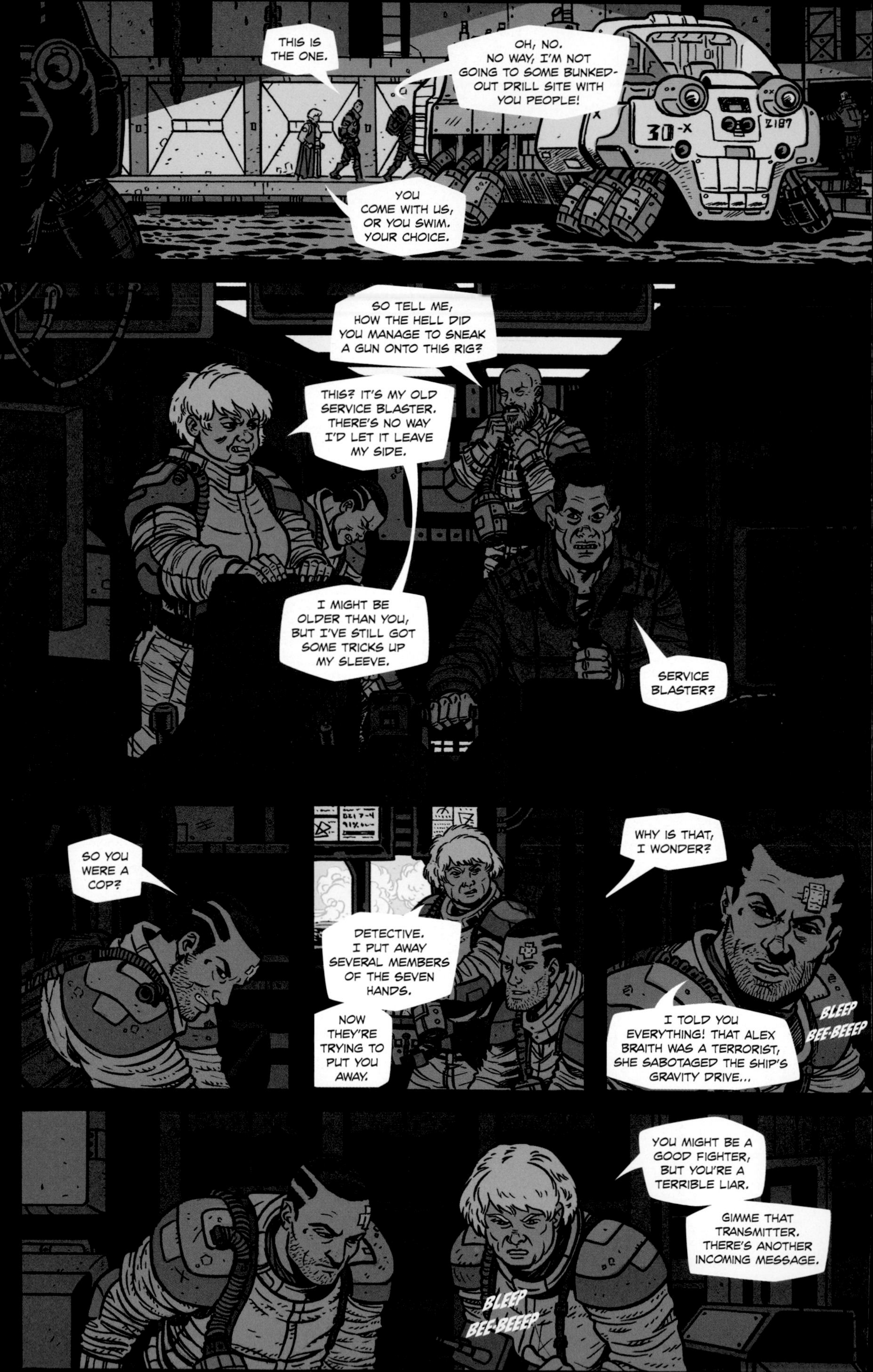
THIS IS THE ONE.
OH, NO. NO WAY, I'M NOT GOING TO SOME BUNKED-OUT DRILL SITE WITH YOU PEOPLE!
30-X
Z187
YOU COME WITH US, OR YOU SWIM. YOUR CHOICE.
SO TELL ME, HOW THE HELL DID YOU MANAGE TO SNEAK A GUN ONTO THIS RIG?
THIS? IT'S MY OLD SERVICE BLASTER. THERE'S NO WAY I'D LET IT LEAVE MY SIDE.
I MIGHT BE OLDER THAN YOU, BUT I'VE STILL GOT SOME TRICKS UP MY SLEEVE.
SERVICE BLASTER?
SO YOU WERE A COP?
DETECTIVE. I PUT AWAY SEVERAL MEMBERS OF THE SEVEN HANDS.
NOW THEY'RE TRYING TO PUT YOU AWAY.
WHY IS THAT, I WONDER?
I TOLD YOU EVERYTHING! THAT ALEX BRAITH WAS A TERRORIST, SHE SABOTAGED THE SHIP'S GRAVITY DRIVE...
BLEEP BEE-BEEEP
YOU MIGHT BE A GOOD FIGHTER, BUT YOU'RE A TERRIBLE LIAR.
GIMME THAT TRANSMITTER. THERE'S ANOTHER INCOMING MESSAGE.
BLEEP BEE-BEEEP

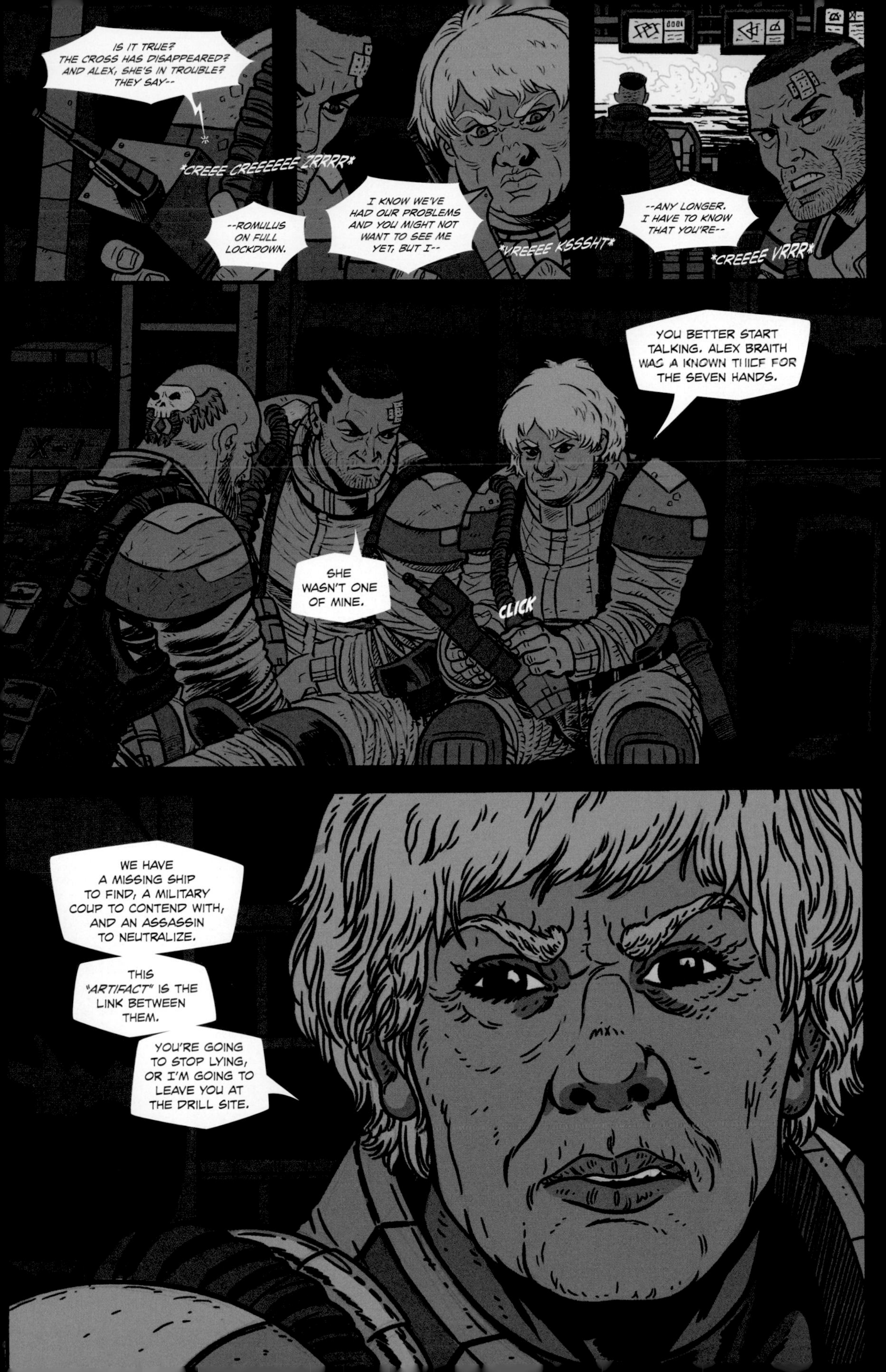
IS IT TRUE? THE CROSS HAS DISAPPEARED? AND ALEX, SHE'S IN TROUBLE? THEY SAY--
*CREEE CREEEEEE ZRRRR*
--ROMULUS ON FULL LOCKDOWN.
I KNOW WE'VE HAD OUR PROBLEMS AND YOU MIGHT NOT WANT TO SEE ME YET, BUT I--
*VREEEE KSSSHT*
--ANY LONGER. I HAVE TO KNOW THAT YOU'RE--
*CREEEE VRRR*
YOU BETTER START TALKING. ALEX BRAITH WAS A KNOWN THIEF FOR THE SEVEN HANDS.
SHE WASN'T ONE OF MINE.
CLICK
WE HAVE A MISSING SHIP TO FIND, A MILITARY COUP TO CONTEND WITH, AND AN ASSASSIN TO NEUTRALIZE.
THIS "ARTIFACT" IS THE LINK BETWEEN THEM.
YOU'RE GOING TO STOP LYING, OR I'M GOING TO LEAVE YOU AT THE DRILL SITE.

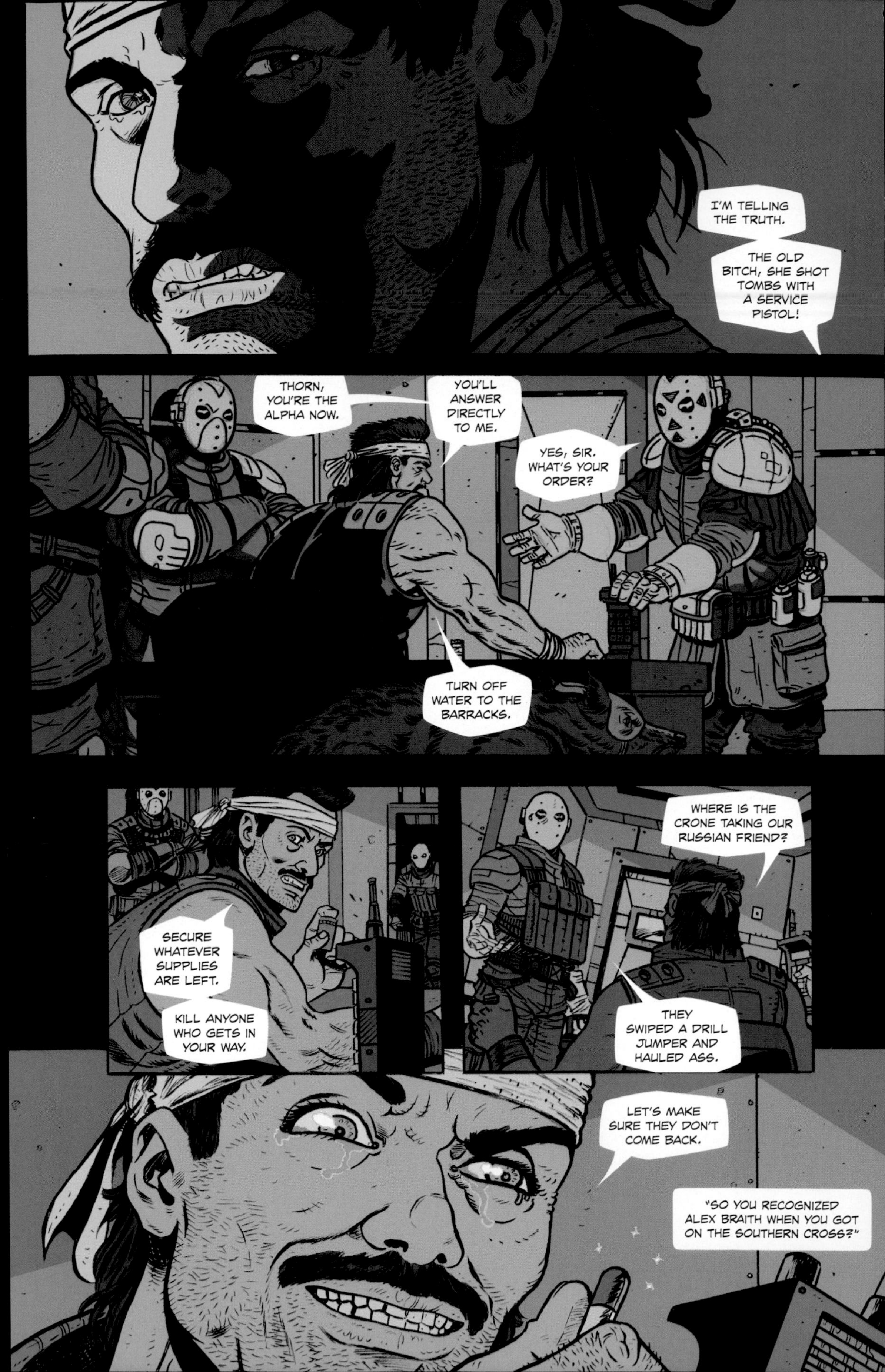
I'M TELLING THE TRUTH.
THE OLD BITCH, SHE SHOT TOMBS WITH A SERVICE PISTOL!
THORN, YOU'RE THE ALPHA NOW.
YOU'LL ANSWER DIRECTLY TO ME.
YES, SIR. WHAT'S YOUR ORDER?
TURN OFF WATER TO THE BARRACKS.
SECURE WHATEVER SUPPLIES ARE LEFT.
KILL ANYONE WHO GETS IN YOUR WAY.
WHERE IS THE CRONE TAKING OUR RUSSIAN FRIEND?
THEY SWIPED A DRILL JUMPER AND HAULED ASS.
LET'S MAKE SURE THEY DON'T COME BACK.
"SO YOU RECOGNIZED ALEX BRAITH WHEN YOU GOT ON THE SOUTHERN CROSS?"

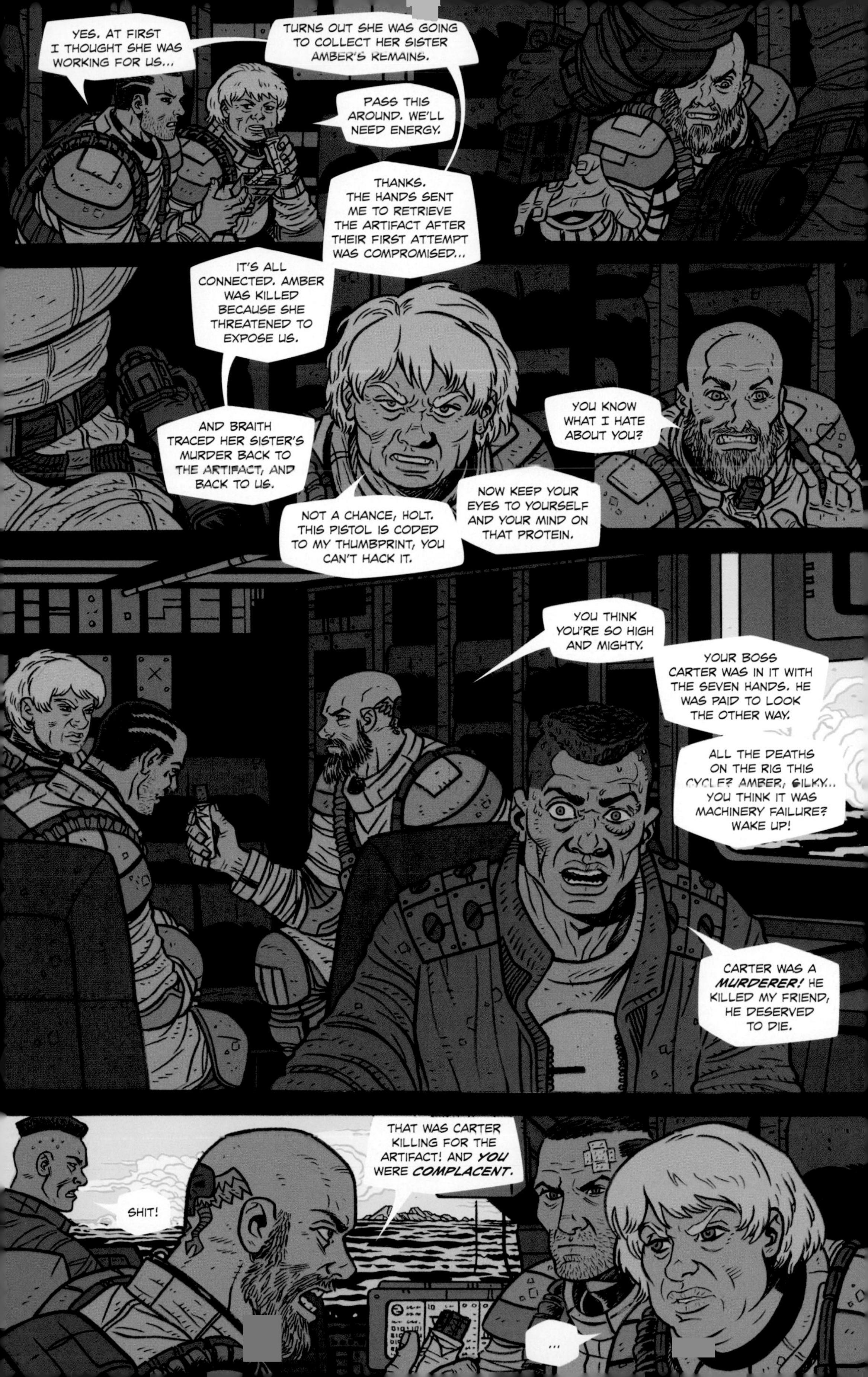
YES. AT FIRST I THOUGHT SHE WAS WORKING FOR US...
TURNS OUT SHE WAS GOING TO COLLECT HER SISTER AMBER'S REMAINS.
PASS THIS AROUND. WE'LL NEED ENERGY.
THANKS. THE HANDS SENT ME TO RETRIEVE THE ARTIFACT AFTER THEIR FIRST ATTEMPT WAS COMPROMISED...
IT'S ALL CONNECTED. AMBER WAS KILLED BECAUSE SHE THREATENED TO EXPOSE US.
AND BRAITH TRACED HER SISTER'S MURDER BACK TO THE ARTIFACT, AND BACK TO US.
YOU KNOW WHAT I HATE ABOUT YOU?
NOT A CHANCE, HOLT. THIS PISTOL IS CODED TO MY THUMBPRINT, YOU CAN'T HACK IT.
NOW KEEP YOUR EYES TO YOURSELF AND YOUR MIND ON THAT PROTEIN.
YOU THINK YOU'RE SO HIGH AND MIGHTY.
YOUR BOSS CARTER WAS IN IT WITH THE SEVEN HANDS. HE WAS PAID TO LOOK THE OTHER WAY.
ALL THE DEATHS ON THE RIG THIS CYCLE? AMBER, SILKY... YOU THINK IT WAS MACHINERY FAILURE? WAKE UP!
CARTER WAS A *MURDERER!* HE KILLED MY FRIEND, HE DESERVED TO DIE.
SHIT!
THAT WAS CARTER KILLING FOR THE ARTIFACT! AND *YOU* WERE *COMPLACENT*.
...

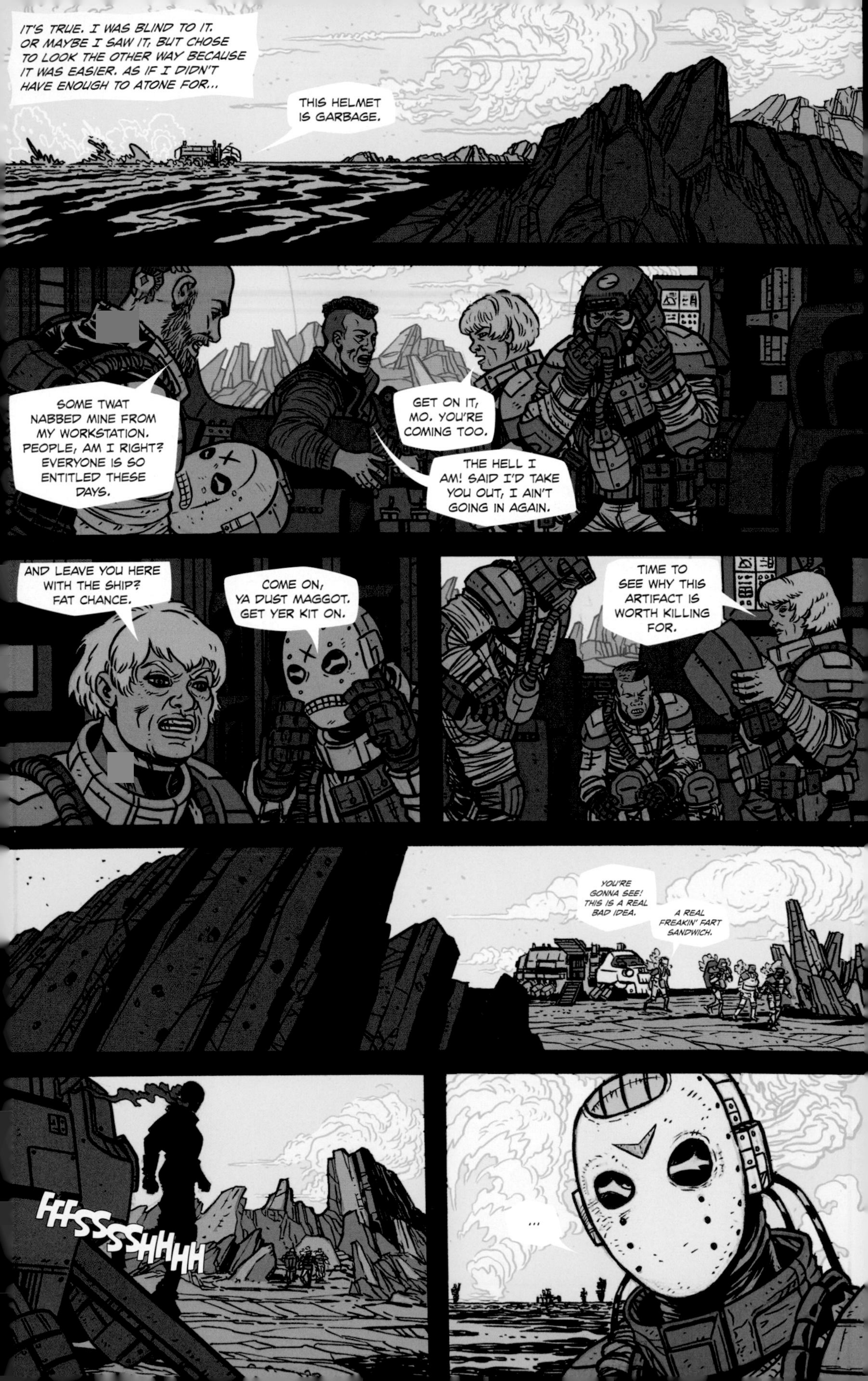
IT'S TRUE. I WAS BLIND TO IT. OR MAYBE I SAW IT, BUT CHOSE TO LOOK THE OTHER WAY BECAUSE IT WAS EASIER. AS IF I DIDN'T HAVE ENOUGH TO ATONE FOR...
THIS HELMET IS GARBAGE.
SOME TWAT NABBED MINE FROM MY WORKSTATION. PEOPLE, AM I RIGHT? EVERYONE IS SO ENTITLED THESE DAYS.
GET ON IT, MO. YOU'RE COMING TOO.
THE HELL I AM! SAID I'D TAKE YOU OUT, I AIN'T GOING IN AGAIN.
AND LEAVE YOU HERE WITH THE SHIP? FAT CHANCE.
COME ON, YA DUST MAGGOT. GET YER KIT ON.
TIME TO SEE WHY THIS ARTIFACT IS WORTH KILLING FOR.
YOU'RE GONNA SEE! THIS IS A REAL BAD IDEA.
A REAL FREAKIN' FART SANDWICH.
FFFSSSSHHHH
...

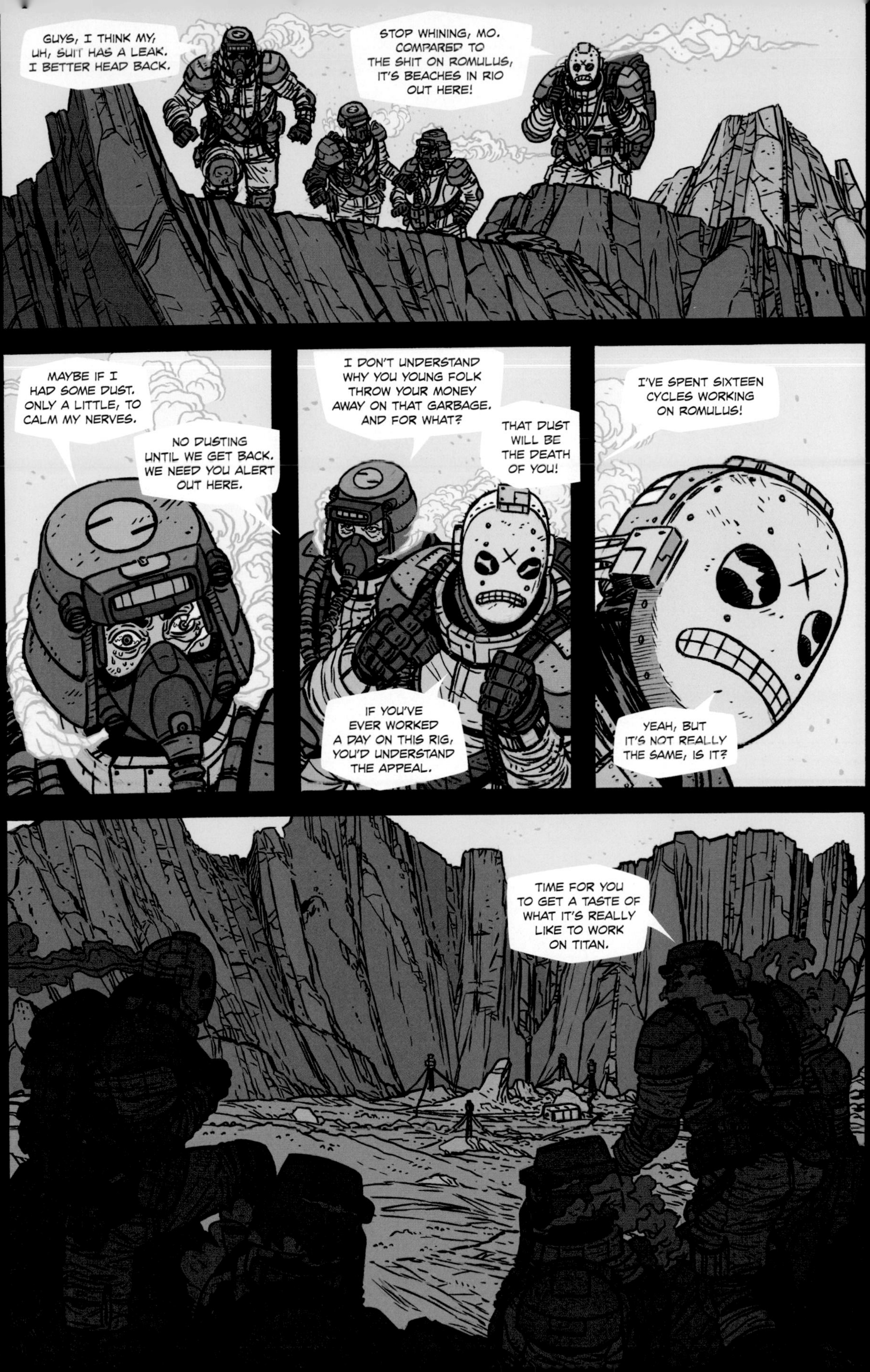
GUYS, I THINK MY, UH, SUIT HAS A LEAK. I BETTER HEAD BACK.
STOP WHINING, MO. COMPARED TO THE SHIT ON ROMULUS, IT'S BEACHES IN RIO OUT HERE!
MAYBE IF I HAD SOME DUST. ONLY A LITTLE, TO CALM MY NERVES.
NO DUSTING UNTIL WE GET BACK. WE NEED YOU ALERT OUT HERE.
I DON'T UNDERSTAND WHY YOU YOUNG FOLK THROW YOUR MONEY AWAY ON THAT GARBAGE. AND FOR WHAT?
THAT DUST WILL BE THE DEATH OF YOU!
IF YOU'VE EVER WORKED A DAY ON THIS RIG, YOU'D UNDERSTAND THE APPEAL.
I'VE SPENT SIXTEEN CYCLES WORKING ON ROMULUS!
YEAH, BUT IT'S NOT REALLY THE SAME, IS IT?
TIME FOR YOU TO GET A TASTE OF WHAT IT'S REALLY LIKE TO WORK ON TITAN.

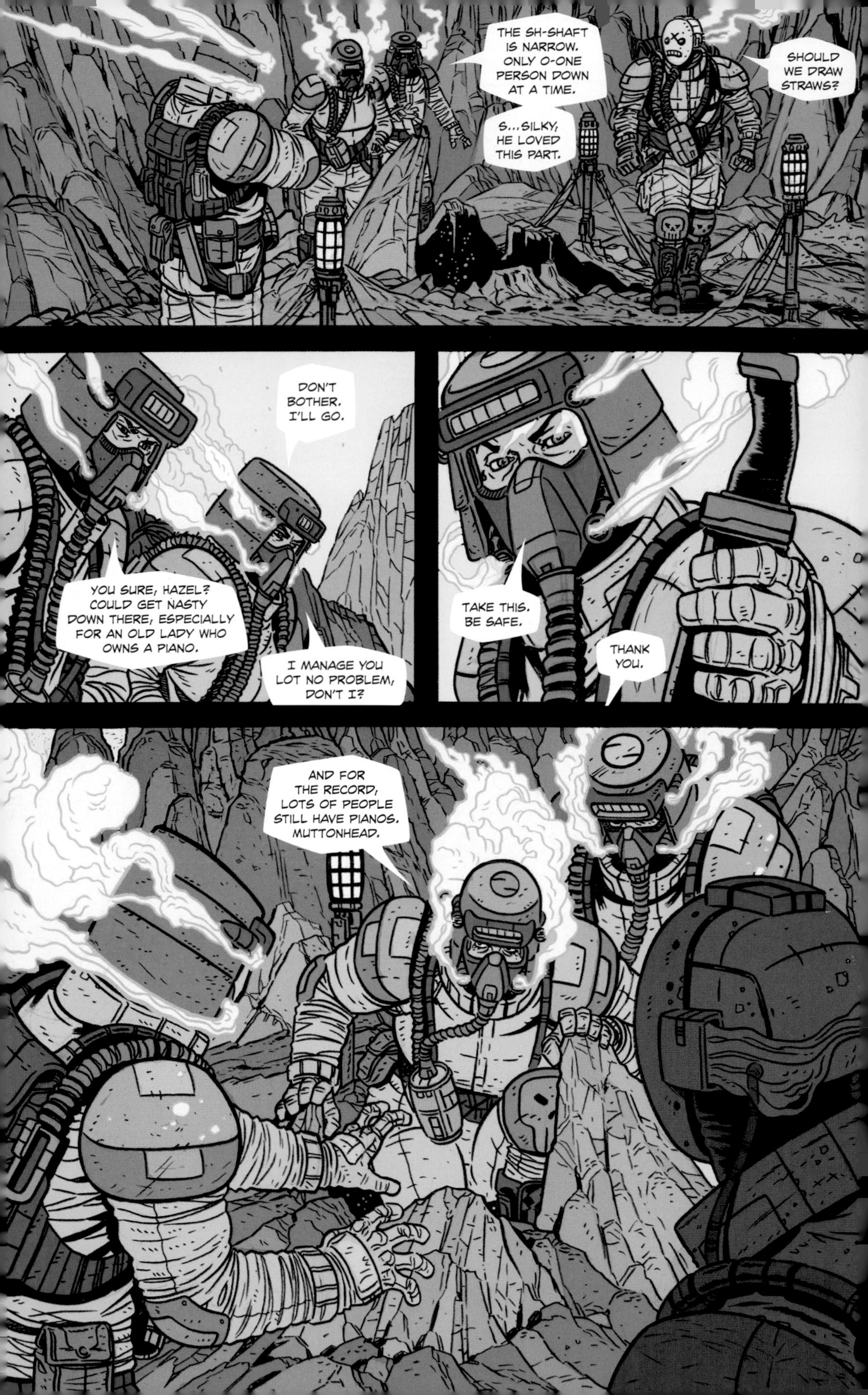
THE SH-SHAFT IS NARROW. ONLY O-ONE PERSON DOWN AT A TIME.
S...SILKY, HE LOVED THIS PART.
SHOULD WE DRAW STRAWS?
DON'T BOTHER. I'LL GO.
YOU SURE, HAZEL? COULD GET NASTY DOWN THERE, ESPECIALLY FOR AN OLD LADY WHO OWNS A PIANO.
I MANAGE YOU LOT NO PROBLEM, DON'T I?
TAKE THIS. BE SAFE.
THANK YOU.
AND FOR THE RECORD, LOTS OF PEOPLE STILL HAVE PIANOS. MUTTONHEAD.

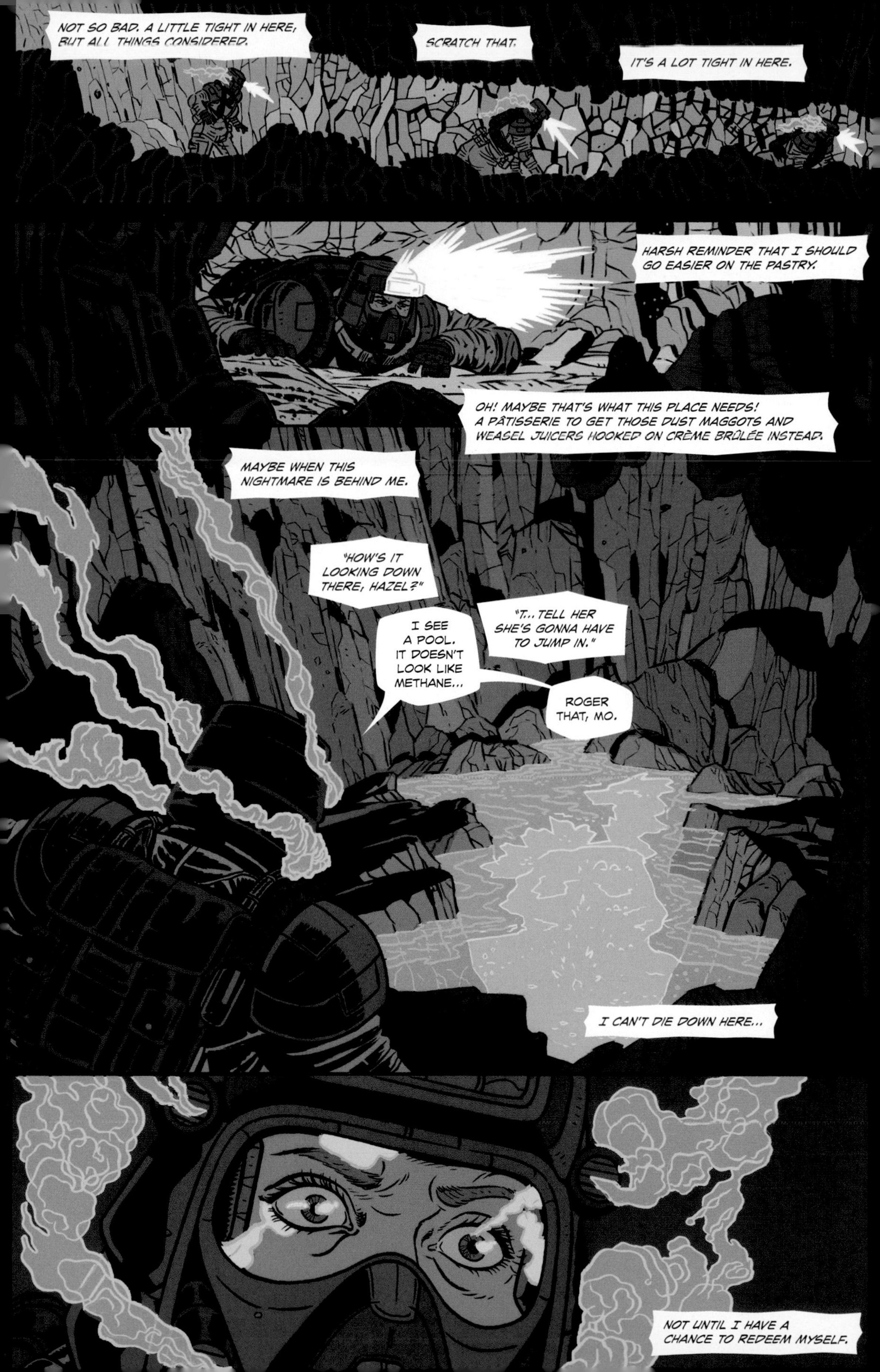
NOT SO BAD. A LITTLE TIGHT IN HERE, BUT ALL THINGS CONSIDERED.
SCRATCH THAT.
IT'S A LOT TIGHT IN HERE.
HARSH REMINDER THAT I SHOULD GO EASIER ON THE PASTRY.
OH! MAYBE THAT'S WHAT THIS PLACE NEEDS! A PÂTISSERIE TO GET THOSE DUST MAGGOTS AND WEASEL JUICERS HOOKED ON CRÈME BRÛLÉE INSTEAD.
MAYBE WHEN THIS NIGHTMARE IS BEHIND ME.
"HOW'S IT LOOKING DOWN THERE, HAZEL?"
I SEE A POOL. IT DOESN'T LOOK LIKE METHANE...
"T...TELL HER SHE'S GONNA HAVE TO JUMP IN."
ROGER THAT, MO.
I CAN'T DIE DOWN HERE...
NOT UNTIL I HAVE A CHANCE TO REDEEM MYSELF.

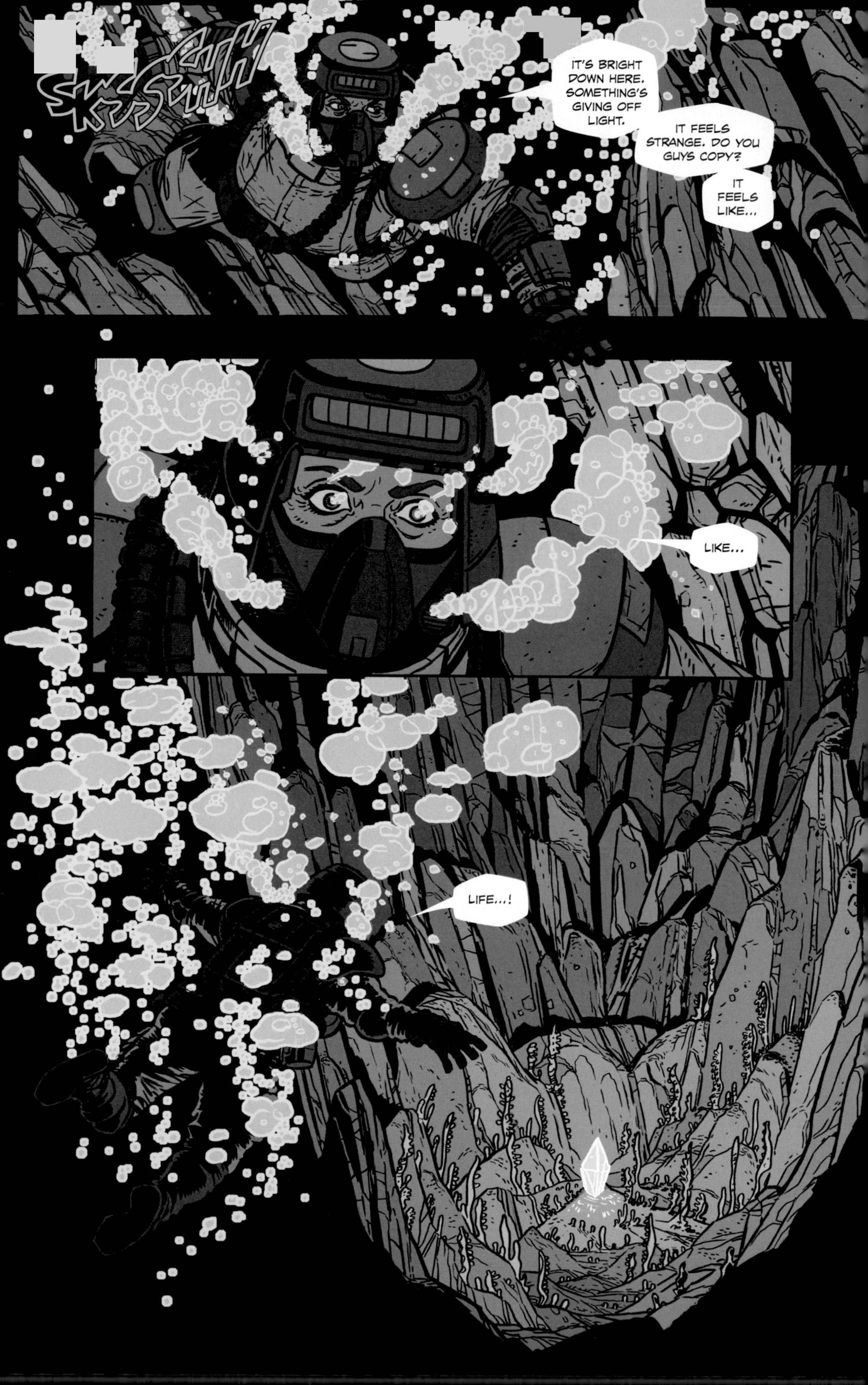
IT'S BRIGHT DOWN HERE. SOMETHING'S GIVING OFF LIGHT.
IT FEELS STRANGE. DO YOU GUYS COPY?
IT FEELS LIKE...
LIKE...
LIFE...!

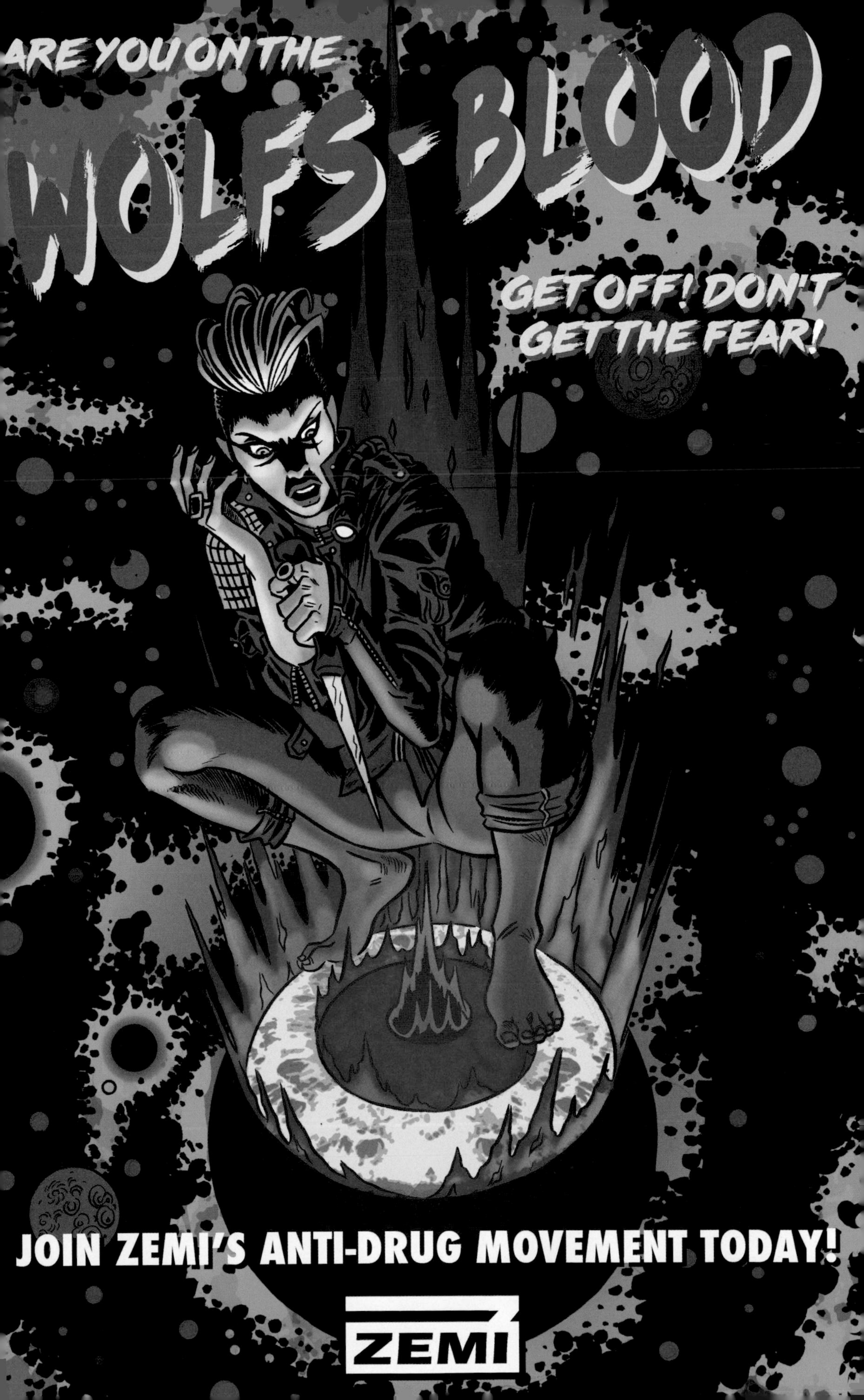
ARE YOU ON THE
WOLFS-BLOOD
GET OFF! DON'T GET THE FEAR!
JOIN ZEMI'S ANTI-DRUG MOVEMENT TODAY!
ZEMI

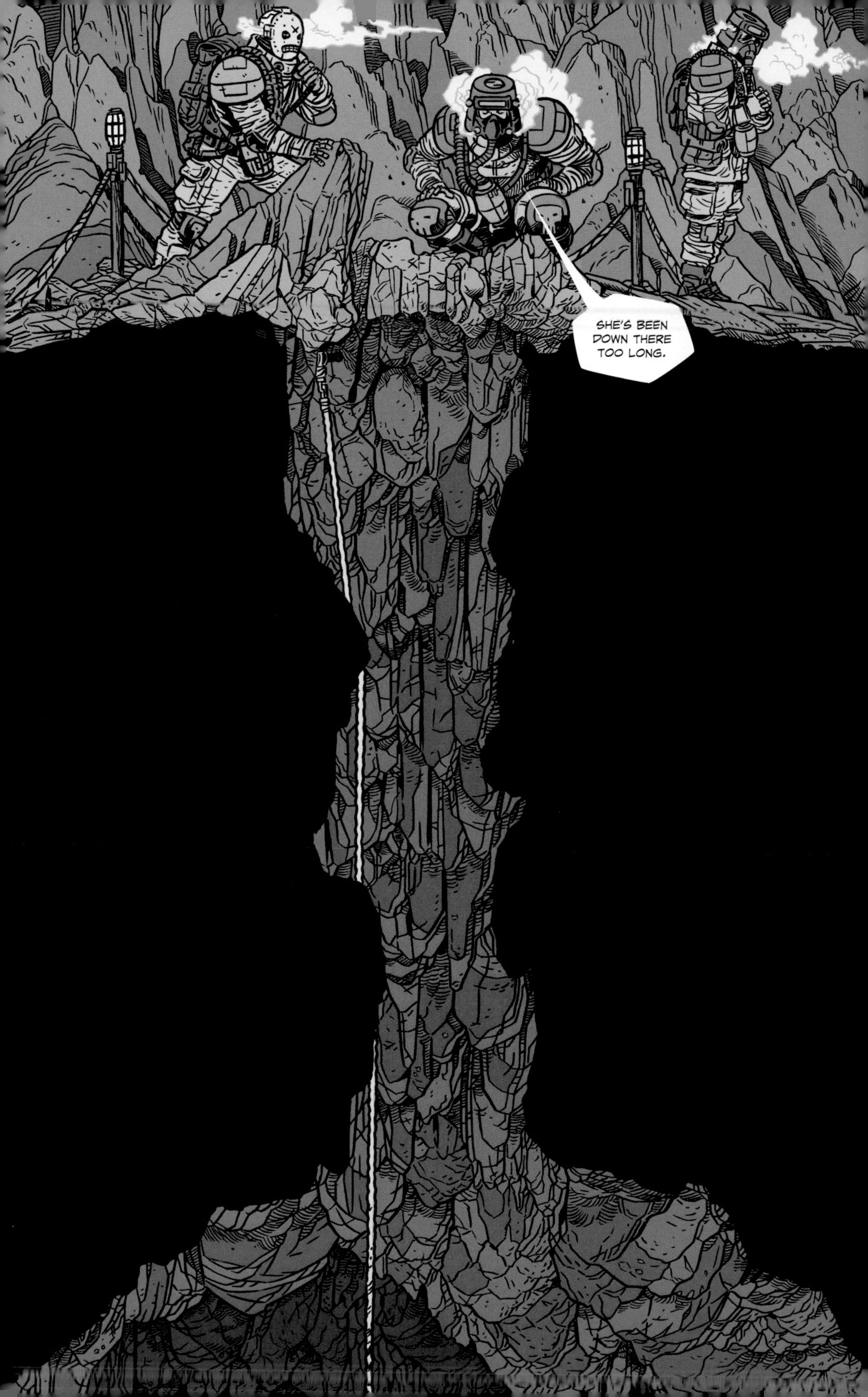
SHE'S BEEN DOWN THERE TOO LONG.

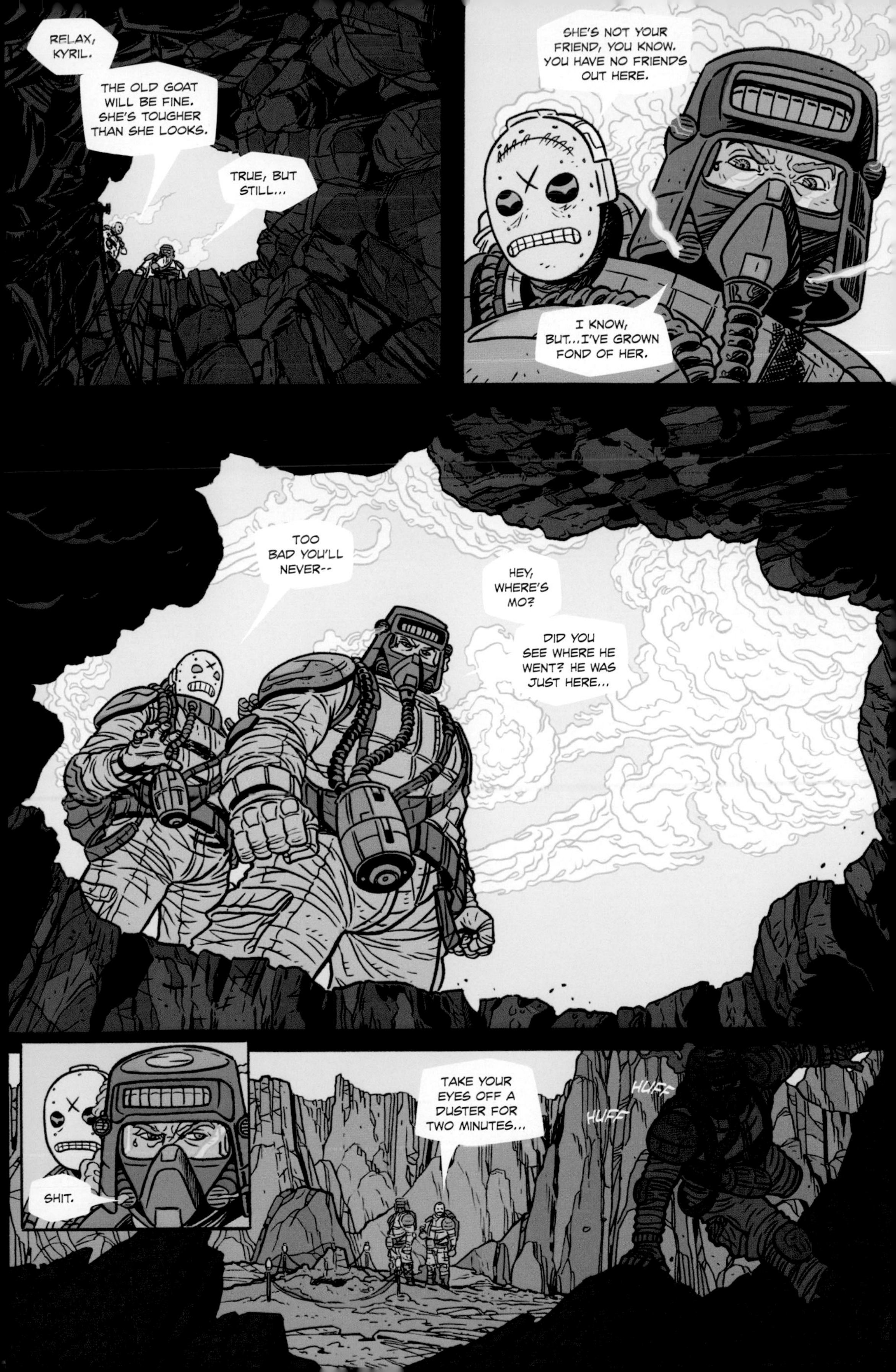
RELAX, KYRIL.
THE OLD GOAT WILL BE FINE. SHE'S TOUGHER THAN SHE LOOKS.
TRUE, BUT STILL...
SHE'S NOT YOUR FRIEND, YOU KNOW. YOU HAVE NO FRIENDS OUT HERE.
I KNOW, BUT...I'VE GROWN FOND OF HER.
TOO BAD YOU'LL NEVER--
HEY, WHERE'S MO?
DID YOU SEE WHERE HE WENT? HE WAS JUST HERE...
SHIT.
TAKE YOUR EYES OFF A DUSTER FOR TWO MINUTES...
HUFF
HUFF

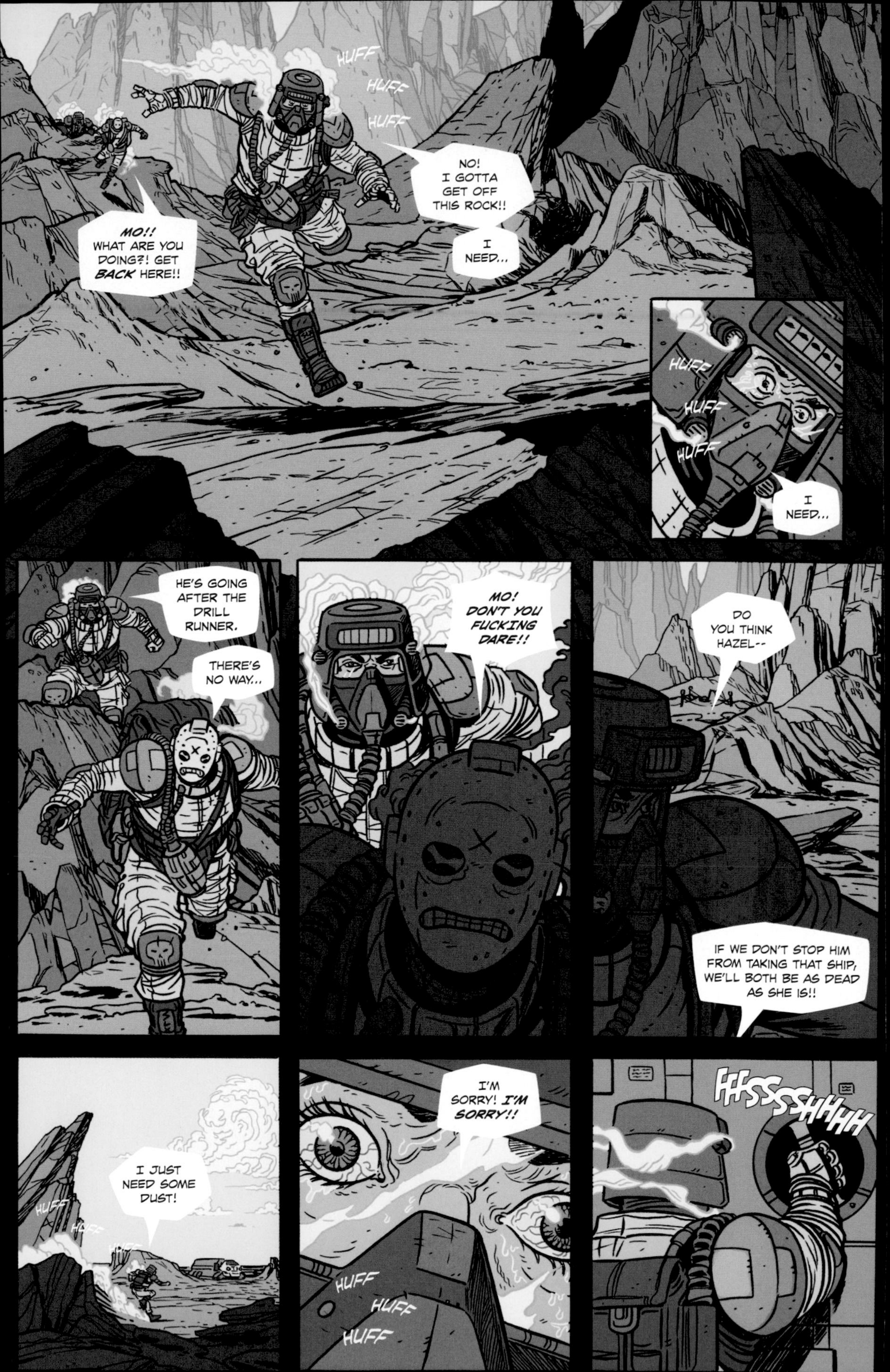
HUFF
HUFF
HUFF
MO!! WHAT ARE YOU DOING?! GET BACK HERE!!
NO! I GOTTA GET OFF THIS ROCK!!
I NEED...
HUFF
HUFF
HUFF
I NEED...
HE'S GOING AFTER THE DRILL RUNNER.
THERE'S NO WAY...
MO! DON'T YOU FUCKING DARE!!
DO YOU THINK HAZEL--
IF WE DON'T STOP HIM FROM TAKING THAT SHIP, WE'LL BOTH BE AS DEAD AS SHE IS!!
I JUST NEED SOME DUST!
HUFF
HUFF
HUFF
I'M SORRY! I'M SORRY!!
HUFF
HUFF
HUFF
FFFSSSSHHHH

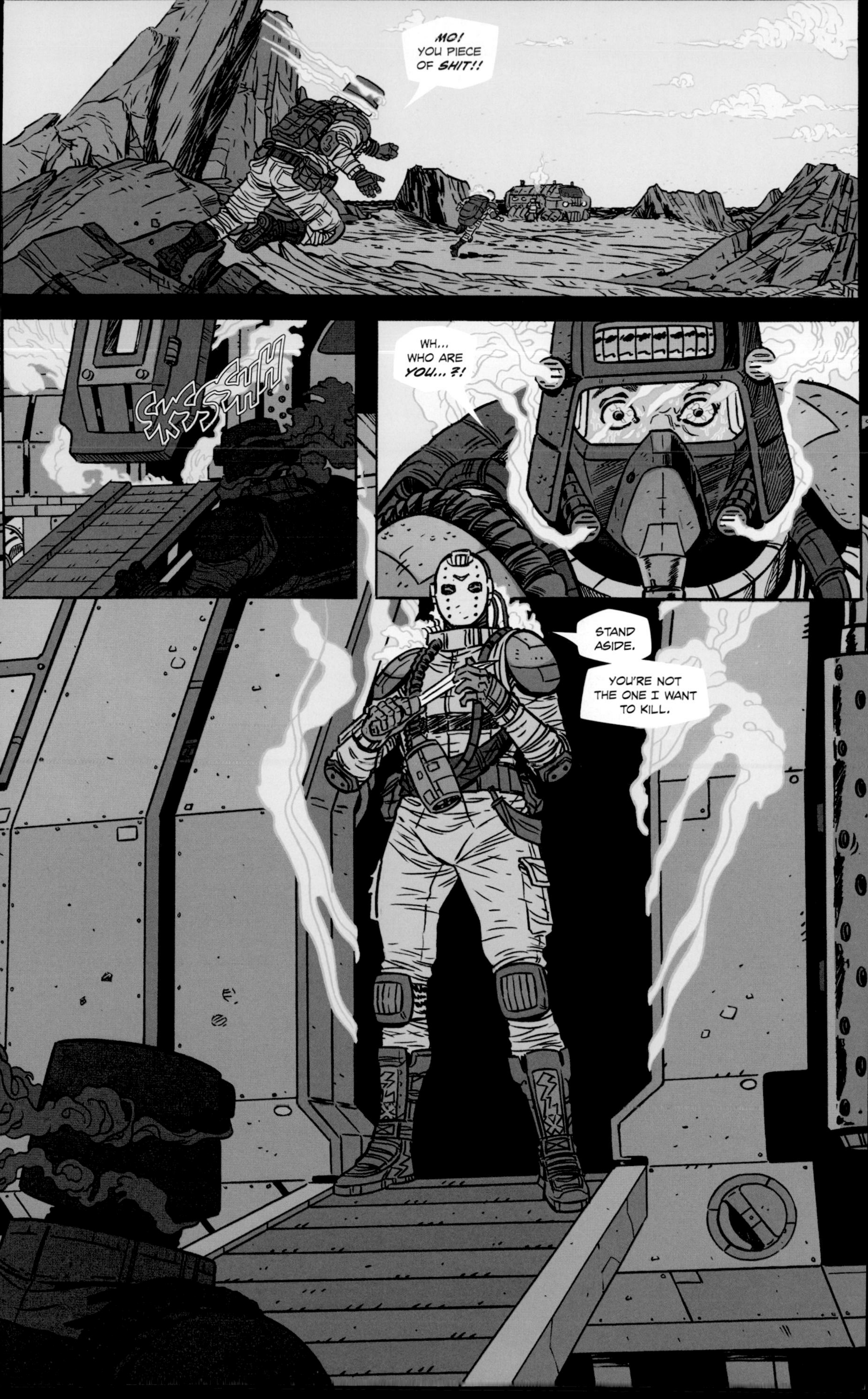
MO! YOU PIECE OF SHIT!!
SKSSHH
WH... WHO ARE YOU...?!
STAND ASIDE.
YOU'RE NOT THE ONE I WANT TO KILL.

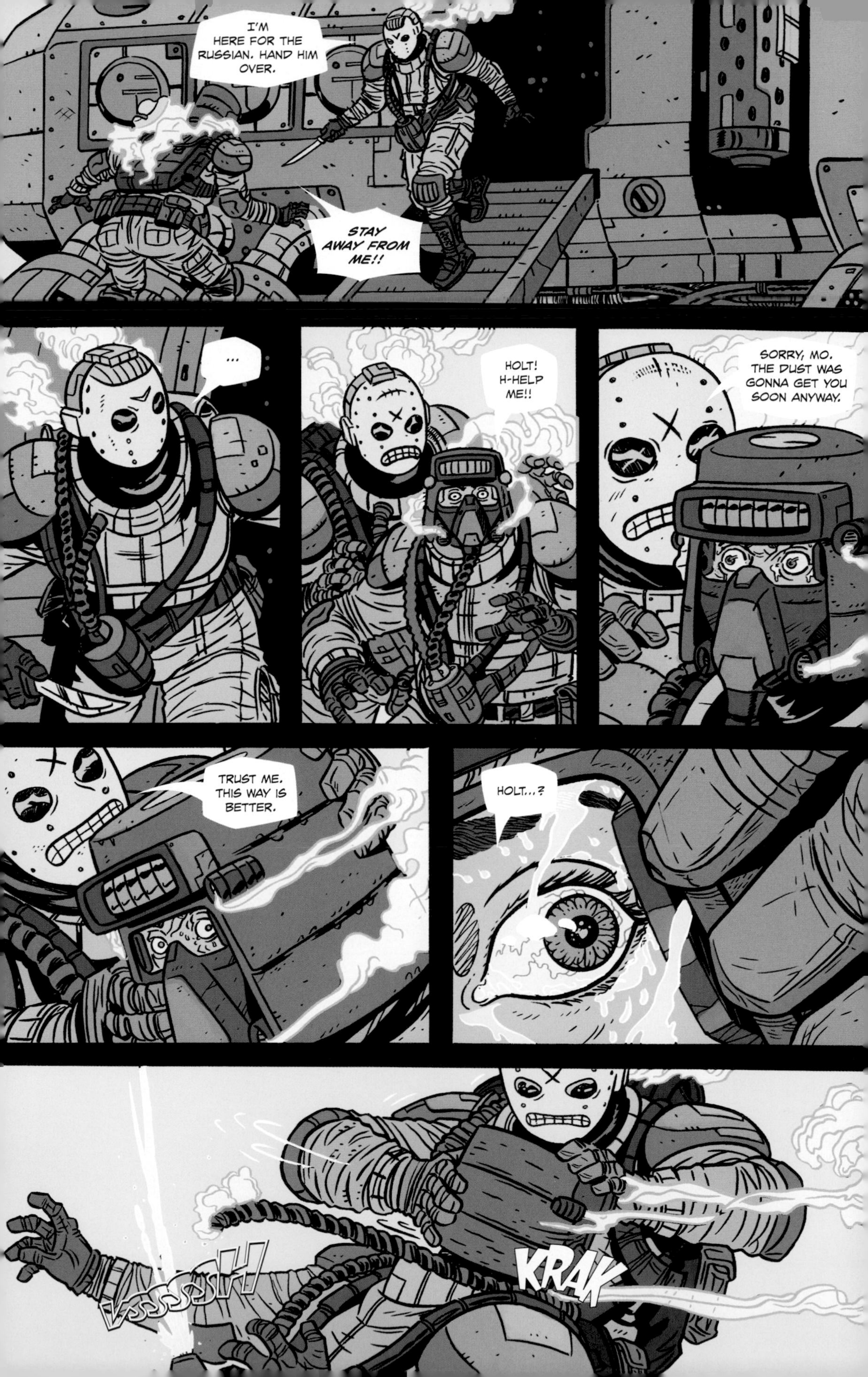
I'M HERE FOR THE RUSSIAN. HAND HIM OVER.
STAY AWAY FROM ME!!
...
HOLT! H-HELP ME!!
SORRY, MO. THE DUST WAS GONNA GET YOU SOON ANYWAY.
TRUST ME. THIS WAY IS BETTER.
HOLT...?
KRAK

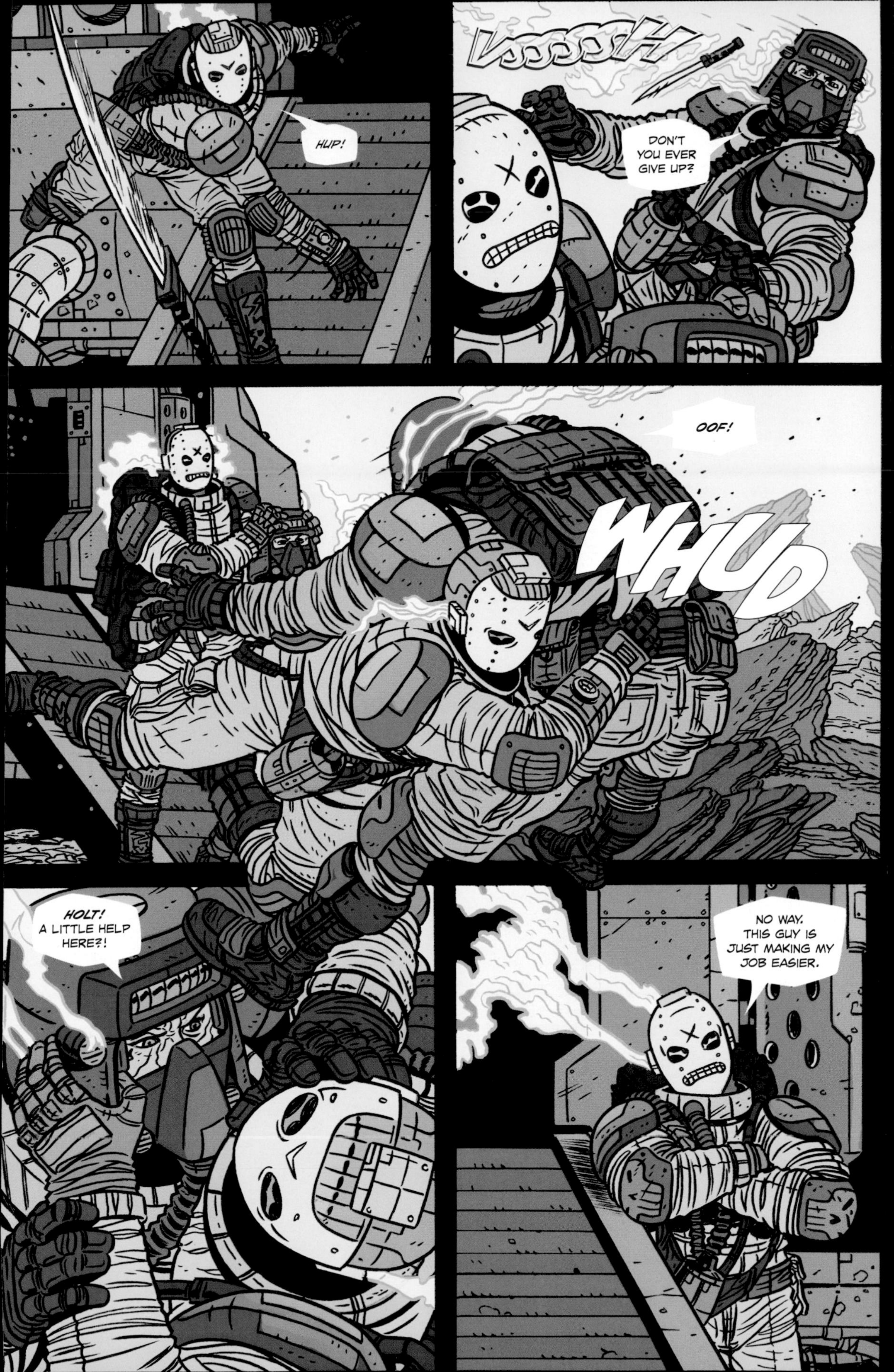
HUP!
VSSSSH!
DON'T YOU EVER GIVE UP?
OOF!
WHUD
HOLT! A LITTLE HELP HERE?!
NO WAY. THIS GUY IS JUST MAKING MY JOB EASIER.

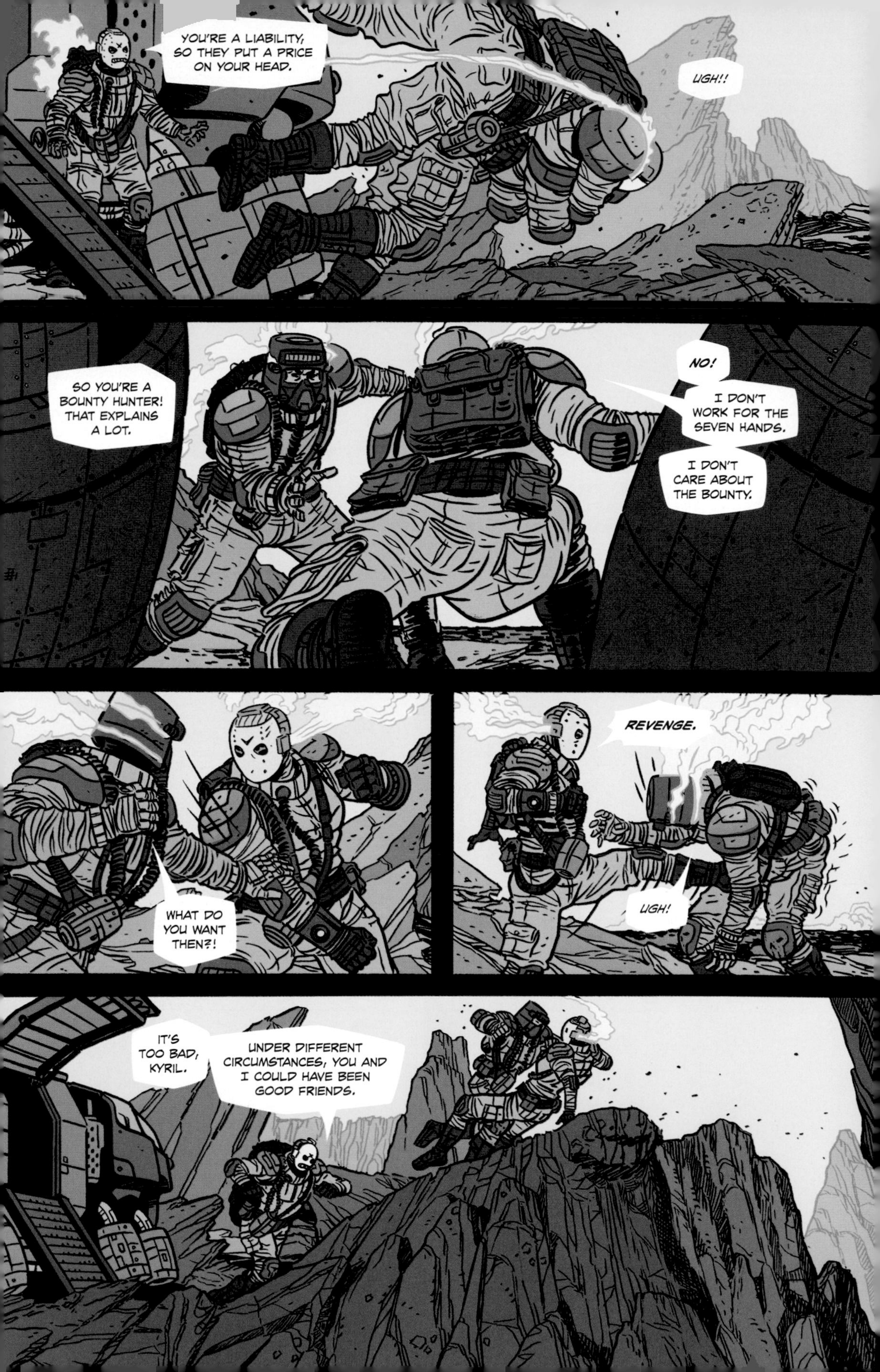
YOU'RE A LIABILITY; SO THEY PUT A PRICE ON YOUR HEAD.
UGH!!
SO YOU'RE A BOUNTY HUNTER! THAT EXPLAINS A LOT.
NO!
I DON'T WORK FOR THE SEVEN HANDS.
I DON'T CARE ABOUT THE BOUNTY.
WHAT DO YOU WANT THEN?!
REVENGE.
UGH!
IT'S TOO BAD, KYRIL.
UNDER DIFFERENT CIRCUMSTANCES, YOU AND I COULD HAVE BEEN GOOD FRIENDS.

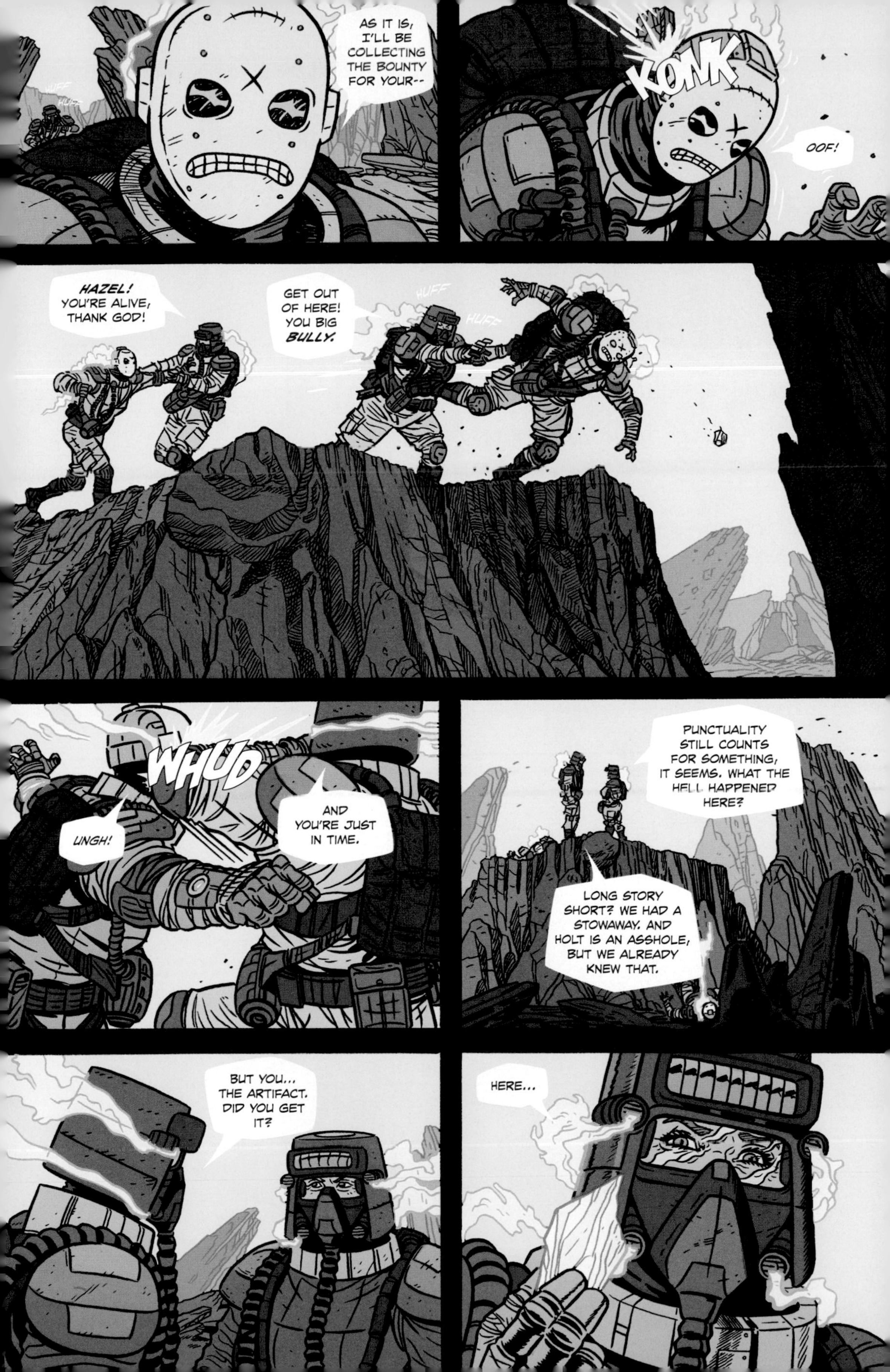

AS IT IS, I'LL BE COLLECTING THE BOUNTY FOR YOUR--
HUFF
HUFF
KONK
OOF!
HAZEL! YOU'RE ALIVE, THANK GOD!
GET OUT OF HERE! YOU BIG BULLY.
HUFF
HUFF
WHUD
UNGH!
AND YOU'RE JUST IN TIME.
PUNCTUALITY STILL COUNTS FOR SOMETHING, IT SEEMS. WHAT THE HELL HAPPENED HERE?
LONG STORY SHORT? WE HAD A STOWAWAY. AND HOLT IS AN ASSHOLE, BUT WE ALREADY KNEW THAT.
BUT YOU... THE ARTIFACT. DID YOU GET IT?
HERE...

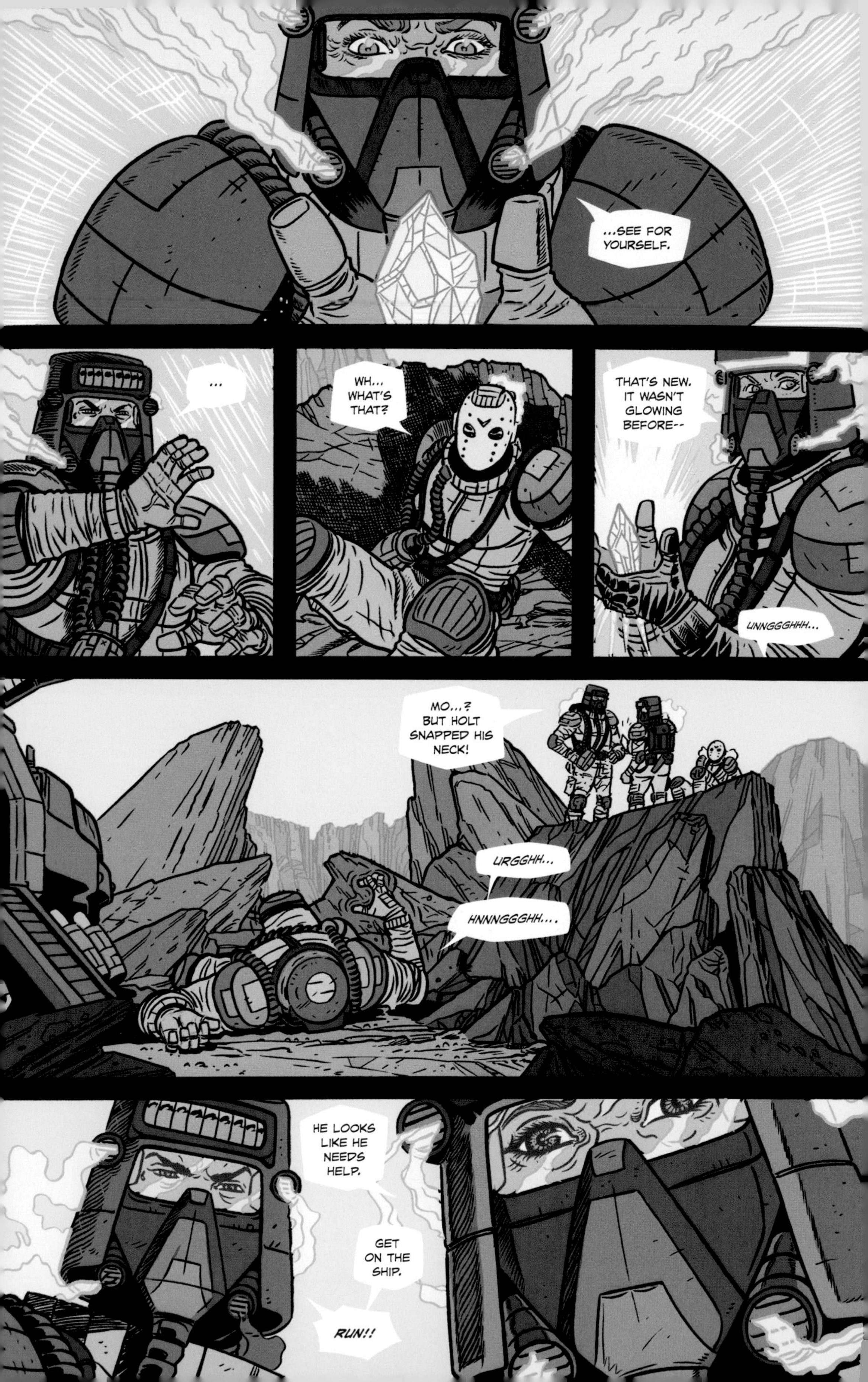
...SEE FOR YOURSELF.
...
WH... WHAT'S THAT?
THAT'S NEW. IT WASN'T GLOWING BEFORE--
UNNGGGHHH...
MO...? BUT HOLT SNAPPED HIS NECK!
URGGHH...
HNNNGGGHH....
HE LOOKS LIKE HE NEEDS HELP.
GET ON THE SHIP.
RUN!!

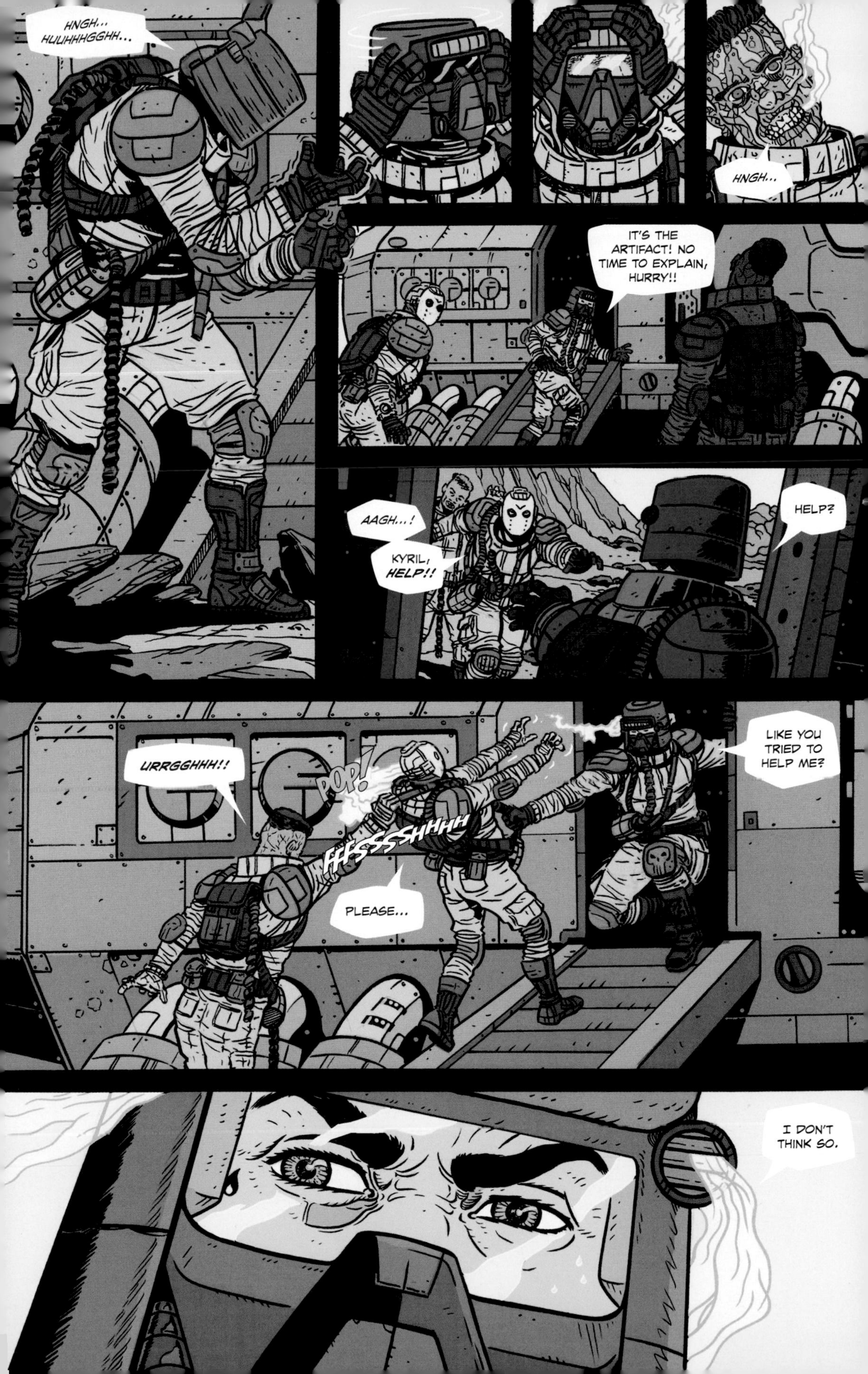
HNGH... HUUHHHGGHH...
HNGH...
IT'S THE ARTIFACT! NO TIME TO EXPLAIN, HURRY!!
AAGH...!
KYRIL, HELP!!
HELP?
URRGGHHH!!
POP!
FFFSSSSHHHH
PLEASE...
LIKE YOU TRIED TO HELP ME?
I DON'T THINK SO.

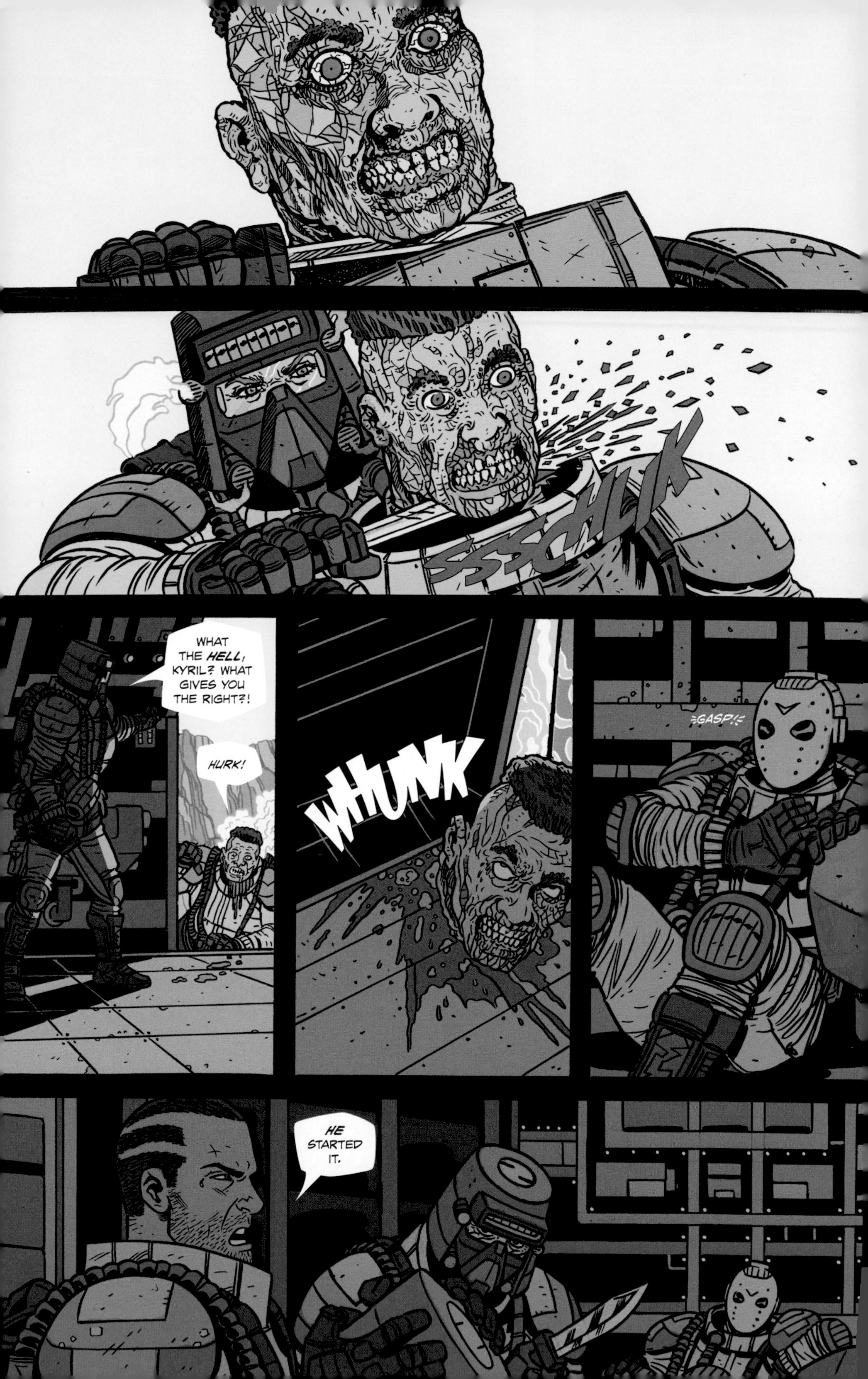
SSSCHLIK
WHAT THE HELL, KYRIL? WHAT GIVES YOU THE RIGHT?!
HURK!
WHUNK
GASP!
HE STARTED IT.

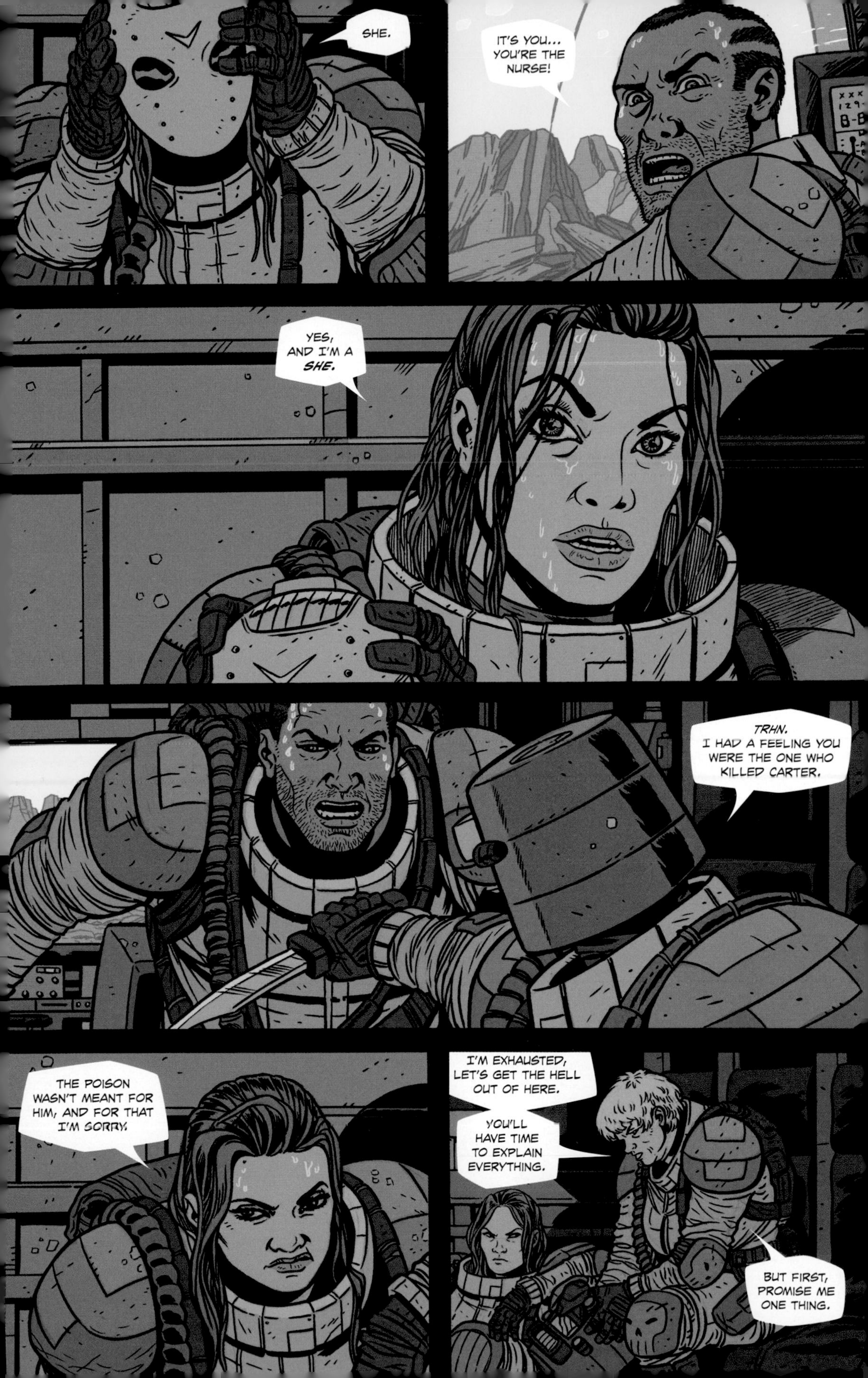
SHE.
IT'S YOU... YOU'RE THE NURSE!
YES, AND I'M A *SHE.*
*TRHN.* I HAD A FEELING YOU WERE THE ONE WHO KILLED CARTER.
THE POISON WASN'T MEANT FOR HIM, AND FOR THAT I'M SORRY.
I'M EXHAUSTED, LET'S GET THE HELL OUT OF HERE.
YOU'LL HAVE TIME TO EXPLAIN EVERYTHING.
BUT FIRST, PROMISE ME ONE THING.

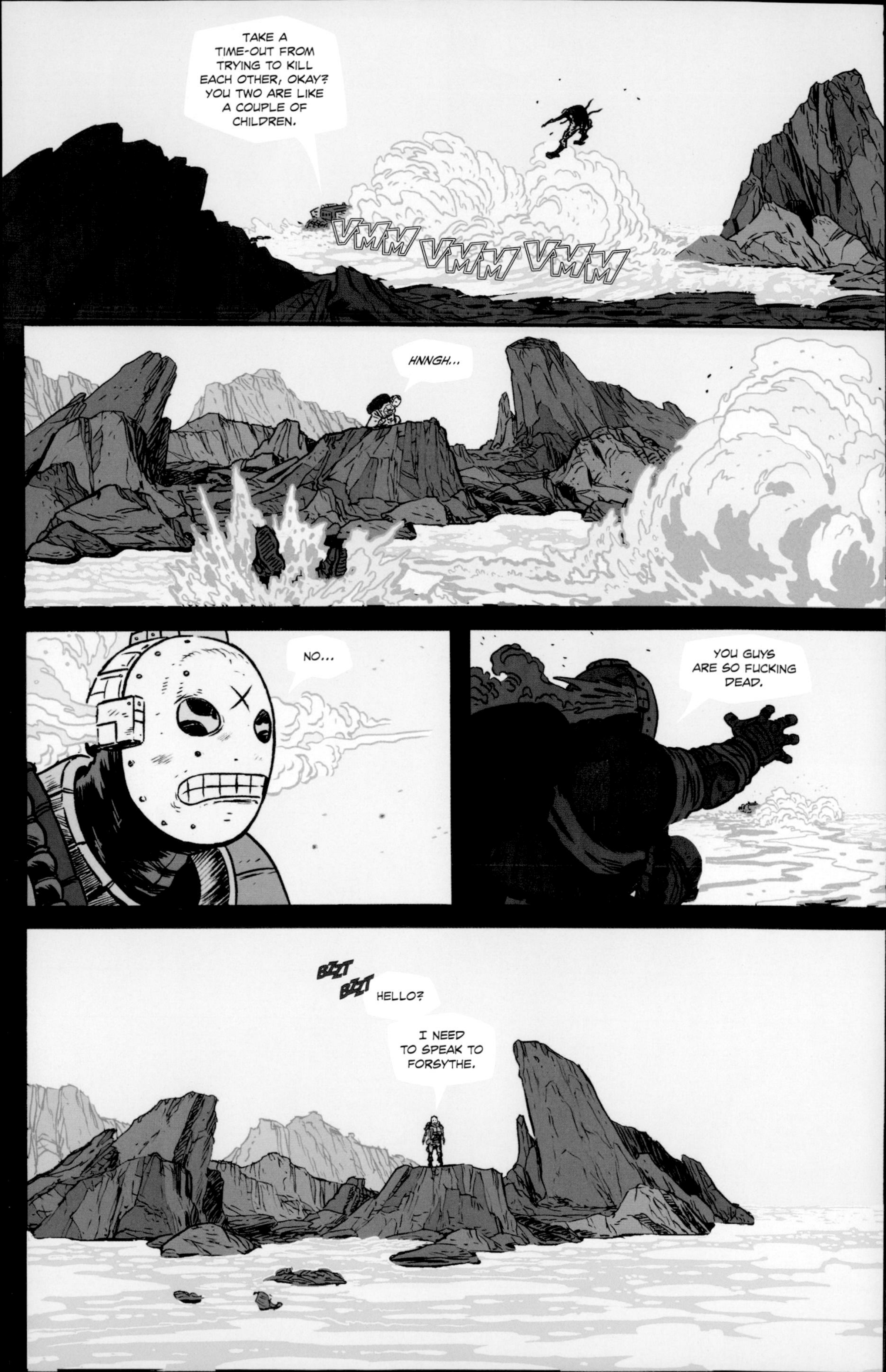
TAKE A TIME-OUT FROM TRYING TO KILL EACH OTHER, OKAY? YOU TWO ARE LIKE A COUPLE OF CHILDREN.
VMMM VMMM VMMM
HNNGH...
NO...
YOU GUYS ARE SO FUCKING DEAD.
BZZT BZZT
HELLO?
I NEED TO SPEAK TO FORSYTHE.

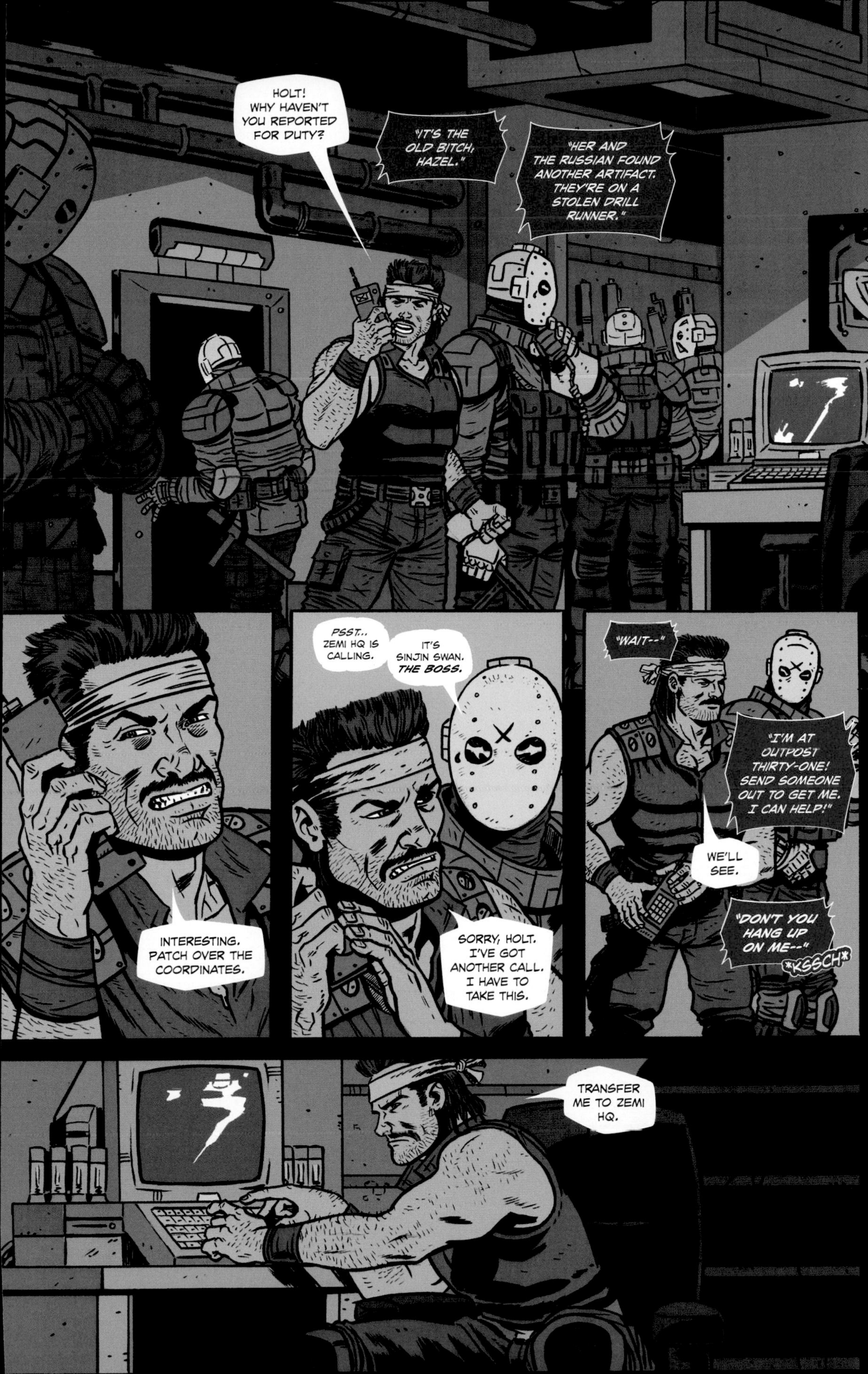
HOLT! WHY HAVEN'T YOU REPORTED FOR DUTY?
"IT'S THE OLD BITCH, HAZEL."
"HER AND THE RUSSIAN FOUND ANOTHER ARTIFACT. THEY'RE ON A STOLEN DRILL RUNNER."
INTERESTING. PATCH OVER THE COORDINATES.
PSST... ZEMI HQ IS CALLING.
IT'S SINJIN SWAN. THE BOSS.
SORRY, HOLT. I'VE GOT ANOTHER CALL. I HAVE TO TAKE THIS.
"WAIT--"
"I'M AT OUTPOST THIRTY-ONE! SEND SOMEONE OUT TO GET ME. I CAN HELP!"
WE'LL SEE.
"DON'T YOU HANG UP ON ME--"
*KSSCH*
TRANSFER ME TO ZEMI HQ.

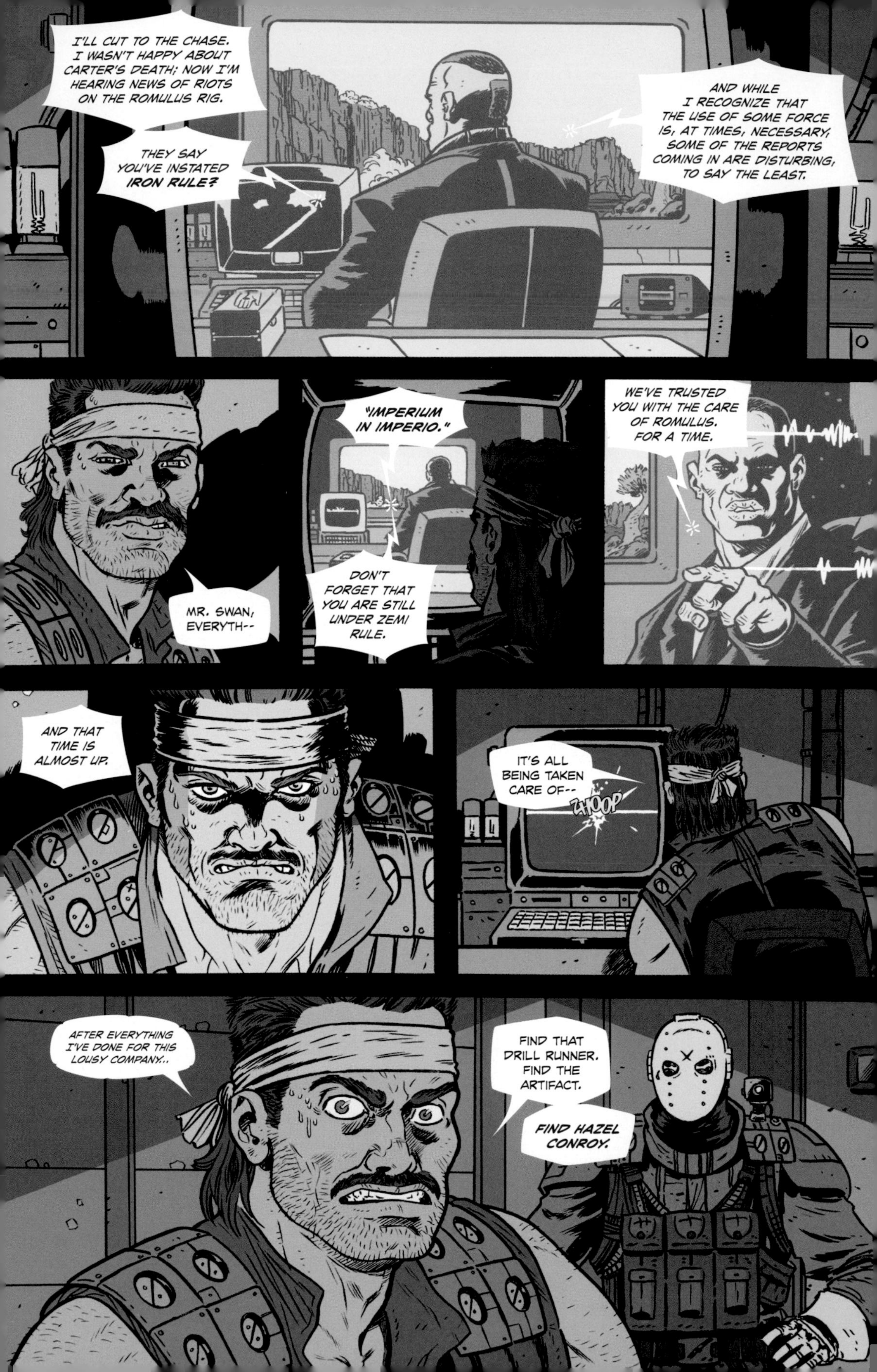
I'LL CUT TO THE CHASE. I WASN'T HAPPY ABOUT CARTER'S DEATH; NOW I'M HEARING NEWS OF RIOTS ON THE ROMULUS RIG.
THEY SAY YOU'VE INSTATED IRON RULE?
AND WHILE I RECOGNIZE THAT THE USE OF SOME FORCE IS, AT TIMES, NECESSARY, SOME OF THE REPORTS COMING IN ARE DISTURBING, TO SAY THE LEAST.
MR. SWAN, EVERYTH--
"IMPERIUM IN IMPERIO."
DON'T FORGET THAT YOU ARE STILL UNDER ZEMI RULE.
WE'VE TRUSTED YOU WITH THE CARE OF ROMULUS. FOR A TIME.
AND THAT TIME IS ALMOST UP.
IT'S ALL BEING TAKEN CARE OF--
ZHOOP
AFTER EVERYTHING I'VE DONE FOR THIS LOUSY COMPANY...
FIND THAT DRILL RUNNER. FIND THE ARTIFACT.
FIND HAZEL CONROY.

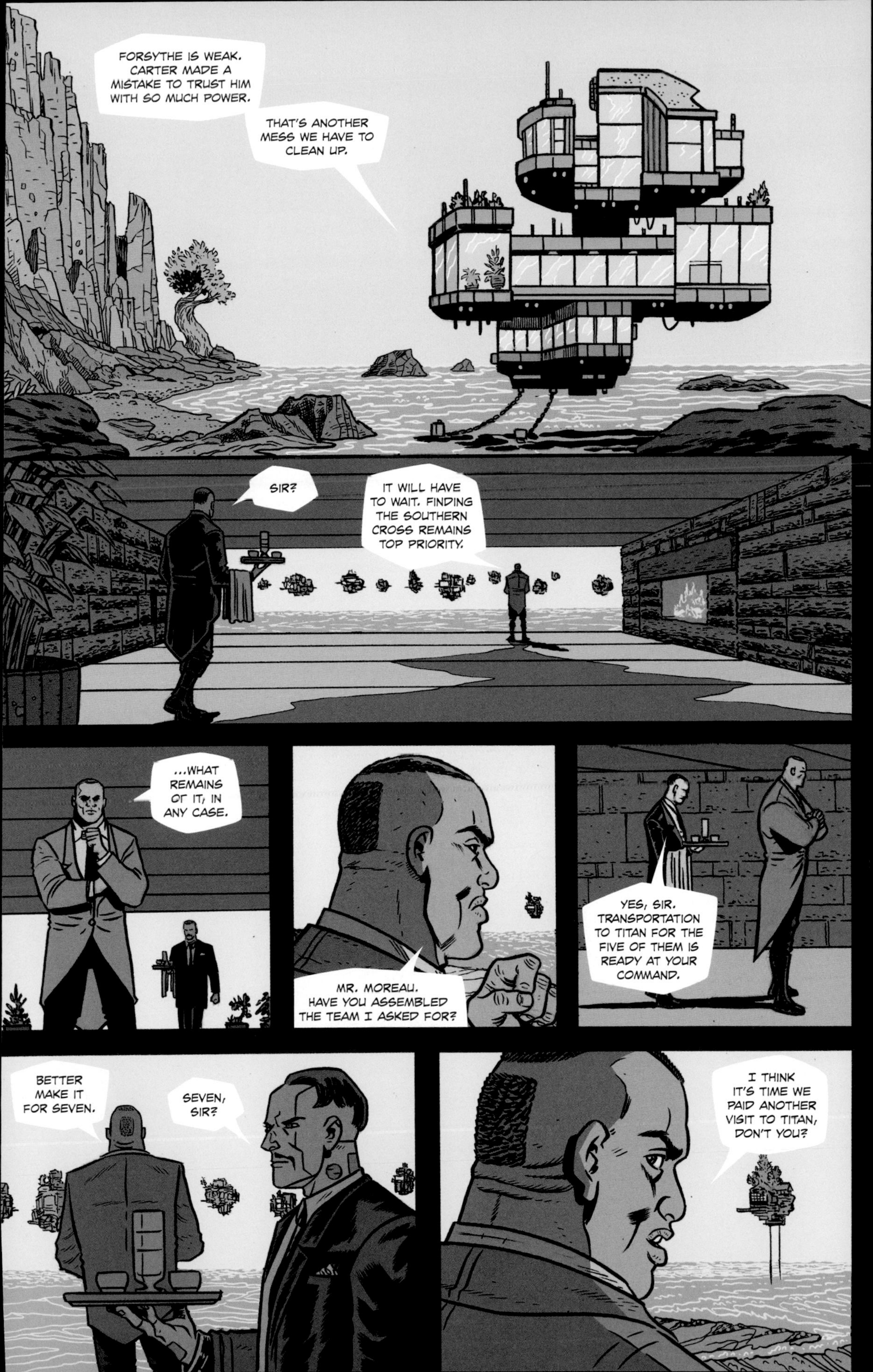
FORSYTHE IS WEAK. CARTER MADE A MISTAKE TO TRUST HIM WITH SO MUCH POWER.
THAT'S ANOTHER MESS WE HAVE TO CLEAN UP.
SIR?
IT WILL HAVE TO WAIT. FINDING THE SOUTHERN CROSS REMAINS TOP PRIORITY.
...WHAT REMAINS OF IT, IN ANY CASE.
MR. MOREAU. HAVE YOU ASSEMBLED THE TEAM I ASKED FOR?
YES, SIR. TRANSPORTATION TO TITAN FOR THE FIVE OF THEM IS READY AT YOUR COMMAND.
BETTER MAKE IT FOR SEVEN.
SEVEN, SIR?
I THINK IT'S TIME WE PAID ANOTHER VISIT TO TITAN, DON'T YOU?

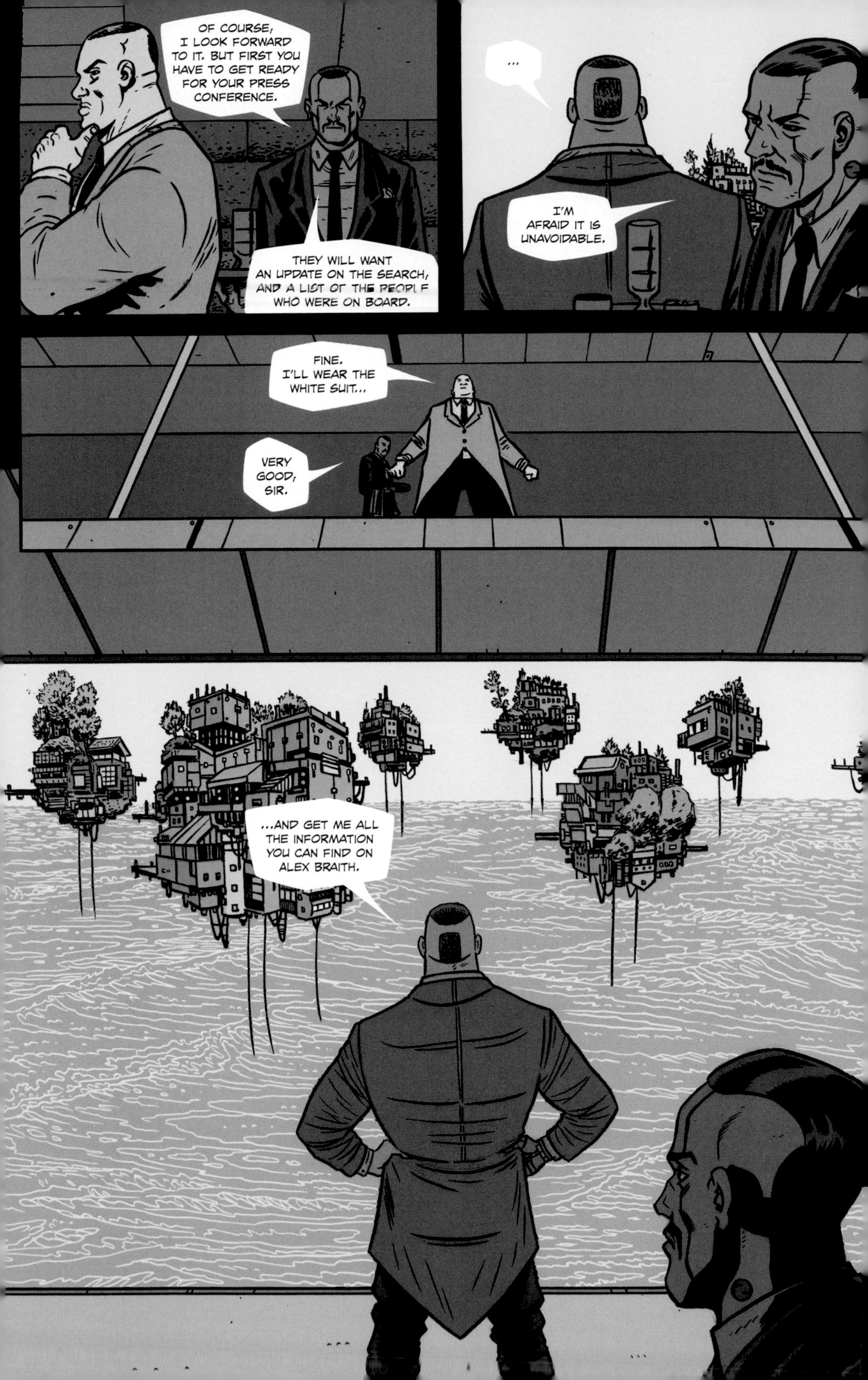
OF COURSE, I LOOK FORWARD TO IT. BUT FIRST YOU HAVE TO GET READY FOR YOUR PRESS CONFERENCE.
THEY WILL WANT AN UPDATE ON THE SEARCH, AND A LIST OF THE PEOPLE WHO WERE ON BOARD.
...
I'M AFRAID IT IS UNAVOIDABLE.
FINE. I'LL WEAR THE WHITE SUIT...
VERY GOOD, SIR.
...AND GET ME ALL THE INFORMATION YOU CAN FIND ON ALEX BRAITH.

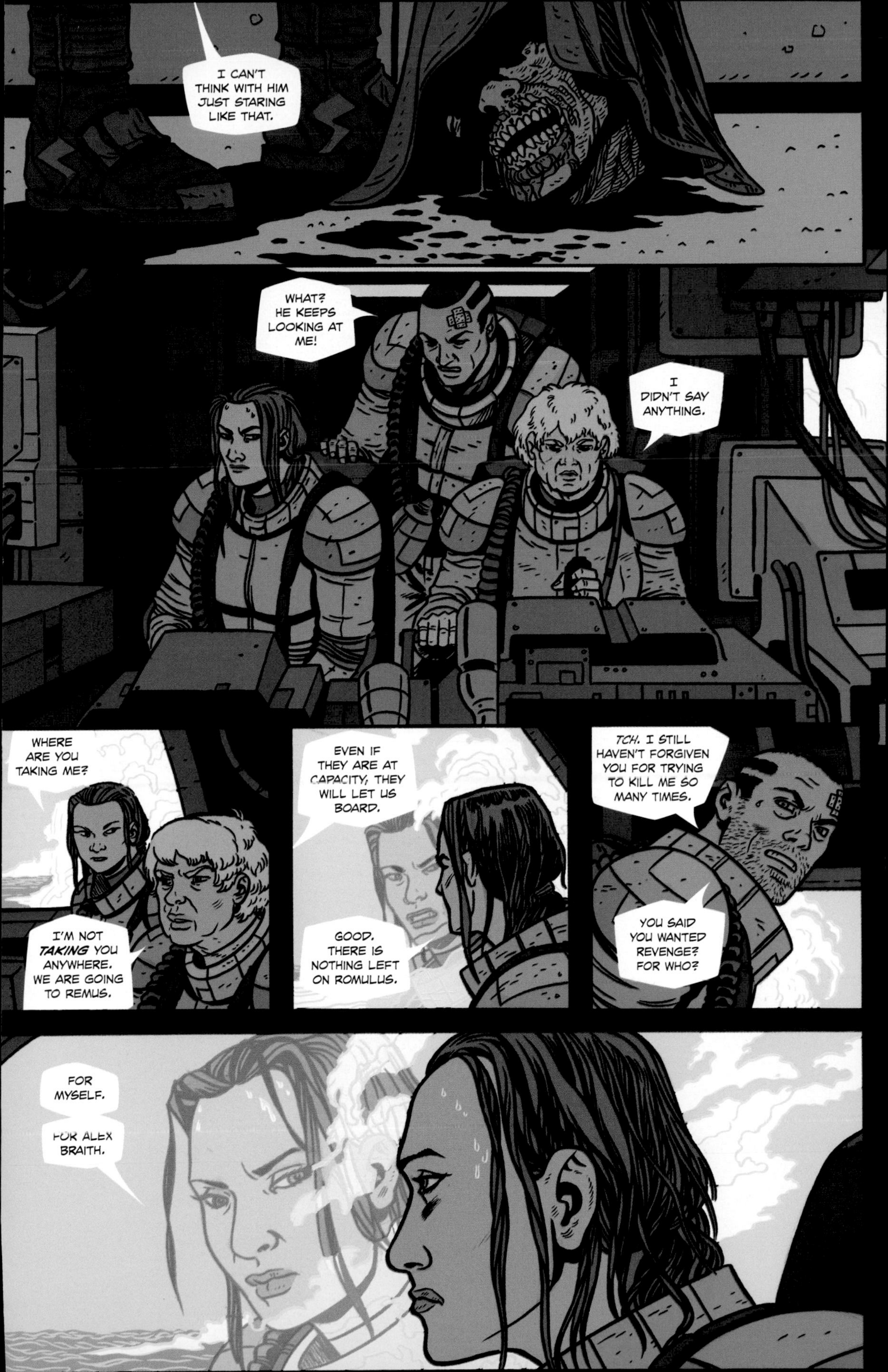
I CAN'T THINK WITH HIM JUST STARING LIKE THAT.
WHAT? HE KEEPS LOOKING AT ME!
I DIDN'T SAY ANYTHING.
WHERE ARE YOU TAKING ME?
I'M NOT *TAKING* YOU ANYWHERE. WE ARE GOING TO REMUS.
EVEN IF THEY ARE AT CAPACITY, THEY WILL LET US BOARD.
GOOD. THERE IS NOTHING LEFT ON ROMULUS.
*TCH.* I STILL HAVEN'T FORGIVEN YOU FOR TRYING TO KILL ME SO MANY TIMES.
YOU SAID YOU WANTED REVENGE? FOR WHO?
FOR MYSELF.
FOR ALEX BRAITH.

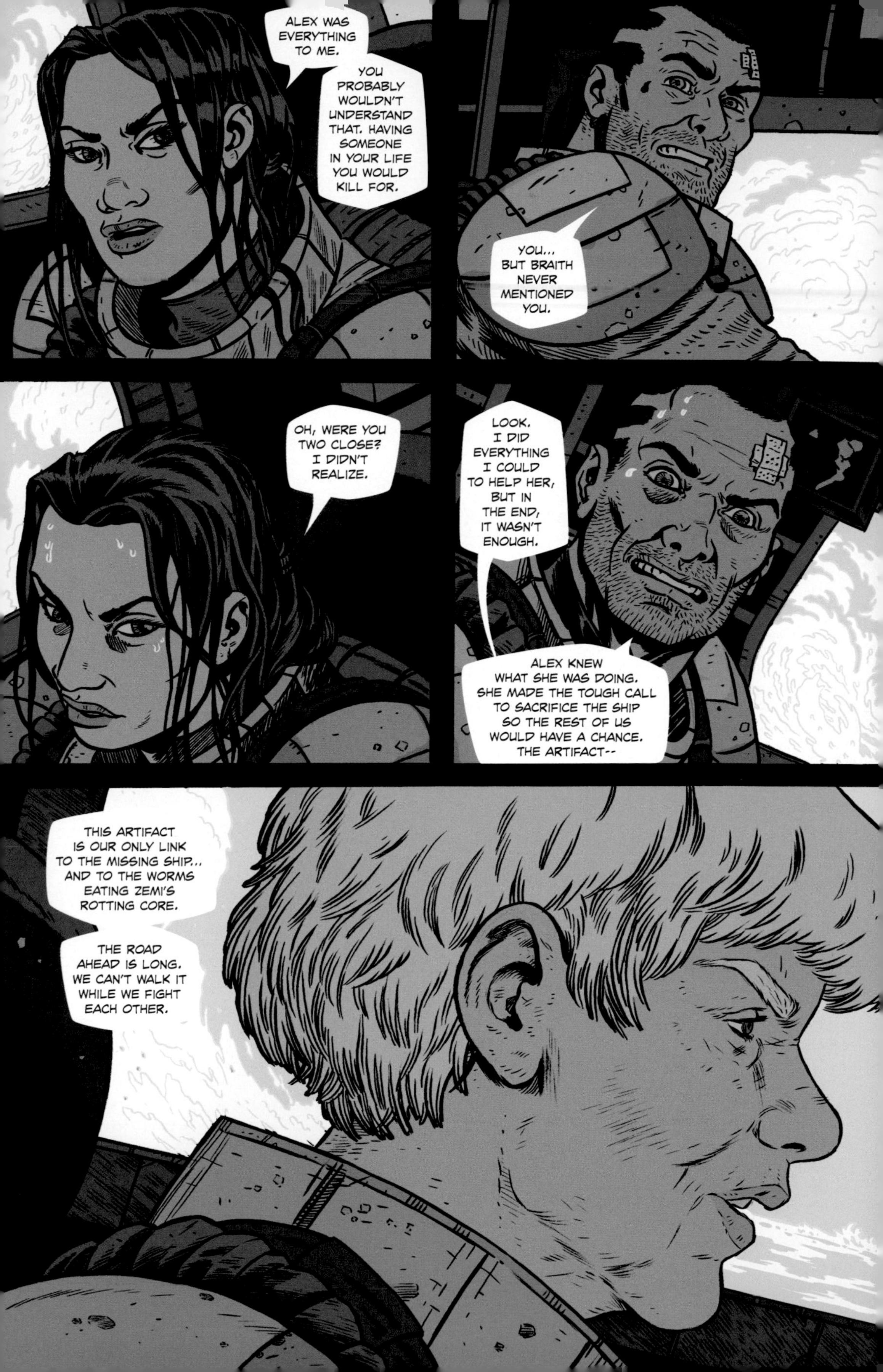
ALEX WAS EVERYTHING TO ME.
YOU PROBABLY WOULDN'T UNDERSTAND THAT. HAVING SOMEONE IN YOUR LIFE YOU WOULD KILL FOR.
YOU... BUT BRAITH NEVER MENTIONED YOU.
OH, WERE YOU TWO CLOSE? I DIDN'T REALIZE.
LOOK. I DID EVERYTHING I COULD TO HELP HER, BUT IN THE END, IT WASN'T ENOUGH.
ALEX KNEW WHAT SHE WAS DOING. SHE MADE THE TOUGH CALL TO SACRIFICE THE SHIP SO THE REST OF US WOULD HAVE A CHANCE. THE ARTIFACT--
THIS ARTIFACT IS OUR ONLY LINK TO THE MISSING SHIP... AND TO THE WORMS EATING ZEMI'S ROTTING CORE.
THE ROAD AHEAD IS LONG. WE CAN'T WALK IT WHILE WE FIGHT EACH OTHER.

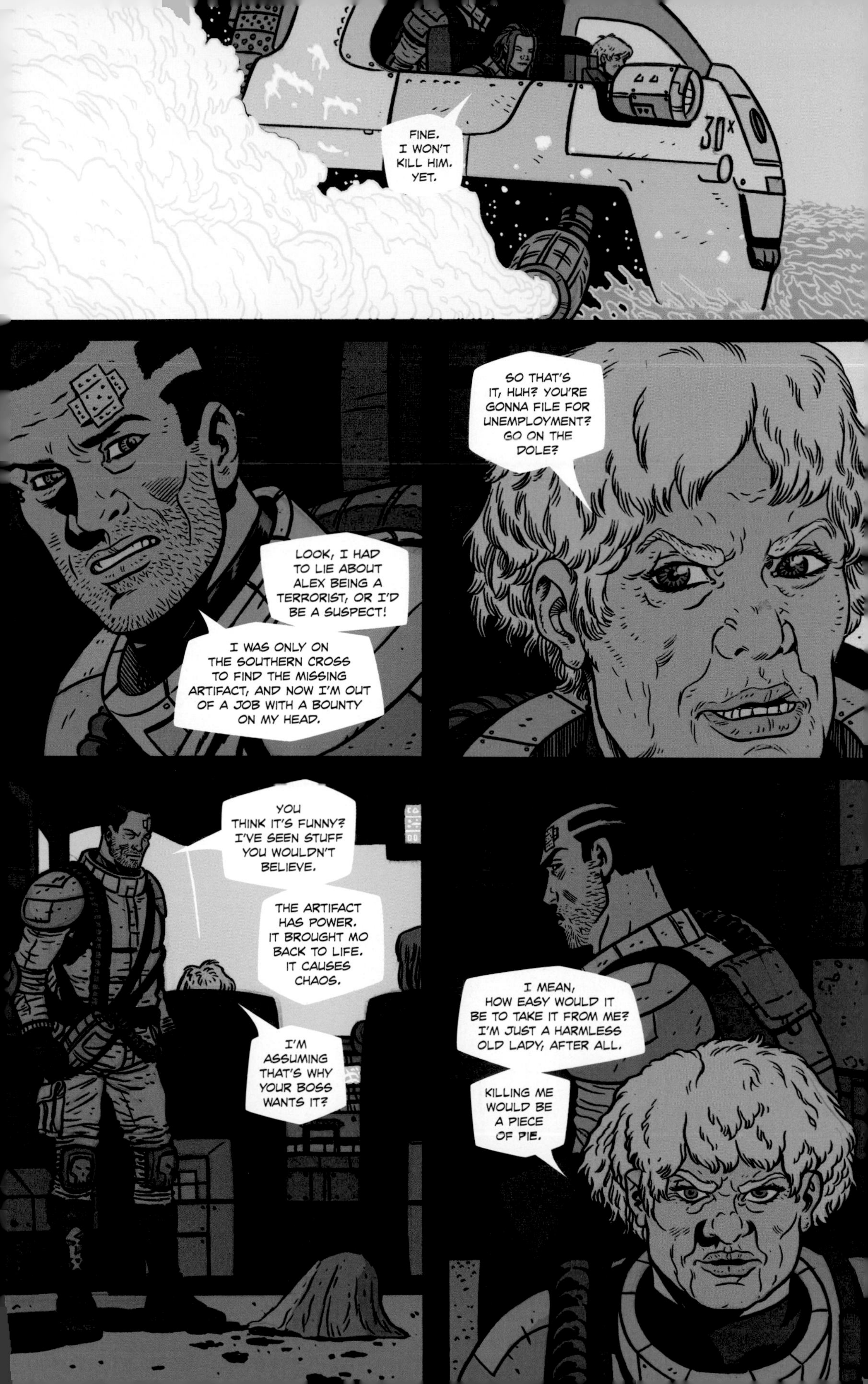
FINE. I WON'T KILL HIM. YET.
30x
LOOK, I HAD TO LIE ABOUT ALEX BEING A TERRORIST, OR I'D BE A SUSPECT!
I WAS ONLY ON THE SOUTHERN CROSS TO FIND THE MISSING ARTIFACT, AND NOW I'M OUT OF A JOB WITH A BOUNTY ON MY HEAD.
SO THAT'S IT, HUH? YOU'RE GONNA FILE FOR UNEMPLOYMENT? GO ON THE DOLE?
YOU THINK IT'S FUNNY? I'VE SEEN STUFF YOU WOULDN'T BELIEVE.
THE ARTIFACT HAS POWER. IT BROUGHT MO BACK TO LIFE. IT CAUSES CHAOS.
I'M ASSUMING THAT'S WHY YOUR BOSS WANTS IT?
I MEAN, HOW EASY WOULD IT BE TO TAKE IT FROM ME? I'M JUST A HARMLESS OLD LADY, AFTER ALL.
KILLING ME WOULD BE A PIECE OF PIE.

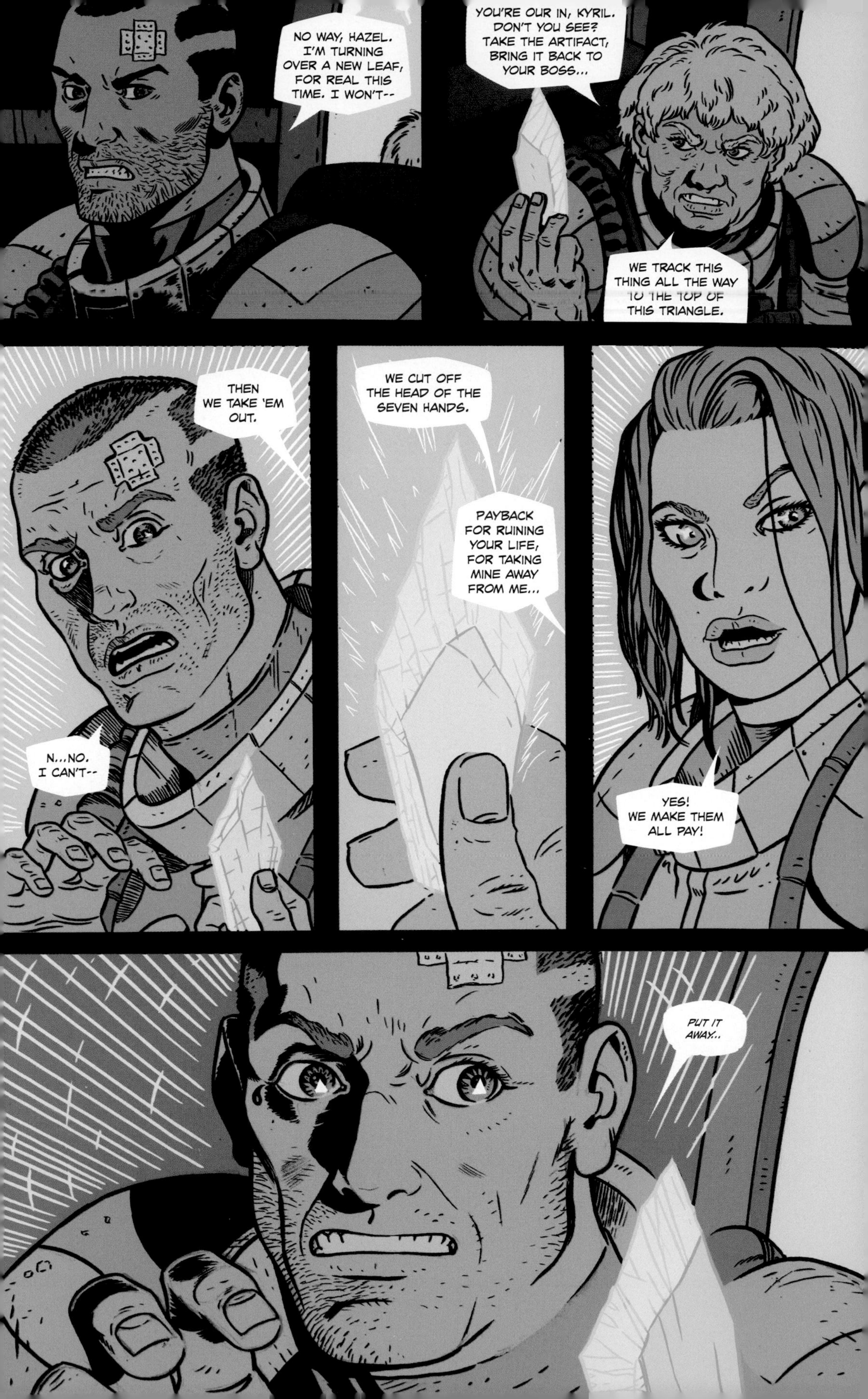
NO WAY, HAZEL. I'M TURNING OVER A NEW LEAF, FOR REAL THIS TIME. I WON'T--
YOU'RE OUR IN, KYRIL. DON'T YOU SEE? TAKE THE ARTIFACT, BRING IT BACK TO YOUR BOSS...
WE TRACK THIS THING ALL THE WAY TO THE TOP OF THIS TRIANGLE.
THEN WE TAKE 'EM OUT.
N...NO. I CAN'T--
WE CUT OFF THE HEAD OF THE SEVEN HANDS.
PAYBACK FOR RUINING YOUR LIFE, FOR TAKING MINE AWAY FROM ME...
YES! WE MAKE THEM ALL PAY!
PUT IT AWAY...

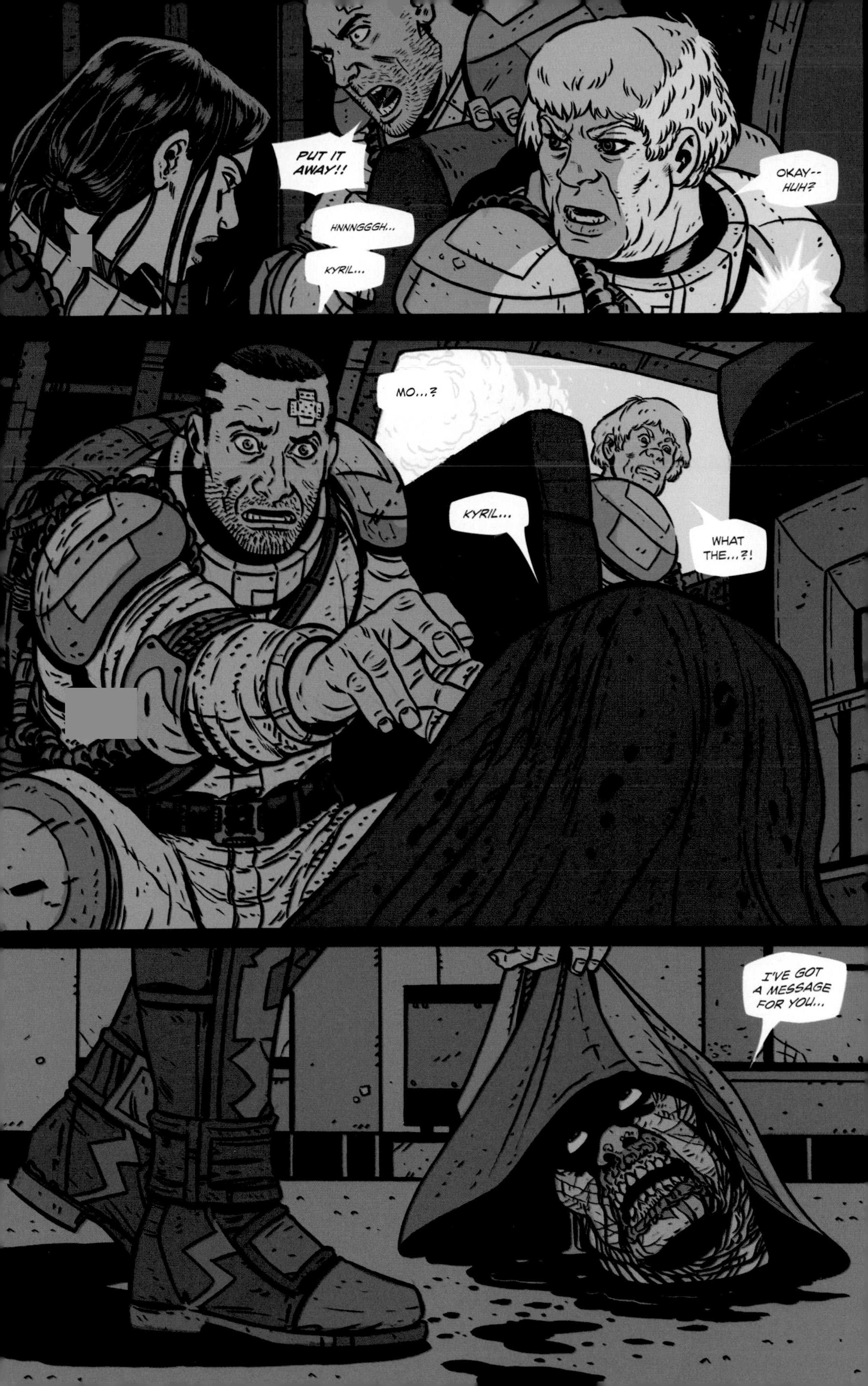
PUT IT AWAY!!
HNNNGGGH...
KYRIL...
OKAY-- HUH?
MO...?
KYRIL...
WHAT THE...?!
I'VE GOT A MESSAGE FOR YOU...

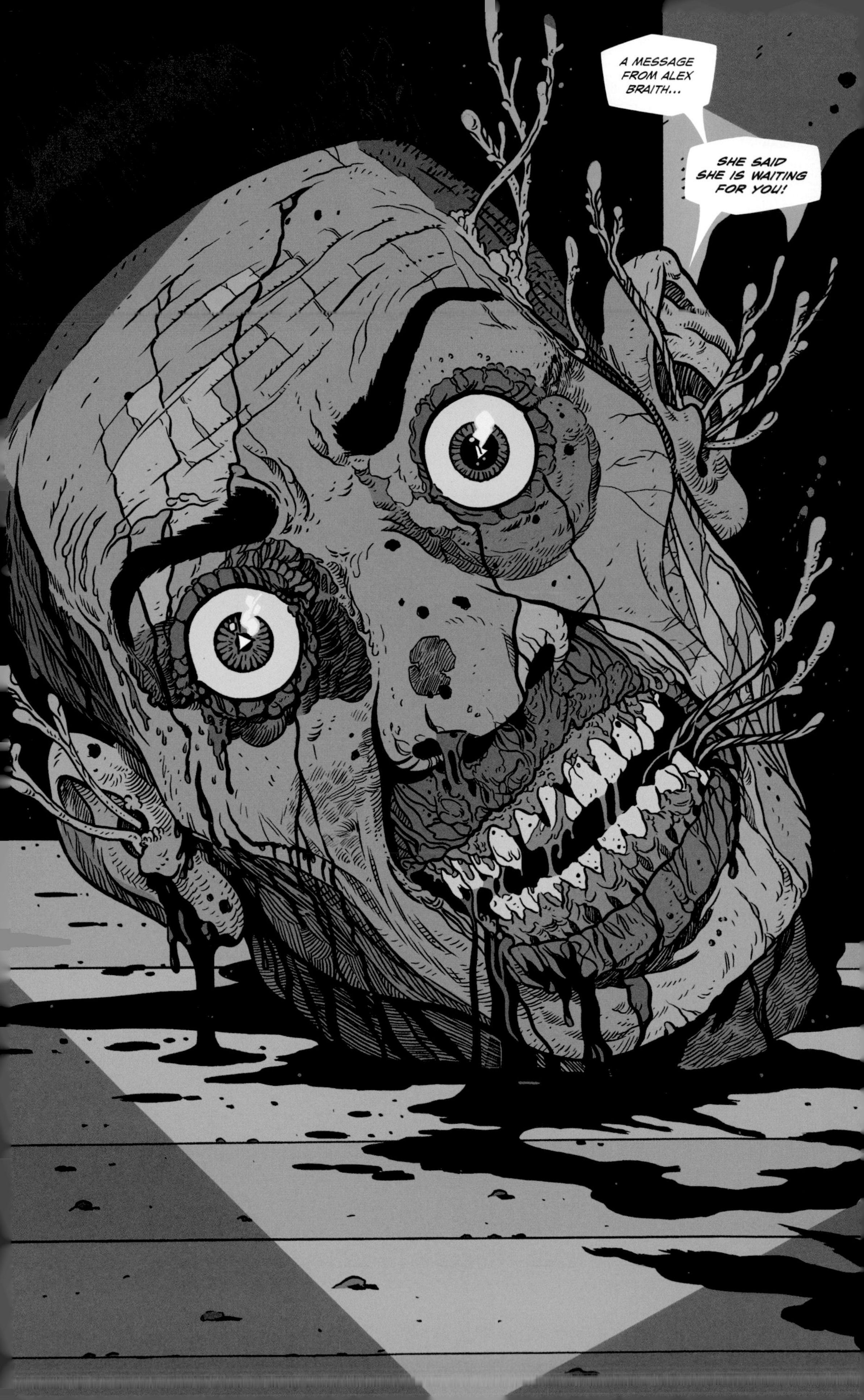
A MESSAGE FROM ALEX BRAITH...
SHE SAID SHE IS WAITING FOR YOU!

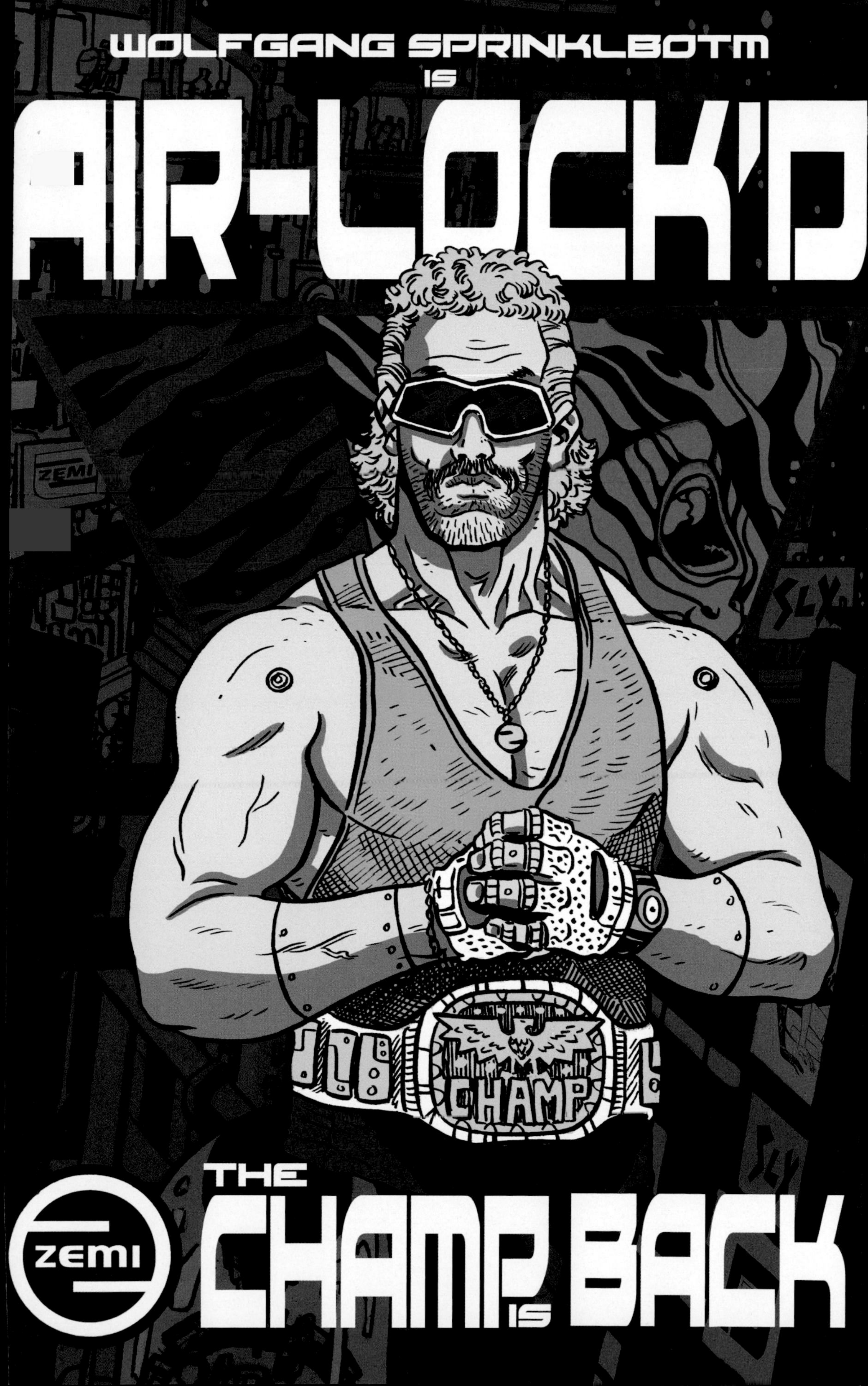
WOLFGANG SPRINKLBOTM
IS
AIR-LOCK'D
ZEMI
SLX
CHAMP
ZEMI
THE
CHAMP IS BACK

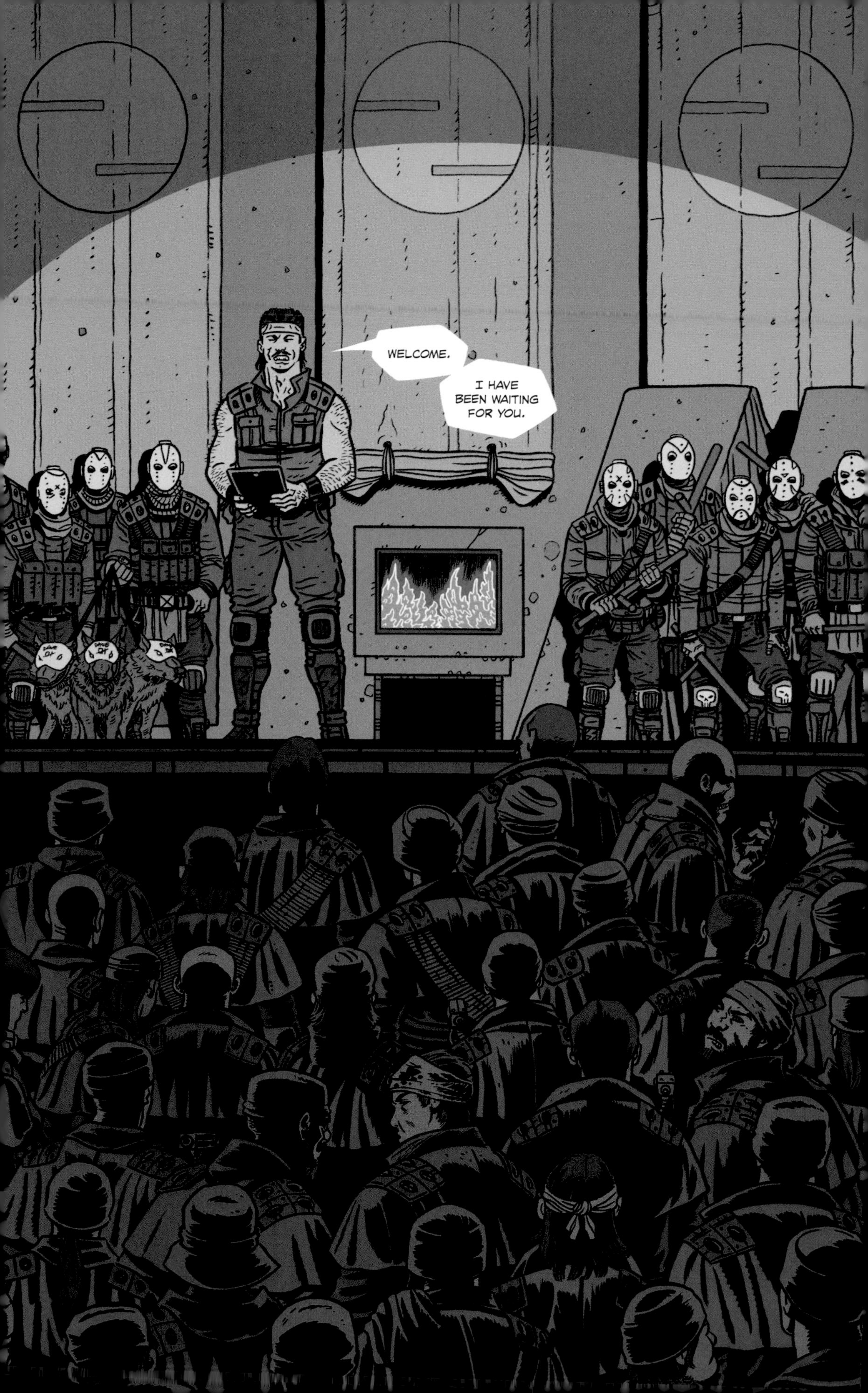
WELCOME.
I HAVE BEEN WAITING FOR YOU.

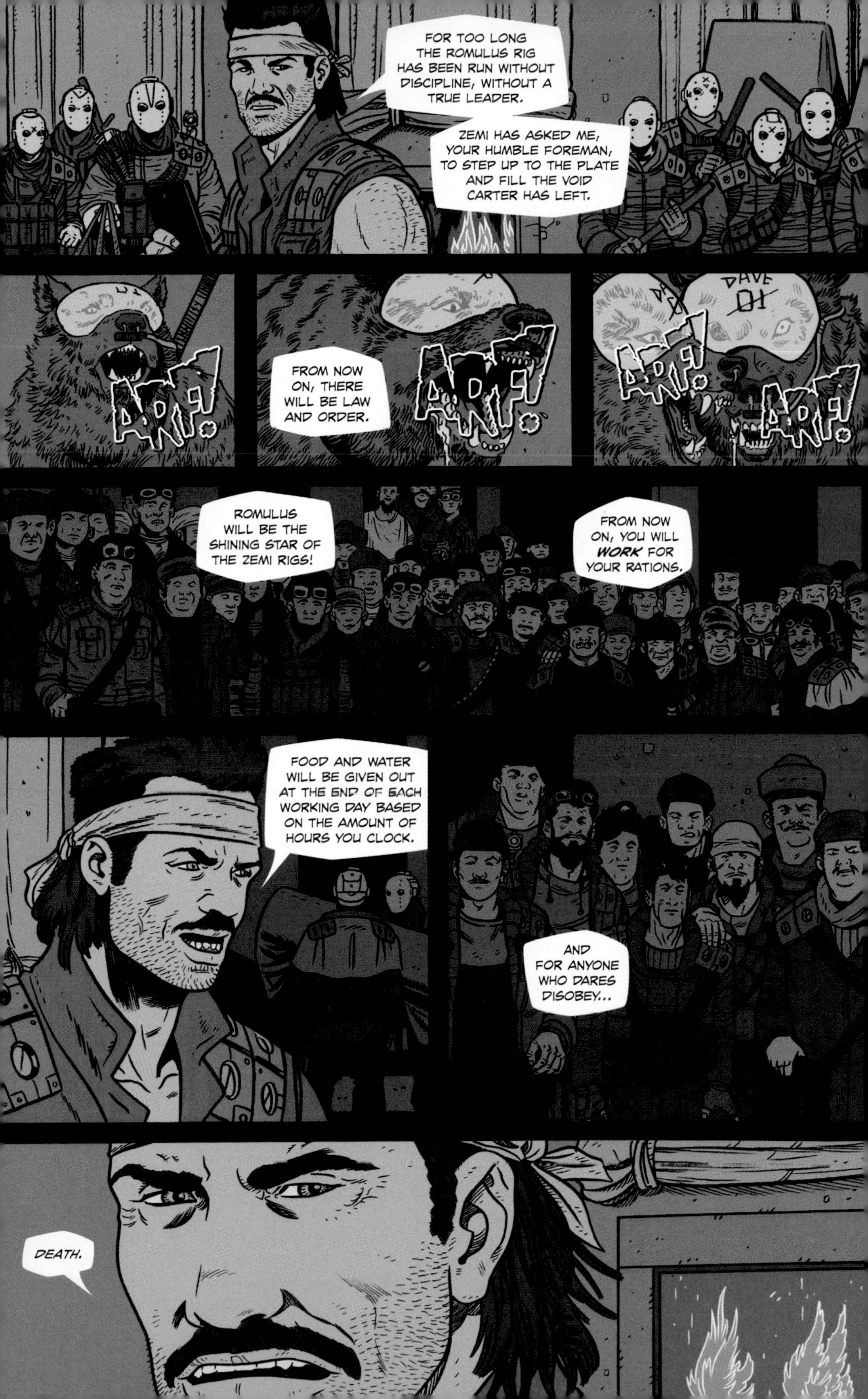
FOR TOO LONG THE ROMULUS RIG HAS BEEN RUN WITHOUT DISCIPLINE, WITHOUT A TRUE LEADER.
ZEMI HAS ASKED ME, YOUR HUMBLE FOREMAN, TO STEP UP TO THE PLATE AND FILL THE VOID CARTER HAS LEFT.
ARF!
FROM NOW ON, THERE WILL BE LAW AND ORDER.
ARF!
DAVE 01
ARF!
ARF!
ROMULUS WILL BE THE SHINING STAR OF THE ZEMI RIGS!
FROM NOW ON, YOU WILL WORK FOR YOUR RATIONS.
FOOD AND WATER WILL BE GIVEN OUT AT THE END OF EACH WORKING DAY BASED ON THE AMOUNT OF HOURS YOU CLOCK.
AND FOR ANYONE WHO DARES DISOBEY...
DEATH.

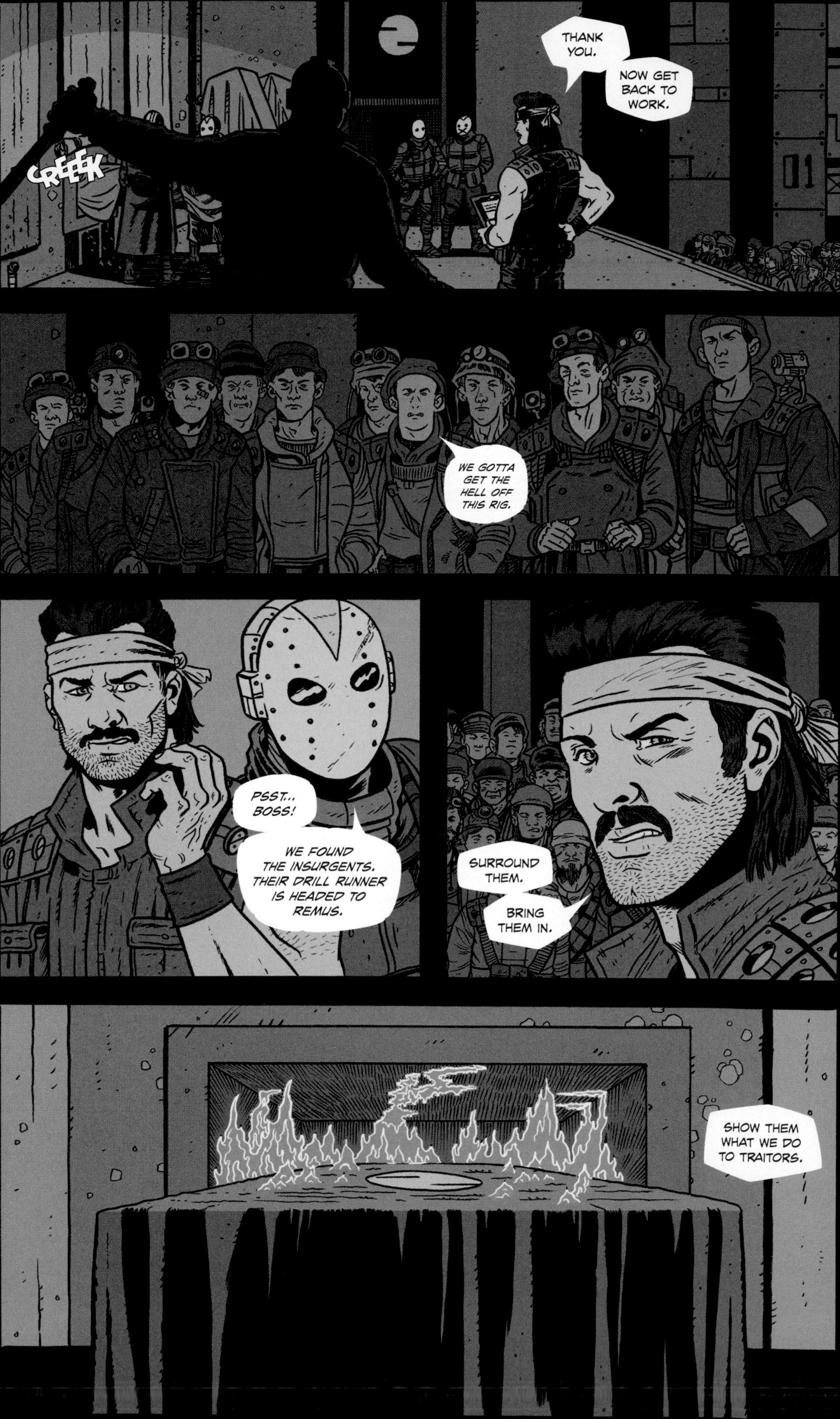
CREEEK
THANK YOU.
NOW GET BACK TO WORK.
WE GOTTA GET THE HELL OFF THIS RIG.
PSST... BOSS!
WE FOUND THE INSURGENTS. THEIR DRILL RUNNER IS HEADED TO REMUS.
SURROUND THEM.
BRING THEM IN.
SHOW THEM WHAT WE DO TO TRAITORS.

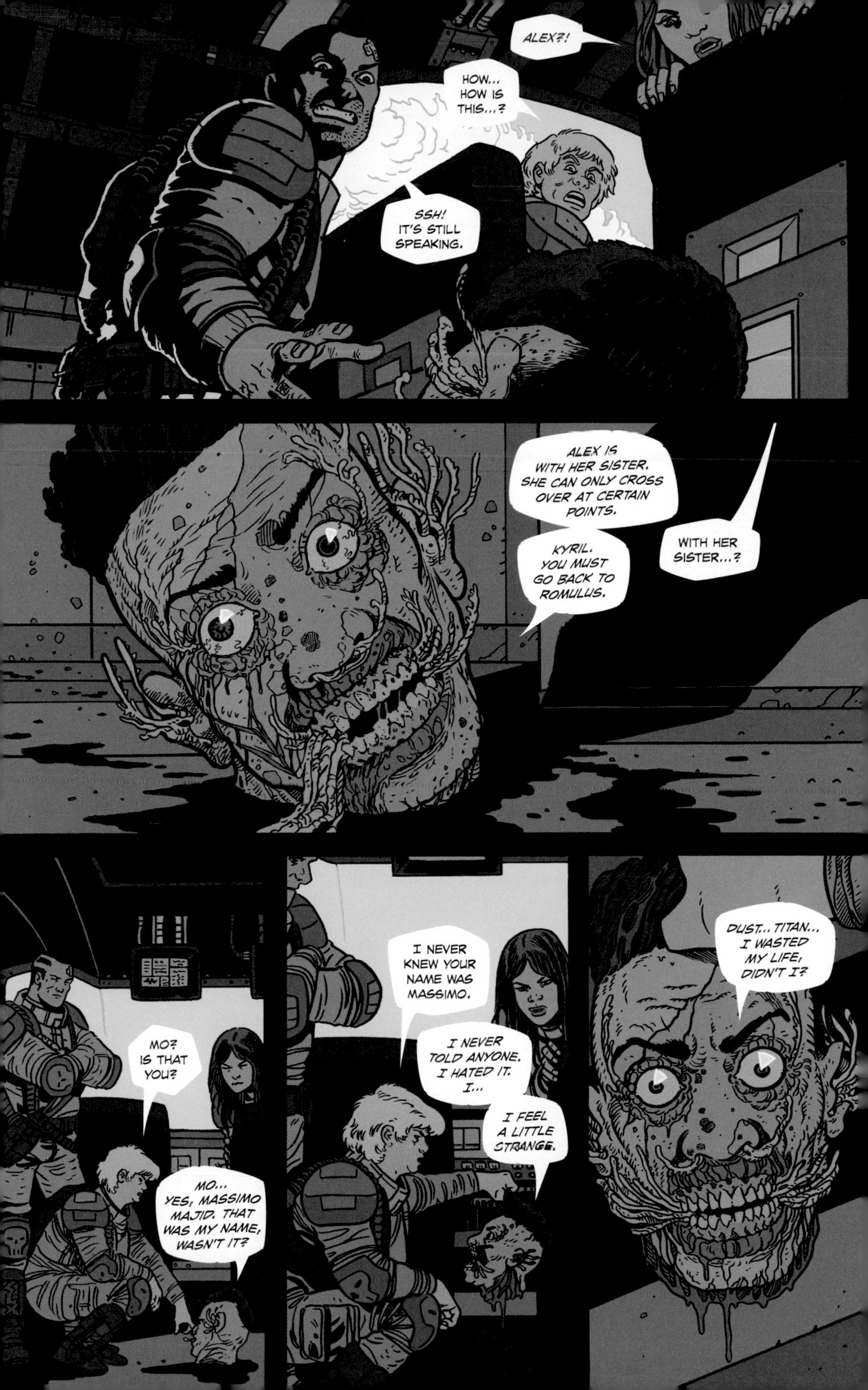
ALEX?!
HOW... HOW IS THIS...?
SSH! IT'S STILL SPEAKING.
ALEX IS WITH HER SISTER. SHE CAN ONLY CROSS OVER AT CERTAIN POINTS.
KYRIL. YOU MUST GO BACK TO ROMULUS.
WITH HER SISTER...?
MO? IS THAT YOU?
MO... YES, MASSIMO MAJID. THAT WAS MY NAME, WASN'T IT?
I NEVER KNEW YOUR NAME WAS MASSIMO.
I NEVER TOLD ANYONE. I HATED IT. I...
I FEEL A LITTLE STRANGE.
DUST... TITAN... I WASTED MY LIFE, DIDN'T I?

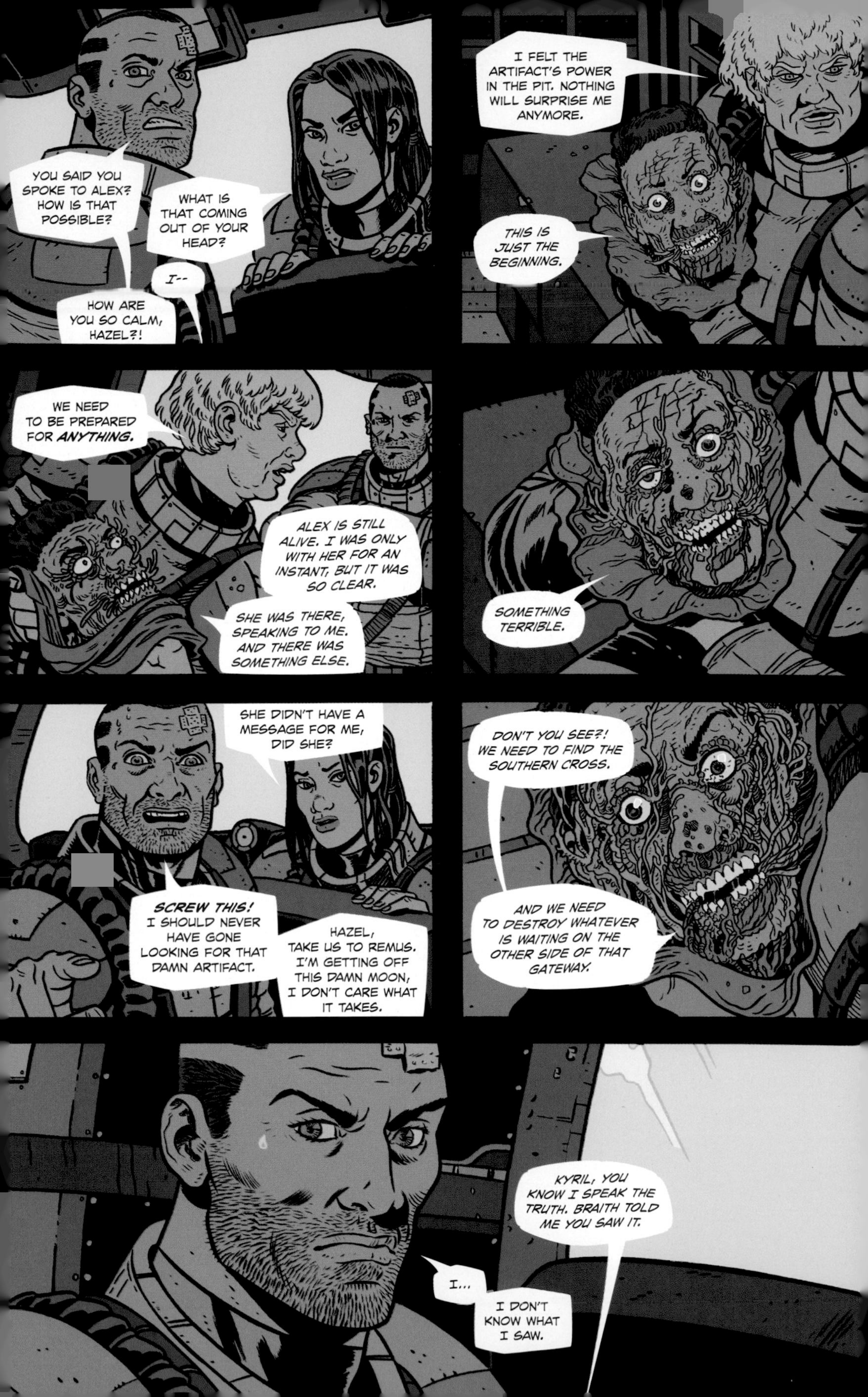
YOU SAID YOU SPOKE TO ALEX? HOW IS THAT POSSIBLE?
WHAT IS THAT COMING OUT OF YOUR HEAD?
I--
HOW ARE YOU SO CALM, HAZEL?!
I FELT THE ARTIFACT'S POWER IN THE PIT. NOTHING WILL SURPRISE ME ANYMORE.
THIS IS JUST THE BEGINNING.
WE NEED TO BE PREPARED FOR ANYTHING.
ALEX IS STILL ALIVE. I WAS ONLY WITH HER FOR AN INSTANT, BUT IT WAS SO CLEAR.
SHE WAS THERE, SPEAKING TO ME. AND THERE WAS SOMETHING ELSE.
SOMETHING TERRIBLE.
SHE DIDN'T HAVE A MESSAGE FOR ME, DID SHE?
SCREW THIS! I SHOULD NEVER HAVE GONE LOOKING FOR THAT DAMN ARTIFACT.
HAZEL, TAKE US TO REMUS. I'M GETTING OFF THIS DAMN MOON, I DON'T CARE WHAT IT TAKES.
DON'T YOU SEE?! WE NEED TO FIND THE SOUTHERN CROSS.
AND WE NEED TO DESTROY WHATEVER IS WAITING ON THE OTHER SIDE OF THAT GATEWAY.
KYRIL, YOU KNOW I SPEAK THE TRUTH. BRAITH TOLD ME YOU SAW IT.
I...
I DON'T KNOW WHAT I SAW.

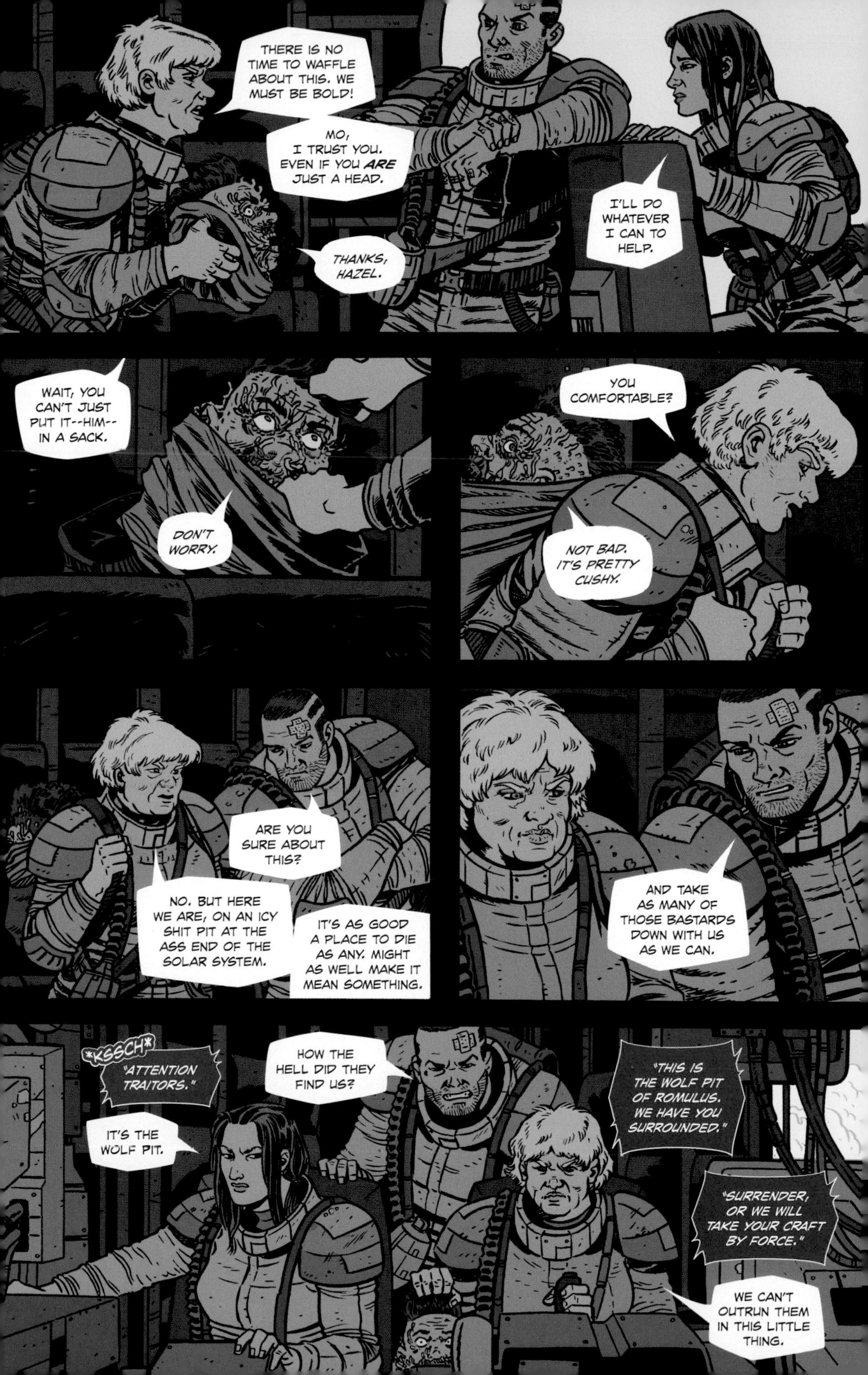
THERE IS NO TIME TO WAFFLE ABOUT THIS. WE MUST BE BOLD!
MO, I TRUST YOU. EVEN IF YOU ARE JUST A HEAD.
THANKS, HAZEL.
I'LL DO WHATEVER I CAN TO HELP.
WAIT, YOU CAN'T JUST PUT IT--HIM--IN A SACK.
DON'T WORRY.
YOU COMFORTABLE?
NOT BAD. IT'S PRETTY CUSHY.
ARE YOU SURE ABOUT THIS?
NO. BUT HERE WE ARE, ON AN ICY SHIT PIT AT THE ASS END OF THE SOLAR SYSTEM.
IT'S AS GOOD A PLACE TO DIE AS ANY. MIGHT AS WELL MAKE IT MEAN SOMETHING.
AND TAKE AS MANY OF THOSE BASTARDS DOWN WITH US AS WE CAN.
*KSSCH*
"ATTENTION TRAITORS."
HOW THE HELL DID THEY FIND US?
IT'S THE WOLF PIT.
"THIS IS THE WOLF PIT OF ROMULUS. WE HAVE YOU SURROUNDED."
"SURRENDER, OR WE WILL TAKE YOUR CRAFT BY FORCE."
WE CAN'T OUTRUN THEM IN THIS LITTLE THING.

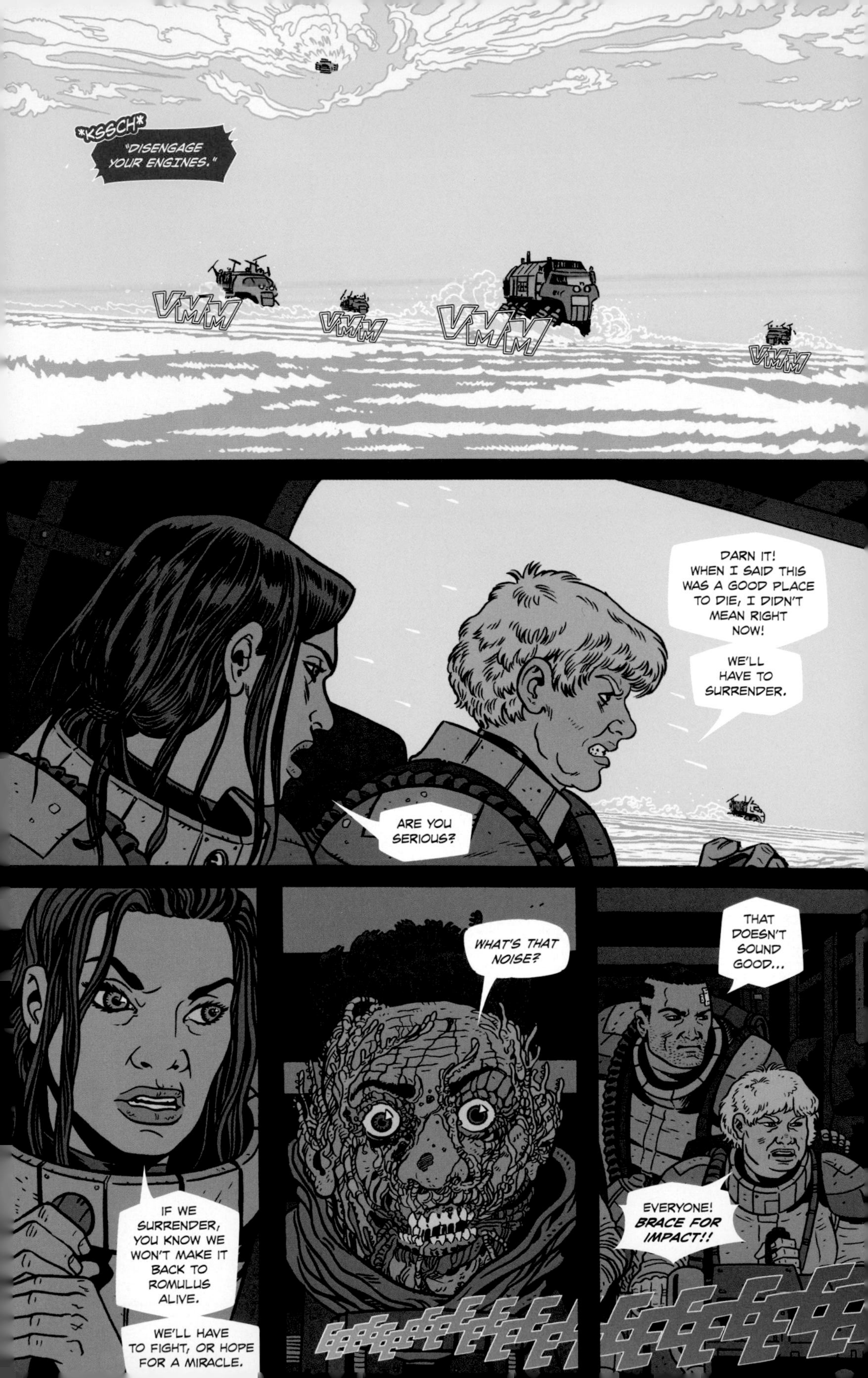
*KSSCH*
"DISENGAGE YOUR ENGINES."
VMMM
VMMM
VMMM
VMMM
DARN IT! WHEN I SAID THIS WAS A GOOD PLACE TO DIE, I DIDN'T MEAN RIGHT NOW!
WE'LL HAVE TO SURRENDER.
ARE YOU SERIOUS?
IF WE SURRENDER, YOU KNOW WE WON'T MAKE IT BACK TO ROMULUS ALIVE.
WE'LL HAVE TO FIGHT, OR HOPE FOR A MIRACLE.
WHAT'S THAT NOISE?
THAT DOESN'T SOUND GOOD...
EVERYONE! BRACE FOR IMPACT!!

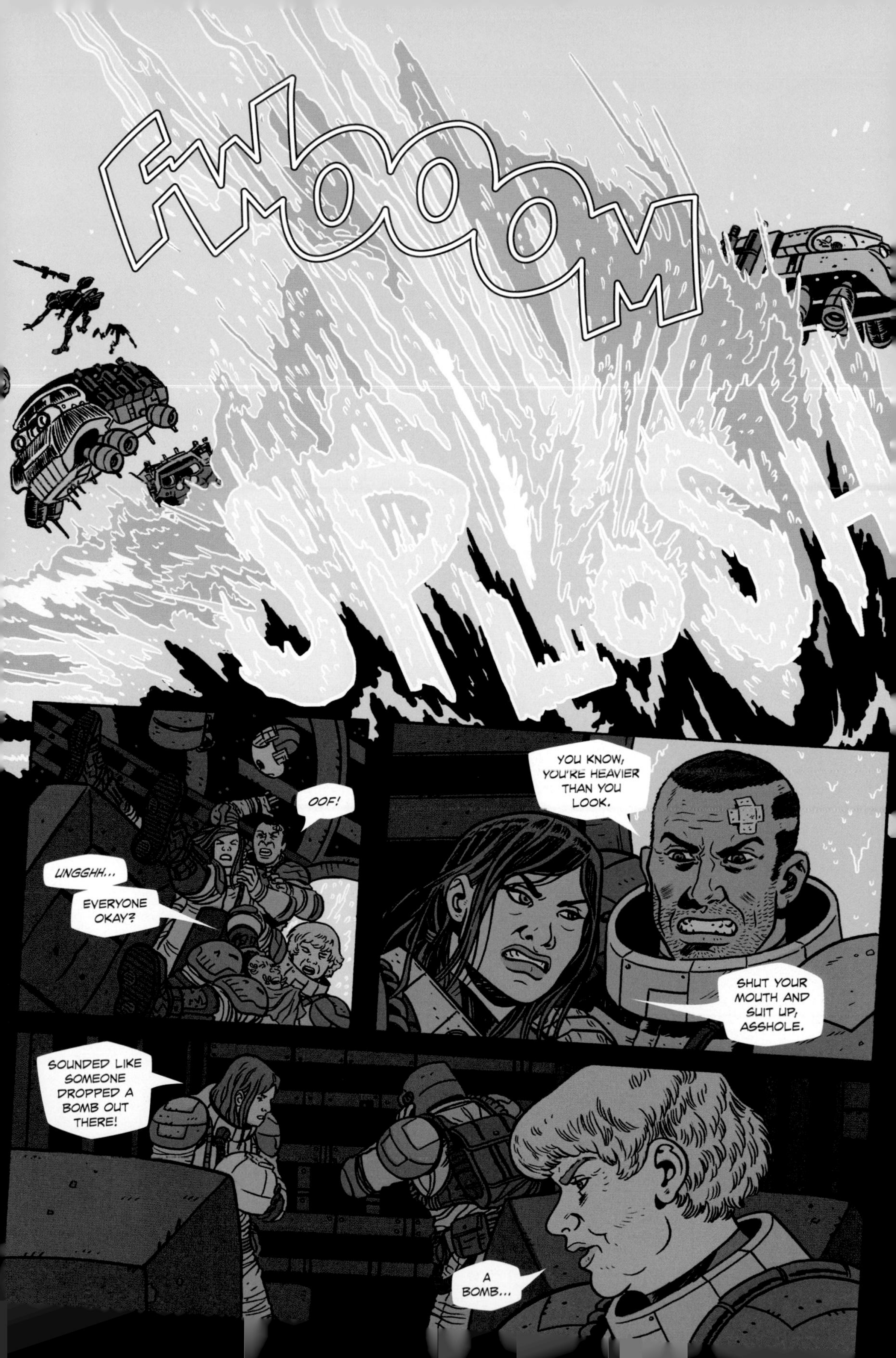
FWOOOOM
SPLOSH
OOF!
UNGGHH...
EVERYONE OKAY?
YOU KNOW, YOU'RE HEAVIER THAN YOU LOOK.
SHUT YOUR MOUTH AND SUIT UP, ASSHOLE.
SOUNDED LIKE SOMEONE DROPPED A BOMB OUT THERE!
A BOMB...

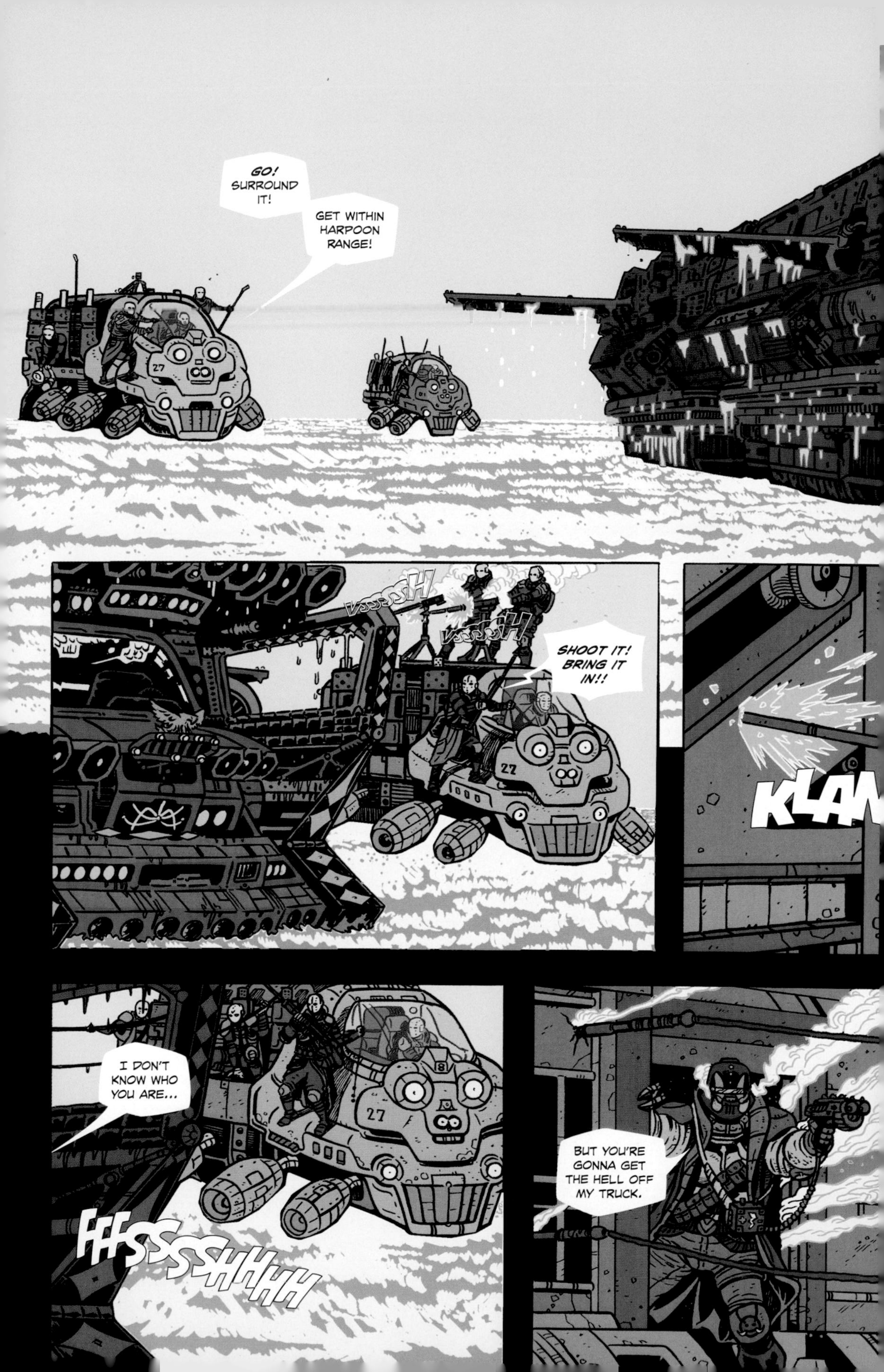
GO! SURROUND IT!
GET WITHIN HARPOON RANGE!
VSSSSSH
VSSSSSH
SHOOT IT! BRING IT IN!!
KLAN
I DON'T KNOW WHO YOU ARE...
FFFSSSSHHHHH
BUT YOU'RE GONNA GET THE HELL OFF MY TRUCK.

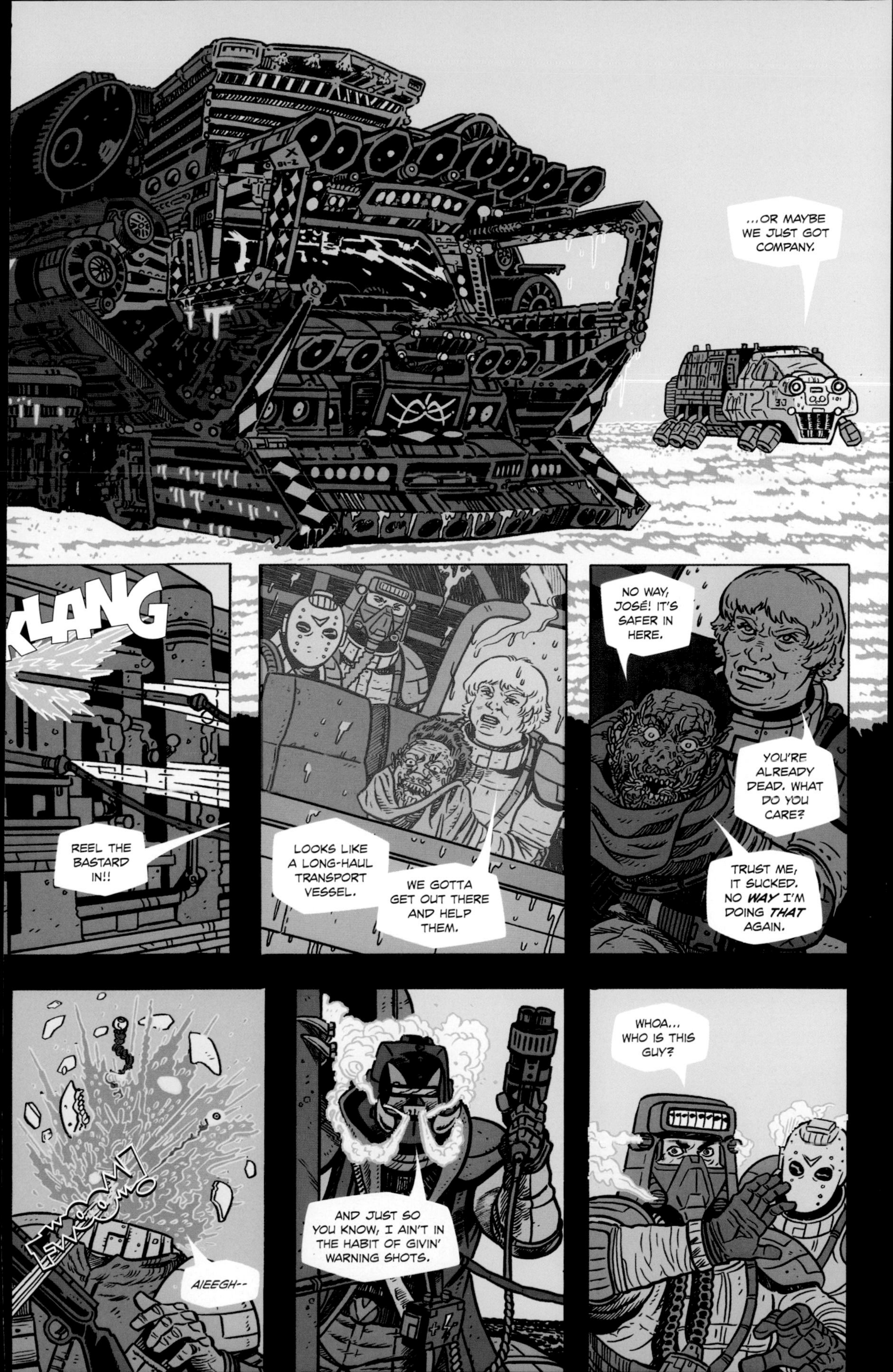
...OR MAYBE WE JUST GOT COMPANY.
KLANG
REEL THE BASTARD IN!!
LOOKS LIKE A LONG-HAUL TRANSPORT VESSEL.
WE GOTTA GET OUT THERE AND HELP THEM.
NO WAY, JOSÉ! IT'S SAFER IN HERE.
YOU'RE ALREADY DEAD. WHAT DO YOU CARE?
TRUST ME, IT SUCKED. NO *WAY* I'M DOING *THAT* AGAIN.
AIEEGH--
AND JUST SO YOU KNOW, I AIN'T IN THE HABIT OF GIVIN' WARNING SHOTS.
WHOA... WHO IS THIS GUY?

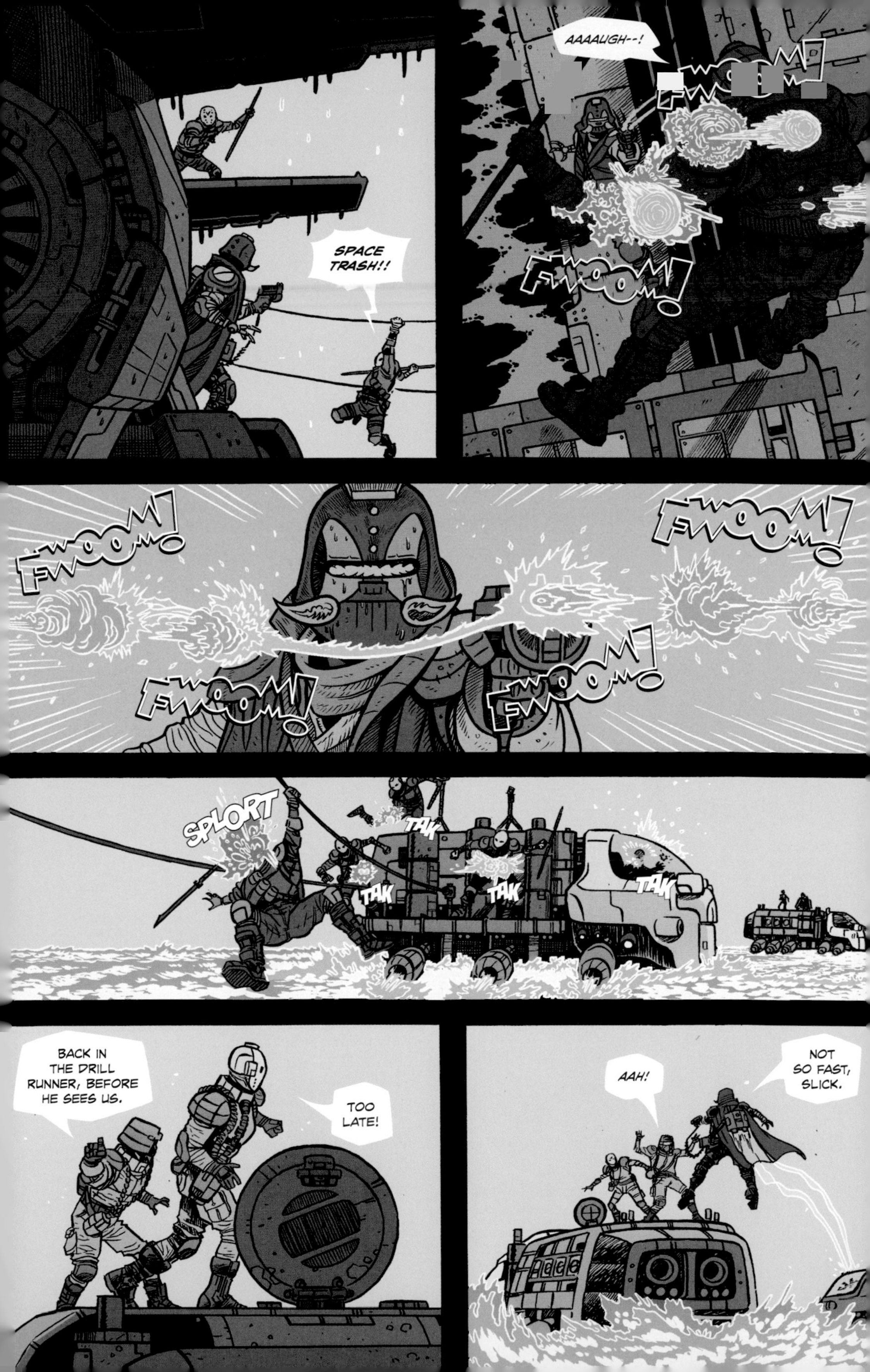

SPACE TRASH!!
AAAAUGH--!
FWOOM!
FWOOM!
FWOOM!
FWOOM!
FWOOM!
FWOOM!
SPLORT
TAK
TAK
TAK
TAK
BACK IN THE DRILL RUNNER, BEFORE HE SEES US.
TOO LATE!
AAH!
NOT SO FAST, SLICK.

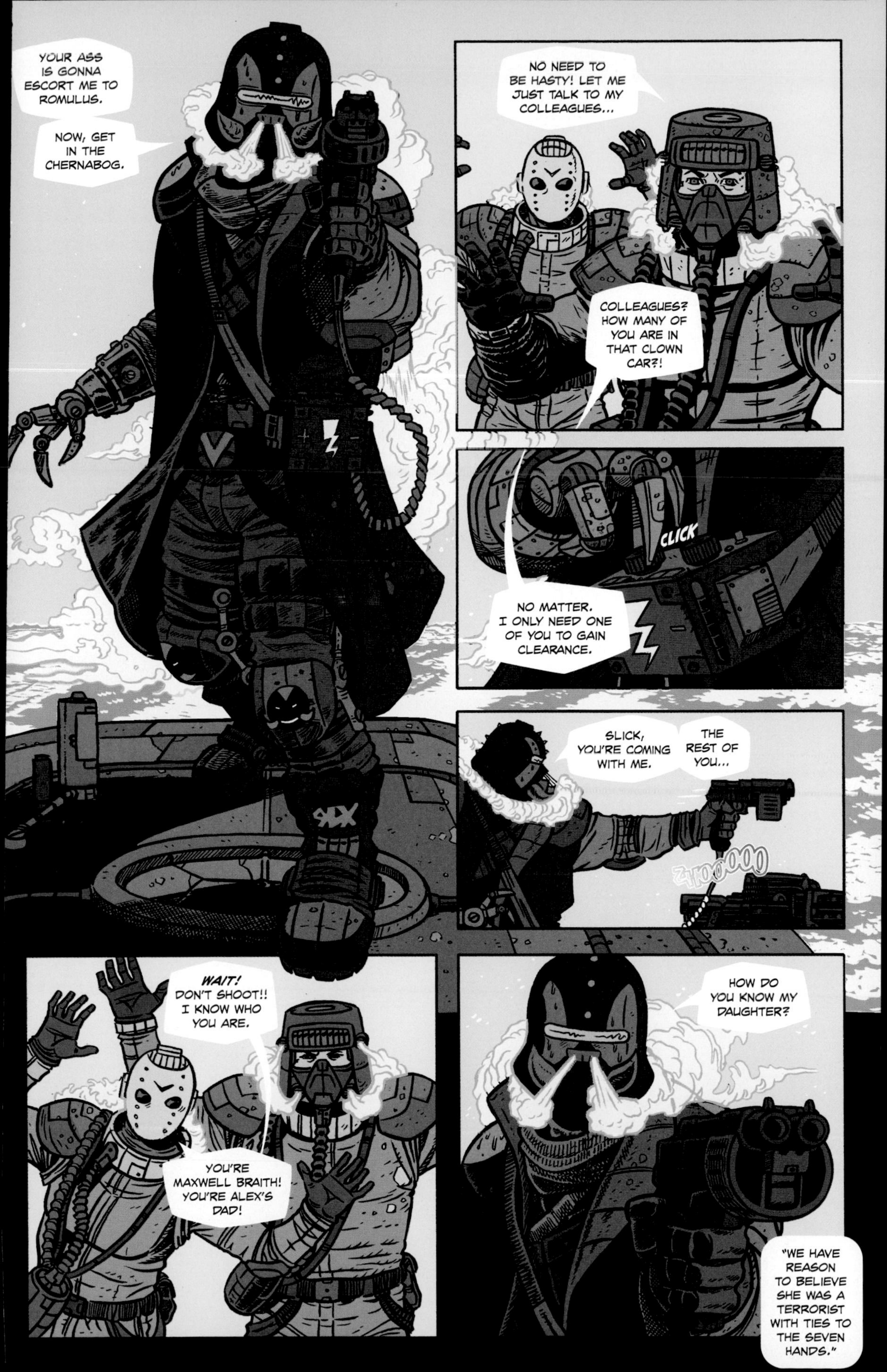

YOUR ASS IS GONNA ESCORT ME TO ROMULUS.
NOW, GET IN THE CHERNABOG.
NO NEED TO BE HASTY! LET ME JUST TALK TO MY COLLEAGUES...
COLLEAGUES? HOW MANY OF YOU ARE IN THAT CLOWN CAR?!
CLICK
NO MATTER. I ONLY NEED ONE OF YOU TO GAIN CLEARANCE.
SLICK, YOU'RE COMING WITH ME.
THE REST OF YOU...
WAIT! DON'T SHOOT!! I KNOW WHO YOU ARE.
YOU'RE MAXWELL BRAITH! YOU'RE ALEX'S DAD!
HOW DO YOU KNOW MY DAUGHTER?
"WE HAVE REASON TO BELIEVE SHE WAS A TERRORIST WITH TIES TO THE SEVEN HANDS."

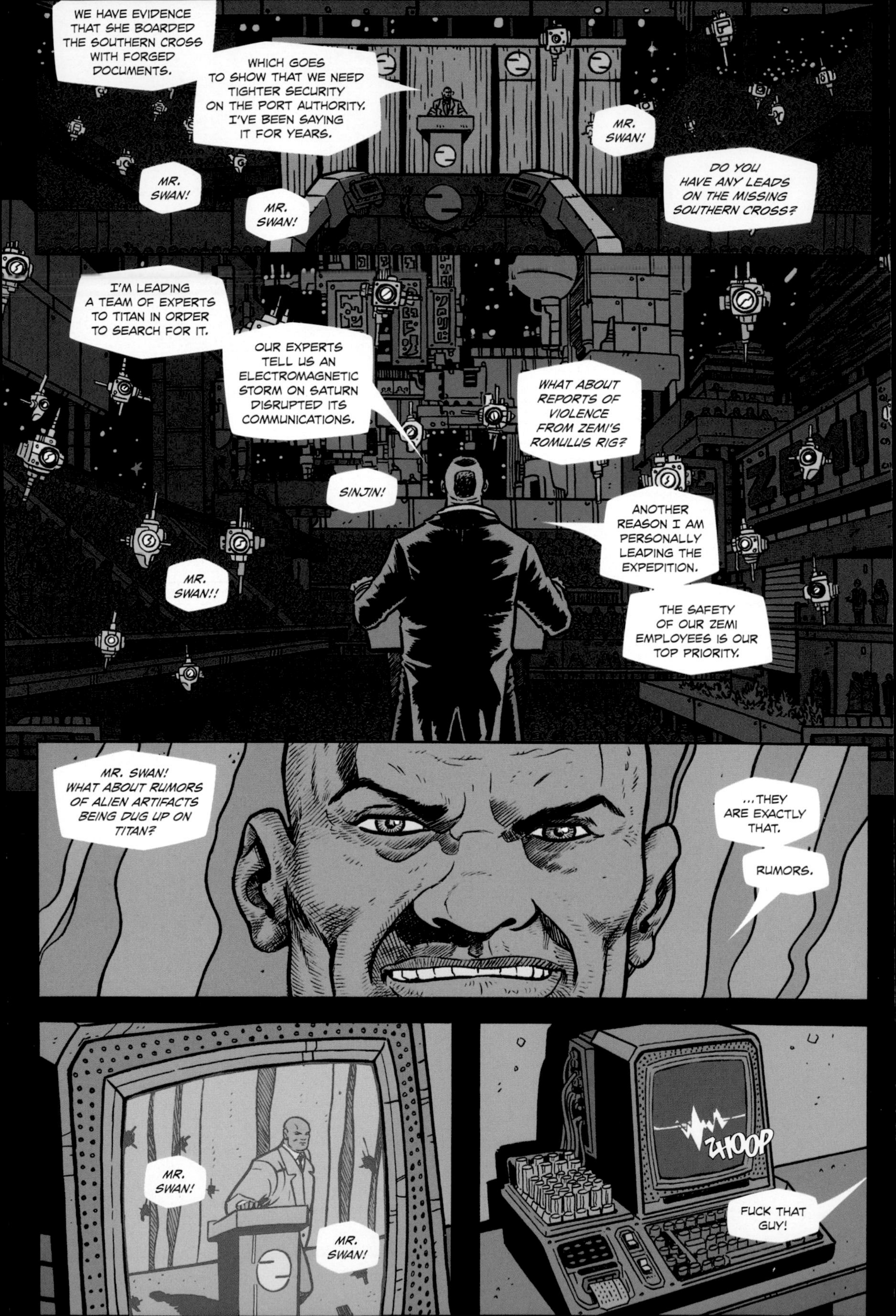
WE HAVE EVIDENCE THAT SHE BOARDED THE SOUTHERN CROSS WITH FORGED DOCUMENTS.
WHICH GOES TO SHOW THAT WE NEED TIGHTER SECURITY ON THE PORT AUTHORITY. I'VE BEEN SAYING IT FOR YEARS.
MR. SWAN!
MR. SWAN!
MR. SWAN!
DO YOU HAVE ANY LEADS ON THE MISSING SOUTHERN CROSS?
I'M LEADING A TEAM OF EXPERTS TO TITAN IN ORDER TO SEARCH FOR IT.
OUR EXPERTS TELL US AN ELECTROMAGNETIC STORM ON SATURN DISRUPTED ITS COMMUNICATIONS.
WHAT ABOUT REPORTS OF VIOLENCE FROM ZEMI'S ROMULUS RIG?
SINJIN!
ANOTHER REASON I AM PERSONALLY LEADING THE EXPEDITION.
MR. SWAN!!
THE SAFETY OF OUR ZEMI EMPLOYEES IS OUR TOP PRIORITY.
ZEMI
MR. SWAN! WHAT ABOUT RUMORS OF ALIEN ARTIFACTS BEING DUG UP ON TITAN?
...THEY ARE EXACTLY THAT.
RUMORS.
MR. SWAN!
MR. SWAN!
ZHOOP
FUCK THAT GUY!

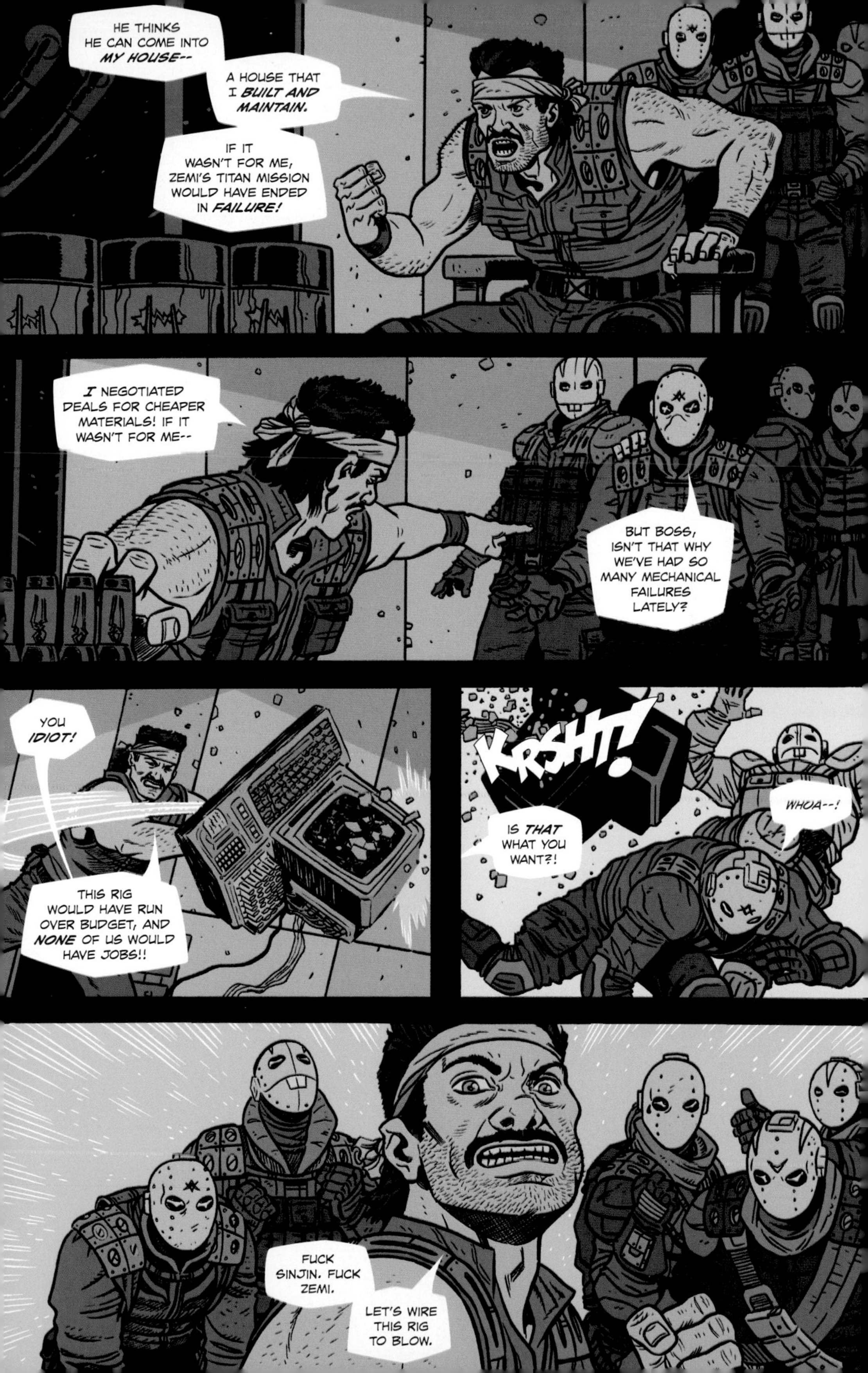
HE THINKS HE CAN COME INTO MY HOUSE--
A HOUSE THAT I BUILT AND MAINTAIN.
IF IT WASN'T FOR ME, ZEMI'S TITAN MISSION WOULD HAVE ENDED IN FAILURE!
I NEGOTIATED DEALS FOR CHEAPER MATERIALS! IF IT WASN'T FOR ME--
BUT BOSS, ISN'T THAT WHY WE'VE HAD SO MANY MECHANICAL FAILURES LATELY?
YOU IDIOT!
THIS RIG WOULD HAVE RUN OVER BUDGET, AND NONE OF US WOULD HAVE JOBS!!
KRSHH!
IS THAT WHAT YOU WANT?!
WHOA--!
FUCK SINJIN. FUCK ZEMI.
LET'S WIRE THIS RIG TO BLOW.

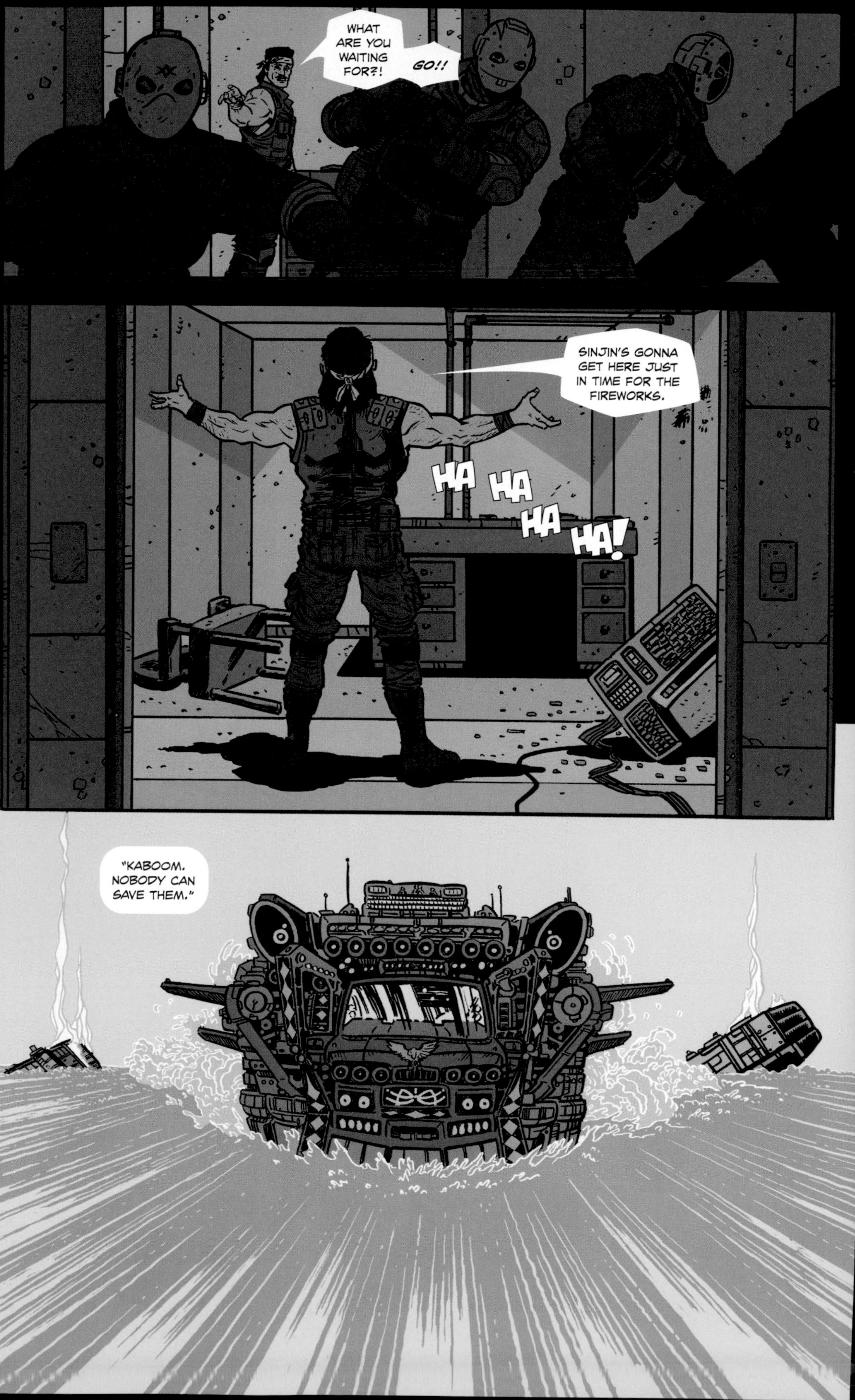
WHAT ARE YOU WAITING FOR?! GO!!
SINJIN'S GONNA GET HERE JUST IN TIME FOR THE FIREWORKS.
HA HA HA HA!
"KABOOM. NOBODY CAN SAVE THEM."

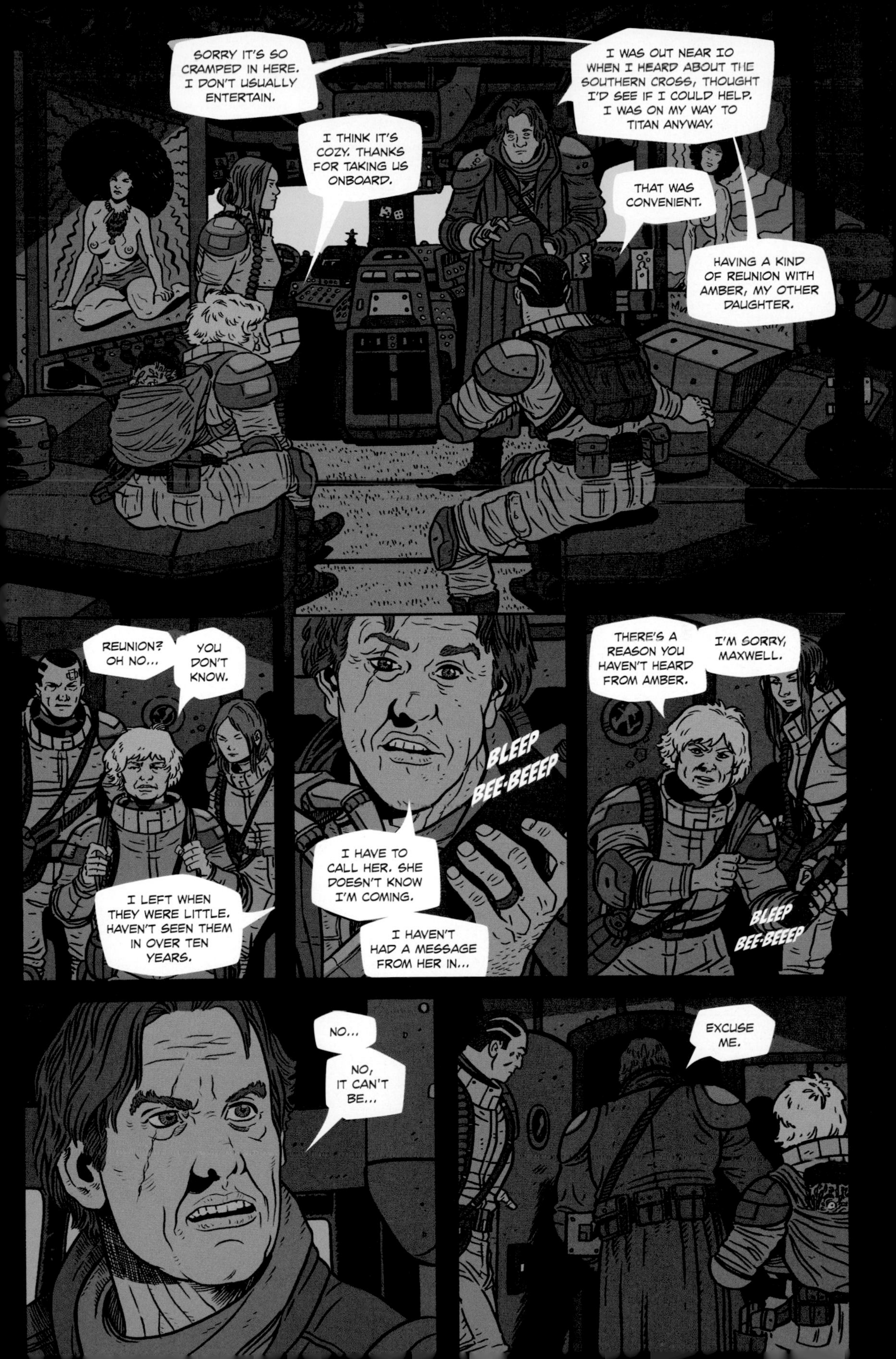
SORRY IT'S SO CRAMPED IN HERE. I DON'T USUALLY ENTERTAIN.
I WAS OUT NEAR IO WHEN I HEARD ABOUT THE SOUTHERN CROSS, THOUGHT I'D SEE IF I COULD HELP. I WAS ON MY WAY TO TITAN ANYWAY.
I THINK IT'S COZY. THANKS FOR TAKING US ONBOARD.
THAT WAS CONVENIENT.
HAVING A KIND OF REUNION WITH AMBER, MY OTHER DAUGHTER.
REUNION? OH NO...
YOU DON'T KNOW.
I LEFT WHEN THEY WERE LITTLE. HAVEN'T SEEN THEM IN OVER TEN YEARS.
BLEEP BEE-BEEEP
I HAVE TO CALL HER. SHE DOESN'T KNOW I'M COMING.
I HAVEN'T HAD A MESSAGE FROM HER IN...
THERE'S A REASON YOU HAVEN'T HEARD FROM AMBER.
I'M SORRY, MAXWELL.
BLEEP BEE-BEEEP
NO...
NO, IT CAN'T BE...
EXCUSE ME.

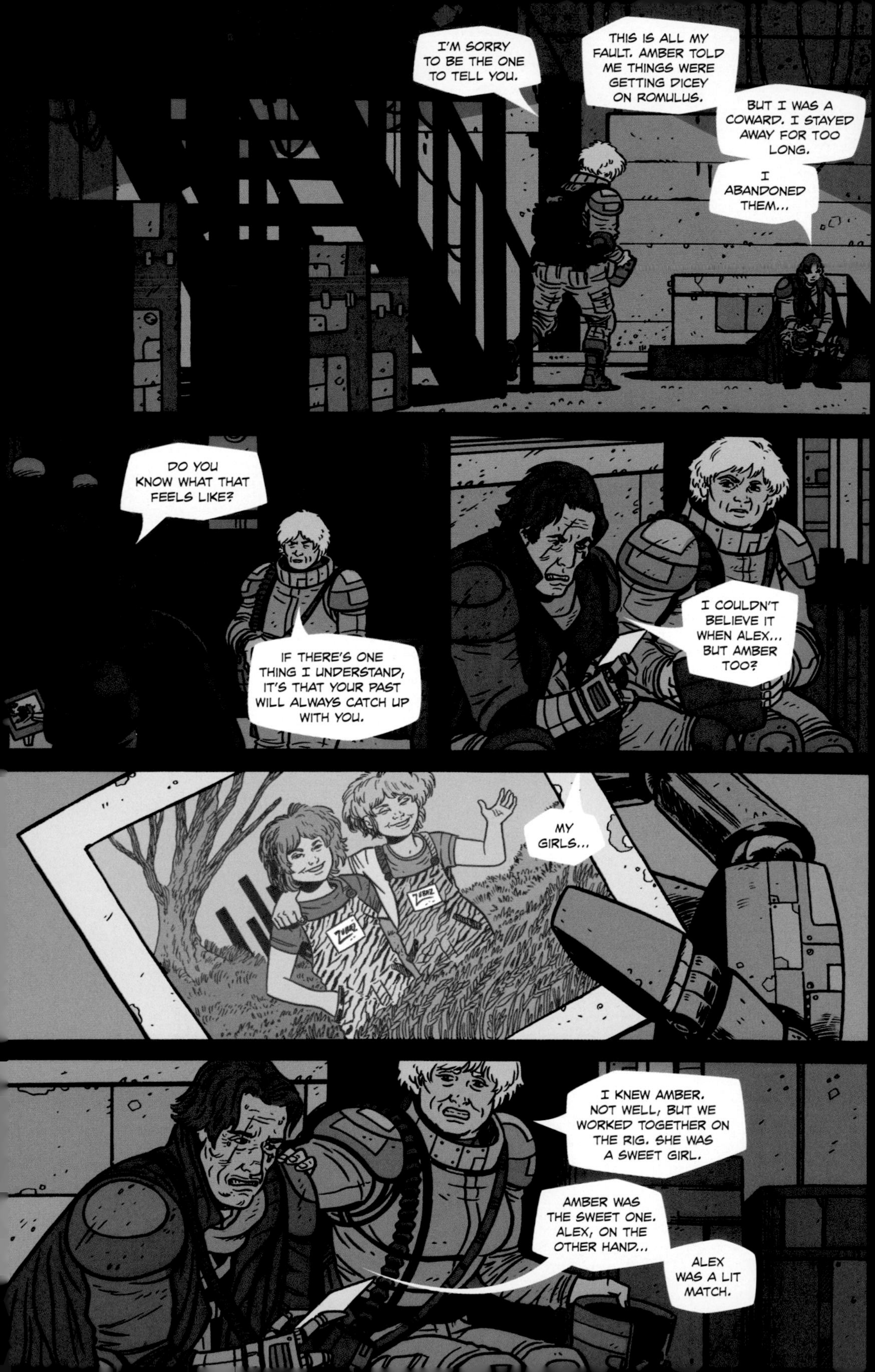
I'M SORRY TO BE THE ONE TO TELL YOU.
THIS IS ALL MY FAULT. AMBER TOLD ME THINGS WERE GETTING DICEY ON ROMULUS.
BUT I WAS A COWARD. I STAYED AWAY FOR TOO LONG.
I ABANDONED THEM...
DO YOU KNOW WHAT THAT FEELS LIKE?
IF THERE'S ONE THING I UNDERSTAND, IT'S THAT YOUR PAST WILL ALWAYS CATCH UP WITH YOU.
I COULDN'T BELIEVE IT WHEN ALEX... BUT AMBER TOO?
MY GIRLS...
I KNEW AMBER. NOT WELL, BUT WE WORKED TOGETHER ON THE RIG. SHE WAS A SWEET GIRL.
AMBER WAS THE SWEET ONE. ALEX, ON THE OTHER HAND...
ALEX WAS A LIT MATCH.

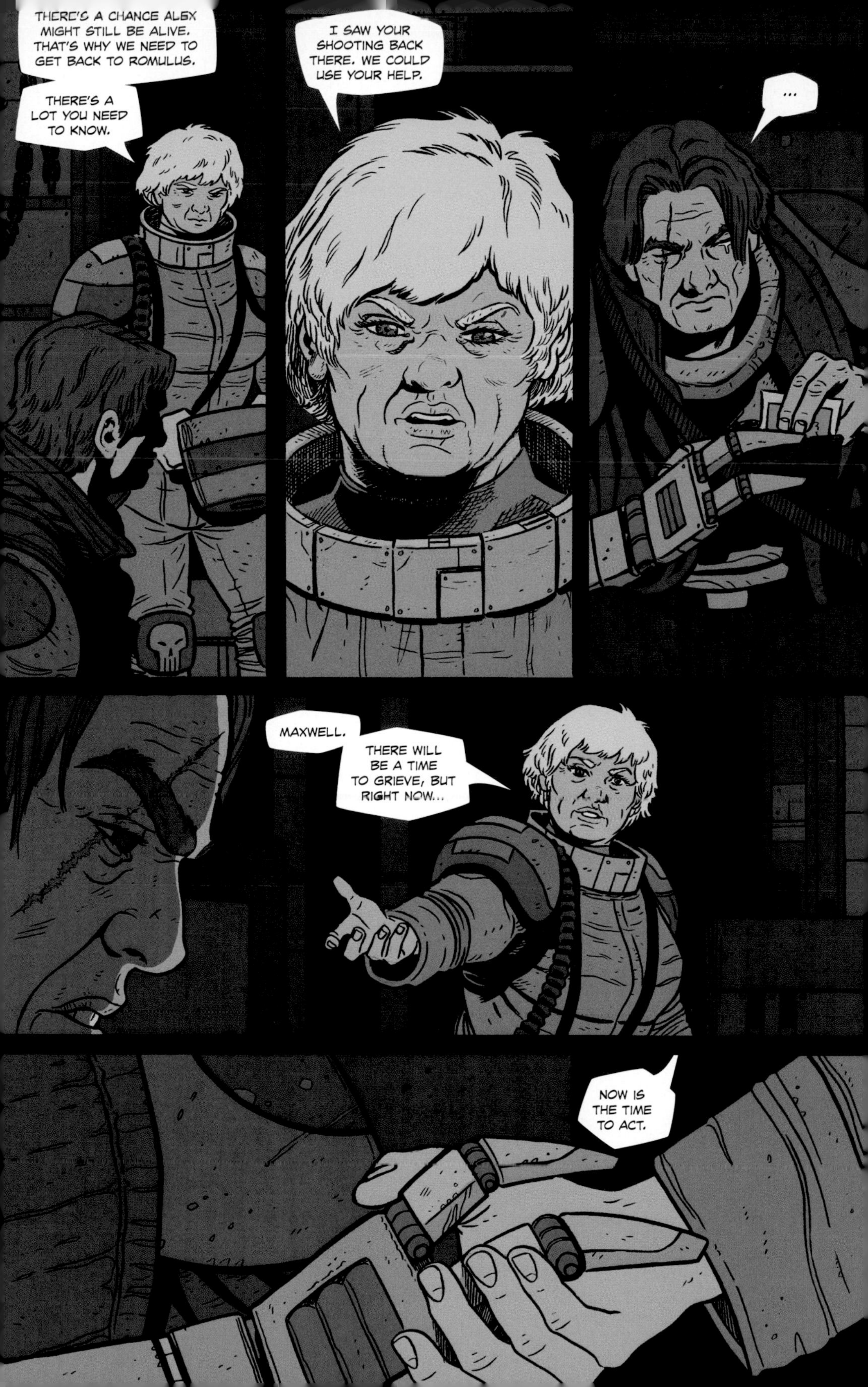
THERE'S A CHANCE ALEX MIGHT STILL BE ALIVE. THAT'S WHY WE NEED TO GET BACK TO ROMULUS.
THERE'S A LOT YOU NEED TO KNOW.
I SAW YOUR SHOOTING BACK THERE. WE COULD USE YOUR HELP.
...
MAXWELL.
THERE WILL BE A TIME TO GRIEVE, BUT RIGHT NOW...
NOW IS THE TIME TO ACT.

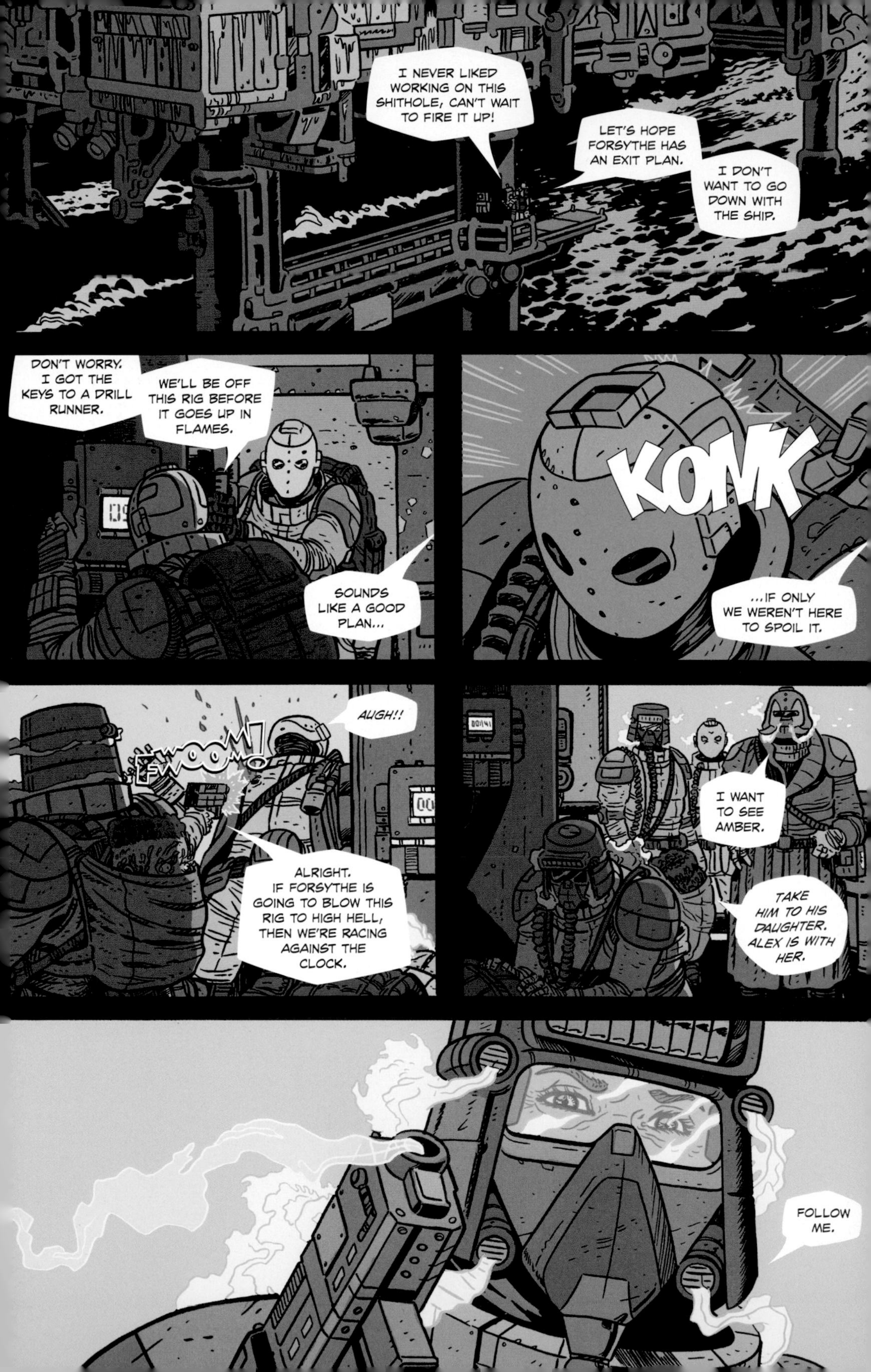
I NEVER LIKED WORKING ON THIS SHITHOLE, CAN'T WAIT TO FIRE IT UP!
LET'S HOPE FORSYTHE HAS AN EXIT PLAN.
I DON'T WANT TO GO DOWN WITH THE SHIP.
DON'T WORRY. I GOT THE KEYS TO A DRILL RUNNER.
WE'LL BE OFF THIS RIG BEFORE IT GOES UP IN FLAMES.
SOUNDS LIKE A GOOD PLAN...
KONK
...IF ONLY WE WEREN'T HERE TO SPOIL IT.
FWOOM!
AUGH!!
ALRIGHT. IF FORSYTHE IS GOING TO BLOW THIS RIG TO HIGH HELL, THEN WE'RE RACING AGAINST THE CLOCK.
I WANT TO SEE AMBER.
TAKE HIM TO HIS DAUGHTER. ALEX IS WITH HER.
FOLLOW ME.

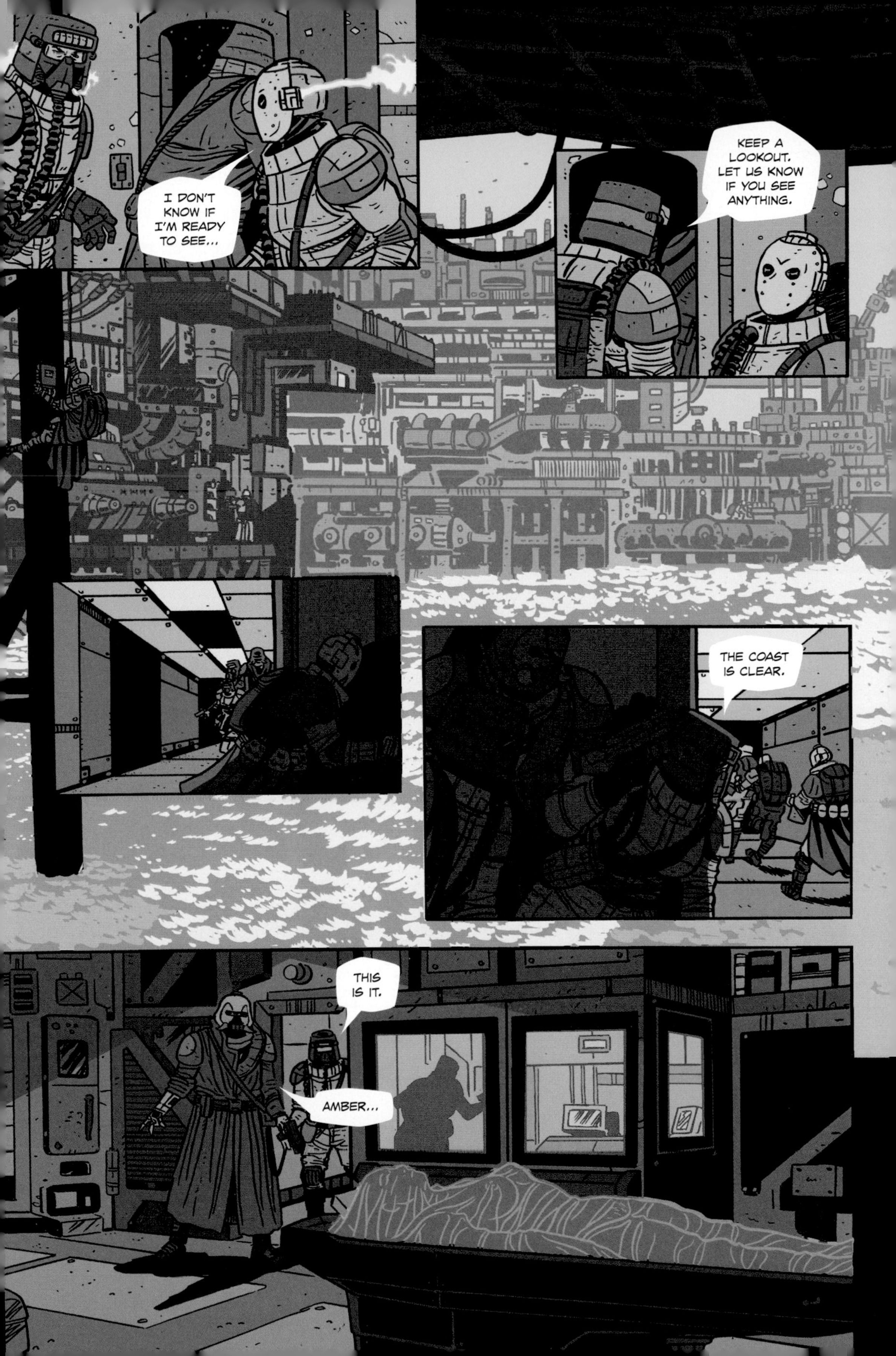
I DON'T KNOW IF I'M READY TO SEE...
KEEP A LOOKOUT. LET US KNOW IF YOU SEE ANYTHING.
THE COAST IS CLEAR.
THIS IS IT.
AMBER...

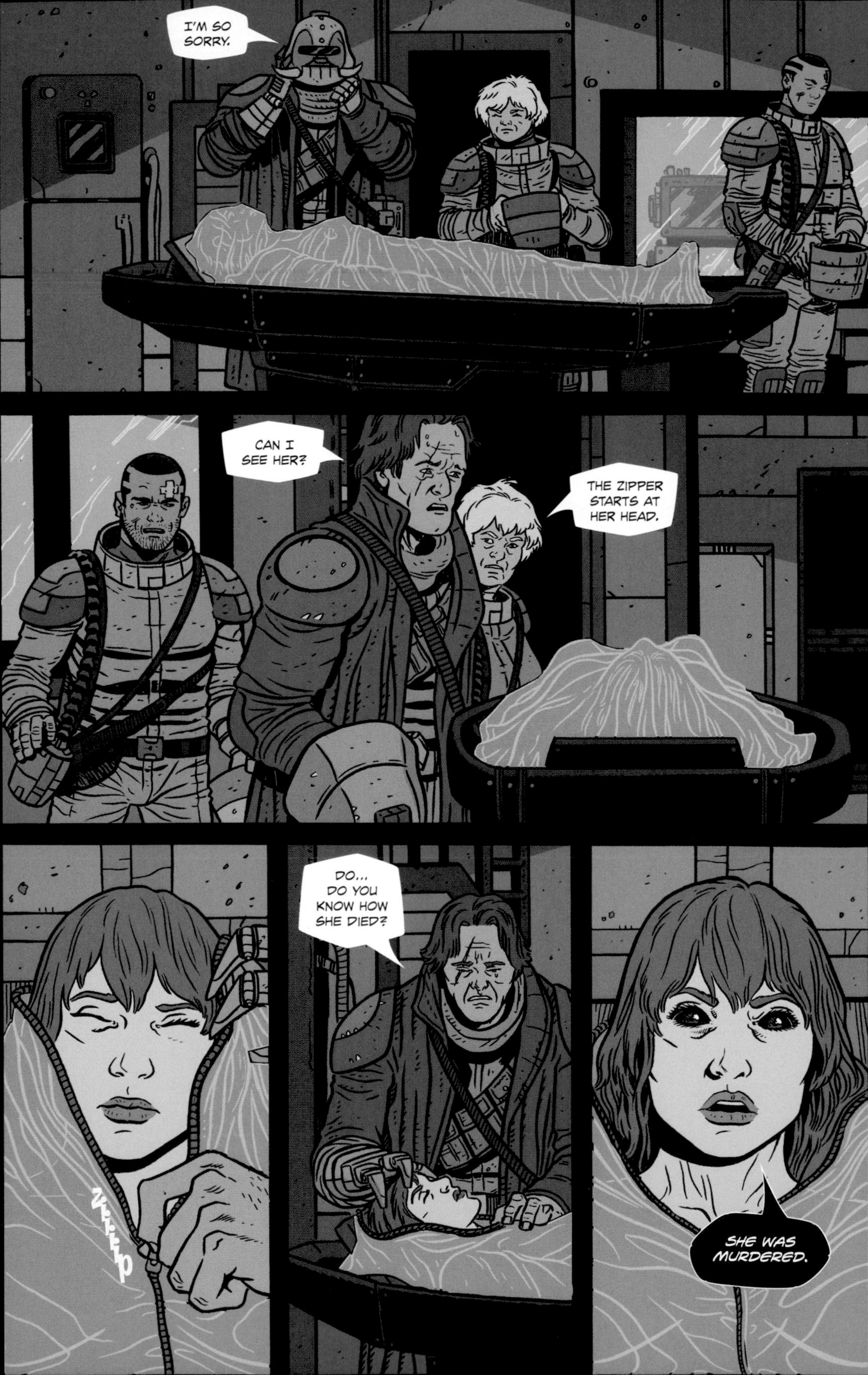
I'M SO SORRY.
CAN I SEE HER?
THE ZIPPER STARTS AT HER HEAD.
ZZZIP
DO... DO YOU KNOW HOW SHE DIED?
SHE WAS MURDERED.

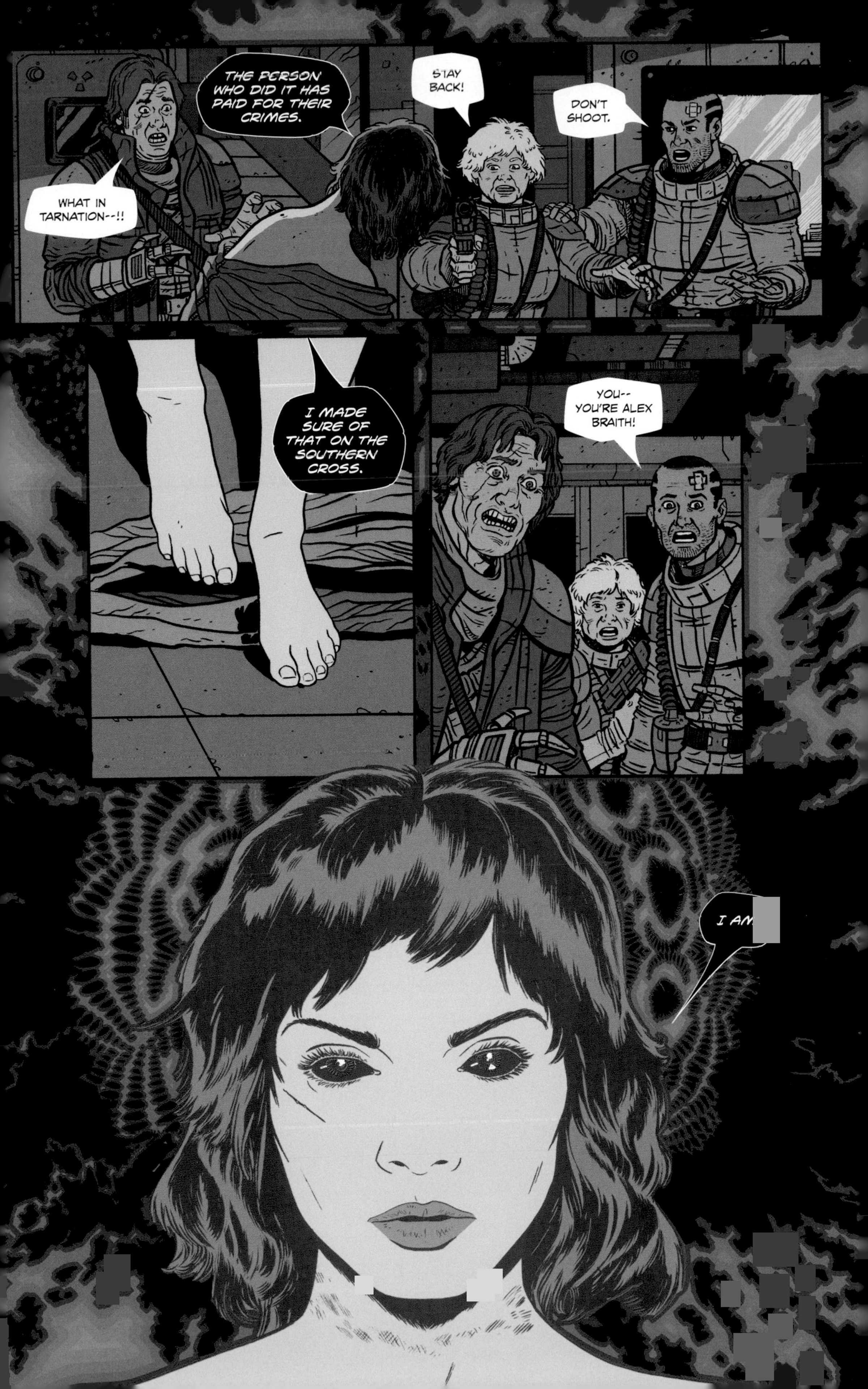
WHAT IN TARNATION--!!
THE PERSON WHO DID IT HAS PAID FOR THEIR CRIMES.
STAY BACK!
DON'T SHOOT.
I MADE SURE OF THAT ON THE SOUTHERN CROSS.
YOU-- YOU'RE ALEX BRAITH!
I AM

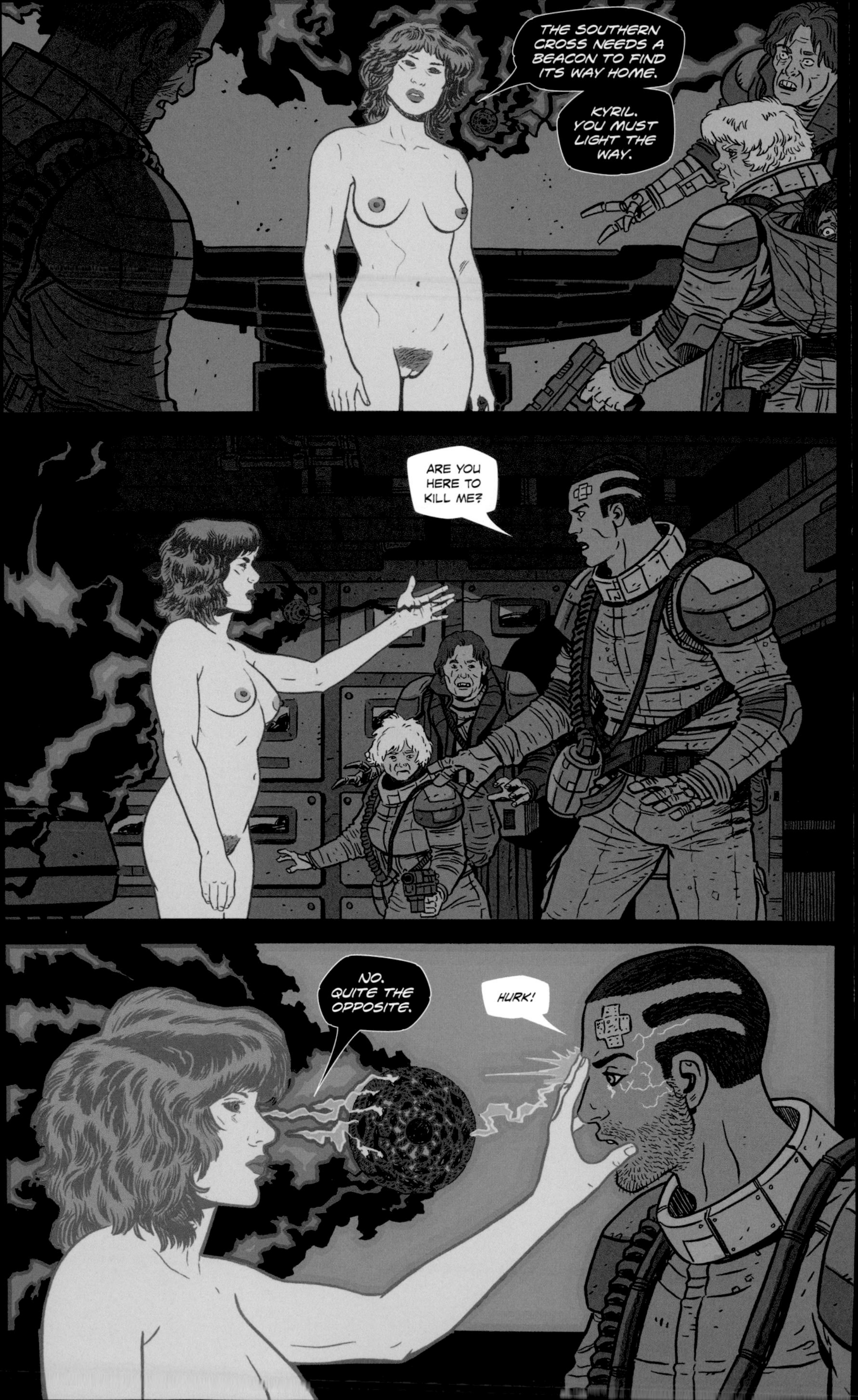
THE SOUTHERN CROSS NEEDS A BEACON TO FIND ITS WAY HOME.
KYRIL. YOU MUST LIGHT THE WAY.
ARE YOU HERE TO KILL ME?
NO. QUITE THE OPPOSITE.
HURK!

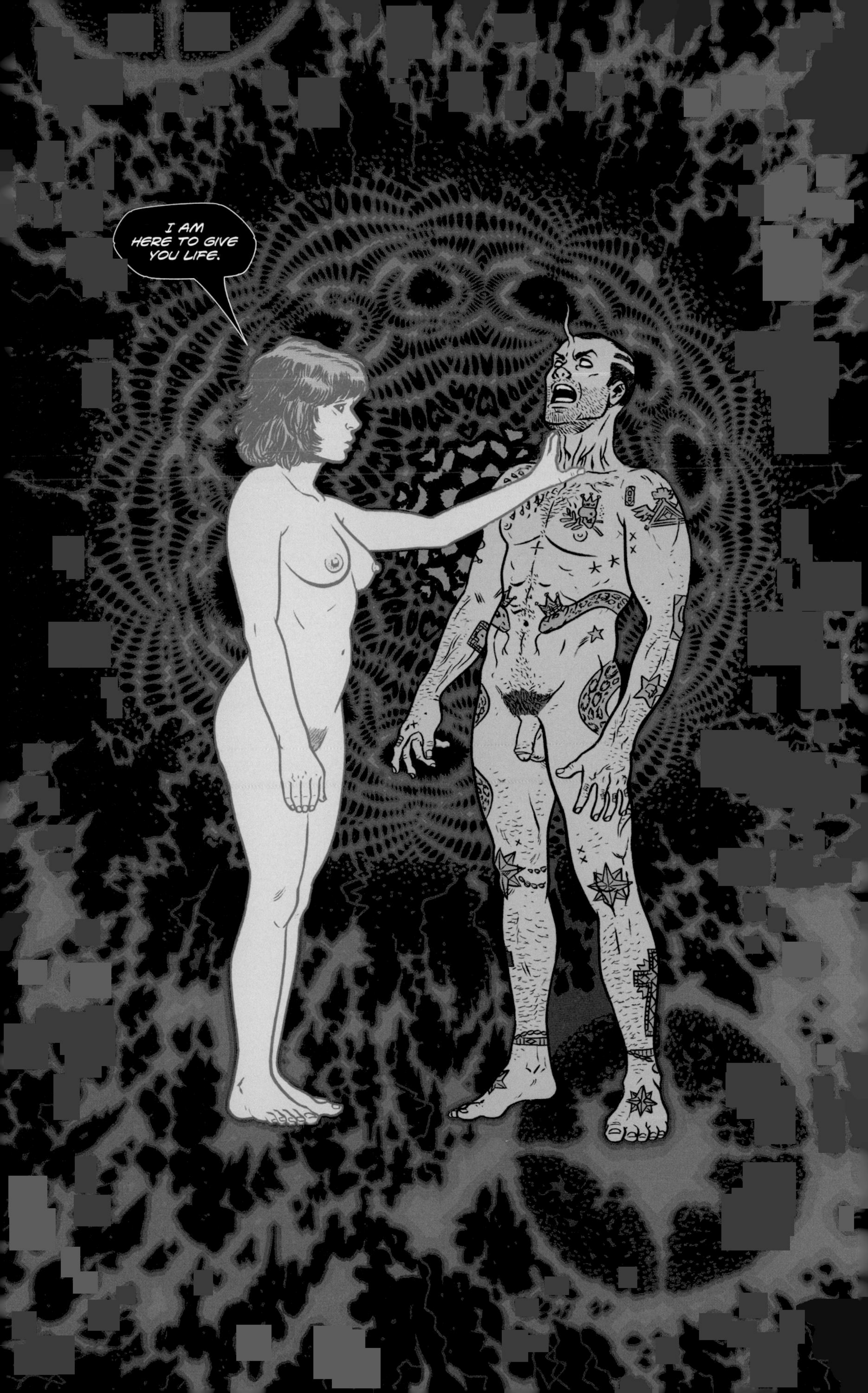
I AM HERE TO GIVE YOU LIFE.

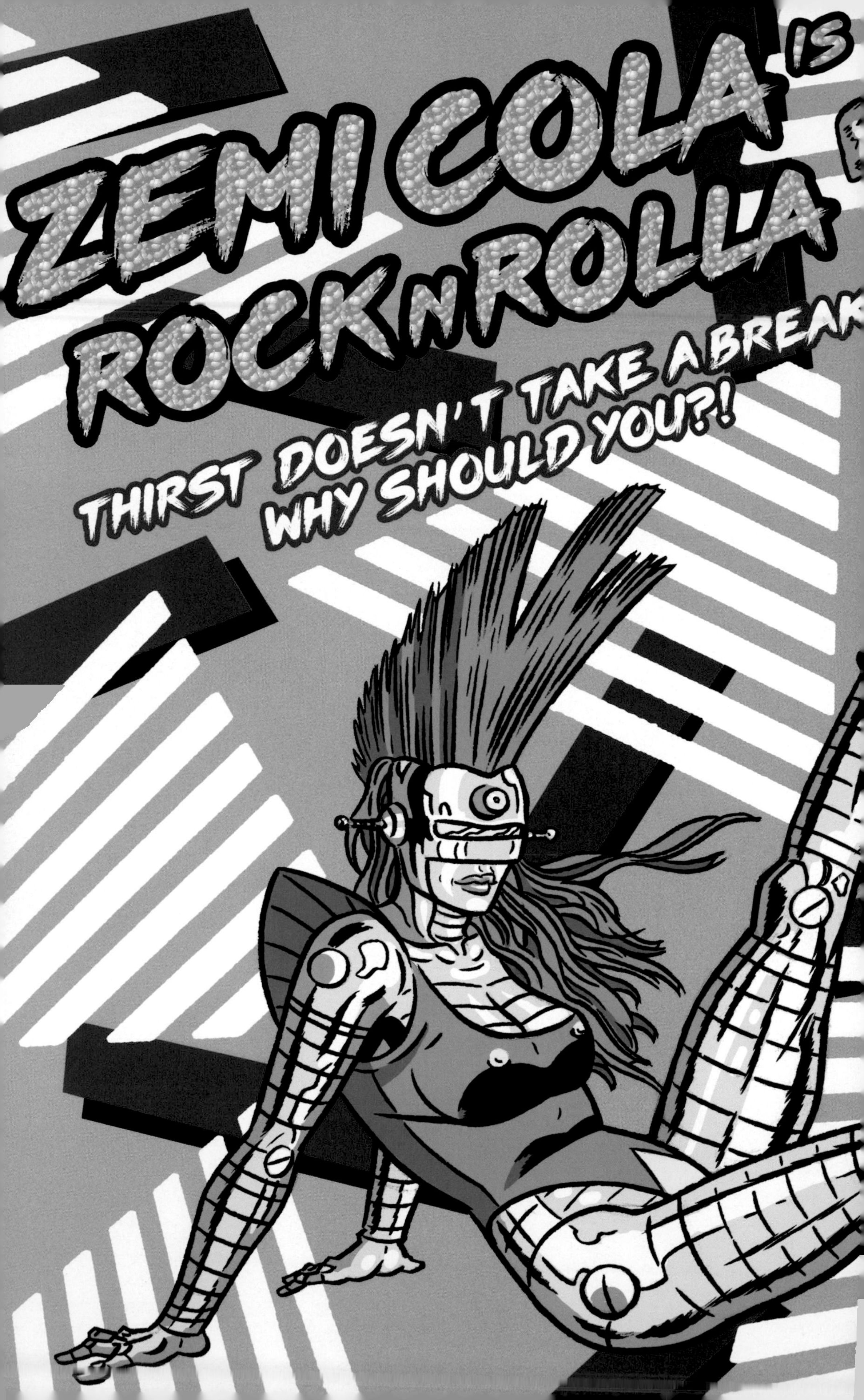
ZEMI COLA IS
ROCK N ROLLA
THIRST DOESN'T TAKE A BREAK
WHY SHOULD YOU?!

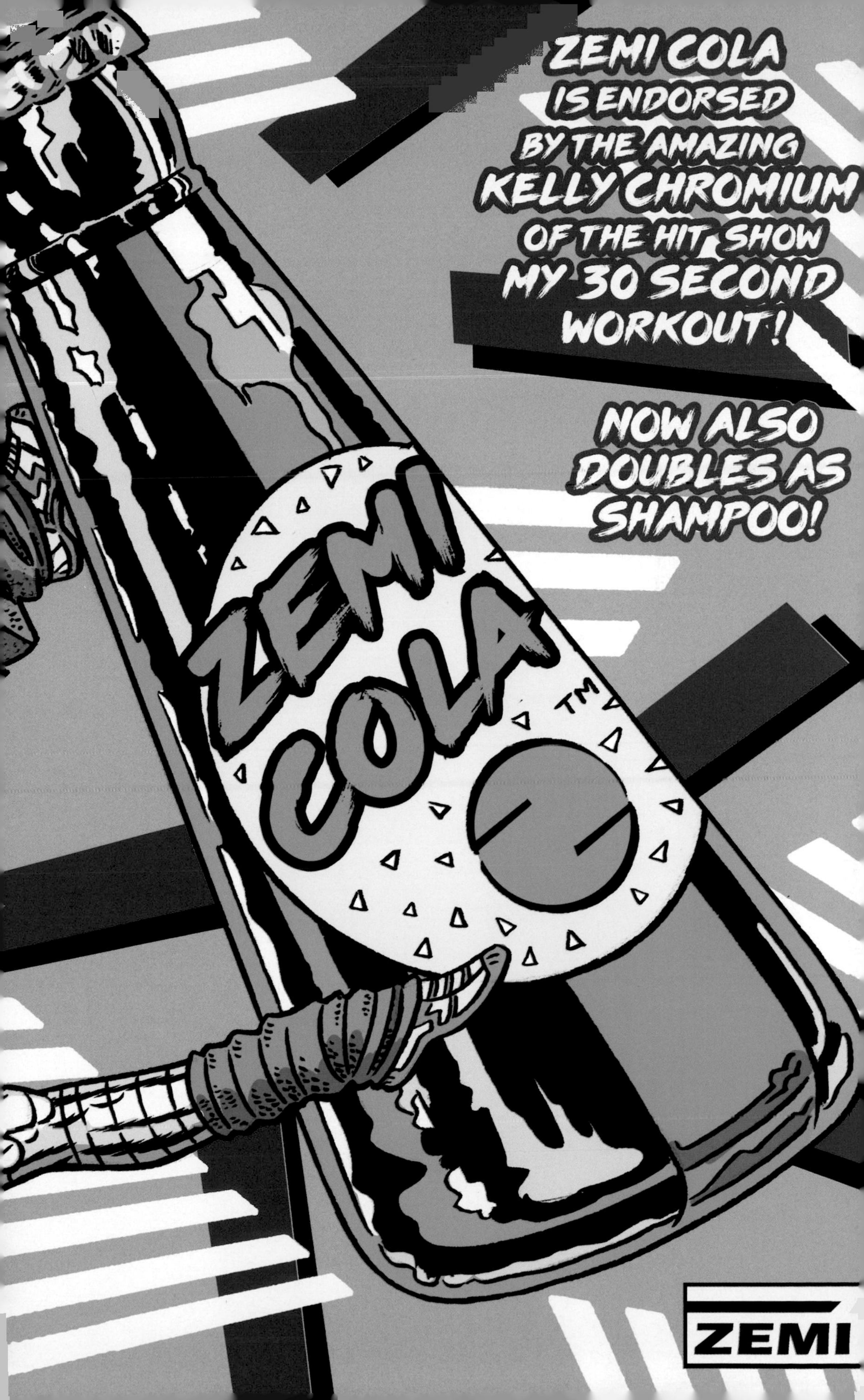
ZEMI COLA IS ENDORSED BY THE AMAZING KELLY CHROMIUM OF THE HIT SHOW MY 30 SECOND WORKOUT!
NOW ALSO DOUBLES AS SHAMPOO!
ZEMI COLA
TM
ZEMI

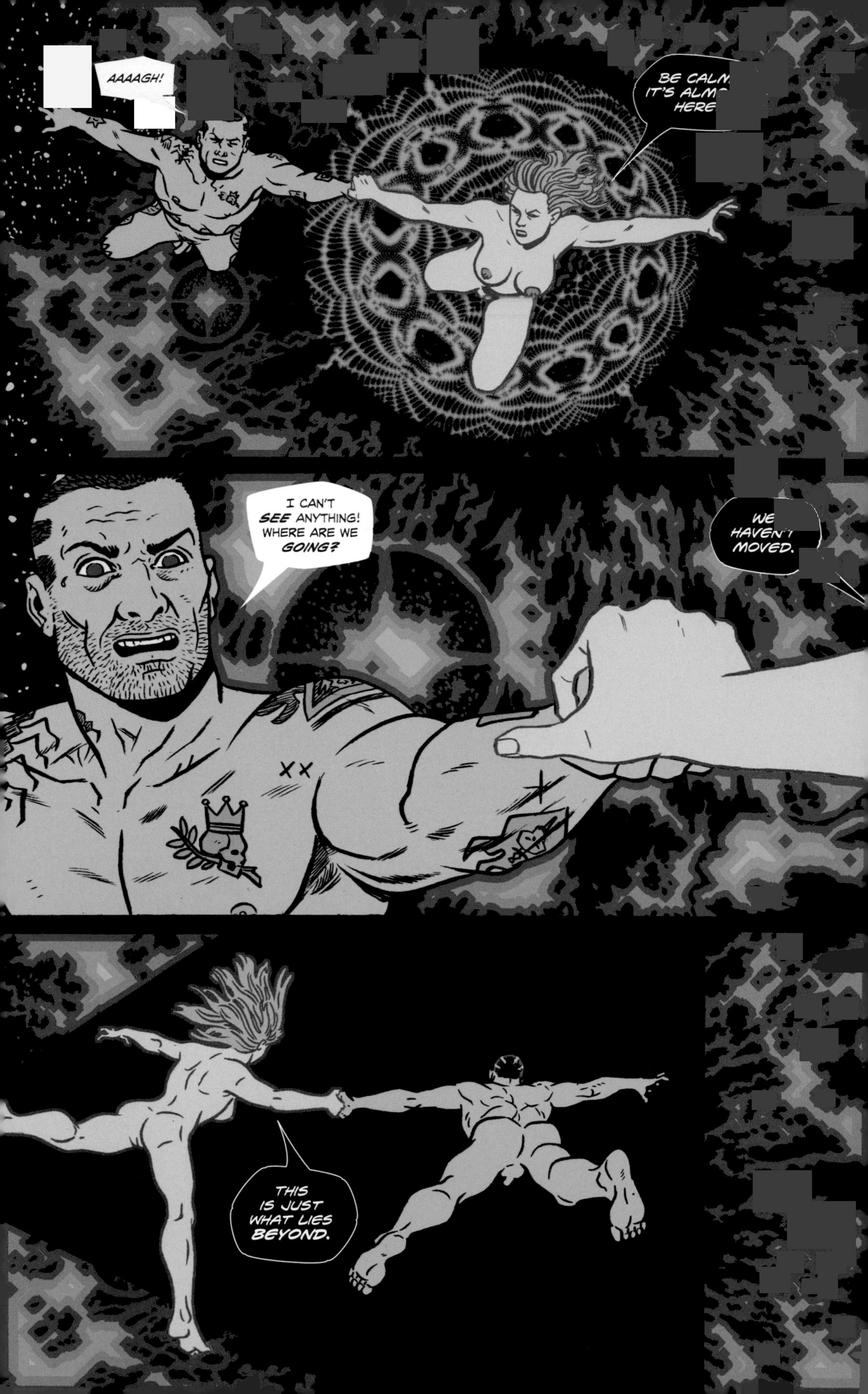
AAAAGH!
BE CALM
IT'S ALM
HERE
I CAN'T **SEE** ANYTHING! WHERE ARE WE **GOING?**
WE
HAVEN
MOVED.
THIS IS JUST WHAT LIES **BEYOND.**

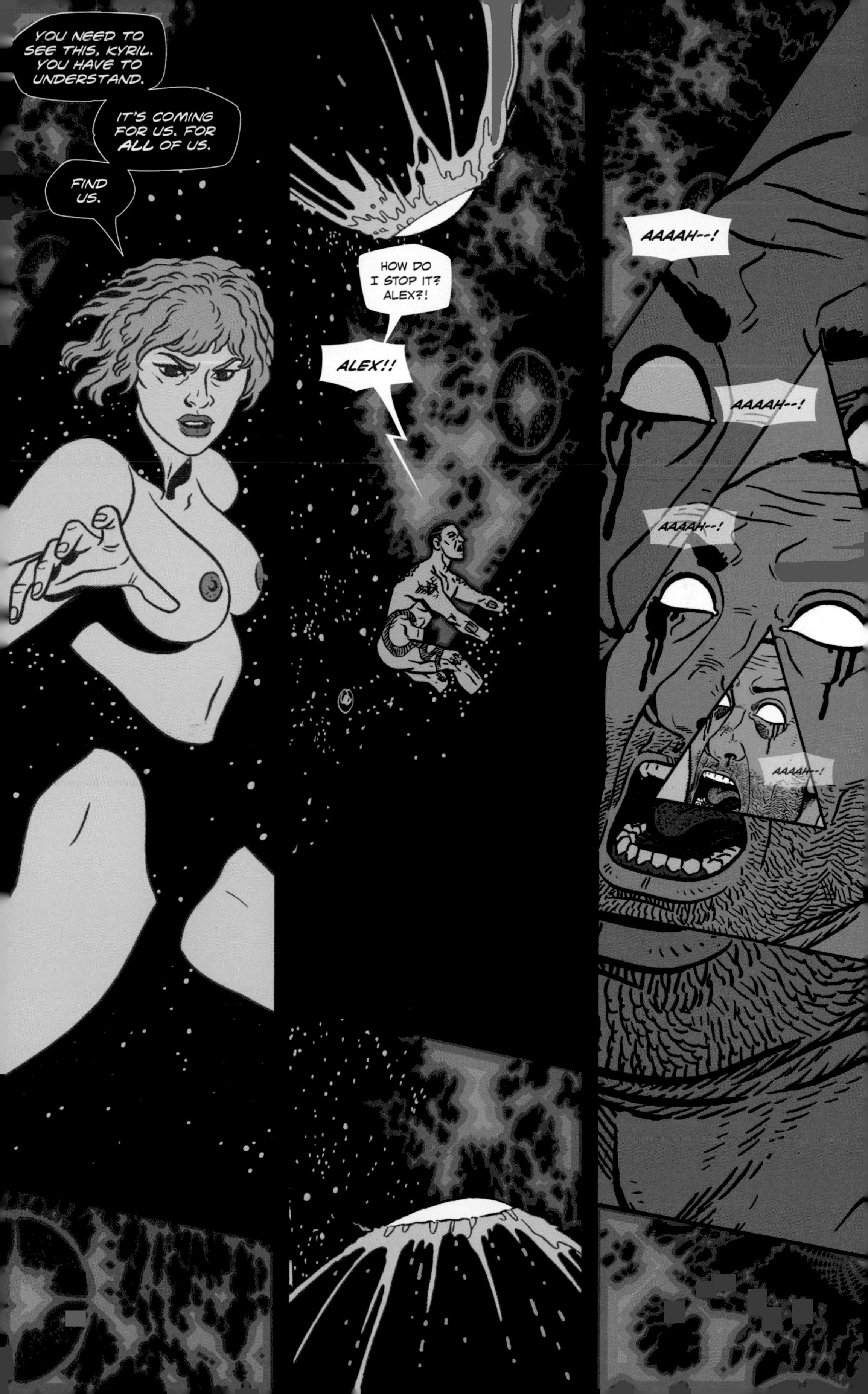
YOU NEED TO SEE THIS, KYRIL. YOU HAVE TO UNDERSTAND.
IT'S COMING FOR US. FOR ALL OF US.
FIND US.
HOW DO I STOP IT? ALEX?!
ALEX!!
AAAAH--!
AAAAH--!
AAAAH--!
AAAAH--!

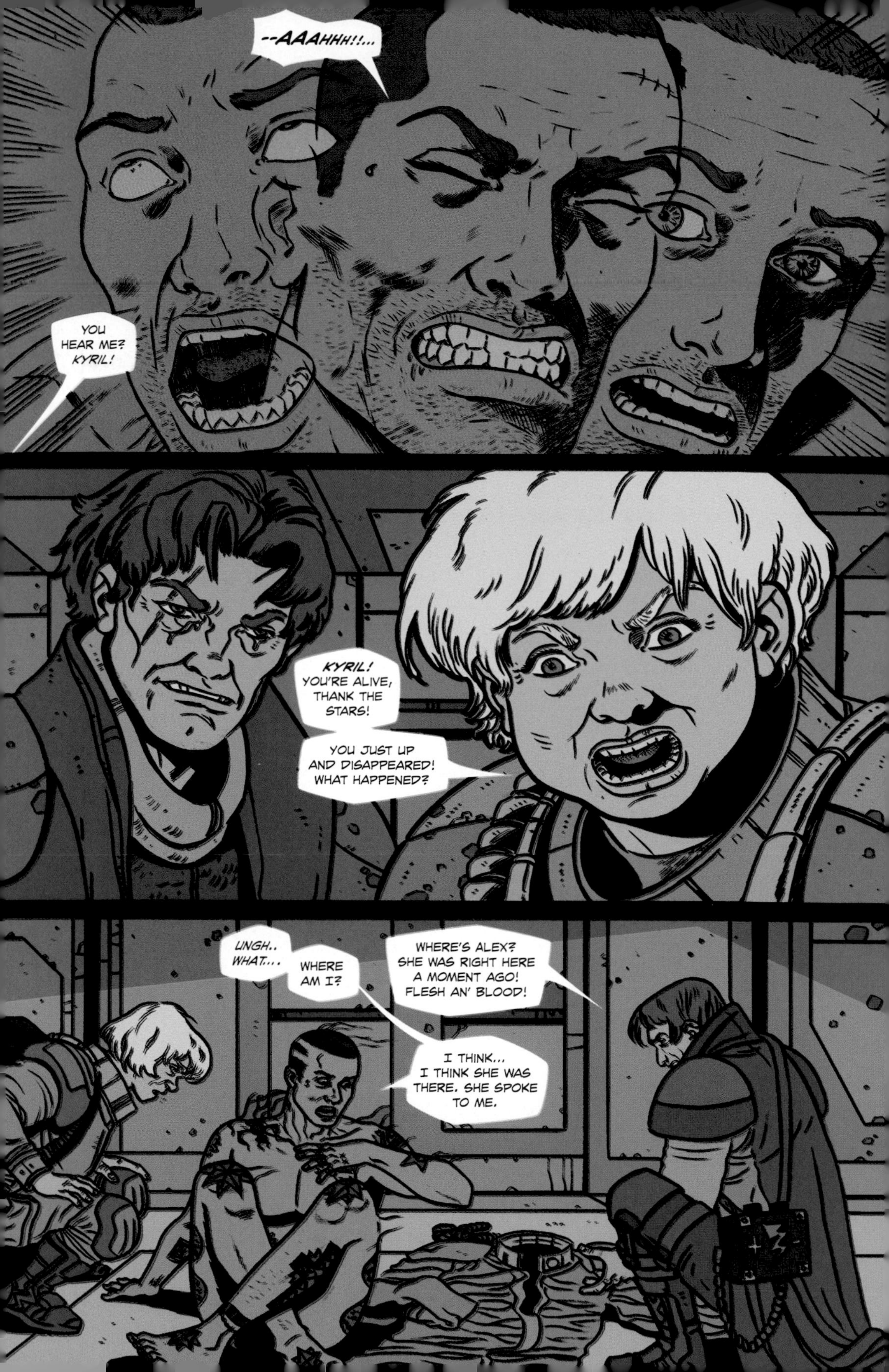
--AAAHHH!!...
YOU HEAR ME? KYRIL!
KYRIL! YOU'RE ALIVE, THANK THE STARS!
YOU JUST UP AND DISAPPEARED! WHAT HAPPENED?
UNGH.. WHAT...
WHERE AM I?
WHERE'S ALEX? SHE WAS RIGHT HERE A MOMENT AGO! FLESH AN' BLOOD!
I THINK... I THINK SHE WAS THERE. SHE SPOKE TO ME.

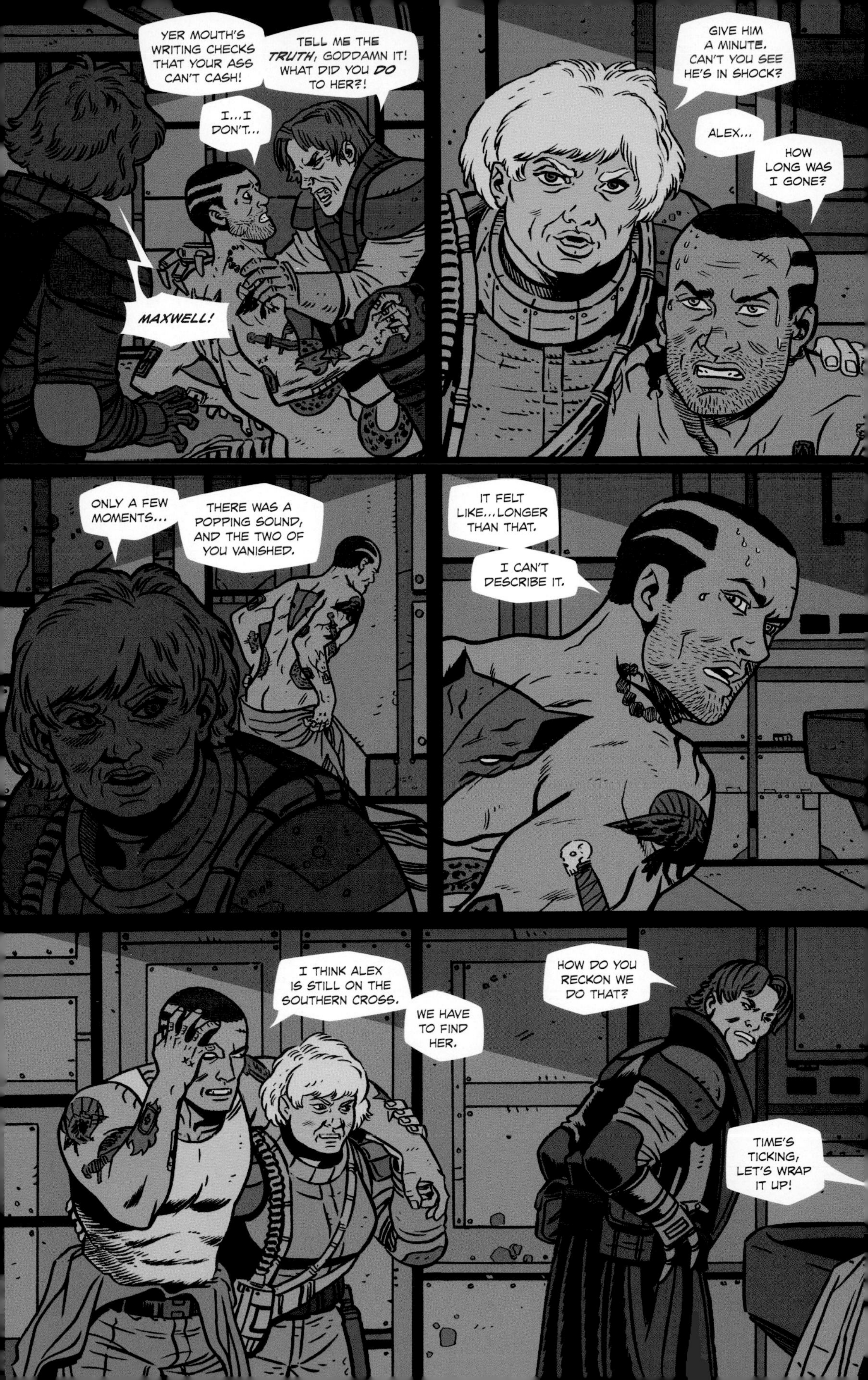
YER MOUTH'S WRITING CHECKS THAT YOUR ASS CAN'T CASH!
TELL ME THE *TRUTH*, GODDAMN IT! WHAT DID YOU *DO* TO HER?!
I...I DON'T...
*MAXWELL!*
GIVE HIM A MINUTE. CAN'T YOU SEE HE'S IN SHOCK?
ALEX...
HOW LONG WAS I GONE?
ONLY A FEW MOMENTS...
THERE WAS A POPPING SOUND, AND THE TWO OF YOU VANISHED.
IT FELT LIKE...LONGER THAN THAT.
I CAN'T DESCRIBE IT.
I THINK ALEX IS STILL ON THE SOUTHERN CROSS.
WE HAVE TO FIND HER.
HOW DO YOU RECKON WE DO THAT?
TIME'S TICKING, LET'S WRAP IT UP!

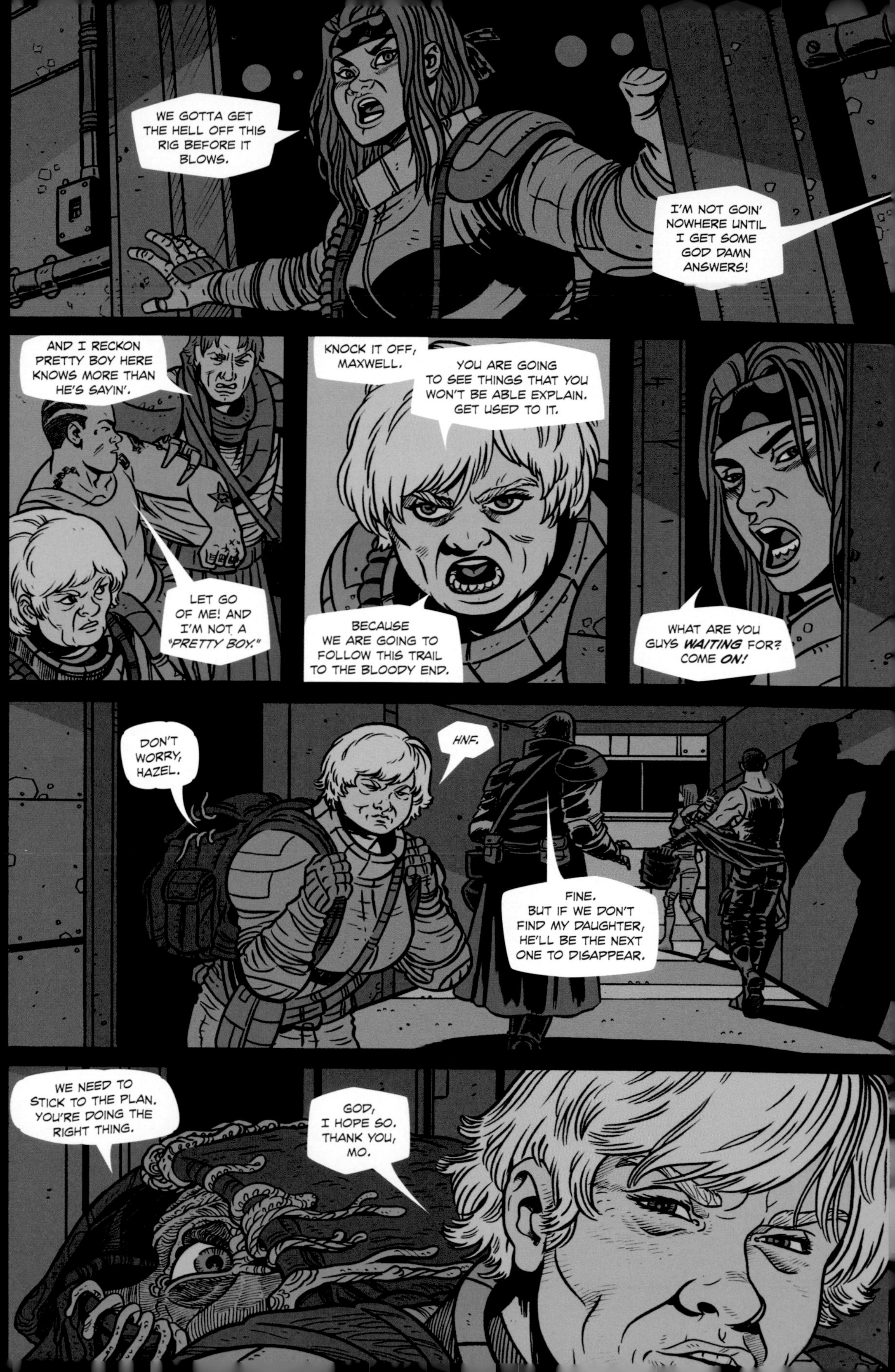
WE GOTTA GET THE HELL OFF THIS RIG BEFORE IT BLOWS.
I'M NOT GOIN' NOWHERE UNTIL I GET SOME GOD DAMN ANSWERS!
AND I RECKON PRETTY BOY HERE KNOWS MORE THAN HE'S SAYIN'.
LET GO OF ME! AND I'M NOT A *"PRETTY BOY."*
KNOCK IT OFF, MAXWELL.
YOU ARE GOING TO SEE THINGS THAT YOU WON'T BE ABLE EXPLAIN. GET USED TO IT.
BECAUSE WE ARE GOING TO FOLLOW THIS TRAIL TO THE BLOODY END.
WHAT ARE YOU GUYS ***WAITING*** FOR? COME ***ON!***
DON'T WORRY, HAZEL.
*HNF.*
FINE. BUT IF WE DON'T FIND MY DAUGHTER, HE'LL BE THE NEXT ONE TO DISAPPEAR.
WE NEED TO STICK TO THE PLAN. YOU'RE DOING THE RIGHT THING.
GOD, I HOPE SO. THANK YOU, MO.

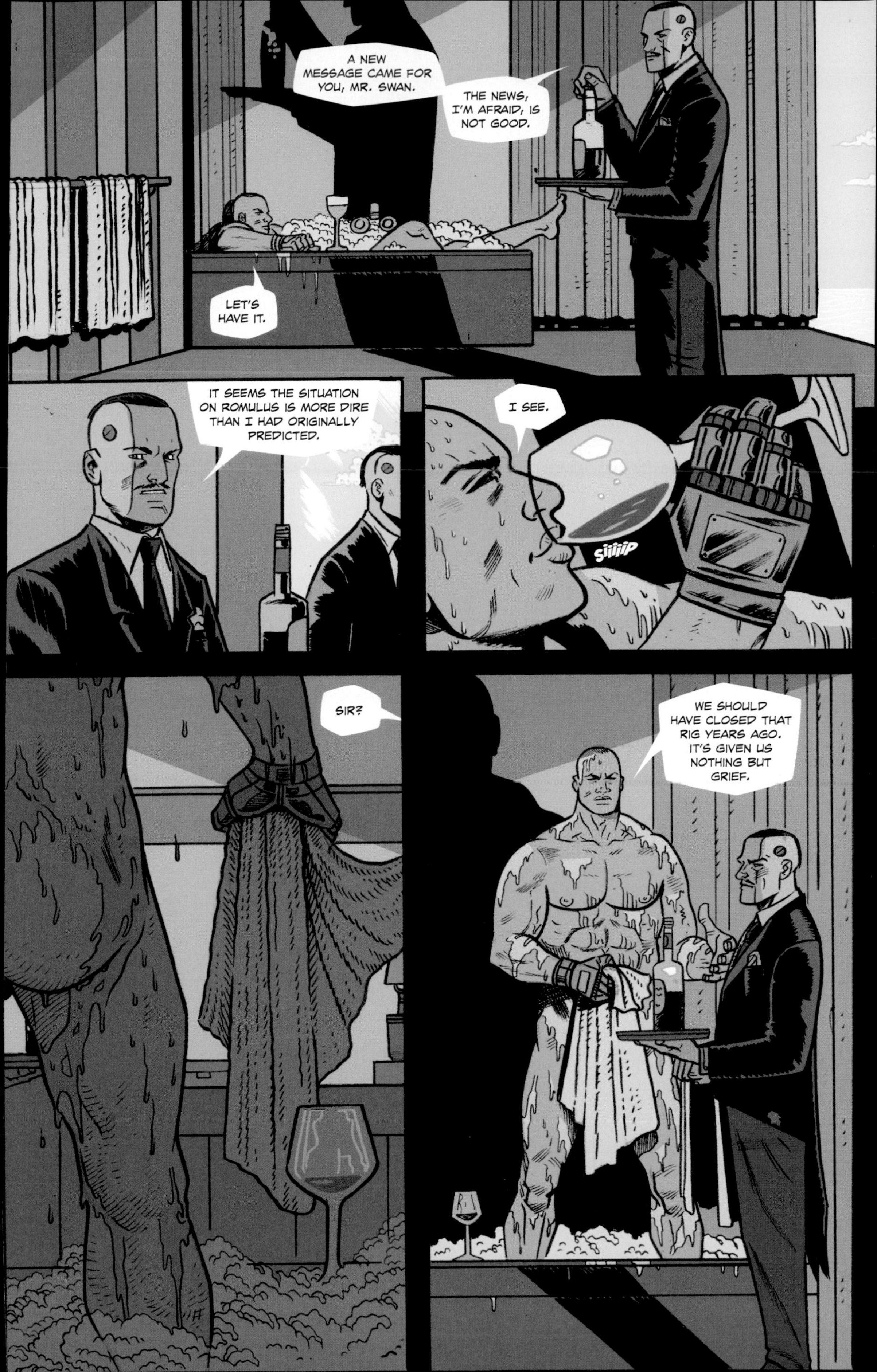
A NEW MESSAGE CAME FOR YOU, MR. SWAN.
THE NEWS, I'M AFRAID, IS NOT GOOD.
LET'S HAVE IT.
IT SEEMS THE SITUATION ON ROMULUS IS MORE DIRE THAN I HAD ORIGINALLY PREDICTED.
I SEE.
SIIIIP
SIR?
WE SHOULD HAVE CLOSED THAT RIG YEARS AGO. IT'S GIVEN US NOTHING BUT GRIEF.

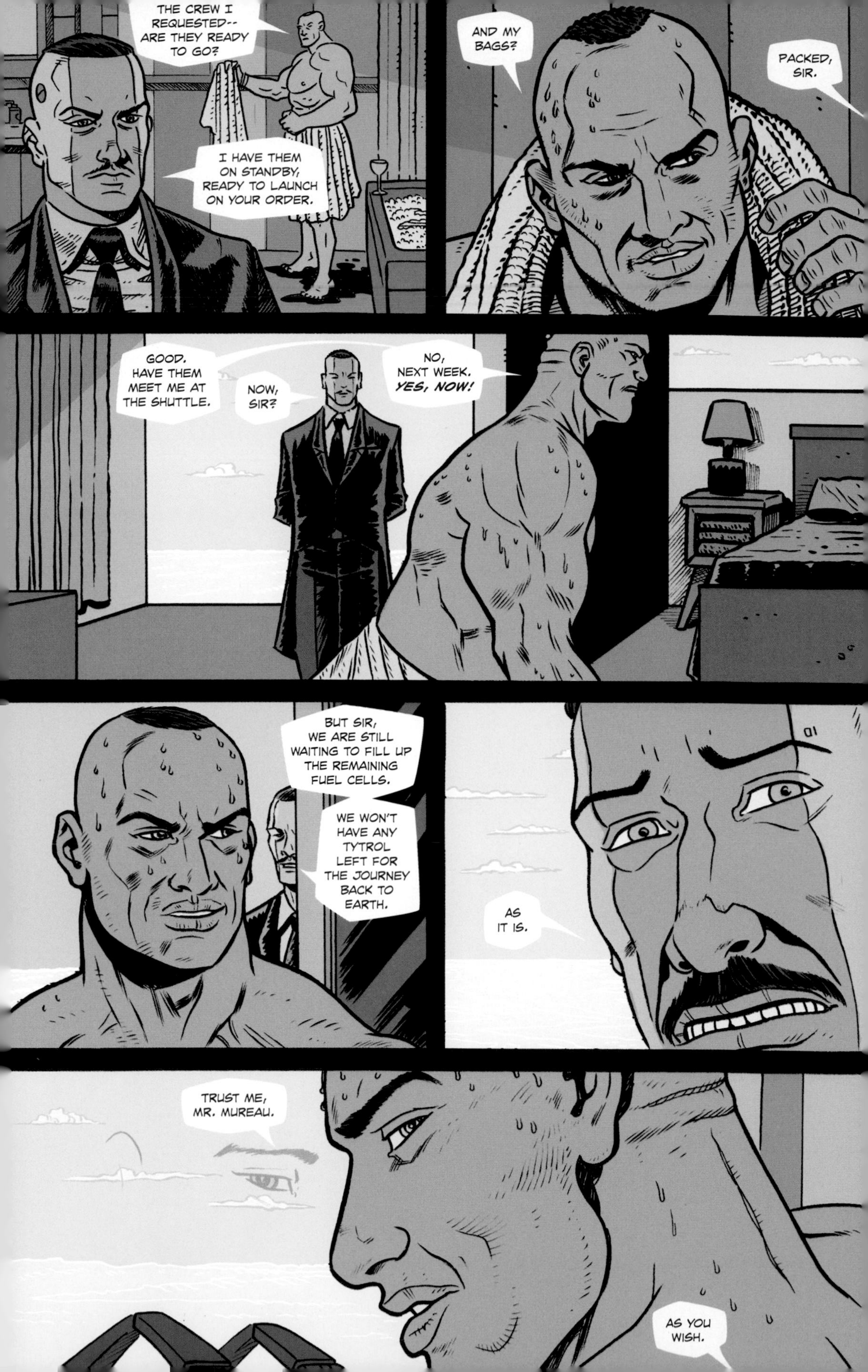
THE CREW I REQUESTED-- ARE THEY READY TO GO?
I HAVE THEM ON STANDBY, READY TO LAUNCH ON YOUR ORDER.
AND MY BAGS?
PACKED, SIR.
GOOD. HAVE THEM MEET ME AT THE SHUTTLE.
NOW, SIR?
NO, NEXT WEEK. YES, NOW!
BUT SIR, WE ARE STILL WAITING TO FILL UP THE REMAINING FUEL CELLS.
WE WON'T HAVE ANY TYTROL LEFT FOR THE JOURNEY BACK TO EARTH.
AS IT IS.
TRUST ME, MR. MUREAU.
AS YOU WISH.

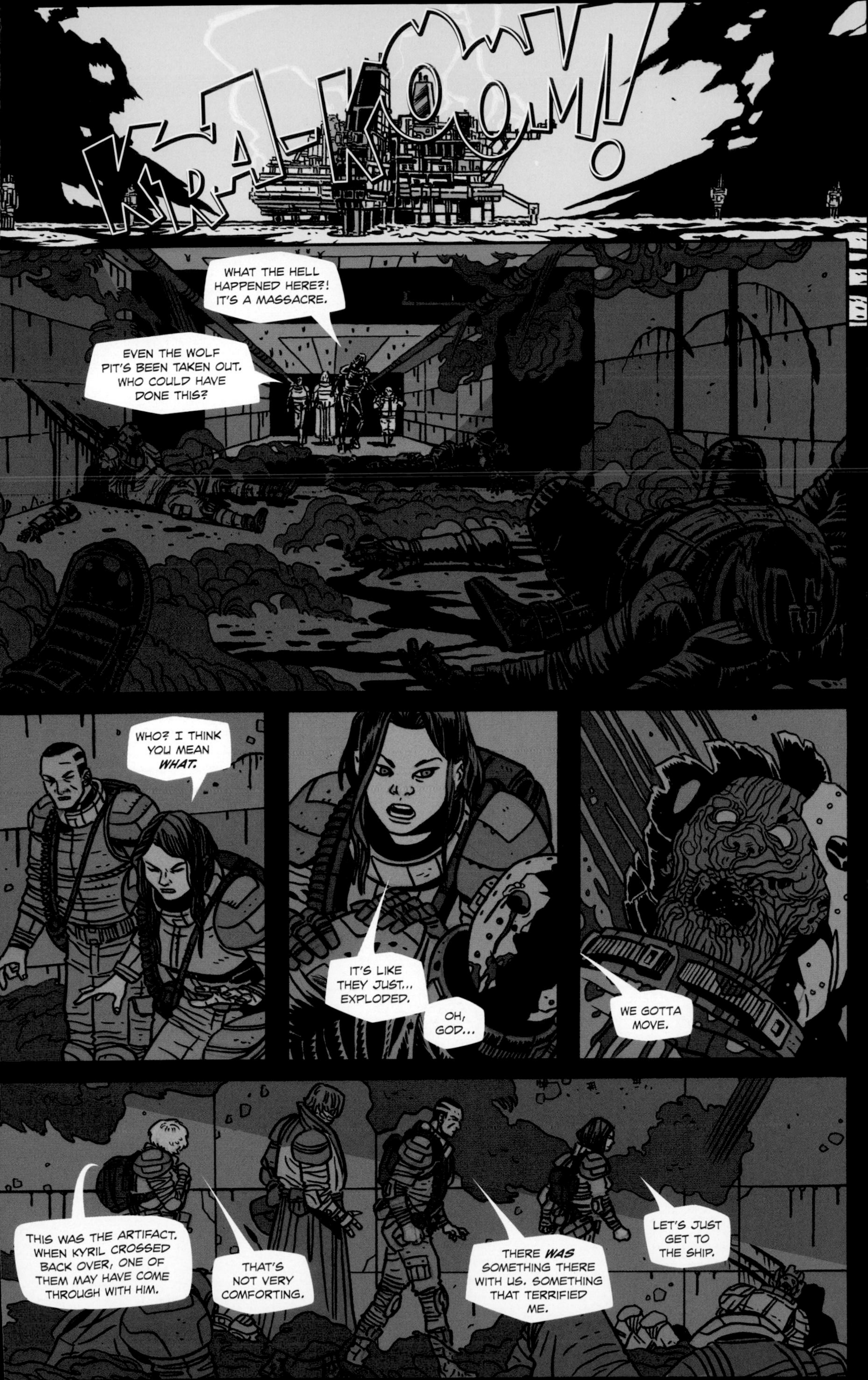
KRA-KOOM!
WHAT THE HELL HAPPENED HERE?! IT'S A MASSACRE.
EVEN THE WOLF PIT'S BEEN TAKEN OUT. WHO COULD HAVE DONE THIS?
WHO? I THINK YOU MEAN WHAT.
IT'S LIKE THEY JUST... EXPLODED.
OH, GOD...
WE GOTTA MOVE.
THIS WAS THE ARTIFACT. WHEN KYRIL CROSSED BACK OVER, ONE OF THEM MAY HAVE COME THROUGH WITH HIM.
THAT'S NOT VERY COMFORTING.
THERE WAS SOMETHING THERE WITH US. SOMETHING THAT TERRIFIED ME.
LET'S JUST GET TO THE SHIP.

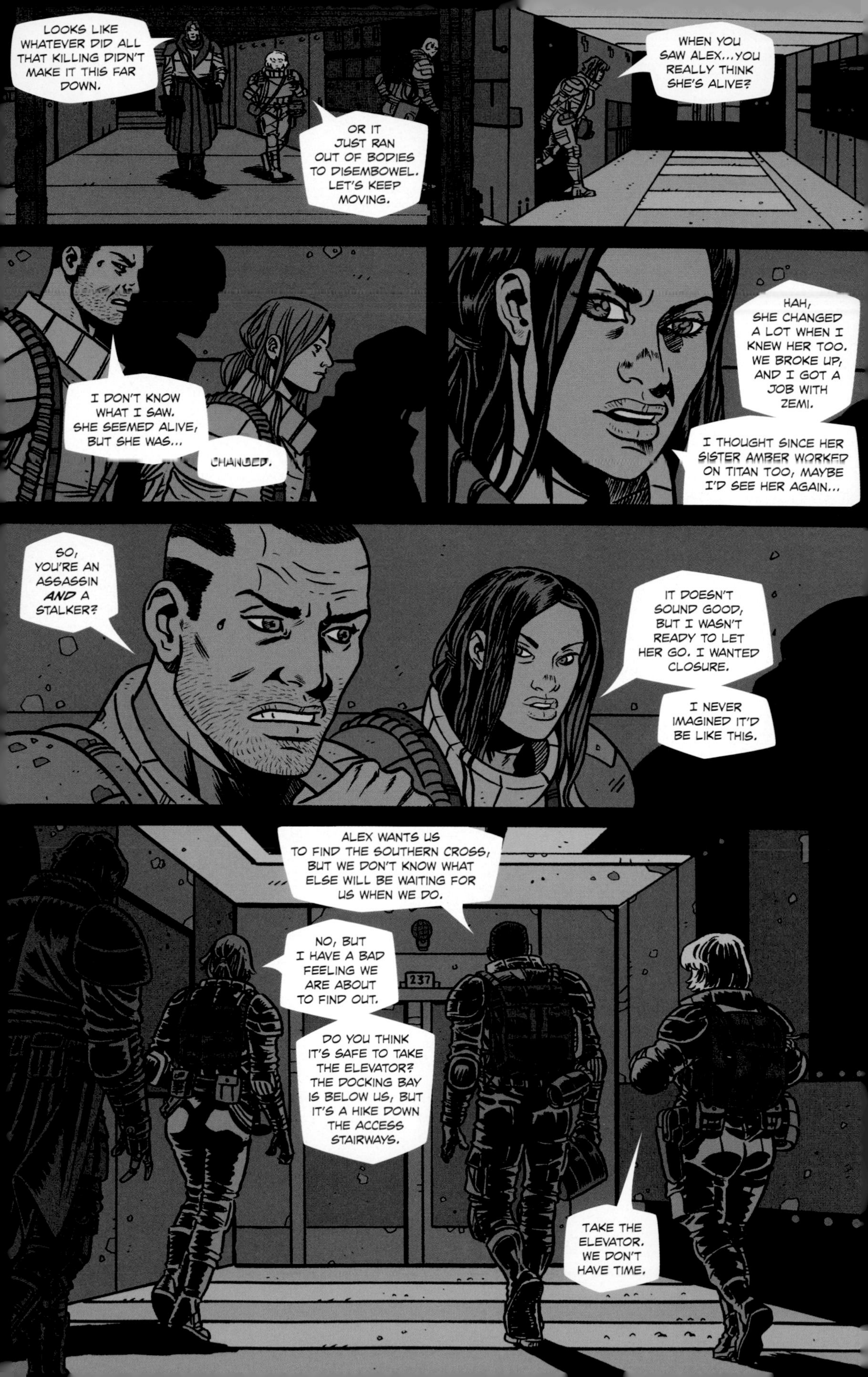
LOOKS LIKE WHATEVER DID ALL THAT KILLING DIDN'T MAKE IT THIS FAR DOWN.
OR IT JUST RAN OUT OF BODIES TO DISEMBOWEL. LET'S KEEP MOVING.
WHEN YOU SAW ALEX...YOU REALLY THINK SHE'S ALIVE?
I DON'T KNOW WHAT I SAW. SHE SEEMED ALIVE, BUT SHE WAS...
CHANGED.
HAH, SHE CHANGED A LOT WHEN I KNEW HER TOO. WE BROKE UP, AND I GOT A JOB WITH ZEMI.
I THOUGHT SINCE HER SISTER AMBER WORKED ON TITAN TOO, MAYBE I'D SEE HER AGAIN...
SO, YOU'RE AN ASSASSIN *AND* A STALKER?
IT DOESN'T SOUND GOOD, BUT I WASN'T READY TO LET HER GO. I WANTED CLOSURE.
I NEVER IMAGINED IT'D BE LIKE THIS.
ALEX WANTS US TO FIND THE SOUTHERN CROSS, BUT WE DON'T KNOW WHAT ELSE WILL BE WAITING FOR US WHEN WE DO.
NO, BUT I HAVE A BAD FEELING WE ARE ABOUT TO FIND OUT.
237
DO YOU THINK IT'S SAFE TO TAKE THE ELEVATOR? THE DOCKING BAY IS BELOW US, BUT IT'S A HIKE DOWN THE ACCESS STAIRWAYS.
TAKE THE ELEVATOR. WE DON'T HAVE TIME.

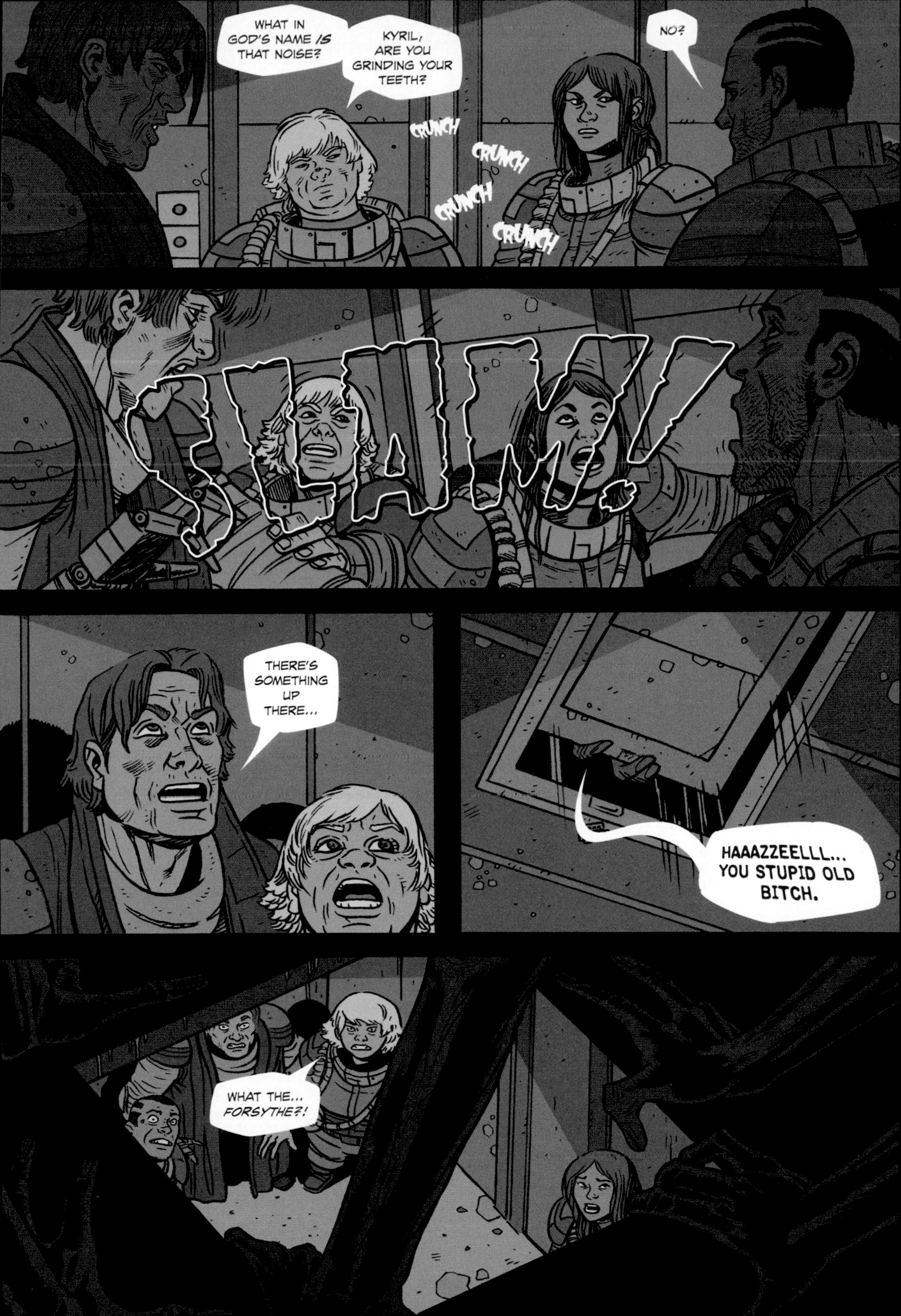
WHAT IN GOD'S NAME *IS* THAT NOISE?
KYRIL, ARE YOU GRINDING YOUR TEETH?
NO?
CRUNCH
CRUNCH
CRUNCH
CRUNCH
SLAM!
THERE'S SOMETHING UP THERE...
HAAAZZEELLL... YOU STUPID OLD BITCH.
WHAT THE... *FORSYTHE?!*

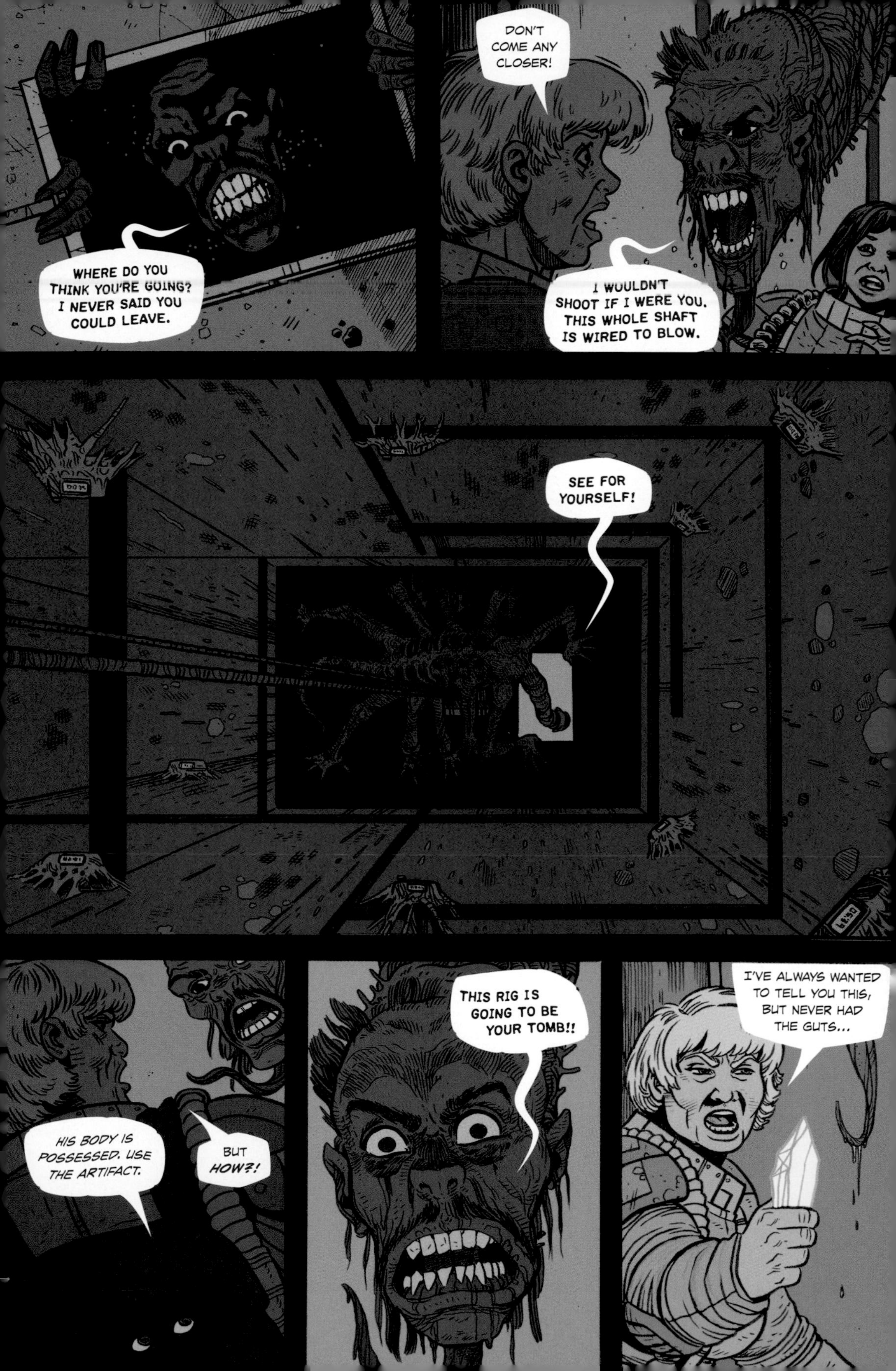
WHERE DO YOU THINK YOU'RE GOING? I NEVER SAID YOU COULD LEAVE.
DON'T COME ANY CLOSER!
I WOULDN'T SHOOT IF I WERE YOU. THIS WHOLE SHAFT IS WIRED TO BLOW.
SEE FOR YOURSELF!
HIS BODY IS POSSESSED. USE THE ARTIFACT.
BUT HOW?!
THIS RIG IS GOING TO BE YOUR TOMB!!
I'VE ALWAYS WANTED TO TELL YOU THIS, BUT NEVER HAD THE GUTS...

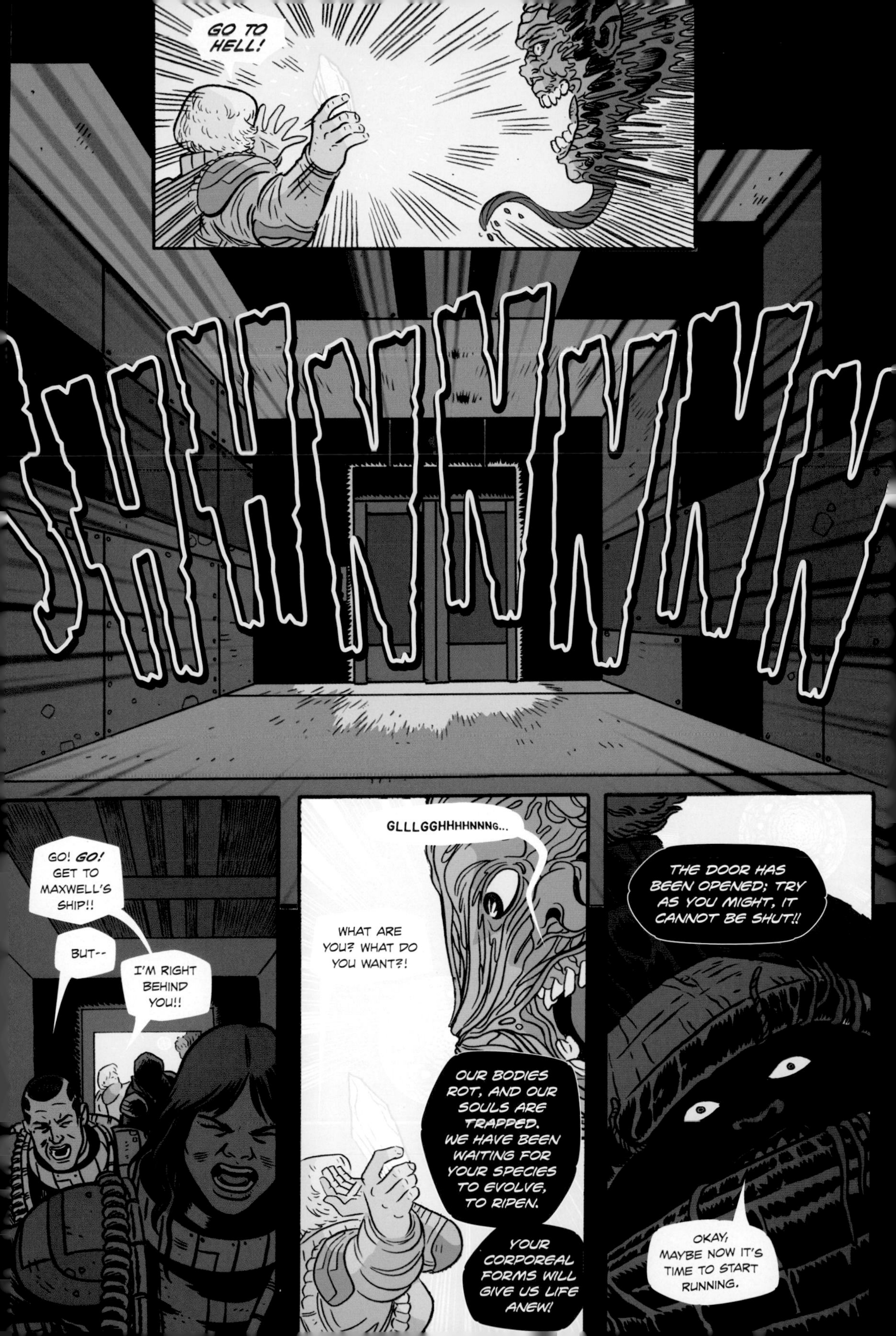

GO TO HELL!
SHHNNWNNK
GO! GO! GET TO MAXWELL'S SHIP!!
BUT--
I'M RIGHT BEHIND YOU!!
GLLLGGHHHHNNNG...
WHAT ARE YOU? WHAT DO YOU WANT?!
OUR BODIES ROT, AND OUR SOULS ARE TRAPPED. WE HAVE BEEN WAITING FOR YOUR SPECIES TO EVOLVE, TO RIPEN.
YOUR CORPOREAL FORMS WILL GIVE US LIFE ANEW!
THE DOOR HAS BEEN OPENED; TRY AS YOU MIGHT, IT CANNOT BE SHUT!!
OKAY; MAYBE NOW IT'S TIME TO START RUNNING.

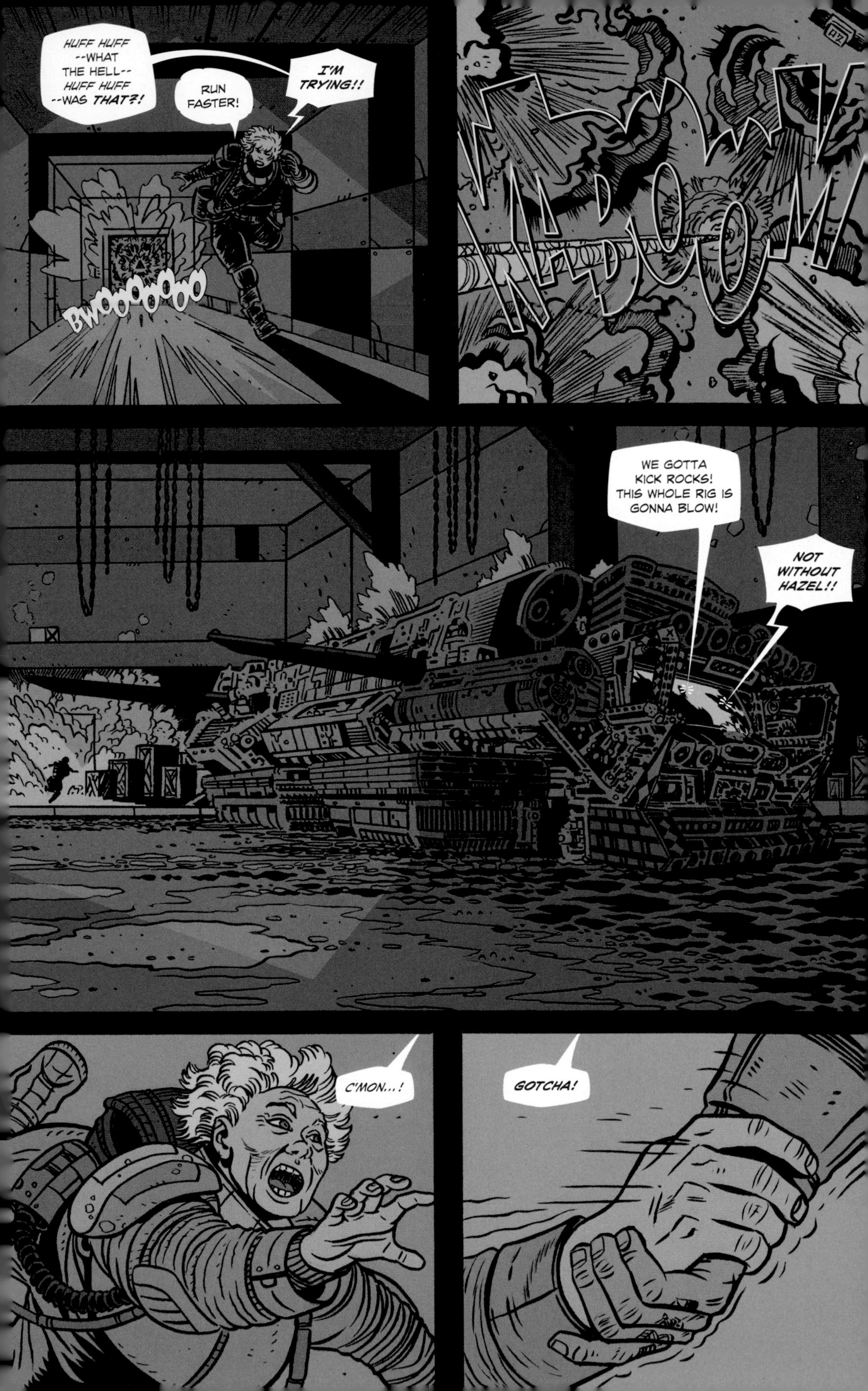
HUFF HUFF --WHAT THE HELL-- HUFF HUFF --WAS THAT?!
RUN FASTER!
I'M TRYING!!
BWOOOOOOO
WE GOTTA KICK ROCKS! THIS WHOLE RIG IS GONNA BLOW!
NOT WITHOUT HAZEL!!
C'MON...!
GOTCHA!

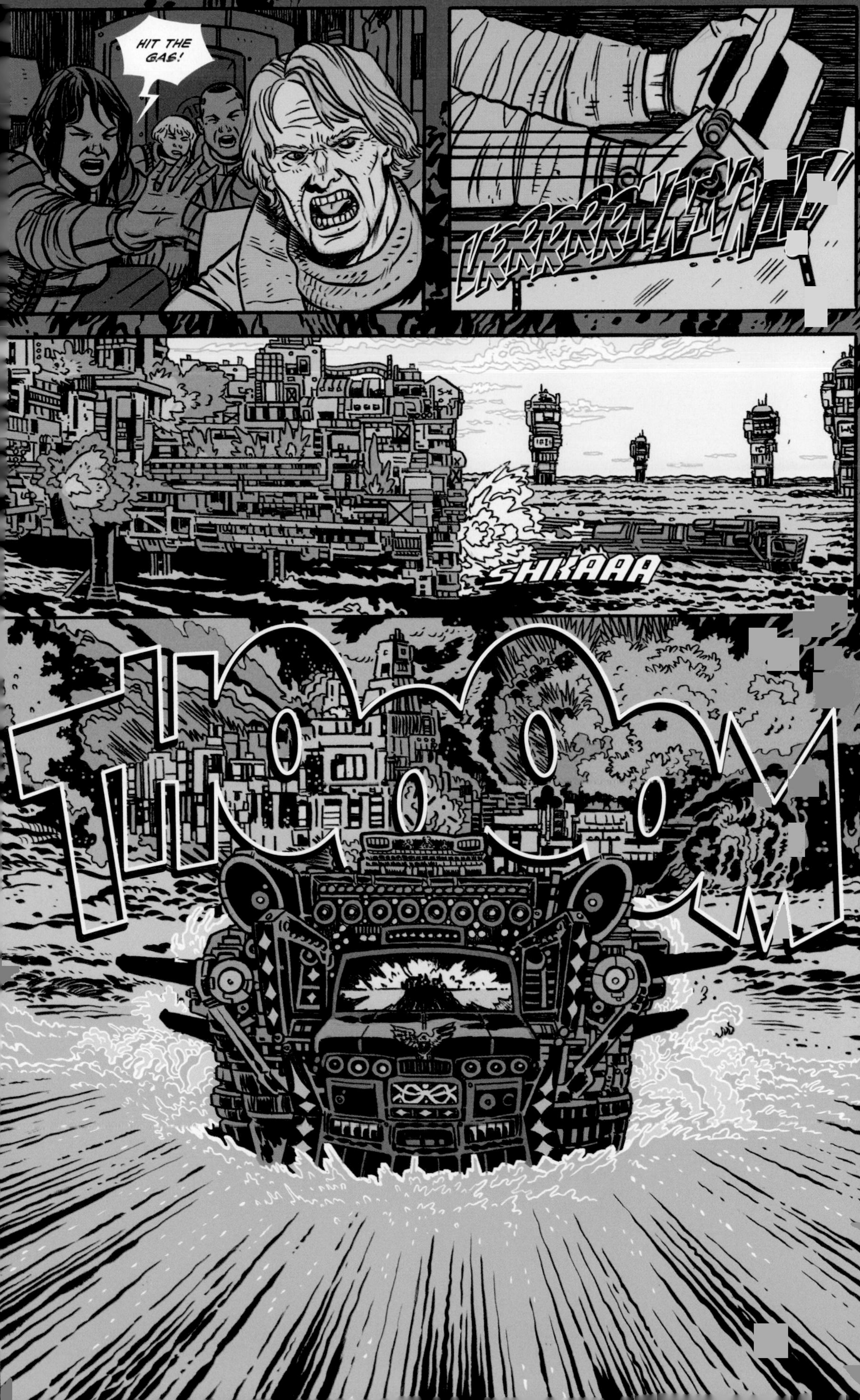
HIT THE GAS!
UKRRRRRRNNNNNNN!
SHKAAA
THOOOOOM

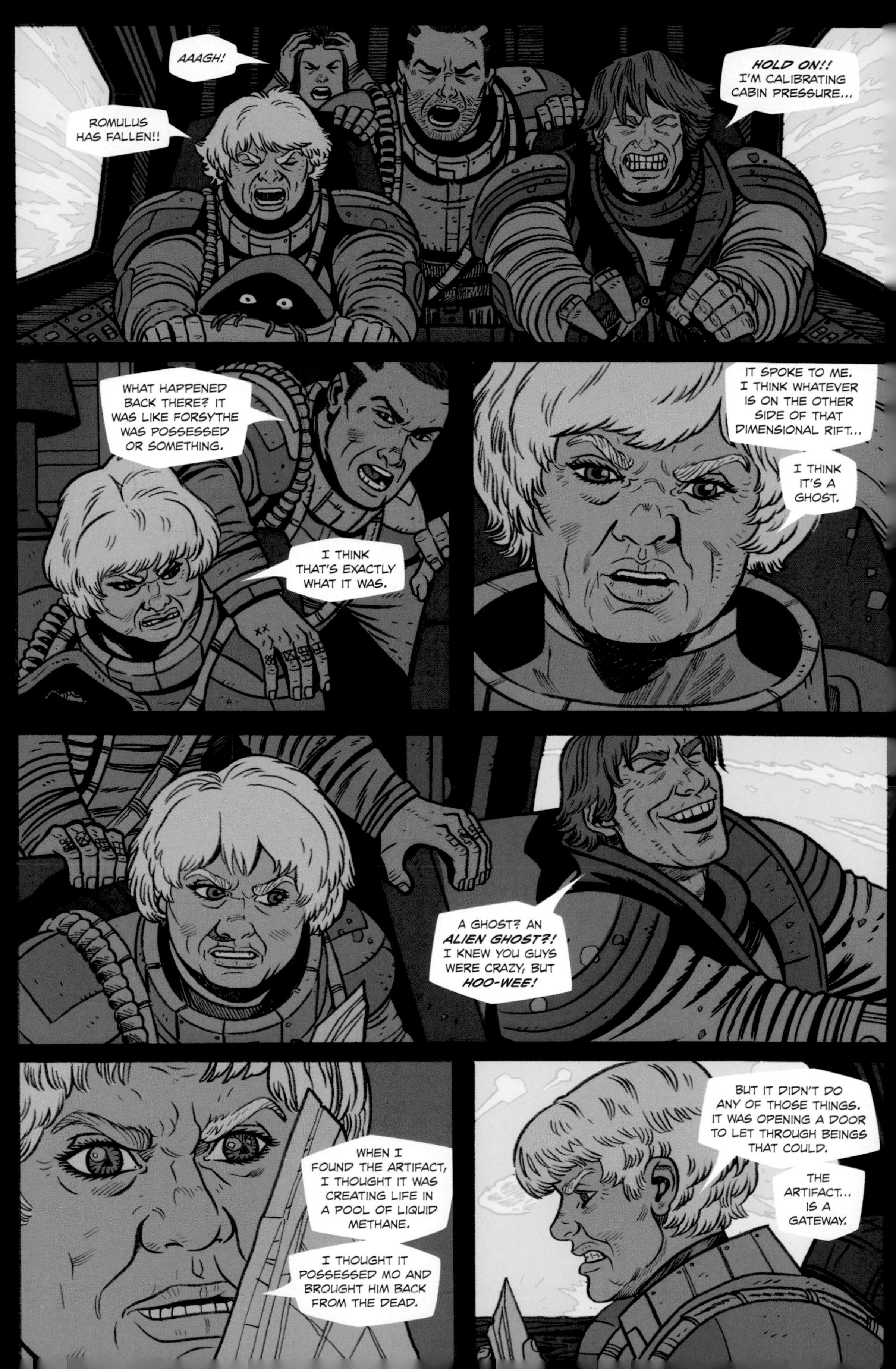
AAAGH!
ROMULUS HAS FALLEN!!
HOLD ON!! I'M CALIBRATING CABIN PRESSURE...
WHAT HAPPENED BACK THERE? IT WAS LIKE FORSYTHE WAS POSSESSED OR SOMETHING.
I THINK THAT'S EXACTLY WHAT IT WAS.
IT SPOKE TO ME. I THINK WHATEVER IS ON THE OTHER SIDE OF THAT DIMENSIONAL RIFT...
I THINK IT'S A GHOST.
A GHOST? AN ALIEN GHOST?! I KNEW YOU GUYS WERE CRAZY, BUT HOO-WEE!
WHEN I FOUND THE ARTIFACT, I THOUGHT IT WAS CREATING LIFE IN A POOL OF LIQUID METHANE.
I THOUGHT IT POSSESSED MO AND BROUGHT HIM BACK FROM THE DEAD.
BUT IT DIDN'T DO ANY OF THOSE THINGS. IT WAS OPENING A DOOR TO LET THROUGH BEINGS THAT COULD.
THE ARTIFACT... IS A GATEWAY.

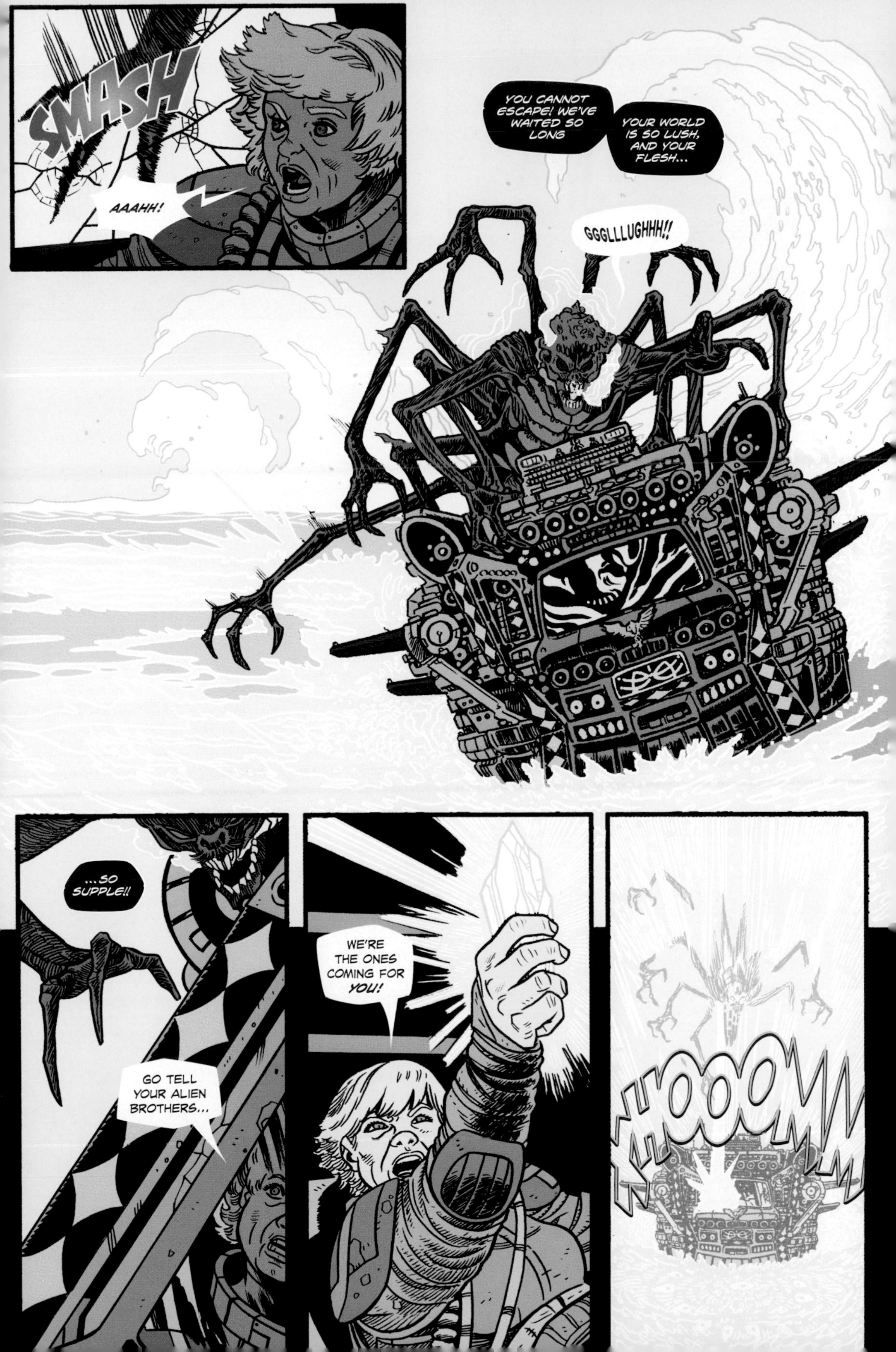
SMASH
AAAHH!
YOU CANNOT ESCAPE! WE'VE WAITED SO LONG
YOUR WORLD IS SO LUSH, AND YOUR FLESH...
GGGLLLUGHHH!!
...SO SUPPLE!!
GO TELL YOUR ALIEN BROTHERS...
WE'RE THE ONES COMING FOR YOU!
KHOOOMM

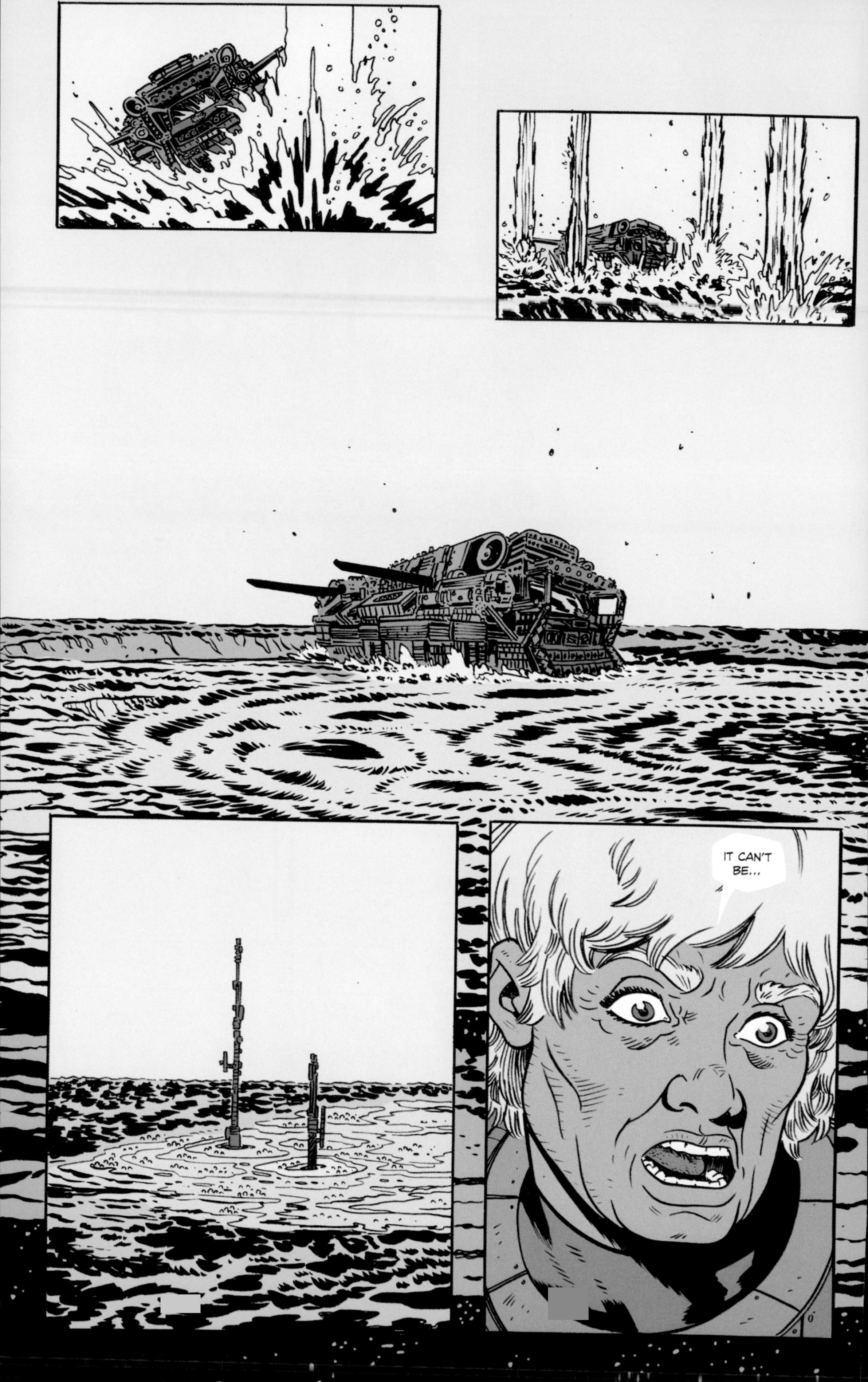
IT CAN'T BE...

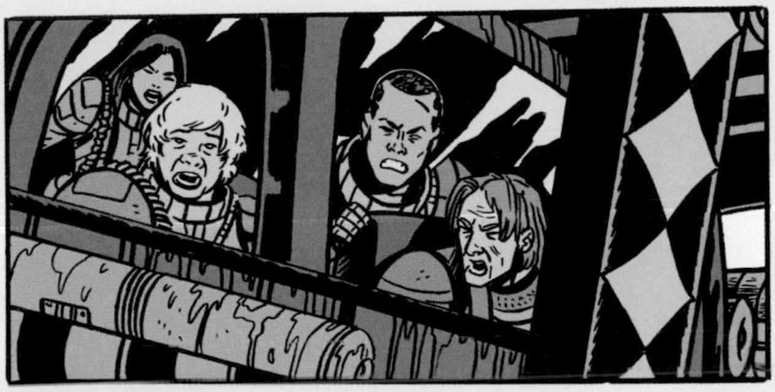

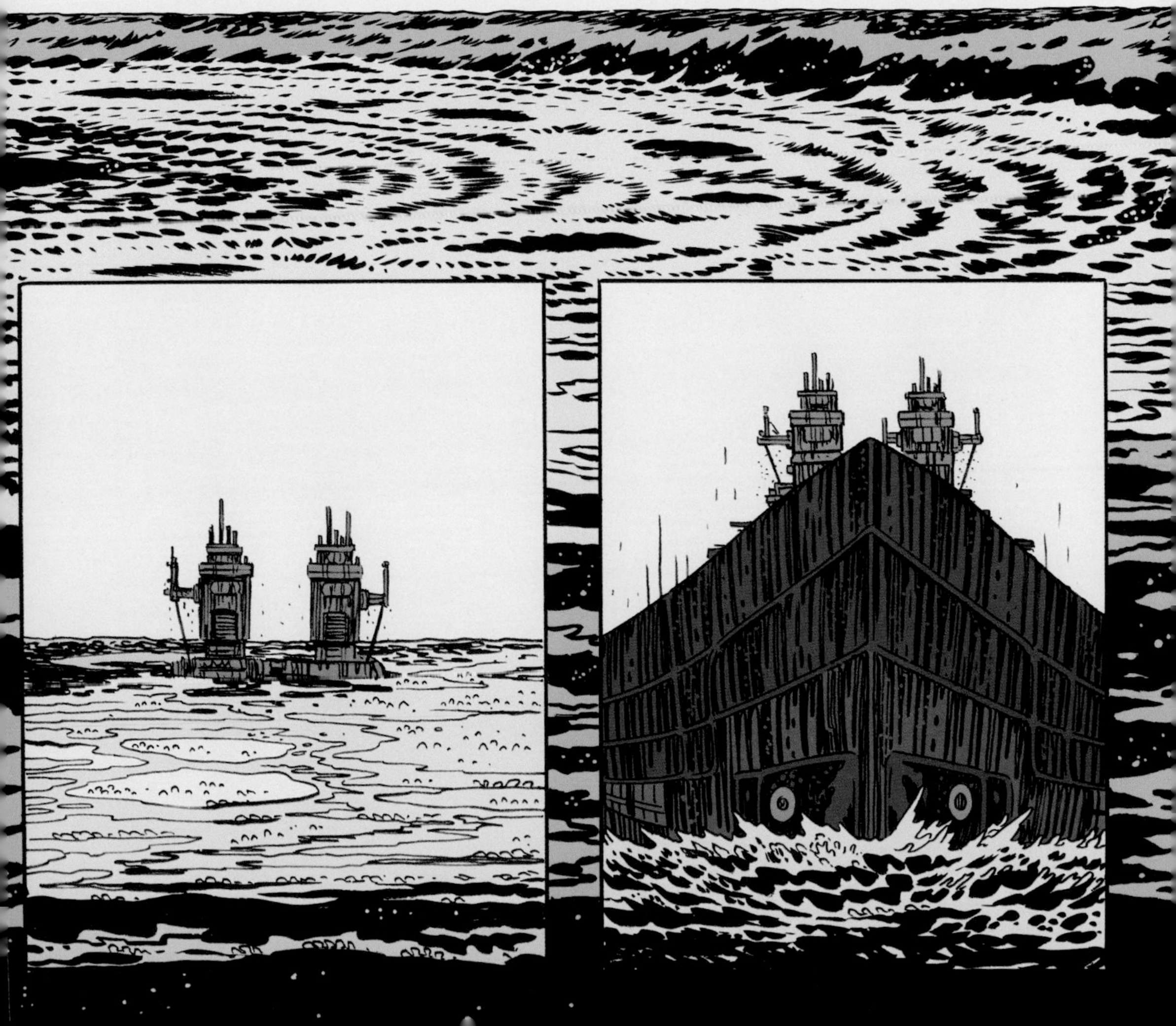

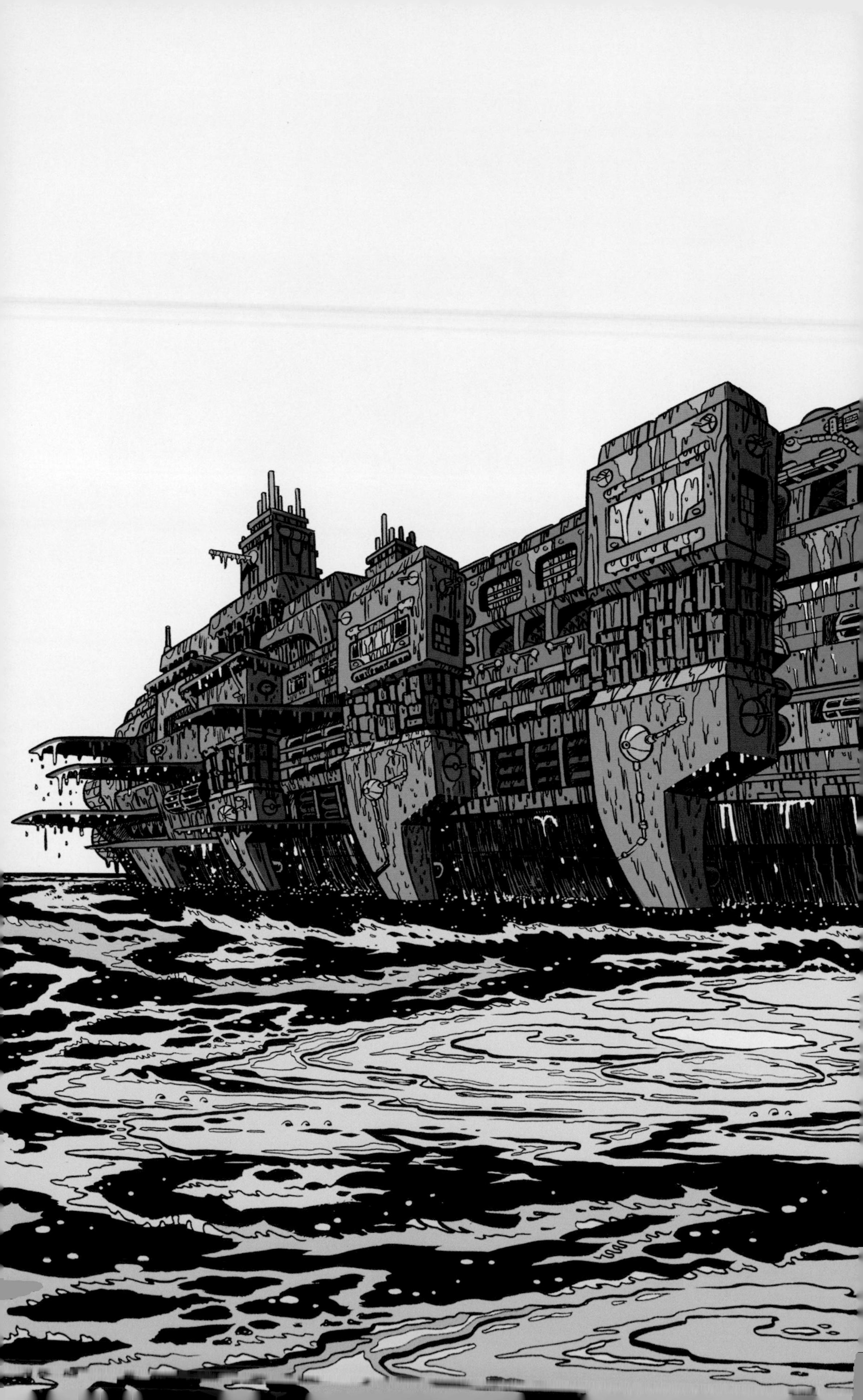

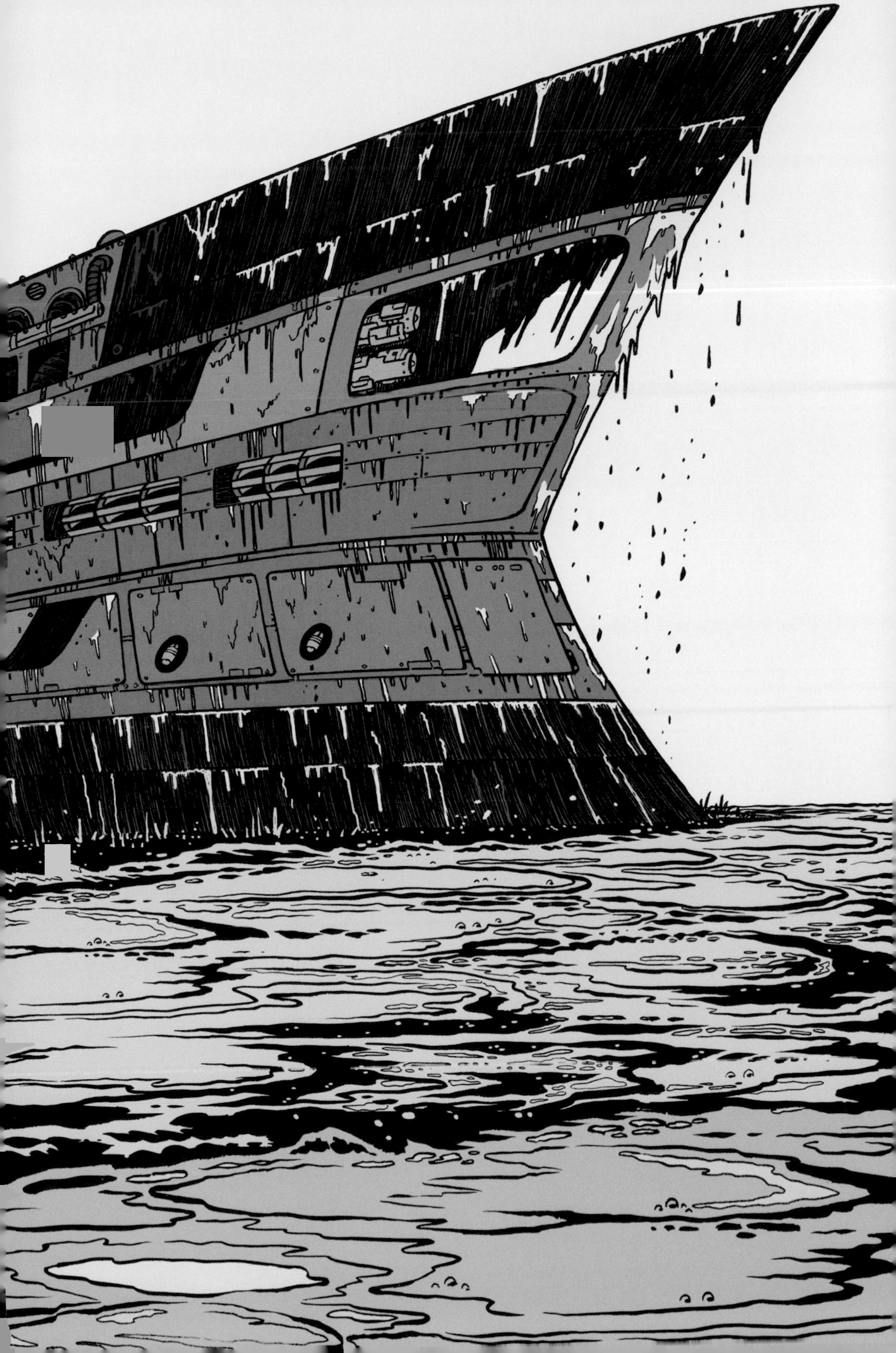

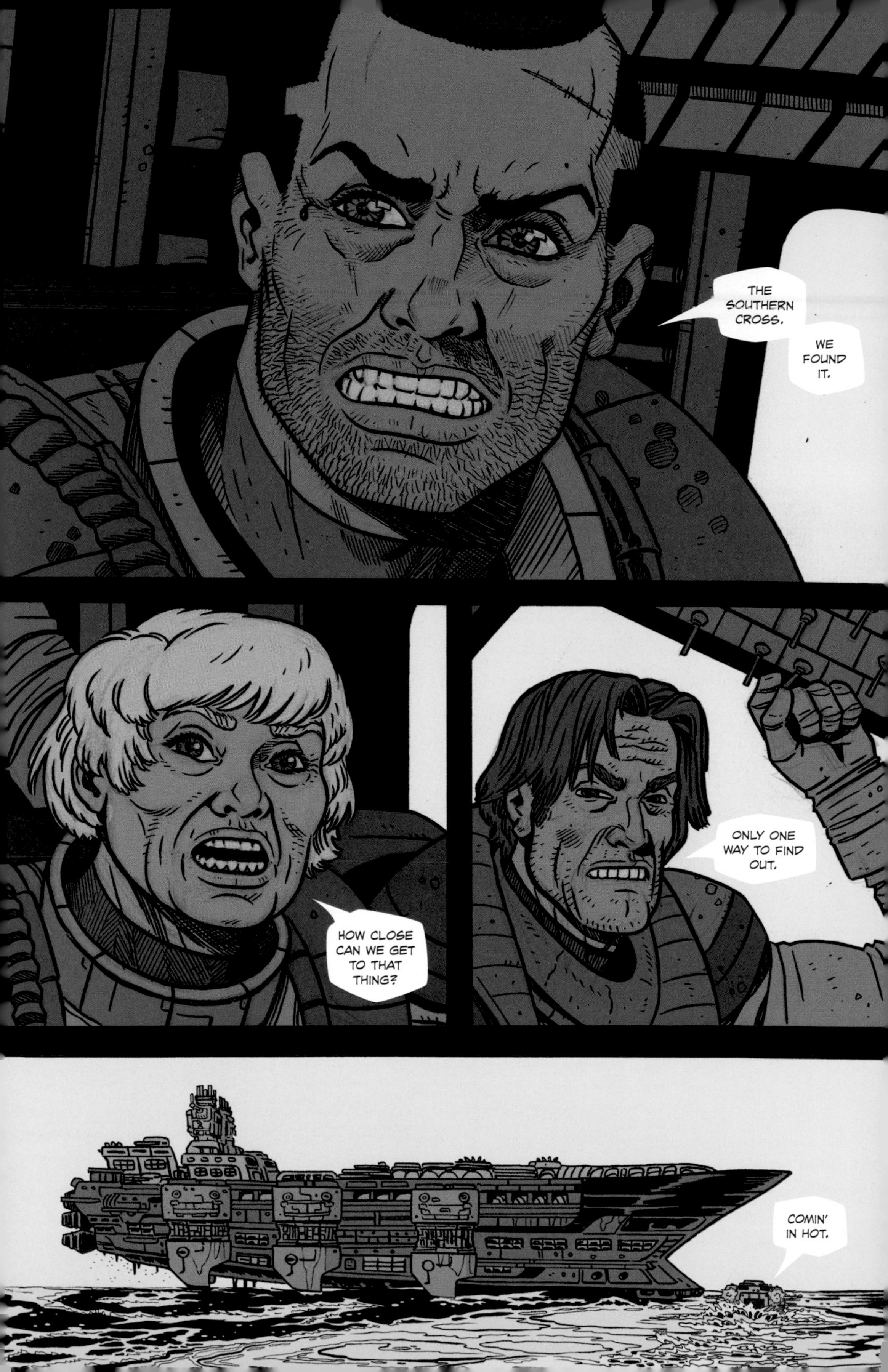
THE SOUTHERN CROSS.
WE FOUND IT.
HOW CLOSE CAN WE GET TO THAT THING?
ONLY ONE WAY TO FIND OUT.
COMIN' IN HOT.

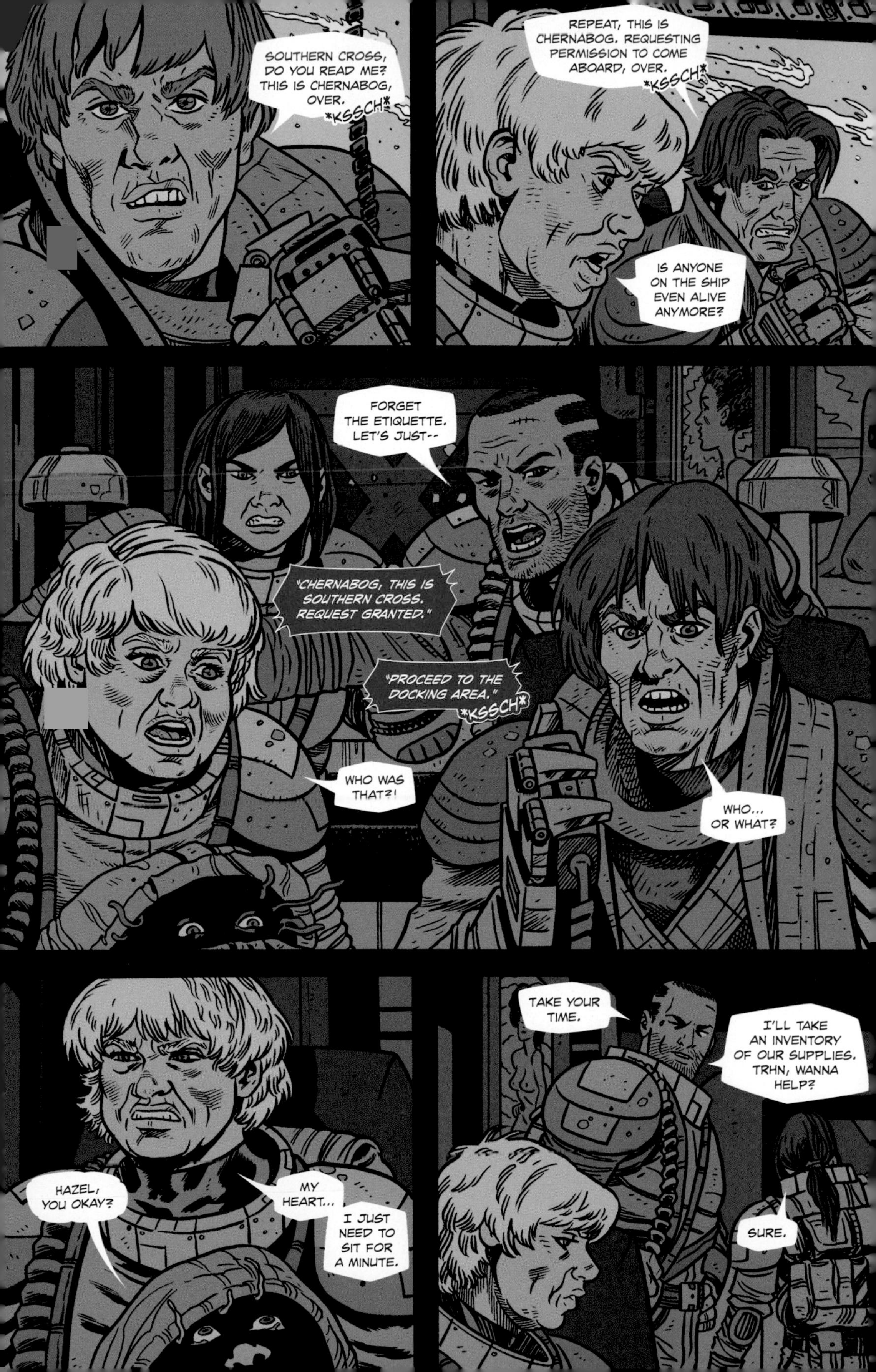
SOUTHERN CROSS, DO YOU READ ME? THIS IS CHERNABOG, OVER.
*KSSCH*
REPEAT, THIS IS CHERNABOG. REQUESTING PERMISSION TO COME ABOARD, OVER.
*KSSCH*
IS ANYONE ON THE SHIP EVEN ALIVE ANYMORE?
FORGET THE ETIQUETTE. LET'S JUST--
"CHERNABOG, THIS IS SOUTHERN CROSS. REQUEST GRANTED."
"PROCEED TO THE DOCKING AREA."
*KSSCH*
WHO WAS THAT?!
WHO... OR WHAT?
HAZEL, YOU OKAY?
MY HEART...
I JUST NEED TO SIT FOR A MINUTE.
TAKE YOUR TIME.
I'LL TAKE AN INVENTORY OF OUR SUPPLIES. TRHN, WANNA HELP?
SURE.

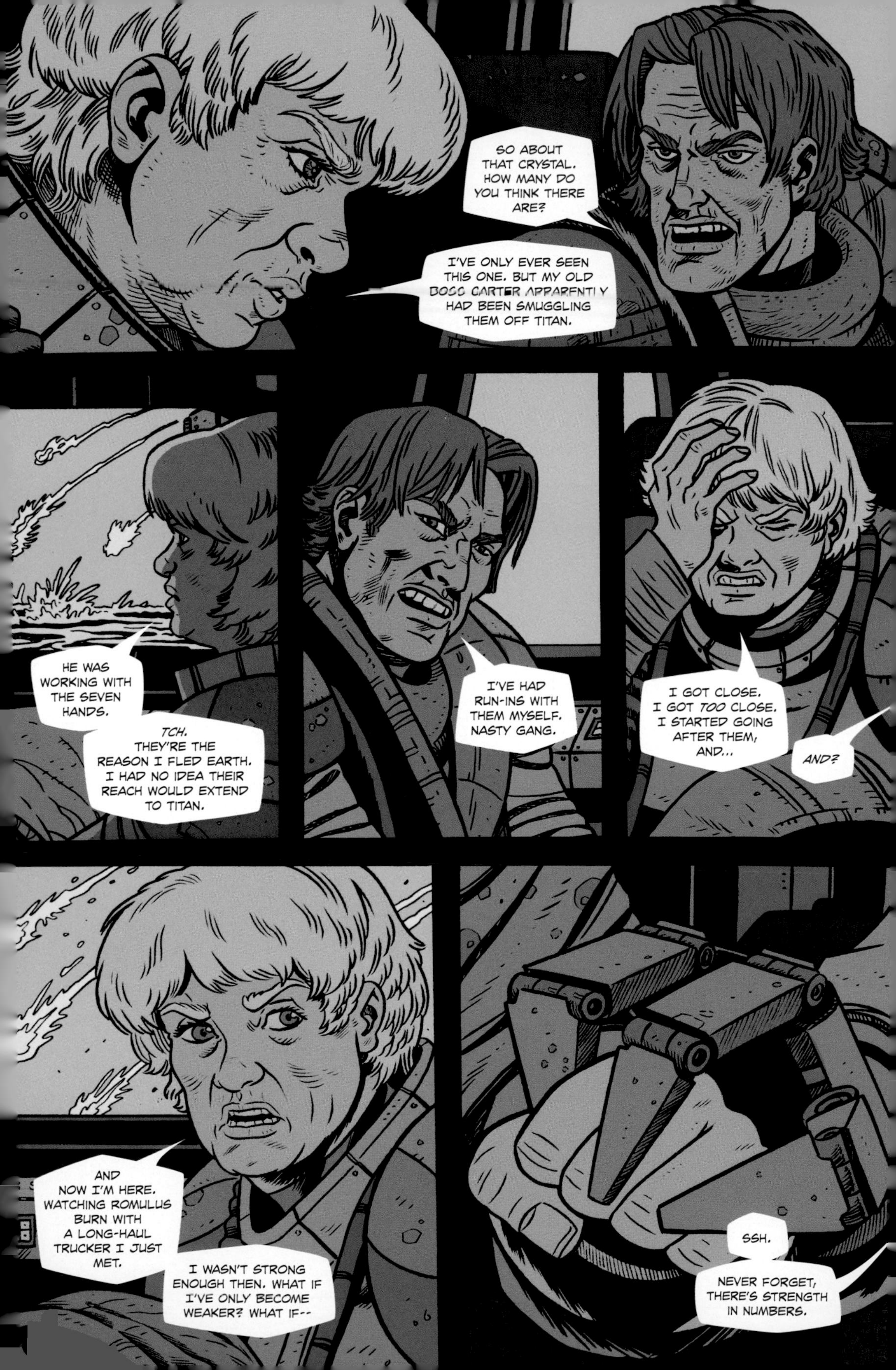
SO ABOUT THAT CRYSTAL. HOW MANY DO YOU THINK THERE ARE?
I'VE ONLY EVER SEEN THIS ONE. BUT MY OLD BOSS CARTER APPARENTLY HAD BEEN SMUGGLING THEM OFF TITAN.
HE WAS WORKING WITH THE SEVEN HANDS.
TCH. THEY'RE THE REASON I FLED EARTH. I HAD NO IDEA THEIR REACH WOULD EXTEND TO TITAN.
I'VE HAD RUN-INS WITH THEM MYSELF. NASTY GANG.
I GOT CLOSE. I GOT TOO CLOSE. I STARTED GOING AFTER THEM, AND...
AND?
AND NOW I'M HERE. WATCHING ROMULUS BURN WITH A LONG-HAUL TRUCKER I JUST MET.
I WASN'T STRONG ENOUGH THEN. WHAT IF I'VE ONLY BECOME WEAKER? WHAT IF--
SSH.
NEVER FORGET, THERE'S STRENGTH IN NUMBERS.

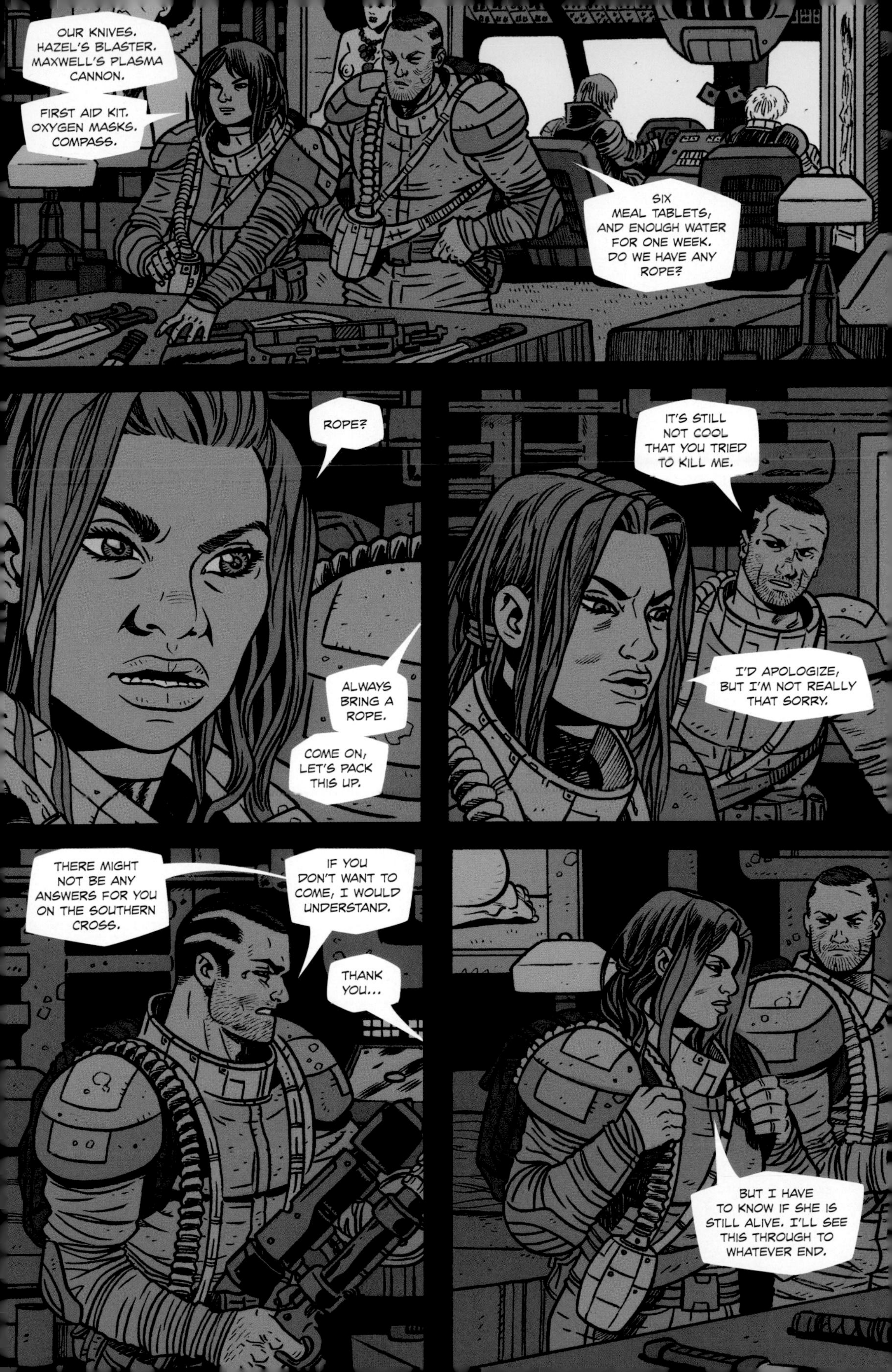
OUR KNIVES. HAZEL'S BLASTER. MAXWELL'S PLASMA CANNON.
FIRST AID KIT. OXYGEN MASKS. COMPASS.
SIX MEAL TABLETS, AND ENOUGH WATER FOR ONE WEEK. DO WE HAVE ANY ROPE?
ROPE?
ALWAYS BRING A ROPE.
COME ON, LET'S PACK THIS UP.
IT'S STILL NOT COOL THAT YOU TRIED TO KILL ME.
I'D APOLOGIZE, BUT I'M NOT REALLY THAT SORRY.
THERE MIGHT NOT BE ANY ANSWERS FOR YOU ON THE SOUTHERN CROSS.
IF YOU DON'T WANT TO COME, I WOULD UNDERSTAND.
THANK YOU...
BUT I HAVE TO KNOW IF SHE IS STILL ALIVE. I'LL SEE THIS THROUGH TO WHATEVER END.

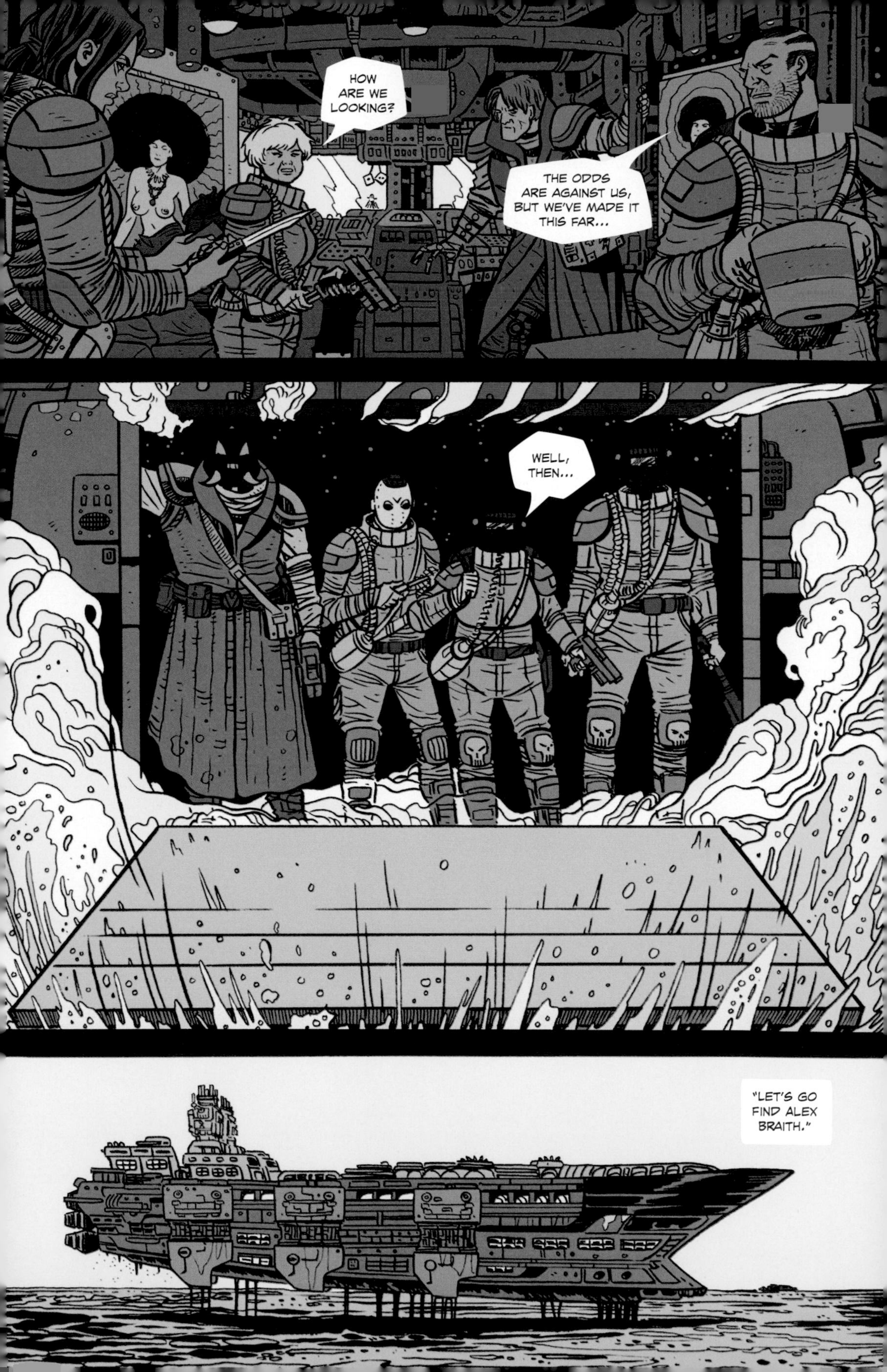
HOW ARE WE LOOKING?
THE ODDS ARE AGAINST US, BUT WE'VE MADE IT THIS FAR...
WELL, THEN...
"LET'S GO FIND ALEX BRAITH."

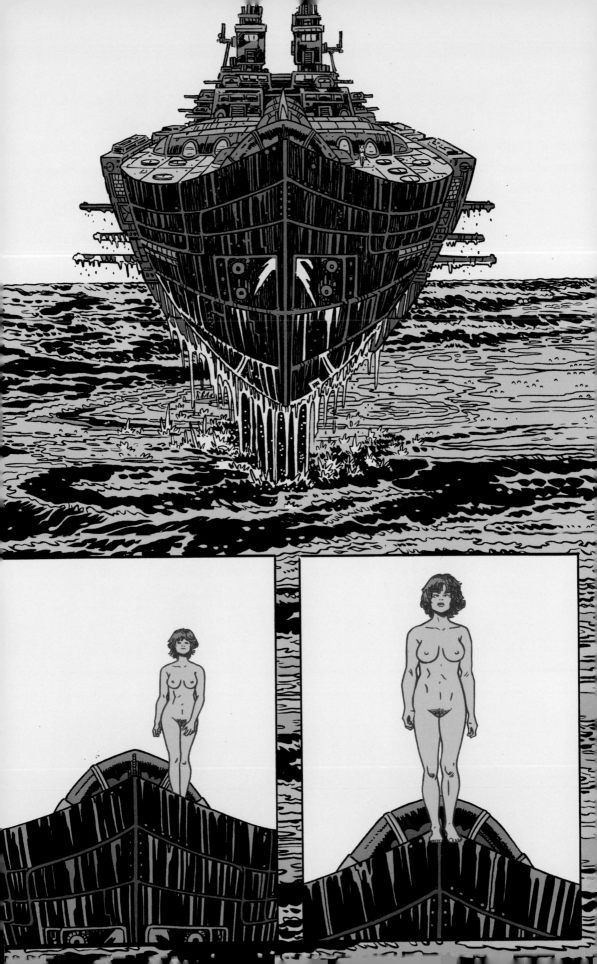

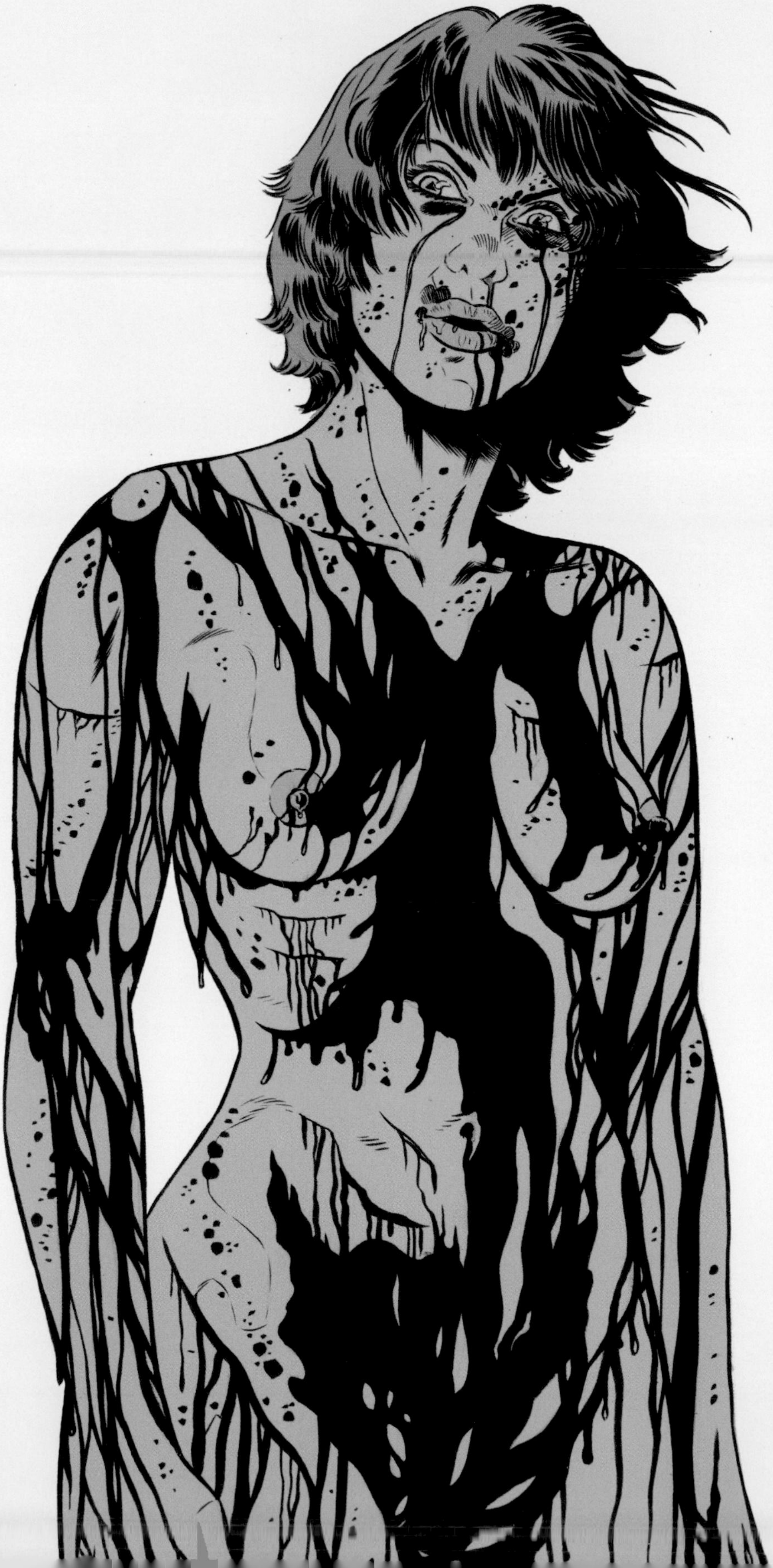

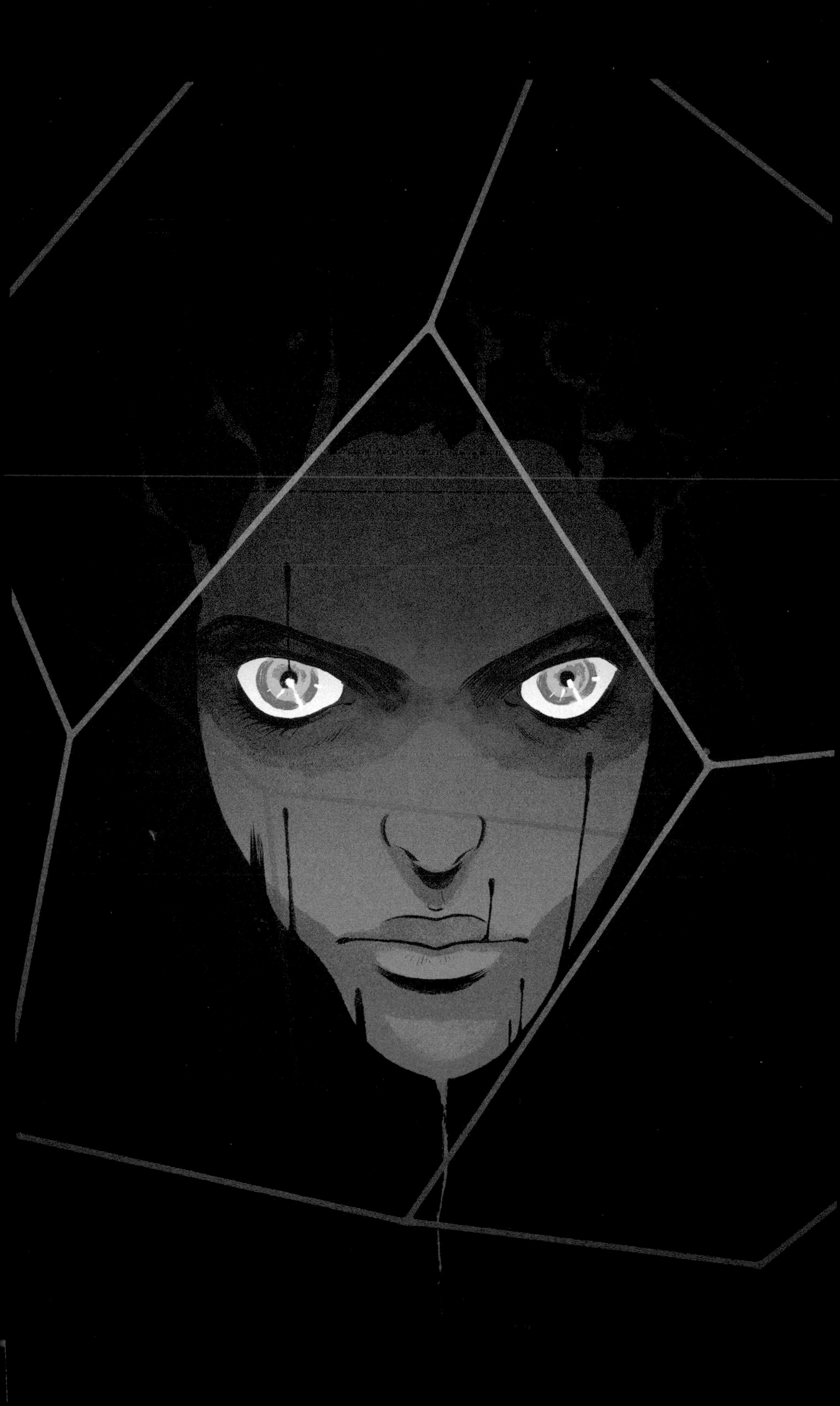

ISSUE 07 COVER | BECKY CLOONAN

ISSUE 08 COVER | BECKY CLOONAN

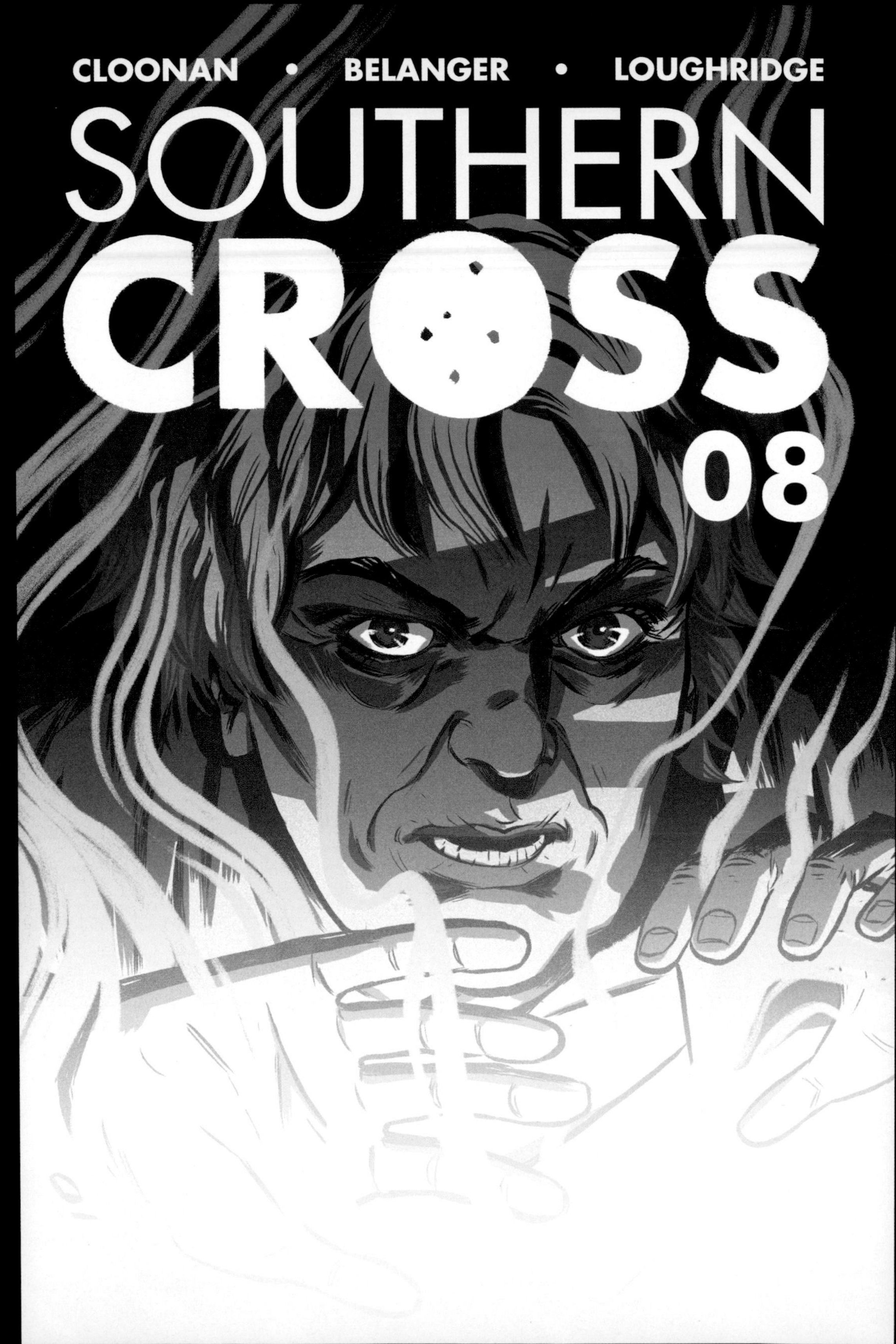
CLOONAN • BELANGER • LOUGHRIDGE
SOUTHERN
CROSS
08

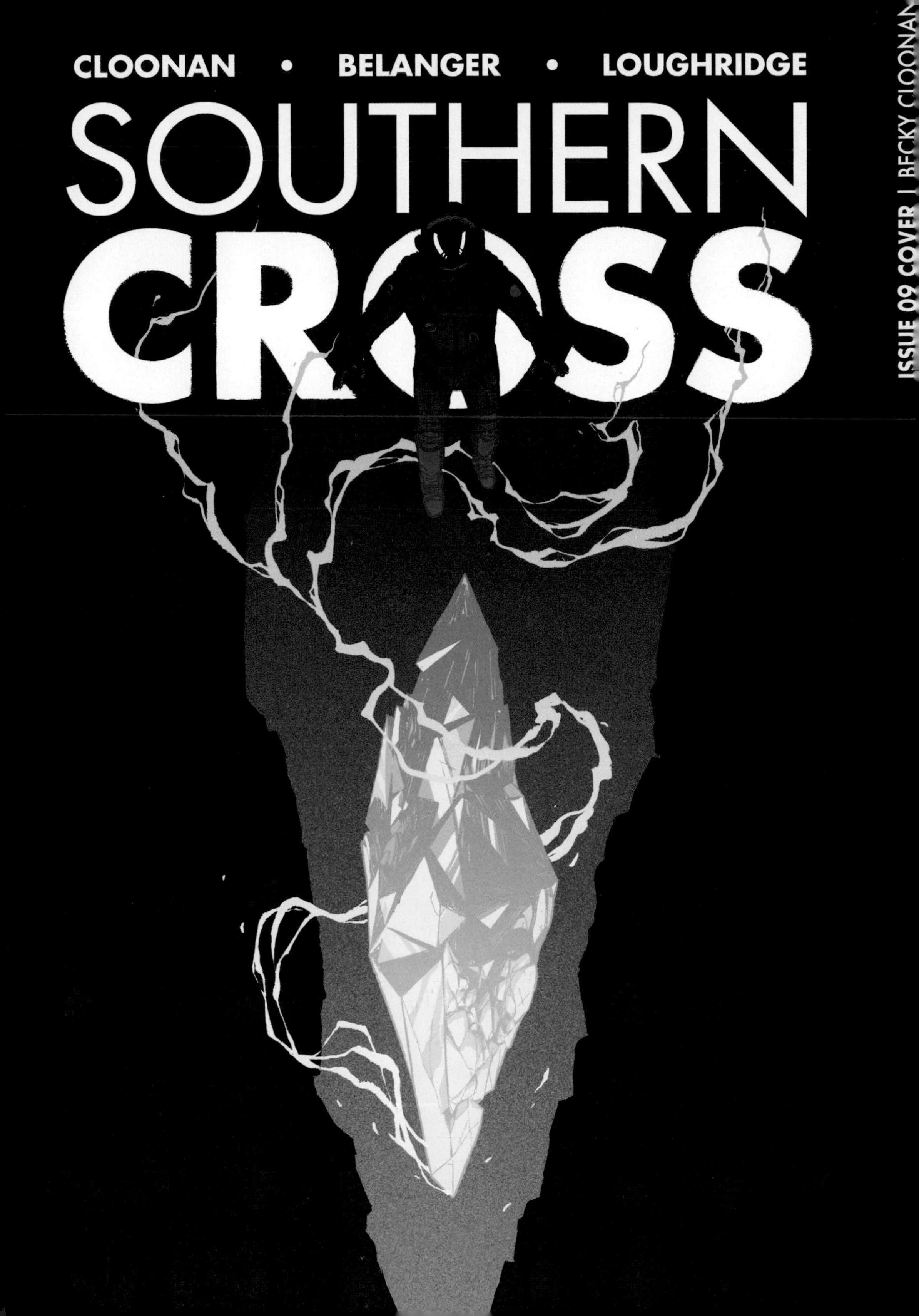
CLOONAN • BELANGER • LOUGHRIDGE
SOUTHERN
CROSS
ISSUE 09 COVER | BECKY CLOONAN

ISSUE 10 COVER | BECKY CLOONAN

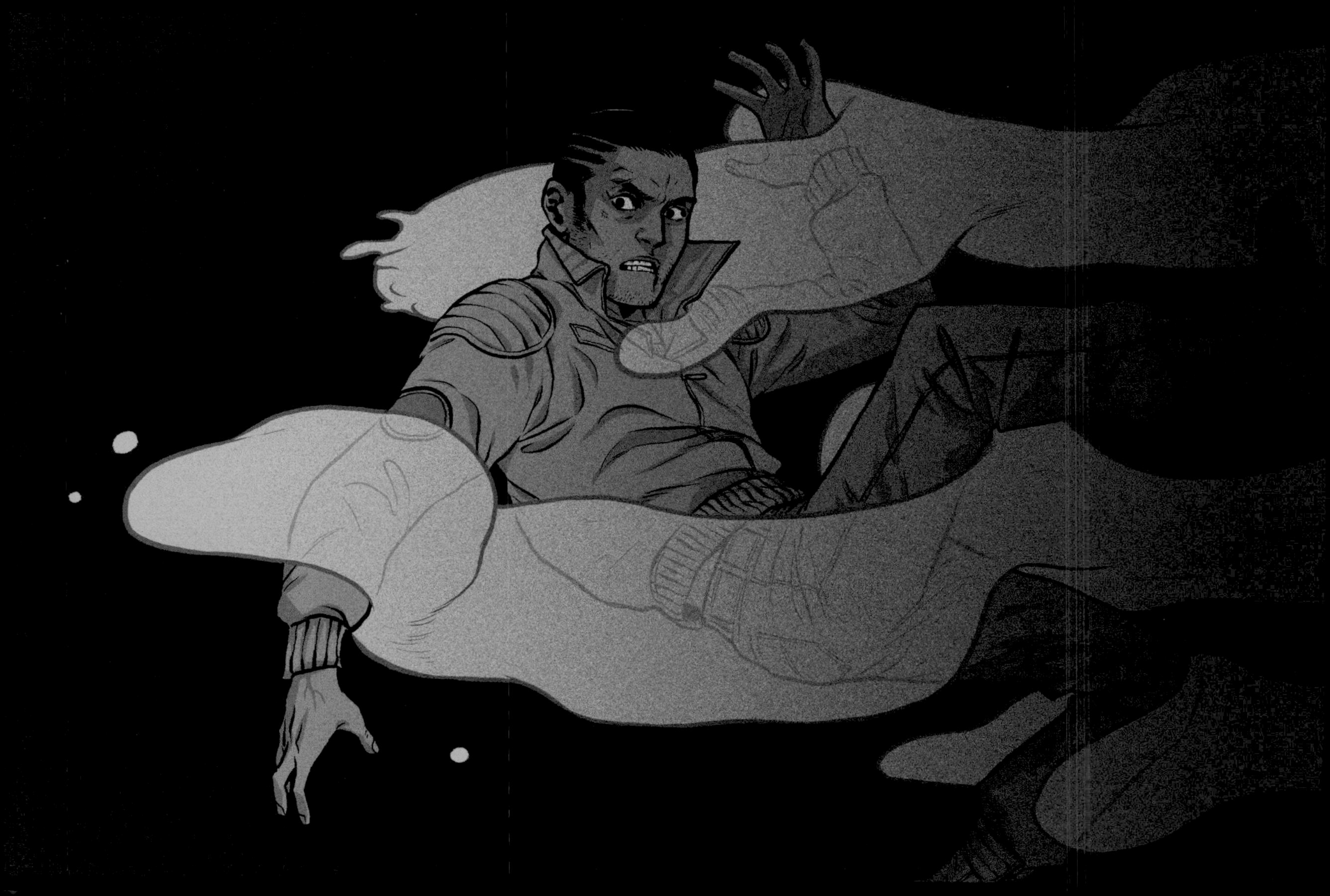

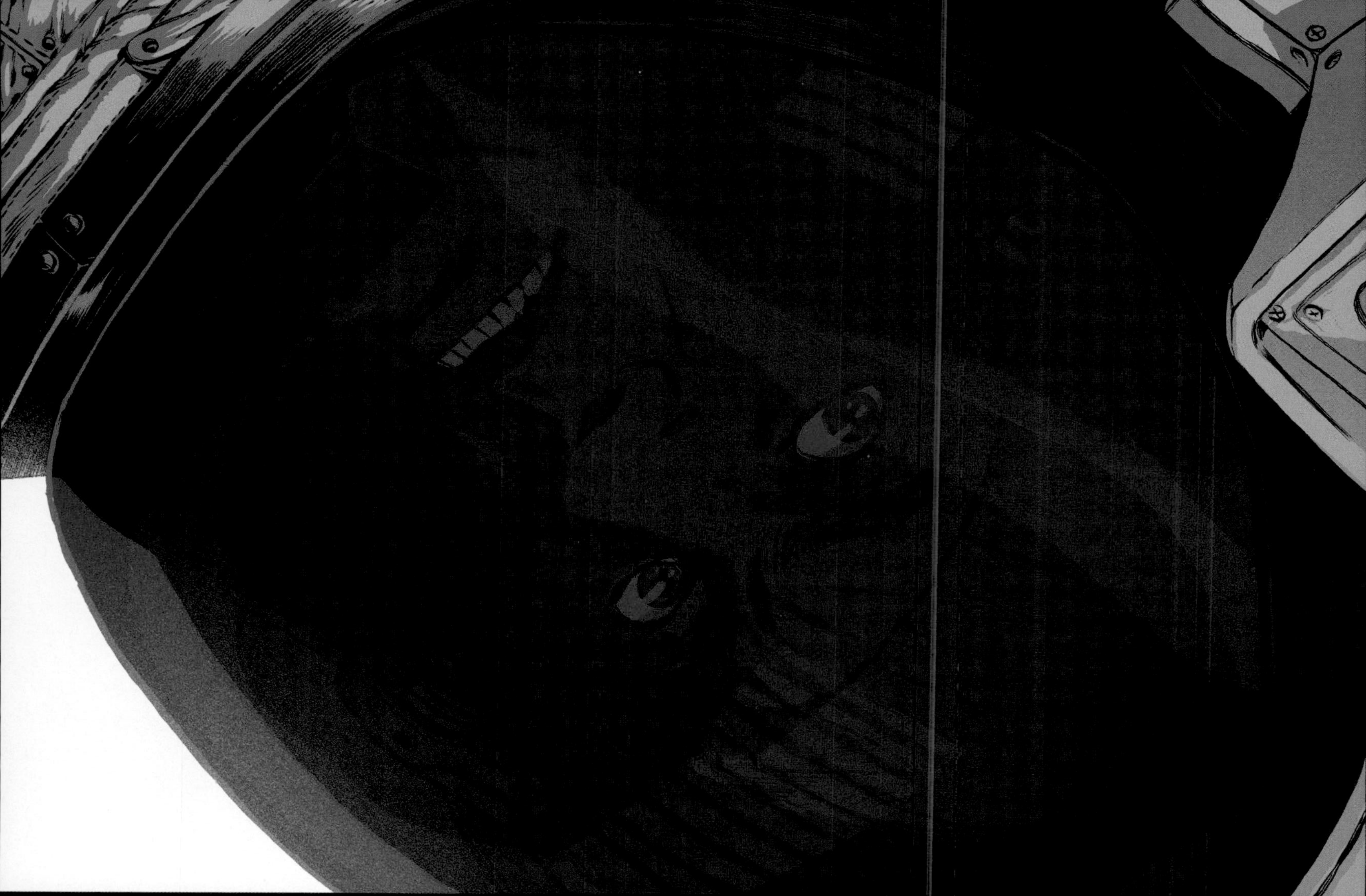

**ISSUE 11 COVER** | BECKY CLOONAN

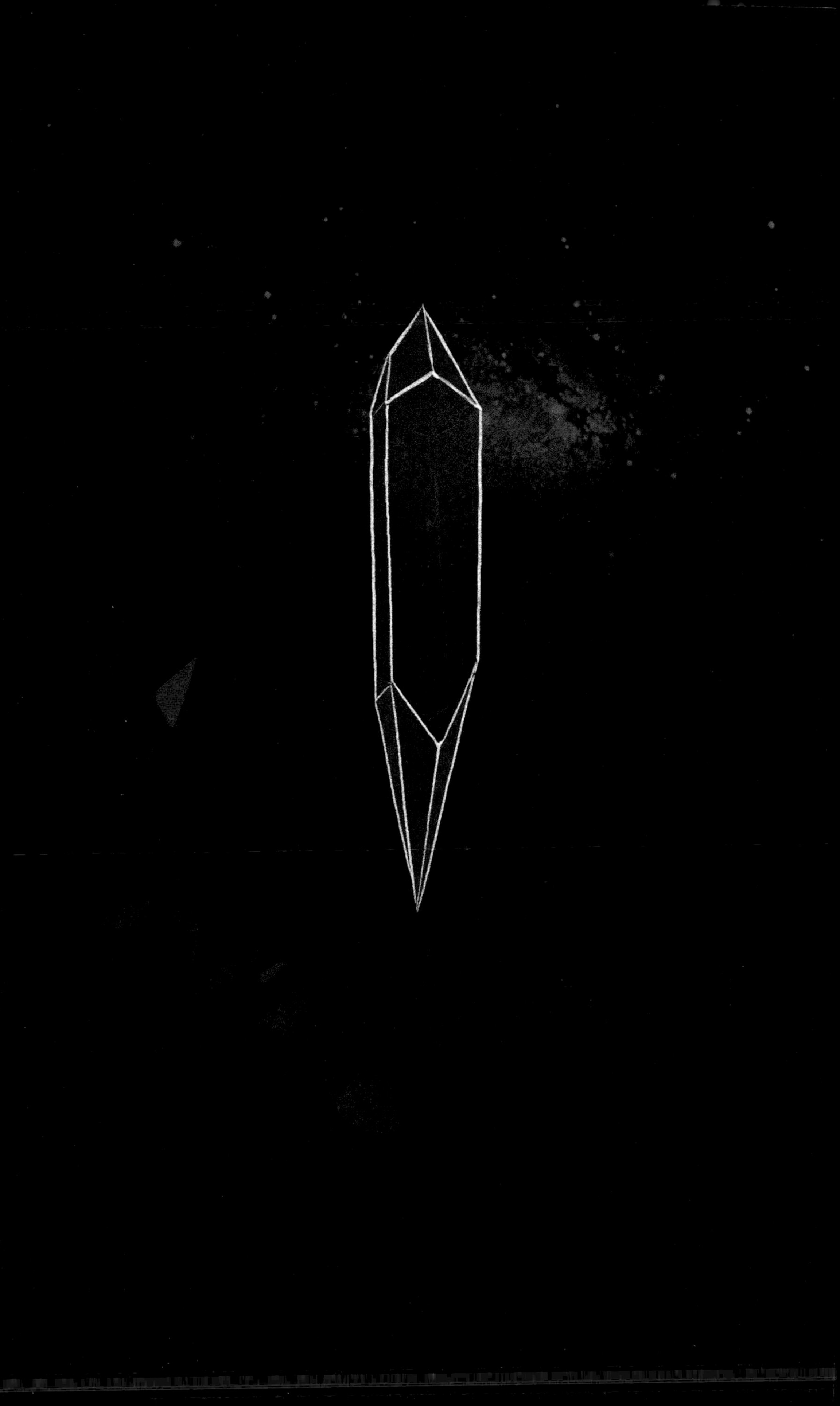

ISSUE 12 COVER | BECKY CLOONAN

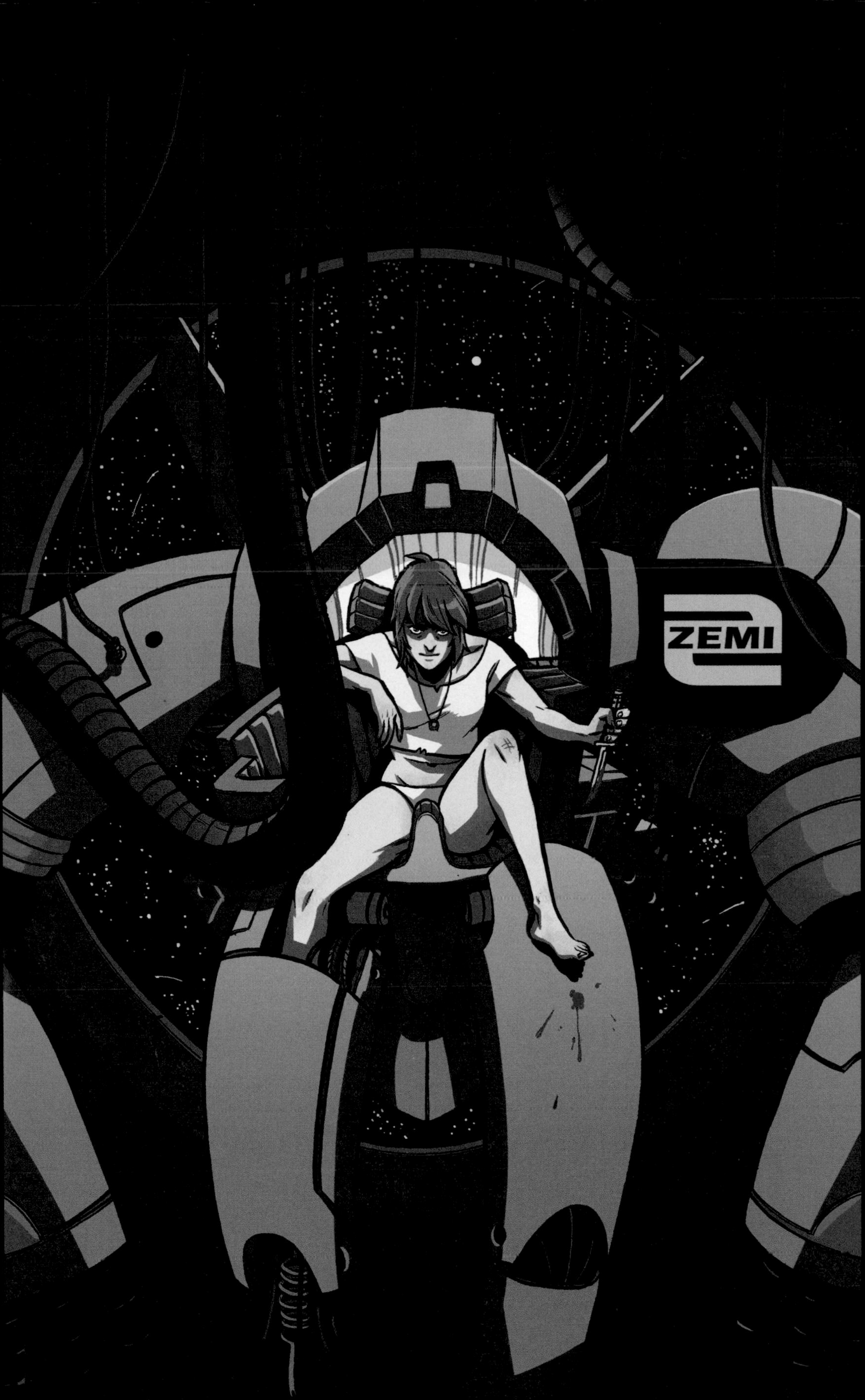
ZEMI

UNUSED COVER | BECKY CLOONAN

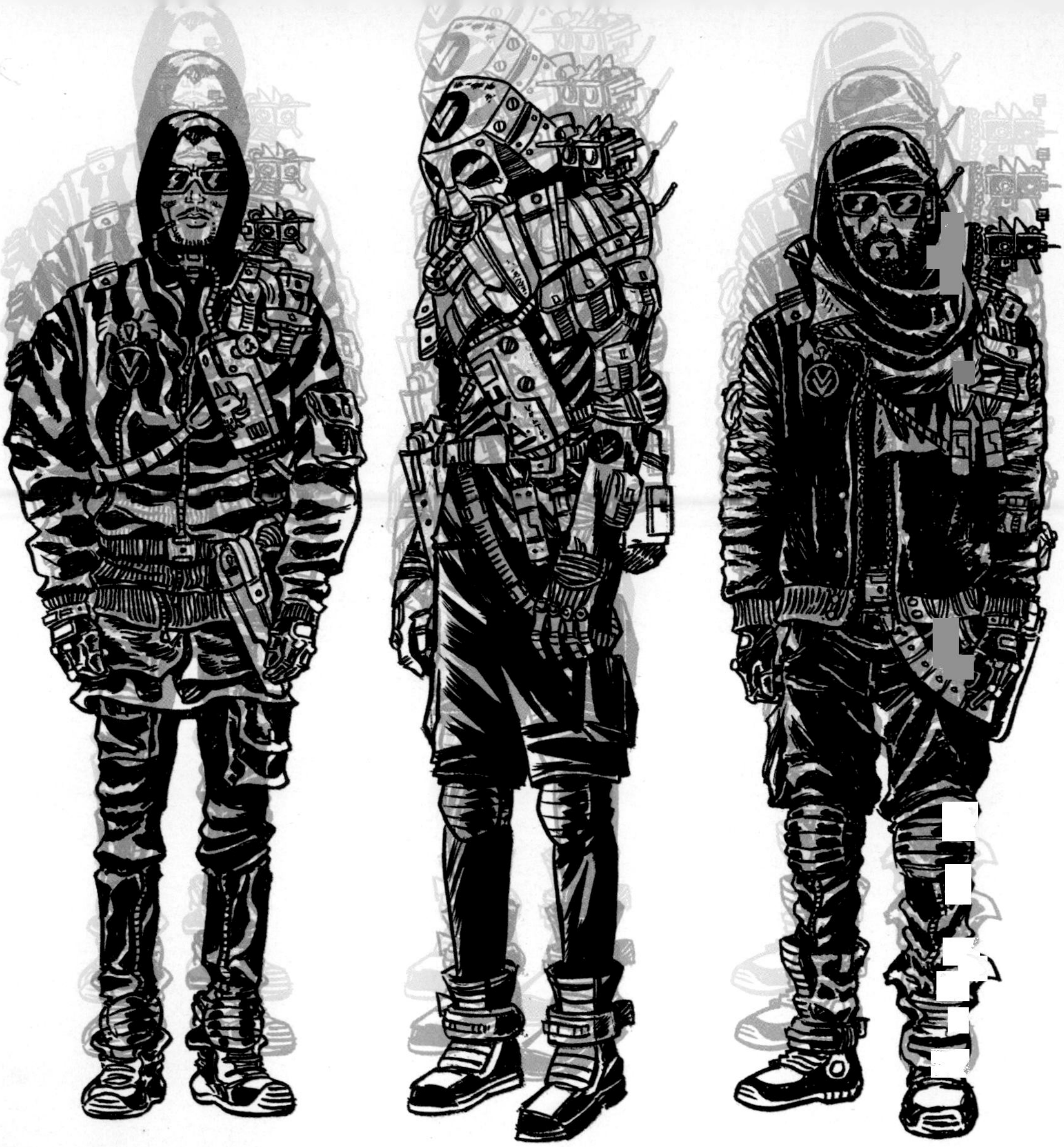

# PILOTS OF THE SOUTHERN CROSS

**BECKY CLOONAN**
Becky Cloonan is a writer/illustrator/necromancer who (at the time of writing) recently gave up her nomadic lifestyle for a home in Austin, Texas. Her first book was published in 2002; since then her profile and workload have steadily risen to include comics for Dark Horse, Marvel, Image, DC, and Vertigo, and a slew of self-published Eisner-winning books. A woman of mystery and reputation, whose reputation is only exceeded by her mystery.

**LEE LOUGHRIDGE**
Lee Loughridge is an artist best known for his work as a colorist on the *Batman Adventures* titles. Loughridge was nominated for the International Horror Guild Award for best illustrated narrative in 2001 for his work on the comic edition of *The House on the Borderland*. He was also nominated for a Hugo Award for his work on *Fables, War and Pieces*. He resides in Southern California where the sun has given him skin like a turkey and the libido of said turkey.

**ANDY BELANGER**
Hailing from the frozen hellscape of Montreal, Andy Bélanger spends his nights illustrating for comics, video games, and TV. Each night in the waning hours of darkness, he seeks out demonic forces in order to join their hellish crusade. Bélanger has worked for DC Comics, Wildstorm, Image, Devil's Due, and Boom!. He also illustrated the four-volume adventure *Kill Shakespeare* for IDW, and self-published an unholy bible titled *Black Church*. He works at Studio Lounak with his canine companion Prince and a creeper cat named Harley.

**SERGE LaPOINTE**
It can be said without a doubt that Serge LaPointe is the best inker, colourist, and letterer in Verdun. In his spare time, he acts as art director, project manager, and designer for the Montreal-based Studio Lounak, which he co-founded in 2010 with Fabrice Forestier and Gautier Langevin. French Canadian born and raised, he resides in Verdun with the love of his life, two Lego maniacs, and a fish.